1 6/02

DATE DUE

JUL 1 0 2002			
AUG 1 9 2002			
AUG 2 8 2002			
SEP 0 9 2002			
SEP 2 8 2002			
OCT 2 6 2002			
NOV 2 3 2002			
GAYLORD			PRINTED IN U.S.A.

Angel
Rock

Angel Rock

Darren Williams

Alfred A. Knopf   *New York*   2002

THIS IS A BORZOI BOOK
PUBLISHED BY ALFRED A. KNOPF

Originally published in Great Britain by HarperCollins, London.

Knopf, Borzoi Books and the colophon are registered
trademarks of Random House, Inc.

ISBN 0-375-41451-7

Manufactured in the United States of America
First American Edition

this one's for S.A.M.

Acknowledgments

I'd like to thank the Eleanor Dark Foundation and the Literature Board of the Australia Council for assistance during the early stages of this novel.

Special thanks to the Williams, Zappulla and Castiglione clans. Thank you to all my supporters, especially Santina, Silvana, Andrew, Merrin, Maggie, Jay, Lorrie, Tony, Paddy, Antony, James and the good people of Brill, Bucks.

Angel Rock

I

1

The first real heat of summer had just steamed into Angel Rock in a welter of frayed tempers and sunburnt noses the afternoon Tom Ferry, almost thirteen years old and still simple-hearted, made his way down to Coop's Universal from where the school bus had left him. The footpath was baking hot and the grass on either side of it full of bindi-eyes and no easier on his bare feet and his progress was punctuated by spells of hopping to recover from one or the other. When he reached the broad expanse of shade under the hotel verandah he dallied for a minute to let his feet cool down properly. He held up his hand and squinted out at the bright day. Fifty yards away the Universal's awning gave the last respite before home. Faded signs—a sunset-orange Coke, an airy blue Bushell's—hung down from it. The sun faded things, it was true, but it also grew them. It was growing *him.* He could really feel it. He didn't feel quite like a boy any more—nothing like Flynn—and he liked the sensation; he liked his body growing, the muscles getting bigger on his bones, the ground getting further away.

He licked his lips and set out. Almost immediately the soles of his feet began to burn again. He ran, sucking in warm air through his rounded lips, laughing it out again, lifting his feet, trying to keep them off the concrete for as long as he could. The shop always seemed an age away on days like these, but he finally reached it and then had to stop and bend over and put his hands on his knees for a while to get his breath back. When he had it he went to the big old deepfreeze that sat just inside the shop's doorway and opened up the lid. Four great half-moons of ice curved out from the sides of the cabinet and he leant over them and plunged his hands and head into the chilled air at its centre. He put his cheek down against the ice and breathed in and felt the cold travel right down into his chest. He laughed at the sensation and waved away the mist with his hands until he could see the box of ice blocks at the bottom of the freezer. He sucked in the sweet, cool smell of them—red ice around ice cream—before reaching down and pulling one out by the tail. He let down the freezer's lid and then ran to the counter at the back of the shop.

"Mrs. Coop!" he yelled. "Mrs. Coop!"

There was no sign of the shopkeeper but in the silence after his yelling he could hear her out the back. The bright light from the open back door reached all the way up the hall and came to rest on the stool sitting in the doorway. She was almost always sitting there whenever Tom came in, fanning herself with a piece of old cardboard. Above her stool, high on the wall, was a dusty bank of brown Bakelite light switches and next to that the electricity meter and the fuse box, and next to that, hanging from a nail, calendar over expired calendar counting back from 1969. Over the counter a sticky mess of old flypaper, bejewelled with blowflies and wasps and beetles, swung gently in the breeze—a grisly record of long-gone summer days. At Tom's feet, alongside the shelves, were the tracks of countless customers worn into the wood. He followed them while he waited for Mrs. Coop to come in, tapping the coin in his hand against the shelves as he went. There was no one else in the shop and the lollies arranged on the counter in coloured boxes seemed to wink at him as he circled. He thought about taking some, gulping them down before Mrs. Coop appeared, but his ears immediately began to burn and he had to think about other things to cool them. He closed his eyes and breathed in the smells of the shop. He imagined a calf walking down between the desks at school, collecting books in its dripping mouth, and he imagined his teacher, Mr. May, pointing to the blackboard with a fishing rod instead of chalk, and then he saw the smooth neck of the girl who sat in front of him in class and he wondered, for the first time in his life, what a kiss might be like.

When he opened his eyes again the ice block in his hand was already beginning to melt. He was about to shout down the hall again when he heard the shopkeeper coming, saw her swaying from side to side because of her bad hip, heard her wheeze. A blue dress with pale yellow flowers covered her bulk and on her hip, like a freshly picked crop, was the basket full of laundry she'd just collected. The deep black line of her cleavage caught Tom's eye and held it for a long second.

"Hello, Mrs. Coop," he said, lifting his chin.

"Hello!" she replied, blinking. "Who's that then?"

"Tom Ferry."

"Ah. Afternoon, Thomas. School's out then?"

"Yep."

"Plans for the weekend?"

"Yep."

"Good boy! What can I do for you then?"

"This," he said, holding up the ice block by its tip. "How much?"

"Thirty-five cents."

"They've gone up!"

"They have?"

Tom looked at the ice block despairingly, then at Mrs. Coop. "But I haven't got that much, and I can't put it back because it's melting already."

Mrs. Coop laughed at him and then made a waving movement with her hand that set the flesh on her arms wobbling.

"Well, you'll just have to owe it to me then," she said. "Or, better yet, when you've finished, you could pull up that grass that's coming up at the front there and that'll settle it, I reckon."

"You sure?"

"Yes. Now go on, get stuck into it before it's just so much coloured water!"

"All right. Thanks, Mrs. Coop. Thanks very much."

Tom turned to go but then he remembered something. "Oh, a pack of Marlboro too, please. For Henry. On his account."

"All right then."

While Mrs. Coop reached for the packet Tom stuck his head out of the doorway. There was grass a foot long coming up between the cracks in the concrete out the front of the shop, all the way from where the awning posts met the ground to where the shop and the footpath met.

"Can I come back and do it tomorrow, Mrs. Coop?" Tom yelled into the shop.

"Course you can," she answered from the gloom. "Go on now."

"All right. See you tomorrow."

"All right. Bye now."

Tom ran down to where the street ended and the ferry ramp began. He sat down on one of the ramp posts and took a big bite out of the ice block but the cold made his forehead ache almost straight away. When the pain had passed he took smaller bites and caught the melting runoff in the cup of his hand. The ferry was on the far bank and he could see the old ferrymaster sitting in his cabin waiting for cars, the twisting streamers from his pipe vanishing into the breeze. Overhead, fat white clouds clippered across the sky and the wind began to pick up, rippling his shirt, cooling him and the day down. School was over for another week and another Apollo was on its way to the moon and that made even Angel Rock seem a more exciting place. Tomorrow, if it was still hot, he'd take Flynn swimming, or maybe fishing, then later, after dinner, they could lie outside on the grass and try to spot it.

He sat looking out across the river and soon forgot where he was, his mind enchanted by images of moon landings and rockets, astronauts and parachuting capsules. He wondered if the Apollo 11 patch he'd ordered from the *Post* would ever arrive. He sat, the ice block dripping onto the ground, until the sound of a commotion filtered through to him. He turned and looked back towards town. The bus from the high school in Laurence had just finished setting down a dozen hot and cranky kids in the main street and now, walking towards him through the rippling heat-waves rising up from the road, was Sonny Steele and his little mate Leonard. He groaned. From about the same spot—just past the bowsers of the Golden Fleece— he'd once seen Jack Webber swing an axe at his brother Joe as if Joe were a tree that needed felling. A summer afternoon just like this one. In the time it had taken him to run to where they faced each other the axe was in Joe—right in his side—though he was still walking, but wrong, like the man up the valley who had polio, and going for his brother with his fists up, the blood draining out of his face. Then Pop Mather, the local copper, had come running up the road and tackled Jack and smacked him one. Then he'd saved Joe's life by jamming his shirt into his wound to keep in the blood. Henry said it was drink and women that had made them fight and he said neither was any good reason to put an axe in someone, especially family.

Tom remembered it as he watched the two older boys increase their pace and he wished wholeheartedly there was an axe handy now. He stood and started walking towards home, jamming the packet of Marlboros down inside the elastic of his shorts. He wouldn't run—he knew there wasn't much point.

When they caught up with him he stopped and turned to face them. Sonny and Leonard stopped too, both dripping with sweat, their mouths open like panting dogs. Sonny stared at him. Sonny had gone to the Catholic primary before high school. Tom thought he must have been like some of the boys in his own class who were always in trouble, who would never do as they were told, whose fathers had short-back-and-sides and wore their trousers up high, whose mothers were heavy and brown-armed and stiff in their floral frocks when they shopped on a Saturday morning. Sonny was one of those. He was nearly three years older than Tom; a foot taller and twice as broad. He had dark curly hair and a curiously flat and featureless face. One eye was dark brown and the other so pale it was almost no colour at all. Tom thought it might once have been blue but had since faded. *Wall-eyed,* Henry called him. He said his family was ignorant and not to bother with him but that was hard when Sonny kept bailing him up. He liked Indians and cover and ambushes and pretending to take scalps. This, however, was no ambush—nothing worthy of Indians— just a crude assault from behind. Tom gritted his teeth, a little twist of fear worming around in his stomach despite his contempt.

"Look at this, a pimple eatin' an ice block!" started Sonny. "Look, Leonard, a big pimple with a mouth!"

Leonard giggled. "Yeah!" he said, his idiot chorus to every joke or comment Sonny ever made. Leonard was so lean and freckled he wouldn't have looked out of place in Africa with the leopards and hyenas.

"What do you want?" Tom asked, sighing.

Sonny raised his eyebrows, hung out a smirk, left it there until Tom's irritation outgrew his nervousness. It was Friday afternoon, the world was changing and he along with it and it was unfair that he had to be standing here again, putting up with Sonny just as he'd always done.

"Give us that, shit-for-brains!" the big boy demanded suddenly, pointing to the ice block. Tom looked at it. There was hardly anything left on the stick and a fly was circling the remains like a tiny vulture.

"Give us your damn ice block I said!" Sonny repeated.

Tom shifted the ice block to his left hand and brought up his right fist and spat on the knuckles as he had seen movie men do and Henry once or twice.

"You'll have to take it off me," he said, and immediately there was a contraction of the world between him and Sonny, as though a vacuum had drawn them together, pushed everything else into the background. It had always been this way—a battle of flesh and wills—and Tom had never bothered to question it before.

The sounds of the world faded and soon he could only hear the blood roaring through his ears, the sky now nothing but a silent exhibition of blue and grey overhead. Sonny leapt at him and grabbed his wrist with one hand and twisted the ice block free with the other while Leonard nipped in and out like a cattle dog and pinched him— hard enough to leave little half-moons of broken skin. Then Sonny used his weight to push him backwards and he teetered, flailing his arms, until Leonard stuck his bony shin behind his knee and sent him sprawling.

"Good, Leonard, good!" Sonny shouted.

He sat down hard on Tom's chest before he could squirm free and proceeded to eat the remains of the ice block. Tom struggled for breath and felt his face grow hot and sweat break out on his forehead. Leonard alternated between looking at Sonny for cues and giving Tom's wrist Chinese burns.

"You . . . fat . . . bastard . . . Steele!" he managed to spit.

Sonny didn't answer, but dribbled red-stained spittle across Tom's face from his pursed lips.

"Open his mouth, Len."

Leonard tried, cautiously, but Tom bit his finger and he retreated, cursing. Tom tried to wriggle free from underneath Sonny, but when he failed miserably it occurred to him that he had other weapons he could use. He thought of a question, something to distract him. The question he came up with seemed straightforward and reasonable, and something he wouldn't have minded having the answer to.

"Why do you do this, Sonny?" he spat, panting.

Sonny stared at him for a moment and then looked up and down the street. The time limit on his fun was fast running out. There were adults about who might spot him at any moment. He looked down at Tom again. He seemed to be giving the question serious considera-tion, but then he flipped Tom over onto his stomach and held his head down in the grass and gravel. He pushed harder and harder and when grit had worked its way into Tom's eyes and nose, and tears were run-ning down his face Sonny leant in close so his smooth, clammy face— lips edged in sticky red, teeth holed by brown decay—filled Tom's field of vision like a noxious moon.

"Because your father's a *drunk* and your mother's a *rotten whore!*" he hissed, his face contorting.

Tom blinked, frozen for a moment by the malice in Sonny's eyes, but then a car came rolling down the street and in a second Sonny and Leonard were up and away. Tom sat up and rubbed the gravel off his cheek and out of his hair. The old farmer driving by slowed his car to better see him there on the verge, then waved slowly when he saw he was none the worse for wear, just the victim of schoolboy rough-and-tumble. Tom nodded at him and the farmer lifted his finger off the steering wheel and straightened his head. When he'd passed, Tom looked down the road at the backs of Sonny and Leonard. Every so often Sonny would turn and glare at him and spit onto the road.

He brushed the dust and grass off his clothes and walked home along the river, looking across at the water as he always did, just in case something interesting was floating by. When he reached his house after fifteen minutes or so he bent by the tap in the front yard and washed his face and rinsed out his mouth and spat a lot. He ran cold water over the places where Leonard had pinched him. *Chicken bastard!* he fumed, under his breath.

He went inside and set the pack of cigarettes on their end on the kitchen table. They were a little crushed but he knew that a bent cigarette was a smokeable cigarette so he didn't worry about it too much—and at least Sonny hadn't found them. He went and sat down in front of the television and had only been watching it for a few minutes when Mrs. Clark from next door came over with Flynn.

"Hello, Mrs. Clark. Hey, Flynn."

"Hey," said Flynn.

"Tom," said Mrs. Clark. "Flynn's been a good boy today. Haven't you, Flynn?"

Flynn nodded. He was only four and not due to start school until the new year. After Mrs. Clark left he promptly fell asleep on the couch with his mouth open. Tom set the fan in front of him and turned it on and then he went into their room and pulled his Junior Dictionary from the bookcase and went and sat out on the verandah in one of the busted cane chairs and opened up the book on his lap. He didn't have a clue what *whore* really meant but the fact that Sonny had said it meant it couldn't be anything good, and was probably some sort of disease or something, maybe something that killed you. He looked up the word in the dictionary, but, as he wasn't sure how to spell it, struggled. There was *hoar*, which was to do with frost, and there was *horology*, but that was the art or science of making timepieces or of measuring time. Under the silent *w*'s there was only *whole*, which meant a whole lot of things, and *who're*, a contraction of *who are*, which seemed close, but he was fairly certain Sonny had not meant his mother was a *who are* because that didn't make sense. He put the dictionary down, locked his hands behind his head like Henry sometimes did and looked out across the river. The long reeds by the bank dipped in the breeze but apart from that nothing much else was moving. He sat and looked and his eyelids were just beginning to droop when he heard a car coming up the road from town. It was the Holden, with his mother at the wheel. He bent and picked up the dictionary and took it back to his room, a feeling of guilt flowing through him like it was one of the magazines Henry kept in the shed.

When she came up the stairs he was back sitting in the cane chair by the front door. She bent and kissed him on the cheek. He thought she looked very tired.

"Where's Flynn?"

"Asleep."

"Good . . . listen. I have to go back to work in an hour or so. And I have to work tomorrow. When Henry comes home could you get his tea?"

Tom looked down at his toes and frowned at them. His mother put her hand on his head and stroked his hair.

"I know. I'm sorry. But I have to go. We need the money. You know we do."

He nodded. "Yep."

"Good boy. I bought some sausages. Just do some potatoes and some peas with them. Make sure Flynn eats his peas."

"Yep."

"All right. I'm going to have a shower now and change my clothes." She kissed him on the forehead. "You're a good boy, Tom. What would I do without you."

He looked up at her. Sometimes just the smell of her was enough to make him feel better, but when she smiled the way she sometimes did—a little sad, yet laced with mischief—it made him remember how it was when it had just been the two of them; before Henry, and before Flynn. He liked to think she remembered those times too, at least once in a while.

He followed her inside the house and went and sat down beside his little brother. He listened as his mother moved around the house and watched as the fan lifted Flynn's fine yellow hair and set it down again. After a while his mother came back and put her hand on his shoulder.

"All right, Tom, bye now. Be good. Henry shouldn't be long." Before she had finished the sentence there was a knock at the door, loud enough to wake Flynn.

"Bloody hell," his mother muttered.

"What?" said Flynn, half opening his eyes.

Tom glanced at him. When he turned back to his mother she was already halfway up the hall.

"Yes? Hello?" he heard her say.

Flynn, sleepy-eyed, slipped off the couch and headed for the door. Tom followed him. There was a man standing on their verandah. Flynn stopped in his tracks and stared at him and Tom did the same.

The man had thick, grey whiskers and long matted hair to his shoulders. His hands were large and brown, the nails yellow, a black semicircle of dirt at their ragged ends. Even though the afternoon was still very warm he wore a woollen jumper with slack, gaping holes, and a filthy tweed coat over that. He wore a wide-brimmed hat and he looked down at them with eyes dark as stones.

"Any spare food, missus?" he said. "I could eat a horse if one were spare."

Flynn giggled. The man looked down at him and Flynn stopped.

"I may have something," said Ellie Gunn, walking back towards the kitchen. Tom and his brother stayed where they were. The man looked from side to side as if watching out for something and then he looked down at them again.

"What's yer name then?" he asked Flynn, in a voice rough as ironbark.

"Flynn," said Flynn. "What's yours?"

"Ah . . . Billy," said the man, as if he didn't have need of it very often. He nodded, said the name again, but softly this time: "*Billy.*"

Tom's mother returned with something wrapped in foil and something in a brown paper bag. He could smell what was in the foil—cold chicken—and his mouth began to water.

"This is all I've got handy, I'm afraid," said his mother, passing the man the food.

"Bless you, missus," he said, taking it. He nodded to her, nodded to the boys, then turned and walked down the path and through the gate, closing it carefully behind him.

"What was he, Mum?" asked Flynn, after he'd walked away.

"A tramp. A swaggie. That's what he was." She picked up her son and swung him back and forth. "You be a good boy for your brother now and I'll be here when you wake up."

"All right."

Tom watched her walk out to the car and climb in, then reverse back out into the road. She just sat there for a few moments then, looking forward. Tom peered up the road but he couldn't see the swaggie. His mother looked their way after a while and waved, then put the car into gear and moved off. Tom waved goodbye and walked out to the gate to watch her go. The car rolled away down the long straight then disappeared round the bend. He walked out onto the road and looked both ways but there was no sign of the tramp. He ran around to the side of the house and stopped at the corner and leant into the cool boards. There he was, walking diagonally across the cow paddock next to the house. As Tom watched, the man threw a chicken bone over his shoulder, and a few strides later he looked back towards the house. Tom ducked back and waited for what seemed like whole minutes before edging along the boards again and peeking around the corner. Too late. The man had gone. Up into the trees maybe.

He walked down into the back yard and watched the trees a little longer and then he turned and went inside. Flynn was back on the couch with his thumb in his mouth, his eyes already closing. Tom went and sat down in the cane chair out front. He put his chin in his hand and before he knew it he was dreaming of his mother putting out washing on a long, long line.

When Tom woke the sunset was reflected in the eastern sky before him and a great cloud of birds was wheeling around over the river. Henry Gunn was walking up the path with the chainsaw resting on his shoulder, his clothes and boots coated with sawdust, his forehead pale where his hat kept the sun off. As he passed through the door he ruffled his stepson's hair. Along the inside of his forearm Tom saw the long jagged scar where a chainsaw had kicked out of a tree once and caught him. The scars where the stitches had been were nearly an inch wide and looked as though someone had laced up the skin like a boot. Henry stopped just inside the doorway and asked him where his mother was. Tom told him and Henry scowled and headed for the bathroom.

Tom made tea while Henry washed away the stink and dirt of his day's work. When the food was ready Tom piled up their three plates with sausages, mashed potatoes, peas. Henry came in and sat down and started to eat. He never made them say grace like their mother did. Tom and Flynn followed suit and tucked in. In between mouthfuls Henry said: "I need you for the snigging tomorrow, Tom. They're closing off the coupe where I got all those good logs last week and Bloody John broke his arm today."

Tom's heart sank. Ordinarily he would have been interested in the details of a broken arm but not on a Friday, not when Henry wanted him to work on a Saturday.

"What about Flynn?" he spluttered, his mouth full.

"What about him?"

"Mum's got to work tomorrow."

"Ah. Mrs. Clark'll have to look after 'im."

Tom waited a few moments. "No, Mrs. Clark can't. She's got to go to Laurence tomorrow."

Henry threw his fork down on the table. "Blast!" he shouted. Flynn jumped.

"I'll look after him," said Tom. "He could help me bag the sawdust."

"No, you're helping me."

Tom could feel his whole Saturday slipping away. "But what about Mr. Riley?"

"He can wait a day for his bloody sawdust can't he!"

"But—"

"Christ Jesus, Tom, no more! I can't afford to pay some bastard, and I need to get those bloody logs out!"

Tom didn't say any more and they continued to eat in silence. He couldn't think of any more cards to play, not without his mother there. Flynn started to giggle and spit mashed potato down the front of his shirt.

"Flynn!" shouted Tom. "What are you doing?"

"He can come too," said Henry, chewing and staring at Flynn. "He'll be all right in the cab."

Tom looked from his stepfather to Flynn and back again, but he bit his lip and said no more. When they had eaten and the table was cleared Henry fetched the chainsaw from the front verandah and sat it on the table under the light. He fitted the sharpening jig to the arm and proceeded to put the edge back onto each tooth in the chain. Flynn settled on the couch in front of the television and put his thumb in his mouth as before.

"Make sure Flynn has his bath before he goes to bed," Henry muttered, his mind on what he was doing.

"Yep."

As Tom washed the dishes he fumed and thought of Sonny Steele again. Another question began to form in his mind but this one had a much more dangerous shape than the one he'd asked Sonny. When he finished the dishes he turned round and watched Henry sharpen the blades for a while. Every so often Henry's hand would slow down and his chin would dip and his eyelids droop and then he would catch himself and shake his head and continue. Tom felt a little light-headed, but then he took a deep breath, held it for three, asked his question straight after.

"Henry?"

"Mmmm?"

"What's a whore?"

Henry didn't answer immediately but looked up at him sharply with his full attention, the chainsaw, the file in his hand forgotten.

"Where'd you hear that?"

Tom gulped. He couldn't lie to Henry when his eyes were like that, his voice so low and blunt.

"Sonny."

"Steele? What—he call *you* that or something?" Henry's forehead rippled into deep furrows. Tom could see a few spots where he hadn't rinsed the soap off properly.

"No."

"Then why'd he say it?"

Tom didn't answer.

"Answer me, or so help me!"

"I don't know why he said it!"

"Repeat to me—exactly—what the little cunt said. *Exactly.*"

Tom tried to swallow the lump in his throat. He felt a bit dizzy, and reckless, as if he were about to unleash something as furious and unstoppable as a storm from the tip of his tongue.

"Mum," he whispered. "He said: *your mother's a whore.* That's what he said."

He braced himself for a belting when Henry leapt up, but it didn't come. The big man's thighs caught the edge of the table and lifted it up and the chainsaw and the tools went banging and clattering to the floor. Henry didn't even seem to notice. The storm Tom had un-leashed, still smelling of soap and with his hair still damp, pulled his work boots back on and pounded out the front door. Tom watched him climb up into the truck and roar off down the road in a spray of gravel. He felt a cold flitter of fear down in his gut, even worse than the one he'd felt that afternoon—a flash of what might happen to anyone who got in Henry's way maybe—but also the sure knowledge that this storm, as well as sweeping over Sonny, might well wheel round and break on him in turn.

2

H ey, Darcy! Darcy Steele! Goody-bloody-two-shoes! Show us your tits!"

The boys were much older than they, long-haired and pimply, and Grace Mather had been apprehensive when she'd first seen them appear, but Darcy just gave a breathy laugh and took in a lungful of air before responding.

"Rack off, bastard arseholes!" she shouted.

Grace nearly wet herself laughing, but it was nervous, wild laughter, more likely to end in dizziness than anything else. The boys stood by the side of the road for a while longer, one chopping at the long grass with a stick to make himself feel better, but then they walked on and disappeared down behind the Agricultural Hall.

"They would have come for me if you hadn't been here," said Darcy.

"I didn't stop them."

"Yes, you did. Pop's your dad. That's why they didn't chase me. Because you're here."

Grace half shrugged, unconvinced. "Have they chased you before?"

"Yeah. Heaps of times."

"Why didn't you tell me? What did you do?"

"I run. I'm faster than them."

"Have they ever caught you?"

"Once."

"What happened?"

"They wanted to see my tits, my fanny. I said they could if they showed me their dicks."

Grace looked at her friend, her eyes wide.

"Did they?"

"One did. The other was too chicken. But I ran away before it was my turn. Ha!"

"What did it look like?" Grace whispered.

Darcy screwed up her face and grinned. "Remember that time we helped the nurse with all the kindie boys?"

"Yeah."

"Well, it was like that. Like a grub. A pink grub. But . . ."

"But what?"

"Bigger . . . and hairy!"

Darcy laughed along with Grace. When they stopped they were racked with giggles until Darcy shouted *Come on!* and took off up the road. Grace followed. She seemed to be doing a lot of following lately, but even though she was older than Darcy by a few months it didn't really bother her. Every Saturday Darcy always wanted to be doing things, never wanted to just sit and talk like they'd used to, but there was less and less to do in Angel Rock that they hadn't already done and Darcy was becoming more and more restless. Lately Grace had been reading books and telling Darcy things that might interest her to try and keep her happy. Saturday last she'd told her all about Huck Finn and his raft and now Darcy wanted to build her own and float away down the river just like him.

They walked along to the sawmill as they'd planned and ducked through the hole in the fence. No one worked there on Saturdays any more. Tom Ferry collected sawdust for the butcher there some weekends but there was no sign of him. They wandered around through the stacks of timber looking for material, toiling in the hot morning sun for an hour until they had a pallet, various other odds and ends of wood, four empty oil drums, bits and pieces of rope and a torn scrap of red cloth that the timbermen nailed to the end of logs when they were carried on the roads.

They tramped across the open paddock between the back of the sawmill and the riverbank carrying their finds, but when they came to the pallet they found that it was far too big for the hole in the fence no matter which way they tried it.

"Goddamn it," said Darcy.

They sat and looked at the pallet and wiped the sweat off their foreheads with their sleeves.

"It's the best bit. We can't leave it."

"I could get Pop to help us," said Grace.

"You can't ask him! He'd probably arrest us!" Darcy laughed but Grace could barely raise a grin.

"We'll just have to try with what we've got," said Darcy.

They walked over to the river and gazed at the pile. It didn't look like much of a raft. Darcy tried to tie one of the drums to a plank of wood but the rope was much too short.

"Goddamn it!" she said again, and pushed a drum down the bank. It splashed into the dark water and then floated away. The girls looked at one another for a moment and then, piece by piece, threw all the wood and the remaining drums into the river. When everything was gone they sat down and watched the line of flotsam drift away downstream.

"Boats might hit them," said Darcy, a little wistfully, after a few minutes had passed.

Grace nodded. "Yeah. Boats might sink. We better go before someone sees."

"They might go all the way out to sea."

"Yeah. All the way to Sydney. Come on," said Grace, her heart beginning to pound.

"What do you think it's like there?" asked Darcy, making no move.

"Where?"

"Sydney."

"I don't know. Lots of buildings, lots of houses, lots of people."

Darcy nodded. "I'm going there one day."

"That's good. Now come on!"

Darcy shrugged, but then got to her feet and slapped the grass off her dress. They walked back up to the road but still saw no one. Along from the mill they stopped by the rail platform and drank from the tap down the side of the old stationmaster's office, wetting their brows and washing the dust off their hands and arms. In the distance a train's horn sounded. They climbed up onto the platform and sat down on an old luggage trolley and peered southwards. Before long they caught a glimpse of the train away down the valley, ploughing through the heat haze like a ship. Darcy stood up. Grace's stomach rumbled and she looked at her watch.

"Think I can beat it?" said Darcy, shading her eyes with her hand.

"What? The train?"

"Yeah. To the tree."

Grace looked up the tracks to the tree—maybe a hundred yards away—then back in the direction the train was coming, then up at Darcy. Standing there in the dust, barefoot, with her fingers splayed in the curve of her waist and her hip out, with the red log flag bunched in her other hand and the sun right behind her golden head, her best friend looked like she could do anything she put her mind to, and beat any train under the sun.

"Ah . . . m-maybe," she answered, stammering. "If it slows around the bend."

"Pah!"

Darcy crouched and waited for the train, a sly grin not shifting from her mouth. The driver sounded the horn as the train approached. It came on, huge and metallic, belching diesel smoke, glinting in the sun. Grace took two steps back from the tracks and nearly called to her friend to take care. When the train reached her Darcy sprang away, racing away alongside the tracks, laughing and lifting the flag up over her head and waving it to and fro like a banner. The passengers in the train stared at her as they passed and then some boys opened a door to yell and whoop. As they did Darcy reached the tree and collapsed, laughing, in a heap on the grass, ruby-cheeked and with her hair clinging to her damp face and neck. Grace, catching her up, flopped down on her back beside her, breathing hard, the solid blue sky overhead brimming with little points of light that spun before her eyes. They lay there, giggling, until Darcy slapped Grace on the thigh.

"Did I beat it?"

"Yeah, you did!"

Darcy lifted up her arms and made fists of her hands.

"Champion!" she yelled, but a moment later she was on her feet again, pulling Grace up by the arm.

"Come on," she said. "I'm too hot now. Let's go for a swim!"

◇❈◇❈◇

They walked down to the ferry, running the last stretch, jumping on just as the ramp was lifting. The ferrymaster growled at them. Darcy poked her tongue out at him. Grace thought she saw him grin but it was hard to tell through his beard. When the ferry reached the town side of the river they ducked the rail and ran up the street, up past the convent and the school, through the weedy paddock behind, past the old house with its huge ramparts of overgrown hedge and saplings growing up through the verandah, then through a fenced yard dotted with tobacco bushes and tall thistles, the scruffy pony in it taking only a few steps out from under the shade of a tree before they'd slipped through the fence on the other side and disappeared down through the bushes to the creek.

There was no one at the waterhole. Most kids swam in the river off the jetty or up at the dam. Grace didn't like any place much, but the day was too hot to be fussy. Darcy pulled her dress over her head and kicked off her underpants. Grace looked around.

"Don't worry, nobody's here."

Grace nodded nervously and began to undress.

"You're getting boobs now," Darcy said, nodding her head towards Grace's chest and making her blush. "It's about time."

"Mum says I'm a late bloomer."

"Blooming late, that's all!"

Grace blushed.

"You'll have to wear a bra then."

"I don't like them."

"Me neither. Who needs 'em."

Darcy turned and climbed down the bank and slipped into the water. Grace left her underpants on and followed. In under the trees the water was cool and her skin rippled into goosebumps and her teeth chattered for a few moments as she lowered herself into the water. She soon forgot about her half-naked state and began to paddle around the pool and enjoy the sensation of the water against her skin, how good it felt compared to the hot and sticky air.

After swimming around the pool a few times Darcy clambered up the far bank and jumped off an overhanging rock into the water, the sound of the splash loud under the leafy canopy.

"Come on! You try!" she called to Grace after she'd surfaced.

Grace resisted, but after a campaign of pleading from Darcy she relented and climbed the bank. She stood on the rock for a minute, her arms crossed over her chest, and gathered her nerve. When she jumped she felt the much cooler water in the depths of the hole with her toes and she shivered again when she broke the surface. They took turns jumping until Darcy pointed to the branch of a tree hanging out over the water.

"I'm going to climb up there and jump off," she said.

"Don't be dumb! It's too high!"

"No, it's not. I've seen it done."

Grace watched as Darcy climbed the tree and then wriggled forward along the overhanging limb, her muddy legs hanging down on either side.

"Be careful!" Grace called. "Maybe the water isn't deep enough!"

"Bulldust!"

Darcy manoeuvred herself around the branch and lowered herself down. She swung for a moment or two by her arms and then let go. Grace put her hand over her mouth and held her breath as Darcy's body seemed to just hang in the air for a moment before scything down into the water and making a great splash, the wave from it nearly swamping Grace where she knelt in the shallows.

"See?" spluttered Darcy, when her head broke the surface.

"You can be a real dill sometimes, Darcy Steele," said Grace, shaking her head.

Darcy pulled herself up out onto the bank and sat and shook the water from her hair. Grace followed and sat down beside her.

"Want a smoke?" said Darcy, after a while.

Before Grace could answer she went over to her clothes and rummaged through them, returning with a crumpled pair of cigarettes and a box of matches. She put one in her mouth and lit it, handed it to Grace, then lit the other. Grace put the cigarette to her lips and breathed in while Darcy watched, her face wreathed in smoke.

"Good! You're a natural!"

They sat and smoked until Grace began to feel a little sick. Darcy didn't say anything for a long time. Grace was about to ask her what was wrong when they both heard a sound away through the trees.

"What was that?" whispered Grace. The cigarette fell from her fingers onto the ground, forgotten. Darcy stood and peered across the water at the bushes on the bank. Grace crossed her arms over her chest and began to slide over to where her dress lay. She heard the sound again but this time it was much clearer. There was a strangled laugh, and then a fierce admonition.

"It's my brother," Darcy whispered. "It's Sonny."

She bent and scooped up a handful of mud from the bank and then stepped down into the water and flung it towards the far bank. She threw more, her cigarette poised in the fingers of her left hand, until there was a squeal from the bushes. Sonny and Leonard broke from their cover and crashed through the undergrowth like pademelons. Grace saw Leonard gawping at Darcy's bare breasts and at the dark triangle under her belly.

"I'm telling!" Sonny squawked.

"Haven't done nothin'!" Darcy shouted back. "I'll tell on *you*!"

She bent and dug in the bank for more ammunition then glanced over at Grace.

"Come on! Aren't you going to help?"

"I can't!"

Darcy shrugged and kept flinging mud, even after Sonny and Leonard were well out of range. After a few final sallies she came and stood near Grace and picked up her dress and pulled it over her head.

"They're always doing things like that," she said, pulling on her underpants. Grace felt even sicker.

"Why didn't you cover yourself up?"

Darcy looked surprised by the question. She seemed to think about it for a moment and then gave a little shrug.

"I don't care," she said.

She walked down into the water and washed the worst of the mud from her arms and legs and it dawned on Grace then that she really didn't—didn't care that Sonny had seen, didn't care that Leonard had. She came back up the bank and sat down, pulling her legs up to her chin. Neither said anything for a minute or so, as if the clothes had somehow changed them.

"I should go," Grace said, eventually. "My mum'll have lunch ready. You can come if you want."

"No. I'll stay here."

"I'll come back later then."

Darcy nodded.

"Remember you have to come and try on your dress," said Grace, as she stood.

"Yeah. I remember."

Grace waited. She felt awkward and didn't know quite why. Darcy was staring at the water and throwing twigs into it.

"I'll see you then," said Grace.

"Yeah. See ya," Darcy whispered.

A shadow fell across her friend's face then and her head lowered and she began to cry. Grace went to her and put an arm round her, then held her head as Darcy set it against her shoulder. She cried for ten minutes or more, and when she was nearly through and just sobbing Grace tried to find out what the problem was. Darcy would only shake her head. Grace stroked her hair and then pulled her close and hugged her.

"What is it?" she asked again, but Darcy wouldn't, or couldn't, answer her. Grace looked at her red eyes and her cheeks wet with tears. She lifted a strand of her damp hair and put it behind her ear. Darcy looked up at her with her sad, blue eyes, then lifted her hands and put them on either side of Grace's face. And then Grace felt her hot, wet mouth as she pressed her lips hard against her cheek. She pulled away and as she did she saw an odd look cross Darcy's face, and she knew without a doubt that it was a reflection of her own dismay. She stood abruptly.

"Gra—"

"I have to go now. If you won't tell me what's wrong . . ."

Darcy bit her lip and said nothing. Finally, Grace had to turn and walk away, her head all confusion, her feelings in a spin. When she glanced over her shoulder her friend was sitting very still, watching her depart. Her face looked very pale in the dappled sunlight. Darcy gave a weak, hopeful smile and then waved, as if hoping with all her heart that she wouldn't be the only one to do so. Grace hesitated, her brow furrowing, but then she lifted her hand and waved it feebly once or twice before turning for home.

3

Tom wiped his hands on his trousers and then jumped up and caught the hook swinging down from the truck's jib hoist. Using his weight, he pulled the hook and the steel cable attached to it down and around the log while Henry watched from the truck's cab and barked orders. He ducked down and jammed the hook under the log where there was a small gap between it and the ground and then he scrambled over the log and burrowed through the earth and leaves with his hand until he felt the hook and could pull it through. If the log was too heavy he'd grab the log-hook and hang off it and roll the log over the cable until the hook appeared. Sometimes Henry had to come and do it. When the cable was looped round the log Henry jabbed at the winch controls and the steel noose slithered and tightened round the log and lifted it off the ground. Tom thought that Henry was nearly always too quick with the winch and didn't give him enough time to get clear. Sometimes he found himself on his backside in the dirt, having dodged the log, holding his hand where the rope had grazed it, or splinters had gone in. He didn't understand the need for all the hurry, always wringing the truck's neck. He could see how Bloody John had broken his arm—it would be easy enough to get it caught either in the loop or under a rolling log, but Henry expected him to be quick, to use his head, and he wasn't going to let him or the job get the better of him.

Flynn stood on the truck's seat and watched him out the rear window. He sometimes shouted to him, calling out *Hey!* or something similar when he slipped over, but other than that he kept still in the seat. He'd already learnt to keep right out of Henry's way. The window was about the same shape as a movie screen but Flynn's fingers were hanging out of this one, unrestrained by the rules of coloured film and light, and Henry's scarred arm and big hand came right out to work the winch. The last time they'd gone to the movies in Laurence the woman hadn't let him and Flynn in because of their bare feet and they'd had to sit for an hour and a half, staring at their tickets, distraught, until their mother returned, and then she'd gone to the woman and given her one hell of a blast. He smiled at the memory, but then put it from his head in case it distracted him.

"Wait there," ordered Henry. Tom, surprised, watched the truck disappear down the track, Flynn's face a pale oval in the window, to where they'd taken the other logs, to where the jinker would pick them up later. He wondered whether *Wait there* was Henry's way of saying he'd done a good job and he should have a break, or that he was completely useless. He sat down under a tree to wait, suddenly feeling a little lonely.

Henry had been gone a long time the night before. Tom had given up waiting for him. He'd gone and lain on his bed, listening to the world outside the house, but had fallen asleep, and only later been woken by the sound of the truck returning, Henry's steady footsteps through the house, all the energy drained away, all the fury. Whatever had happened, whatever he'd said or done at the Steeles', he didn't say. Then, outside in the night, a real storm had brewed, just the faint sound of thunder at first, slowly moving closer, becoming louder, until the house was shuddering, until he'd worried about his mother having to come home through it. The lightning had flashed through the window and then the rain, great sheets of it, had come crashing down on the roof for half an hour, maybe three-quarters, and then it had gone, waltzing away down the valley, leaving the drains gurgling and the air cool and clean. He'd heard the floorboards creak as Henry walked out to the verandah. He'd pictured him standing out there on the step in his singlet, watching the storm go, maybe smoking one of the bent Marlboros. In the last flickers of light through the window he'd seen Flynn in his bed across the room, his mouth a dark O in his face, oblivious to it all.

There'd been no black eyes in the morning light, no grazes on Henry's knuckles which hadn't been there before, but there had been silence and an understanding on Tom's part that he should not mention anything to do with the night before, especially not in front of his mother, whom he hadn't even heard come home. Tom hadn't even dreamt of it.

When Henry returned he jumped down from the truck and proceeded to build a little fire of twigs and bark to boil the billy on. A breeze picked up and blew the firesmoke away through the trees. When the tea was made he opened a tin of biscuits and passed two each to Tom and Flynn. Tom went and sat with his back against the cool trunk of a young bluegum and watched Flynn mess about chasing big red bull ants with a stick. He daydreamed about taking off his shoes and putting his feet in cool creek water. Henry had made both of them wear their school shoes to stop splinters. Tom hardly ever wore his except on special occasions and they were black and shiny and stiff and made his feet feel clumsy and heavy. They hurt his heels but it was worse for Flynn—he'd *never* worn his. Henry said that that was all the more reason Flynn should wear them in before he started school. Tom tried to tell him that hardly anyone wore shoes there but Henry hadn't seemed to hear him.

"Be careful with those bloody things, Flynn," Tom said when Henry went behind a tree to piss. "Don't get bit!"

"I won't," said Flynn, spitting crumbs.

Henry set the transistor radio on the ground when he came back and they listened to a few songs and then the pips sounded and the news came on. The newsreader read out something about birth dates for the conscription. Tom listened and, to his alarm, heard his own—the same day and month, but a different year.

"That's my birthday!"

"What?"

"He just said my birthday!"

"You're too young."

"For what?"

"To fight."

"What if I was old enough?"

Henry shrugged. "You'd have to go," he said.

"What if I didn't want to go?"

Henry looked at him as though he were surprised he could speak. "You'd have to."

"But what if I have to go one day? What if the war's still going when I'm old enough?"

"Well . . . you'd have to go. If I had anything to say about it. If your country needs you, you have to go."

Henry flicked away the leafy tea at the bottom of his cup and then looked at Tom as though one or two more questions might be all right. Tom was about to ask another question when Henry suddenly looked up and shouted at Flynn to be careful. Tom looked over at his brother. He didn't seem in any immediate danger.

"Come on," said Henry, gruffly, after a silence.

When they returned to work Henry felled some more trees that had caught his eye, that he couldn't bear to leave. All Tom had to do was keep out of the way and paint the end of the log with Henry's mark and clear the branches from around the log as Henry lopped them so the truck could get in. They kept working until lunch time and then Henry drove them down to where other gangs were having their lunch in a large cleared area where the forest had been stripped back to the bare earth and the smouldering stumps of felled trees sent light-blue smoke into the air. The men squatted near the fires cooking meat, making tea, and smoking. Tom liked being around the timber-men and listening to their filthy speech and their eerie tales of head-less convicts and moans and cries in the bush in the dead of night. They smelt of tobacco, grease and tree sap and sometimes told stories of themselves or other men and their battles with giant trees, the breaking of arms, legs, necks and backs. They spoke of women as though they were trees and trees as though they were women until Tom couldn't tell one smooth limb from another, and they nearly always had grazes on their arms and legs and nearly always gaps in their grins or bright white false teeth. The older men wore braces over their work shirts or singlets and took no cheek from the young-sters.

He wandered around for a while in the cold ashes and charred earth.

"The surface is fine and powdery," he whispered to himself. *"I can see footprints of my boots . . . in the fine sandy particles."*

Henry called his name after a while and directed him to a fire and told him to watch out for Flynn and fry up some eggs. Henry strode over to the largest group of men—a Commission gang—and squatted amongst them. He plucked a cigarette from his pocket and straightened it out with his fingers and then lit it.

Tom got the pan, eggs and bread from the truck and set to work. It was hot in the sun after the shade of the trees and the sweat ran down his forehead and into his eyes and as he wiped it away with his forearm he grew more irritated. He saw Flynn wandering around the uprooted bole of a huge tree.

"Go and sit in the shade!" Tom shouted to him.

Flynn came over, trailing a stick through the dust. Tom could tell he was irritable as well. They'd both had to get up before the sun for the early start.

"Watch me cook," he said, but this did not seem to excite Flynn much. Tom looked at his brother. He felt sorry for him and then that turned into a fierce surge of protectiveness that rolled up from his gut and swamped everything else.

"Maybe tomorrow we can go fishing," he said, his voice sounding weak and strangled, as though Sonny was pinning him down again.

Flynn's face lit up. "Yeah? Can we?"

"Yep."

"Where?"

"In the river. Where else, knucklehead?"

"Will Dad let us?"

"He'll be asleep in the morning. We'll go then. We'll leave him a bloody note!"

Flynn giggled and seemed to cheer up a little and soon he was singing to himself and crawling around in the dirt under the truck to see what he could find.

The last time Henry had taken them fishing it had rained. *It's not too heavy, not really rain at all,* he'd said. Tom had followed him into the paddock, through the barbed wire, his legs wet from the long, water-loaded grass, his mother behind them in the car with Flynn becoming smaller and smaller. He remembered that his mother had smoked a cigarette that day. The car was a black Holden Special and the smoke had curled out through the chromed window frame. Henry had a wicker fishing creel that hung at his waist from two old leather belts that he'd stitched together with oiled string. In their back yard at home Tom remembered Flynn, only two or three, standing in the basket and holding on to its greasy rim. Tom had carried the short bamboo pole Henry had made for him, an old Alvey reel attached to the bamboo with wire and window putty, and on his head he'd worn a battered old oilskin hat that had leaked cold rain down the back of his neck. He'd looked back before they'd reached the dark curve of trees at the far end of the paddock and seen his mother following at last, her head bowed, her bare feet white against the grass, she and Flynn just small dark shapes against the expanse of grass and trees, connected at the hands, arms like rigging between them, his mother helping Flynn, who'd still been mastering walking, over the rough ground. Flynn had had no hat at all and his thin hair when they'd caught up had been flat against his scalp and his little shirt wet. The river when they'd reached it had been dark, fast flowing and overhung with willow. He remembered the sound of the water rippling through tree roots and black rocks. Henry had sworn that it was a special spot, shown to him by his own father, but they had not caught anything that day, and they had never been back.

After five minutes or so the eggs were nearly cooked. He looked over to where Henry was sitting. He was still talking. Tom called to him but he made no move. He peered at the eggs through the smoke that was suddenly wafting towards him. It got into his eyes and made them water and sting. He lifted the pan and saw that the eggs were exactly how Henry liked them, any longer and they would go hard and rubbery, the way he hated them. He looked around for Flynn but couldn't see him. He swore under his breath—*Bloody shit*—and put the pan in the shade of the truck and then he walked over to Henry and tapped him on the shoulder, acutely aware of the clunky black shoes on his feet. Henry looked at him from the corner of his eye but made no move to come. Tom fidgeted and swore some more but this time silently and to himself. One or two of the other men looked up at him and then back to Henry, who was listening intently to an old-timer going on and on about something. Tom's ears grew hot with frustration and embarrassment. Finally he turned away, shouting *The bloody eggs are ready!* just before he did. When he glanced back some of the men were grinning at him, turning their heads from him to Henry like dogs waiting for a stick to be thrown. He walked back to the truck, the sun burning his already hot neck. He heard Henry's boots crunching through the dirt behind him, and then the soft padding sound they made through the ash.

"Where's Flynn?" he demanded, when he'd caught up.

Tom jumped. He looked around but couldn't see him. He looked under the truck but Flynn wasn't there either. Just then they both heard a little boy's moan coming from the far side of the truck. It was Flynn. He'd taken off his shoes and he was holding his arm with his other hand. His feet and arms were both covered in the crumbly dirt of the clearing. Henry reached him and took hold of his arm and brushed away the dirt. He asked him what the matter was but Flynn could only cry, his tears leaving trails down his dusty cheeks.

"He's burnt his arm," said Henry. "He's gone too near one of these fires and tripped over into some ashes or something. Bloody hell, Tom! I told you to fucking look after him!"

Tom, stunned, opened his mouth to defend himself, but, before he could, Henry shot out his arm and caught him across the ear and the side of the head with his open palm. His ear rang for a moment and then he heard Flynn's crying rise and rise until it was a high-pitched squeal. He saw Henry almost throw Flynn up into the truck and then he heard an order to fetch the pan. The blood was right up in his ears and his cheek was on fire under his hand. He heard laughing and he turned. The men—all the men—were watching. Some were laughing, their shoulders and bellies shaking. They were all looking at him, laughing at him. He picked up the pan and threw the eggs into the fire and then walked to the truck with his head down. Flynn was still bawling. His anger at all of them grew. His brother was burnt. That was nothing to laugh at—there was nothing funny about it. He felt like throwing the pan at their stupid faces, but, instead, he climbed up into the cab, tossed the pan on the floor, and slammed shut the door.

They roared off down the track. Henry said nothing else to him but swore a few more times under his breath. Flynn held his arm and cried big breathy sobs and looked miserable. Tom put his arm round his shoulders—but more for his own comfort than Flynn's. They drove to the nearest town, a little place called Jack's Mountain that had a general store, a post office, a hotel, a few dishevelled-looking houses. Henry found a tap at the side of the hotel and stuck Flynn's arm under it. Flynn watched transfixed as his arm emerged from the dust and the damage could be seen. There were two long red marks, one above the other, beginning to puff out in blisters. Tom couldn't look at Henry.

"It's not too bad," Henry declared. "Keep his arm under there a while longer." He put his hand on Flynn's head.

"You'll be right, tiger," he said. "You'll live." He turned and stomped up the hotel stairs and disappeared inside. Tom waited with Flynn at the tap. When Flynn became impatient he pulled his arm out from under the water but soon afterwards the pain would return and he would put his arm back under again. A dog came and sniffed them both and a kid on a bike rode past and nearly steered into a post looking at them.

"Look at him, Flynn. Nearly crashed into the post," said Tom. Flynn giggled.

The wife of the publican came out to look at Flynn's arm. She tut-tutted and then took him inside. When he came out he had a bright white bandage on his arm and a glass of Coke with a straw in it. She had a glass for Tom as well and a plate of sandwiches. They climbed up into the truck and sat amidst the curled and sun-yellowed racing guides, the dried and miniaturised orange peel, the crushed red Marlboro packets, the smell of sawdust and hot oil. They ate their sandwiches, washed them down with their Cokes, burped. Tom began to think the day might finally be looking up.

Soon Flynn was sound asleep, his mouth open and his head back against the wine-red seat, the band of burnt, freckled skin across his nose and cheeks vivid against the smooth white skin of his neck. Tom sat and listened. He could hear the hotel noises: shouting, laughing, tinny music. The sounds seemed strangely comforting. A breeze filtering down through the trees fanned him through the open window. He put his head back and fell asleep beside his brother and soon he was dreaming. He dreamt he fell off the deck of a great ship and sank down through the sea, the sun disappearing, miles and miles of black elbow-room opening up all around.

Henry woke them by thudding on the door of the truck, right where Tom's head rested. He looked up, his thoughts in a muddle, but not so much that he couldn't see that Henry was good and drunk. He looked out the window at the street. It was much later in the day. Where before there had only been their one truck in the street there were now half a dozen. It seemed work was over for the timbermen for the week. They sat out on the verandah of the hotel, leant against the doorposts and spat into the dust. The boy on the bike was back, but keeping his distance on the other side of the street.

"Mr. McKinnon's going to take you home," said Henry. "I'm stayin' on for a bit longer." He turned and went back into the hotel after mumbling something about waiting by the truck. Tom rubbed his face, shook Flynn, then climbed down from the truck's cab. Flynn followed at his own pace, muttering to himself.

"You sleep a lot," Tom told him.

"Do I?"

"Yep, you do."

"Well, so do you."

"Not as much as you. How's your arm?"

"Good," said Flynn, as though there were nothing wrong with it.

"You hungry?"

"Yeah."

"What do you want to eat?"

"Bacon."

"Oh yeah. Bacon'd be good."

He took Flynn to the tap and let him drink and then he took a few mouthfuls himself. They wandered down to Artie McKinnon's truck to wait. Tom could see Henry inside the hotel. He was laughing and holding up his empty glass and pointing to it. Being inside there obviously put him in a much better mood. Tom looked at the golden glasses of beer in the hands of the men and tried to imagine how cold they were, colder than ice maybe, from the way water dripped from them like it did from trees in the rain. He swore to Flynn he would go in there when he was old enough and drink twenty of them at once but Flynn seemed unimpressed.

Three or four men were drinking quietly in the shade of the hotel's southern wall, admiring an axe one held, when the boys walked by. Tom recognised a few from the clearing.

"Henry's boy," one said, as if Tom were hard of hearing.

"Doesn't treat him good," said a second.

"Maybe it's not your business."

"Maybe not, but he'll be six feet under, Henry doesn't watch out."

"How's that?"

"Henry'll let go a log on him, way he charges about, bull at a gate."

"Henry has a good boy there," said the first man.

"Yep, he's a good boy. Not his boy though."

"No?"

"No. That's Alex Ferry's boy."

"You don't say?"

"That little un's Henry's."

"Ah."

"Henry should watch out, all I'm saying," repeated the second man.

The first man sang out to Tom. "Come here a minute, son!"

Tom thought about ignoring him but then he turned and walked over, his head down, Flynn trailing behind.

"How's the little feller's arm?"

"It's all right."

The man was old and stocky with a small red nose and big ears. The deep, crinkled skin around his eyes made him look like a coolie he'd seen once in a book.

"Your old man, he's all right."

Tom nodded and looked at the gaiters over the man's socks.

"We're all a bit rough and ready but our barks are worse than our bites. You follow?"

Tom nodded.

"Good boy. Hey, here's something for ya."

The man pulled something from his pocket and palmed it before Tom could see what it was.

"What is it?"

"Don't want to guess?"

"No."

"No, I suppose you're gettin' too old to be guessing."

The man held the object out to Tom in his palm and Tom picked it up. It was a harmonica, about three inches long and silver.

"I can't take this."

"You go ahead. You're a good boy, helping your—helping old Henry. I want you to have it. I've got plenty."

"Take it, kid," said the second man. "Anything to stop him playin' it."

Tom was about to protest a little more when the man's attention was caught by another of his mates. One of their number, a huge man with black chops, was stumbling about in the vacant land next to the hotel. A building had once stood where he tottered but had burnt to the ground long ago, charred stumps the only evidence of its dimensions. The man leant to the side and then his leg gave way on him and he fell into the long grass. The men laughed and began to pelt him with small stones from the side of the road and anything else they could lay their hands on.

"Thanks then," said Tom.

The man glanced at him and grinned and raised his hand, gave a slight nod, his eyes concealed almost completely now by the folds of skin around them. He turned to his mate, pointed to the tool he held in his hands, said: "Yeah, she's a good axe that."

Tom walked on, turning the harmonica over in his hands. Flynn held out his hand to look and after a while Tom gave it to him.

"What is it?"

"It's a harmonica."

"What's it for?"

"It's to make music. You blow through the front there."

Flynn put his lips to the instrument and blew and then laughed at the sound he made and then began to make it again and again.

"What do the words say?"

"*The Miniature Boomerang. Albert's System. Tangent Tempered Reeds*," read Tom.

"What's that mean?"

"Something to do with its innards, I think."

"Its gizzards."

"Yep. Its gizzards."

"Why did he give it to you?"

"I don't know."

They waited for Artie McKinnon by his truck for another twenty minutes or so before he appeared, striding down the road with his head down, sucking on the cigarette he seemed to be hiding in his palm. When he saw the boys he jerked his thumb.

"Hop in," he said.

They clambered up into the cab as Artie started the truck and they were soon roaring down the valley road. Artie reeked of beer and smoke. He shouted a few things over the noise of the engine but didn't say much after a while. Tom noticed that he was looking at his watch more and more often, scratching his pointy nose each time. Flynn was leaning forward to work the old indicator hand. Tom grabbed a handful of his shirt so he wouldn't topple forward. Artie became more and more distracted, pressing the accelerator pedal further and further to the floor, the engine wailing its way up and down the hills. After a while they pulled up in a cloud of dust down by the turn-off to Angel Rock. Tom looked over at Artie.

"I'm sorry, fellers, I'll have to drop you here. I'm real late for something."

"Is it far?"

"Nope. You can see the rock from here," he said, pointing out his window. "You just go down this road, take the first right; that goes straight into town. Shouldn't take you twenty minutes."

"All right."

"Thanks, son. Really appreciate it."

Tom was more than glad to get out of the truck. He hopped down after Flynn and shut the door behind them. Artie wasted no more time and took off up the road, sounding the truck's wheezy horn and waving his arm out the window. They watched him go and then waited for the dust to settle.

"Well, come on then," said Tom, setting off, when it had.

"Wrong way, Tom."

"Right way, Flynn. We're not going into town, are we. We're going home. Home's this way, towards the river. This road meets up with ours."

Flynn didn't argue and he followed Tom as he set off along the eastern branch of the crossroads. The afternoon was still and very quiet. The road followed a ridge for a little while and then dropped down into a gully. As Tom thought they might, Flynn's shoes soon began to pinch him and he sat, put the harmonica down, and pulled them off. He would have left all three items behind if Tom hadn't picked them up. When they walked on the sun seemed much lower in the sky than it had been just five minutes before and in under the trees the light was growing dimmer. Tom wasn't worried. He thought the shale road would be easy enough to follow, even after dark, and Artie had said it wasn't far.

They came to where the road split into two and, after thinking about it for a moment, Tom decided on the right fork. The road wound down through a stand of gnarled old swamp gum where the darkness was thickening, great drifts of it piling up in the under-growth. They could hear rustling, whispering sounds coming from behind the roadside trees.

"Is this the right way?" Flynn asked, his voice hesitant.

"Yep. It must be."

Flynn looked doubtful. Tom slipped the watch off his wrist and gave it to him to play with. He'd started to teach Flynn how to tell the time but he seemed happy enough just watching the second hand go round and the luminous dots marking the hours.

"What time is it?"

"I can't tell."

"Try."

Flynn looked at the watch, his lips moving as he laboured with the concepts of big and little, numbers, circles, hands. Tom squeezed at the splinters starting to itch under the skin of his palm. Surely by now they'd be able to see the town, he thought, as what felt like another fif-teen minutes passed. He hadn't seen or heard a car for a long while now and the road was becoming less even and more and more pot-holed and corrugated. He felt a moment of panic but fought it down. He stopped in the middle of the road and turned round. Flynn stopped too.

"I think we've come the wrong way," he said at last. Flynn looked up at him but, thankfully, didn't start to cry.

Back along the road, maybe half an hour before, he had seen the last roadside mailbox, the last gate, the last track leading up to a farm-house. It would be simple enough to go and ask someone the right way—they might even get a lift. Henry need never know, Tom thought. He wouldn't get back home until much later, maybe even tomorrow morning. He turned round, happy with the plan, but as he did he noticed a long, dark shape by the edge of the road. It was just behind a white road marker with a red reflector nailed to it. They must have walked straight past it before and not noticed. He stared until he was sure it was not a shadow and then he moved closer. It was a kangaroo, stretched out, with its smaller front legs above its head, its head between them, its massive hind legs and tail half-obscured by the roadside grass. Tom had seen kangaroos before in the valley, but never one as large. He'd heard stories from the timbermen of the kangaroos of the outback and how they could leap over high fences and how to shoot one and skin it and cut it up and which parts to eat. He thought this one must have been hit by a car. He'd seen many things killed this way and had even been in the truck when Henry had cursed and hit something, but they'd never stopped to see what. One time Tom had turned and peered out into the blackness and seen a strange shape in the red glow of the truck's tail-lights, something stumbling and broken, an outlandish shape spilling its blood and its life out onto the road, and he'd never forgotten the sight.

He approached the roo cautiously, not really a thought in his head about why, but drawn to it all the same. Flynn was dilly-dallying around behind and hadn't noticed what had caught his eye. He was holding his watch arm up to his ear, a self-contained system with himself at the centre, a whole world within the stretch of his arms. Tom turned back to the kangaroo and immediately caught the stench coming off it. The smell was about the same as a rotten cat or dog. Tom screwed up his nose and was about to call to Flynn and continue walking when he felt the kangaroo stiffen and sense him. Not dead after all. He stopped and held his breath. They were only a foot or two away from each other. He heard the animal's chest suck in air and then its entire body quivered, sprang upright, and reared to its full height before him. Tom stepped back and fell over but didn't take his eye off the kangaroo for a moment. The roo's head turned to and fro, its eyes as wide and white as a spooked horse's. There were black and white markings on its face and it had black paws. The fur around one heavily muscled shoulder was much darker and Tom could just see the glistening edges of a putrid wound. Maybe it had been shot, he thought, but before he could think anything else the animal turned clumsily and bounded off into the bush. Tom watched it go—sat and stared into the twilight after it like a sea captain after a mermaid or white whale.

After a moment or two he stood, his and Flynn's predicament forgotten, thinking only of how the kangaroo had come to be injured and how it had come to be by the side of this road.

"Wow," he said to Flynn. "Did you see that? Did you see how big it was?"

He looked around for his brother but the piece of road where he had been was empty; there was no Flynn standing there, no Flynn singing, no Flynn on the grass verge, no Flynn playing a harmonica. Nothing at all and nothing to be heard either. He looked up and around, as if he might be up a tree, or hanging in the air, glowing, like a small moon, but he was gone, and there were only so many times you could look in the same places.

"Flynn!" he yelled. "Come back or you'll get a bloody belting!"

His shouts were swallowed up by the trees and seemed to make no impression. He stopped, listened, and thought he heard the kanga-roo—or maybe Flynn—crashing down through the undergrowth somewhere, but then there was nothing except the faint sound of run-ning water. His hands and feet went cold and when he called his brother's name again he could barely hear himself, his voice was so hoarse, so strangled inside him.

"Flynn!" he croaked, but there was no answer.

He tried to think. Flynn had been behind him. He must have seen the kangaroo and followed it when it leapt away, sliding into the bush behind him and only a few yards away from where he'd been standing. It was the only explanation. He stepped into the bush, calling Flynn's name constantly and trying to watch his step. The floor of the forest was a mess of tree litter and small scratching plants and grasses but the trees were evenly spaced and it was still possible to see quite a dis-tance through them. Away from the road the land sloped sharply away into a gully. He pushed down through the swamp gum scrub until he was standing next to the creek he had heard from the road. Looking down its course, he saw the last of the sun sinking away below the hills in the distance. There were pools, connected by thin trickles of water, stretching away as far as he could see. The thunderstorm the night before seemed to have made little impression on the volume of water but Tom could see where the water had risen, then receded, leaving a watermark of leaves and twigs. He took a quick drink, then stood and yelled Flynn's name again. In the distance, upstream, in a spot where there were fewer trees, he thought he saw something move. He was peering into the gloom, flicking his eyes from left to right, when he saw Flynn's pale legs, or what he thought were Flynn's legs, far ahead.

"Flynn!" he screamed, and the legs seemed to stop and he was certain he saw the white oval of Flynn's face turn to him.

"Stay there!" he yelled, relief flooding through him. He heard a sound like a voice, but he couldn't be sure it wasn't the water. He raced up the creekbed, skidding across the bare rock and crunching through the beds of gravelly wash for about ten minutes until he was sure he was close to where he had seen Flynn. When he arrived there was no sign of him. Nothing at all. He sat down and struck the rock beneath him with his fist and then he burst into tears. He sat there sobbing for ten minutes or so and then there was nothing left to do but keep walking or stop where he was and give up. He wiped his eyes and took some deep breaths and reassured himself as best he could, the cold squid of panic in his belly threatening to grow and grow. He told himself that he wasn't lost, that he could follow the creek back to the road and get help, or he could keep walking and find Flynn and they could walk out together. He licked his lips and then decided to walk. He walked for what felt like nearly an hour before he stopped again. It was pitch dark until the moon rose and helped him, but then clouds came over and soaked up its faint glow and made it so dark he could barely see his feet. He walked a little way up the slope away from the creek and crawled in under an overhanging bush and pulled his knees into his chest. He listened for as long as he could for the sounds of a small boy but heard nothing like them. He was hungry and exhausted and even though it wasn't too cold under the bush he wondered matter-of-factly whether this might be the end of his life. Between bouts of sobbing he felt more than a little annoyed. All the questions he had about things seemed as though they would never be answered and Henry, Sonny, the rest of the world, would win. In the darkness he thought about things until he saw himself and Flynn, clear as day, as though it had already happened, standing by the road, arm out to wave down his mother as she drove by where Artie had dropped them. He saw her staring ahead through the windscreen, wrapped in the hard black skin of the car, the dust billowing up as she roared by, missing them. The sort of dust that clung to trees, bushes, even people if they stood still long enough.

4

After he'd finished his shower and shave Pop Mather went and sat
out on the back step of the station house with a cup of tea. The
morning air was already whet with a summery edge but a whisper of
breeze evaporated water off his damp skin and cooled him. A
butcherbird on the fence watched a dragonfly jig and jag its way over
the lawn. Bees hummed in the orange blossoms. Soft new leaves fluttered in the trees like tassels and ribbons, like echoes of other cele-
brations, other occasions. Births, deaths, marriages. Life churned on
like the will of God, but today was Sunday and it was Pop's day off as
well.

He closed his eyes for a while, then opened them again. Nothing
had changed. He put on his glasses, picked up Homer, began to read.
He'd only finished a few pages when he looked over the top of the
book and saw Ellie Gunn coming across the lawn towards him. He
knew something was wrong by the set of her shoulders and by the way
she was walking, even before he saw the look on her face. He sighed
and put down his book and glasses, a strange feeling in the pit of his
stomach. Ellie was over thirty now and still a peach despite the hard
work she was doing and all the long hours. He'd heard rumours she
and Henry might have to move on soon. He knew he'd be sad to see
her leave and he couldn't say that about every soul in Angel Rock. She
was one of those gentle, generous women who, as far as he could see,
always went for the wrong kind of man. First Tom's father, who'd
stayed barely a month by Ellie's side after young Tom had been born,

and now Henry, who, to give him his due, had stuck around much longer and seemed to be devoted to his young feller and making a go of things.

Ellie stopped when she was only a few yards away from him. Pop thought she looked near collapse. Her face was pale and drawn and her hair was a sight. He jumped up from his chair and took her by the arm.

"What is it, girl?"

"I've been . . . up all night," she managed to say, gulping down air. "I thought the boys were with Henry . . . but when he got home this morning they weren't with him. He doesn't know where they are, Sergeant Mather. He says Artie McKinnon was supposed to . . . He didn't want me to come, but . . ."

He could hear the panic welling up in her voice. He steered her inside and sat her down at the kitchen table. Lil heard the commotion and came and sat down and took Ellie's hand in hers.

"Where's Henry now?" asked Pop.

"He's out looking. He's gone to Artie's."

"Right."

Pop got on the telephone and rang Artie's place. Artie's wife said that he and Henry had gone out looking for the boys.

"If you see either of them, or the boys, ring me here, will you?" he instructed. "Thanks. All right then. Cheers."

"Maybe they've gone fishing or something," Pop said, as he walked back into the kitchen.

"No," Ellie sobbed. "None of the gear's gone."

"Something else then," continued Pop. "Boys can get up to all sorts of things."

Ellie shook her head. Pop put his hand on her shoulder. He could smell the sweet, stale smell of her and he could feel her soft skin through the fabric of her dress.

"Don't worry, love," said his wife. "I'm sure they're all right."

"Yes, don't worry, Ellie. Henry and Artie have probably found 'em already," he said. "We'll just sit tight for a while until we hear. What about a cup of tea?"

They sat for an hour or two waiting for the two men to appear or call. Ellie walked back and forth beside the kitchen table and Lil fussed over her and kept the tea coming. Just after the church bells rang for the morning service Pop saw a movement through the window. Henry and Artie. He strode out to meet the two men with Ellie in his wake. He didn't need to ask the result of their efforts. Henry, bleary-eyed, his shoulders hunched, his dark red hair unkempt, barely lifted his head to acknowledge them. Artie, shamefaced and pasty, stood just behind him, gripping his hat in his hands and playing it like a squeezebox. Ellie stared at them both. She didn't, as Pop thought she might, cry or faint or scream. Instead, she went to the back step and sat down, hard, her eyes glassy, her body trembling. Pop stepped forward to the two men and began whispering fiercely at them.

It was Artie who provided most of the answers to Pop's questions. Henry stood there mutely, looking like a little boy himself despite his thick arms and sun-reddened face. Every so often he would let out a deep breath and shake his head. Pop began to feel a bit sorry for him—he knew how much little Flynn meant to the poor bastard.

"Why'd you drop them by the side of the road like that?" he said, incensed, turning his attention back to Artie.

"I was . . . ah . . . running late."

"What for, for Christ's sake?"

"I . . . ah . . ." Artie's eyes flicked from Pop to the side of Henry's head.

"A woman, Artie? That it? Not Mrs. McKinnon I take it?"

Artie blushed a deep red and stammered something unintelligible.

"Sorry, Sarge," he muttered. "Don't say nothin', will ya?"

"Bloody bleeding hell! You'd better hope those boys are all right, that's all I can say. *Astonishing!*"

He spun round and headed back into the station house. Grace was just emerging from her room as he stormed past on his way to the station proper.

"What's the matter?" she asked him.

"Follow me and I'll tell you," he said, grim-faced.

He was on the phone for three-quarters of an hour getting together the search party. Some of those he rang rang others and by the time everyone had gathered out at the crossroads just before eleven he had a couple of dozen men. He heard one man grumble about losing his Sunday afternoon over some silly lads and Pop shook his head and told him no one had twisted his arm and he was free to go. The man, shamed, stayed put.

Henry stood by his truck staring at the ground and smoking a cigarette. He looked calm but his hand shook as he smoked. He and Artie had already checked every likely place they could think of that morning without any success. Ah well, Pop thought, it's out of his hands now.

He walked into the middle of the road, whistled for everyone's attention and when he had it he asked for their opinions and he listened to where they thought they should start looking for the boys. Most of what they said tallied with where he wanted them so he divided them up into four parties of six each and tried to make sure that there was at least one in each party with a little bit of sense. As he was about to get everyone going the Pope brothers, who lived out along the road to the dam, drove up in their dusty Phantom, the old thing looking like a hearse from another age, a conveyance for some puffed-up dignitary, not a runabout for two old cattlemen. They'd bought the car when they were flush, nearly forty years ago, and had never parted with it. They drove into Angel Rock for church every Sunday. Pop waved them down and they pulled up. Heat was coming off the peaked hood of the Rolls as if there were a fire parked there underneath it.

"You should go a bit faster, get some more air past that radiator," Pop said, leaning in at the window.

"Won't go too fast *up* the damn hill, you fool, only down, and we're not going down are we, we're going up!" said Reg, the cranky one, who was driving.

"Thank you, Sergeant, we'll keep that in mind," said the other brother, Robert, who'd had polio as a child and could barely walk and had more cause to be disagreeable than most but never was. "What can we do for you?" he continued. "What's all the commotion?"

"We're looking for some missing boys."

Pop leant his hip against the side of the car and looked in at them. Both were wearing their hats and threadbare suits. He knew Reg wasn't licensed and his eyes were none too good any more. One day he'd have to take away the keys and he wasn't looking forward to that day at all.

"You didn't see anyone on your way down this morning?"

"No, sir. You see any boys this morning, Reg?"

"No, no boys," Reg muttered.

"What boys are these that are lost?"

"Ellie Gunn's boys."

"Ah. How'd they lose themselves then?"

"Walking home from the crossroads, some time yesterday evening."

"Well, what kind of mug could get lost doing that?" said Reg slowly, his voice scornful.

"All right, Reg, steady on," said Pop quietly. "Their father's just here."

Reg peered past Pop at Henry and screwed up his face.

"Ah, well, *his* father was a silly coot as well," muttered Reg. "Maybe it's in the blood. Whole family never had no common senses."

"Yes. All right then. Thank you, gentlemen. Steady as she goes and you might make it back in one piece. If you do see any boys on your travels you be sure and let me know."

He rapped on the door of the Rolls and turned away before Reg could fire a parting shot. As he did he saw Grace sitting on the step of Artie's truck. She was watching him intently. He sighed to himself. He'd almost forgotten about her. She'd insisted on coming and against his better judgement he had given in. He found it hard to argue with her when she had her mind set on something.

"Come on, you," he said. She came to him, all elbows and knees. He held the door of the car open for her and then they drove down the road a distance to where his party would begin their search. When they arrived he had the four men—Harry Clough, Percy Meaney, Ezra Steele and Artie McKinnon—spread out to within calling distance of each other before setting off across the paddock. Grace stayed close by him and, as he had predicted back home, the jeans she had insisted on wearing were too tight and consequently too hot. Soon her T-shirt was soaked through with perspiration and strands of her hair were plastered to the sides of her ever-reddening face. He went to her side.

"You all right, love?"

"Yep. I'm all right."

"Drink plenty of water," he said to her, and refilled her water bottle from the waterbag slung across his back.

"Thanks."

They soon left the river-flat paddocks behind and started along a track that wound up into the hills. Pop reckoned that if the boys had taken a wrong turn they might have ended up along there somewhere, but there was no answer to their calls and cooees and no one saw any sign that they had been that way. They continued along the track for another hour before Pop signalled a rest. He refilled Grace's water bottle and then he climbed up onto a little rise, took out his binoculars, and scanned the valley. Away across the river he could see one of the other search parties and further still, down to the south, the sun twinkling off car windscreens in Angel Rock's main street. He put down the glasses and rubbed his eyes and muttered a quick invocation to St. Anthony and any of his mates who were handy and had nothing better to be going on with.

By mid-afternoon Grace was nearly spent, but she hid it from her father as a matter of honour. She followed him wearily in under a stand of tall gums. It was cooler in their shade and she immediately felt less faint. She glanced behind her to see if there was any time for a rest before the other men caught up. They were fairly close behind and she sighed inwardly. The six of them were walking in single file across the spur because the bush on each side was too thick. The man immediately behind her, Mr. Meaney, a stocky farmer with very crooked teeth, gave her a shy smile but it was the man following him whose eyes she saw flick from her bottom, up to her eyes, back to her bottom again. She turned and stared at her father's back. Two words sprang into her head and jigged around like butterflies. *He's looking. He's looking* at me. Darcy's *father. Mr. Steele.*

Her bottom suddenly felt enormously big and round and she tried to walk like a boy, keeping her buttocks clenched and her hips as straight as possible. A red flush of indignation lit up her cheeks, neck, and the tips of her ears. She wanted to spin round and tell him to stop but she knew she wouldn't.

They crossed the spur and the bush opened out again and the track ended at a gate in a fence. A creek continued along the flat and three of the men crossed it and spread out along the opposite bank. Pop walked along the near bank and Grace saw with a start that Mr. Steele was now between her and him. She tried to count the men she could see but they kept appearing and disappearing behind trees and then she saw Pop direct her a little further out. She was about to protest, but then marched away when Mr. Steele began drawing closer. She could hear the others calling the boys' names and she kept her head forward, watching the ground in front of her. She could just see Mr. Steele out of the corner of her right eye, although he seemed intent now on the ground before him and didn't even glance in her direction. They continued in the same manner for a quarter of an hour until the trees became more dense and she couldn't see him any more. She kept walking. The calling voices of the others grew fainter and finally seemed to die out altogether. She stopped and listened. Maybe the sound was catching in the trees. She started to walk again and thought she heard Pop shout, but then for a long time there was nothing. The sun dipped in behind a cloud and the stand of trees around her suddenly seemed very dim and eerily quiet. She nearly panicked then and was about to run when a man stepped out from behind a tree, just ahead and to the right of her. At first she thought it was Mr. Steele but, as her heart began thudding in her chest, she saw it was someone else, someone she didn't recognise at all. He was long-haired and dirty and his eyes were wide. They stood, staring at each other, and then Grace heard Pop's voice, away off to the left, calling her name. She glanced away from the man for barely a moment, but when she looked back all she saw was a brief glimpse of his back as he darted away through the trees. She ran to Pop, her heart racing and her legs trembling.

"You all right, sweetheart?"

"Yeah, I . . ."

"Any sign of the boys?"

Grace shook her head.

"All right, stay by me now," he whispered, his hand on her shoulder. "We're nearly home." She nodded, so relieved at the words that she didn't know whether she was about to cry or hug him.

They stopped for a cuppa before covering the last stretch into town. Grace thought it was about three or four o'clock. The crooked-toothed farmer already had the makings out and had built a small fire of twigs underneath a billyful of creek water. Pop squatted and looked at the map with another man and Grace sat down at his side, exhausted, and watched the fire flare into life. The tea-maker handed her a mug of tea when it had been made and smiled at her.

"Thank you, Mr. Meaney," she said and as she did she looked about, her proximity to Pop fuelling her confidence. She wanted to tell him about the man behind the tree, but then Mr. Steele came into the clearing, talking to Artie McKinnon.

"Percy," said Mr. Meaney.

"Pardon?"

"Percy. Call me Percy."

"Oh. Thank you, Percy."

Percy beamed.

"Percy?"

"Yes?"

"There was no one else searching with us, was there? Just the six of us?"

"I believe so. Why?"

"Oh, nothing."

Grace glanced across at Mr. Steele as she sipped her tea. He was looking straight at her, a cigarette only a little thicker than a match-stick in the side of his mouth, a slight grin on his face. She frowned at him and turned away, but when she looked back a little later he was grinning even harder.

It took another hour to get back to Angel Rock and Grace stayed close to her father the whole way. They traipsed wearily into the park and stood around the war memorial just as the sun was sinking behind the Rock. The other search parties were as tired and grubby as they and had found nothing either. Not a thing. While Pop wrote down the names of those available to search the next day Grace walked very slowly back to the station house with her head down. The little kids playing in the street stopped their games for a moment and watched, wide-eyed and silent, as she walked by. Back in the station house her fearfulness during the day seemed almost silly, and she didn't tell Pop about the man that night, or the following day. She pushed the image of him right to the back of her mind and it sat there, almost, but not quite, forgotten.

5

The gully was cool when Tom woke and he shivered a little as he walked down to the water to drink. When he'd filled his belly and cleaned his face he jumped around to get the blood flowing. He felt better and more optimistic than he thought he should be. He set off up the creekbank, water sloshing in his empty stomach, grimly determined to find Flynn, and confident that he would.

He followed the creek for a half-hour or so and then he rounded a long bend and saw Flynn curled up fast asleep in the middle of a stretch of bare rock. He ran over and looked down at him, his relief rendering him speechless. Flynn sniffed in his sleep and then moaned. Two candles of yellow snot sat under his nostrils. Tom bent down and shook him. Flynn opened his eyes sleepily and looked up at his brother.

"What were you doing?" Tom shouted down at him, all his worry suddenly venting itself. "You got yourself bloody lost!"

Flynn started to cry and Tom dropped to his knees and wrapped his arms round him and held him tight.

"Did you see him, Tom?" he said, when his tears had subsided a little.

"Who?"

"The kangaroo."

"Yeah, I saw him! Didn't you hear me calling?"

"Yeah, and I called back, but you didn't come." His dirty little face creased and he began to cry again.

"It's all right," Tom said, unable to shout any more. He patted

Flynn's shoulder. "You're found, and we'll be all right now. We'll walk back up to the road and find a farm."

Flynn nodded and wiped his nose with his forearm.

"Tom?"

"What?"

"I'm hungry."

"Yeah. So am I. Come on, the sooner we go, the sooner we'll eat."

They set off downstream, Tom holding Flynn's hand tightly in his and talking about anything to keep their minds off their predicament.

"You know Ham, the chimpanzee?" Tom asked his brother. "The one they sent up to space in a rocket?"

"No."

"Yes, you do. I've told you about him enough times."

"Oh, yeah."

"Well, when he landed in the sea and they opened up the hatch on his capsule, do you remember what he was doing?"

"No," said Flynn, shaking his head.

"He was eating an apple. He was sitting there at his flippin' flight deck eating an apple."

Flynn laughed and they both felt a little better for a while.

"Tom?"

"Yes?"

"Why'd they send a chim-pan-zee into space?"

"They wanted to see if something alive would be all right up there. Before they sent people. It wouldn't be so bad if a chimpanzee got killed."

"Why not?"

"They don't understand things." Tom shrugged. "They wouldn't get as scared too."

"Oh. Tom?"

"Yes?"

"Will Dad be mad at us?"

"I suppose so. Probably."

They walked for half an hour and Flynn kept grumbling about his stomach. Tom was suddenly dizzy in the head and he had to sit down for a moment to let it pass. Flynn squatted down next to him. He looked worried and then he began to cry again. He was dirty and his shirt was ripped down the front. Tom could see that he'd had a hard night as well, maybe harder than his own.

"Don't be a bloody baby, Flynn," said Tom, very softly, with no venom in his voice.

It took a long while for his brother's tears to stop this time and as Tom waited for him the sun cleared the trees and bathed them in warm yellow light.

"We'll get home, Flynn. I promise we will. Come on, have a drink."

"You promise?"

"Yep. I promise. Come on."

Tom walked his little brother down to the creek and watched as he hung his head over the water and drank, on hands and knees, as though he'd been doing it that way all his life.

They spent half the morning walking back along the creek the way they had come. Tom scanned the banks for any sign of where they had come down from the road but he saw nothing he remembered. The sun was soon scorching into them and their stomachs growled without pause. At about mid-morning they came to a fork in the creek. Tom sat down, despairing, but tried to keep his disappointment from Flynn. He was almost certain he hadn't passed a branch like this the night before. Maybe they'd missed the road altogether. There was nothing for it but to choose a fork of the creek and follow it down to where it must surely join up with the river. He thought about it for a few minutes, chewing his lip, then chose the right fork.

"Come on," he said to Flynn as he started off. "Nearly there."

All that morning they walked by bluegums, tallowwoods and brush-boxes and then, in the middle of the afternoon, the country became much drier and the timber on either side changed to bloodwoods, ironbarks and grey gums, and the ferns and dark-leaved palms gave way to kangaroo grass and blackboys. Cockatoos screeched in the trees as they passed. When Flynn grew tired Tom piggybacked him until his arms ached and his legs trembled. Sometimes when the valley they were in straightened out he saw undulating olive bush stretching ahead as far as he could see. At one point they were quite high and he could make out small clearings in the bush and far ahead a column of pale smoke rising vertically into the cloudless sky. His spirits lifted and he shouted and small birds whirred between trees, startled by the alien noise. They headed for the smoke but never seemed to get any closer to it all that afternoon and then a breeze came and tugged it to and fro until it was indistinguishable against the blue of the sky. Flynn was too tired to notice and only too happy to lie down once again to sleep as darkness fell.

In the morning cryptic-eyed geckoes watched Tom wake and stretch his stiff body. He crawled to the water's edge and drank and then he woke Flynn and made him go to the creek and drink as well. Apart from a handful of bitter-tasting berries they'd had nothing to eat since the publican's wife at Jack's Mountain had made them a sandwich and they were both light-headed and weak from hunger.

"It's a new day and we can make it," Tom whispered to himself.

He was still crouched by the creek when something caught his eye. A fat bluetongue lizard was spread out on a nearby rock, soaking up the morning sun. Tom wiped his mouth, then crawled back a dozen feet and began to search around for a weapon. He scrabbled around in the undergrowth until he found a good-sized stick and then he crept forward, the lizard in his sights. Flynn curled up on the ground and watched him.

"What you doing?" he said.

"Shhh!"

He snuck up on the bluetongue with all the stealth he could muster. When the lizard looked like moving he froze, but when he was barely two yards away it was still in the same spot. He hefted the stick in his hand and wondered how he should attack. The decision was made for him when the lizard curled its body round suddenly to face him, then stuck out its tongue and hissed. Tom leapt up, bringing the stick clubbing down around the lizard—it hissing like a maniac and evading the blows somehow. Tom squeezed his eyes shut and, almost in tears, intensified the barrage until, finally, he felt the stick strike something softer than the rock. He opened his eyes. The blue-tongue's head was bloodied and its legs were doing a slow crawl but getting it nowhere. He sat down, panting and sick to the stomach, and waited for it to die.

He felt Flynn at his shoulder but barely had the strength to turn and look at him, but then he felt his little body slump against him. He turned. Flynn's face was pale and his eyes were right up in his head—he'd fainted dead away. Tom took hold of his arms and pulled him over to the shade of a tree. He brought water from the creek in his cupped hands and wet Flynn's cheeks and lips with it and when he started to come round he went back down to the lizard and wondered how he was going to get to the meat without a knife. A butcherbird lit on a rock in the creek and eyed the bluetongue's carcass.

"Shoo!" said Tom, and waved his arm.

He hunted around for a rock with a sharp edge and when he'd found one he turned the bluetongue over onto its back—the scrape of its little claws against the rock making his skin crawl—and eyed the soft, pale belly. The skin was much tougher than it looked and he had to push down hard with the rock, so hard that a burst of evil-looking shit came squirting out from between the lizard's hind legs. He gagged, turned, retched up the water he'd drunk that morning, and kept retching until nothing more would come. He wiped his mouth and looked down at the rock in his hand. It was streaked with the same dark blood that flecked his hands and forearms and that made him feel even sicker. When he could he looked back at the lizard lying on the rock. Then, in a fit of rage and frustration, he kicked it into the creek. Breathing hard, he turned and walked up to Flynn and grabbed him by the arm.

"Come on, we're going."

They stumbled along for the rest of the morning, Tom holding Flynn's hand, sometimes nearly dragging him along until, finally, he stopped, curled up in a ball, and refused to go any further. Tom pulled the harmonica from his pocket and dangled it before him. Flynn reached out for it and began sobbing.

"Give it!"

"No, you'll have to catch me first."

Tom walked off, holding the harmonica out behind him. Flynn

stood slowly and came after him. Tom kept him going for most of the day with the same trick. They passed through another deep valley filled with tall columns of flooded gum and turpentine, quiet as a cathedral. Then the deep valley was gone and they were in open woodland once more, the creek little more than a trickle beside them. The day was even hotter than the one previous and there was an over-hum of worker bees in the trees around like the sound of heat itself. Every now and then black bird-like shapes fluttered in front of Tom's eyes and he would have to sit, pull up his legs and put his head down until the shapes went away. He had no experience of death and associated it with sudden impacts and rending of flesh, not this gradual fading, ebbing feeling.

Mid-afternoon they stopped to rest again and as Tom lay in the shade he began to think he could smell wood smoke. He closed his eyes and inhaled deeply. Wood smoke. He propped himself up on one elbow and looked over at the timbered country on the far side of the creek. He convinced himself, slowly and surely, that he could see the smoke, lit up by broken sunlight, under some trees just downstream. Flynn was quiet beside him. He was falling behind more often now, wanting to sleep, and Tom was having to almost carry him to keep him going. He was starting to have fits of deep, phlegmy coughing as well.

Tom left him to sleep and started off towards the smoke. He stumbled down until the land levelled out and the trees changed again. The creek they had been following disappeared into a swampy complex of tussocky grass and sedges and deep, narrow sluices of water the colour of strong tea. The swamp now lay between Tom and the smoke, which he could easily see now, rising almost vertically into the sky, a small incline just obscuring its source. He set out across the narrowest part of the swamp towards a stretch of higher ground studded with paperbarks. He slipped and fell more than once when the solid footing afforded by the grass failed him and spun him off into muddy depressions laced with stagnant, silvery water. The mud sucked at his feet and as he struggled to free himself one more time his vision suddenly blurred and starred and he fainted.

When his eyes opened a little later the smell of the swamp was strong in his nostrils and he could hear Flynn wailing. He was near-hysterical by the time Tom managed to return to where he had left him. He took him by the shoulders and told him that he'd gone to look for the smoke and had fainted, that he hadn't abandoned him at all, that he would never do that, but it was a good half-hour before Flynn had calmed down enough for them to continue.

They went down to the swamp with Flynn holding tightly onto Tom's hand and then they skirted the mud and found that the creek continued its course on the swamp's far side. The creek was running in the direction Tom had seen the smoke so they followed it down and down until it entered a steep-sided valley crammed with palms and ferns. The creek formed pools they had to climb round and both were soon scratched and faint from the exertion. They stopped and rested by a pool on grey rocks that jutted out of the earth like the half-buried skulls of giants. Across the water, on the far bank, water dragons warmed themselves in the sun. They sat and watched them and the water and Tom saw tiny flowers float past in the current. Somewhere a tree or bush must have been dropping flowers onto the surface. Some looked like drops of blood under the water as if a murder had taken place in a shady upstream bend. A certain peacefulness stole into Tom's thinking as he sat there, watching the lizards, watching the flowers. It began to replace the gnawing fear and panic which had been close to overwhelming him all day. Although he was very tired and very hungry he welcomed this feeling and its enticement not to worry.

They walked no more that day and as the sun sank behind a saddle in the hills before them—the glow rising up as though a wondrous, golden city existed just beyond the next valley—pale yellow butter-flies came and floated all around them, some dying in the water and floating away downstream, and then something—maybe a platypus—splashed and slipped under the surface of the pool, leaving nothing but long, gentle ripples to kiss each bank. It took a few minutes for the fact to dawn on Tom that the sun was setting in the west and they'd been walking all that day almost directly towards it—in the opposite direction to the one he'd intended. He was about to burst into tears when Flynn began to speak, very softly, beside him.

"I'm hungry, Tom. I want to go home," he said. "I want to see Mum."

"You'll see her."

"You promise?"

"Already have."

"Swear?"

"Yeah."

Tom licked his thumb, straightened Flynn's fringe, then brushed dust off his cheeks.

"You want to look good for Mum, don't you?"

Flynn nodded.

"We must be close to a house or something. A road. Tomorrow we'll find it. Tomorrow we'll get home. I swear we will."

The sun lowered quickly then, and even though it was hard to see, Tom rubbed cool creek water onto the scratches on Flynn's arms and legs and picked specks of dirt and gravel from a deep graze on his own knee. He found a fern and stripped it of its fronds and laid them on the rock and laid Flynn down on them and then curled up round him. He watched him fall asleep, watched his thumb go into his mouth, and then he too closed his eyes. Finches chattered in the bushes and from somewhere up in the hills came the soft, clear tolling of bell-birds.

6

G race leant her head back against the seat and began to see the tricks the light was playing on her. She swung the door to and fro and small horses of reflected light galloped backwards and forwards across the road. It was nearly midday and the heat radiated down through the metal of the car like lightning down a rod but found nowhere to go. The sun burrowed into the car's paint and cracked the colour apart, found a rainbow where you wouldn't expect one, lifted it out for the boiling air to cushion, display like a dusty nugget, spin back out into the day. Everything on either side of the road seemed to be wilting. The road was empty, chalky. The rails running parallel to the road, behind the barbed wire, gleamed like chrome and appeared and disappeared in the heat haze. She looked over at the edge of the trees, where the timber started, where the shadows began, where it might have been just a little cooler. It almost seemed up to the country now, and the sun, to conjure up the boys, to have them step out from the shade and walk directly over to where she sat. They would be dusty, very hungry, and thin. They would probably have cuts on their legs and arms and torn clothes and she would bandage them up and then she and her father would drive them into town and they would sit quite still between them while Pop cracked jokes and she would put her arm across Tom's shoulders and when they arrived in town everyone would come out and crowd around and chatter with excitement and amazement.

They'd been missing for more than a week now. Nearly two hundred men, including blacktrackers and men with dogs, had been brought in to search. It was in all the newspapers—even in Sydney—and on the television and radio stations. She hadn't gone out with Pop again but she had sat by the two-way radio in the station listening to the talk and following the searchers' progress on the big map pinned to the wall. She hadn't even thought about Darcy until she hadn't turned up to have her dress altered, and then she wondered whether her father was being even more strict with her than usual.

She squinted over at the trees again, then turned and perched on her knees to look out the back window, but there was nothing there either, just a red-sided steer plugging slowly across the paddock. Pop stirred from his nap with a loud snort. He opened one of his eyes and looked at her. She knew his mouth would be dry so she jumped out of the car, unhooked the waterbag from the front bumper and handed it in to him. He took a long drink.

"Thanks, love."

He looked at his watch.

"Any sign of the train?"

"No."

"Flamin' thing is later than usual. Should've come past hours ago."

"Maybe it's been derailed. Hit a cow or something."

"Yep. Maybe it has." Pop smiled and leant towards the dashboard. With a trickle of juice from the battery the radio cranked out a bit of music, then a horse race.

"Who have we picked in this one?" Pop reached for the paper, creased open at the form guide, and his glasses, positioning them on the end of his long nose.

"I picked him. Twenty to one. Regular Rocket. But it's the next race."

"Regular Rocket. We'll see," he said, smiling wearily at his daughter. "Let's find some shade. It's more than regulation hot in here."

"We were in the shade before you fell asleep. The shade went that way," she said, pointing.

"Didn't mean to fall asleep. Must be more tired than I thought."

Grace looked at him. He'd been out until well past dark for the last week, rising before the sun. She wasn't surprised he was tired. They climbed from the car and sat where it was throwing a little shade onto the grass verge. They looked out across the river flats towards town, their backs against the warm steel bodywork. The storm over a week ago had done little to break the dry spell they were having. There hadn't been any good rain in months and the usually green paddocks were looking tired and very thirsty. The cattlemen were complaining, the dairymen as well. Everyone else was doing their best to stay cool. There was nothing for it but to wait. The good rain would come—they were too close to the coast for it not to. At least one thing was certain, Pop thought: it *would* come, whether the boys were found, or whether they never were.

He *was* tired. He was bone tired. Waiting for the train, listening to the races, were welcome chances to empty his mind of all the worries, all the impossibilities, all the disappointments of the past few days. There in the stillness, with his eyes closed and the sun against them, was also the place where things sometimes began to make sense, where he often heard the first word of something new. Today, though, there was nothing.

The police radio crackled and there was an echoing squeal and then silence. Pop thought of the noise as a phantom copper, forever on rounds, radio in ghostly hand, maybe whistling softly to himself. In the last week the radio had been constantly alive with voices from dawn to dusk. He'd heard them change from energetic and keen to resigned and anguished. They'd tramped in long ragged lines through dense bush and bivouacked where they'd stood when the daylight failed. He'd had them comb the roads again, on foot and on horse-back, and drag the river with hooks, but still nothing had been found. Henry Gunn, the poor bastard, unable to sleep, had lost his voice completely from calling the boys' names. He'd never seen a man grimmer, a jaw as hard set. He was in some kind of twilight world, along with Ellie, where hope slipped away like time. There was noth-ing he nor anyone else could say to them that was much help. Yester-day he'd had to send most of the searchers home—it had made him sick to do it—and now there was just a man or two with a team of dogs, some of the bushfire brigade lads, and himself—and the occa-sional crackle and sigh from the radio.

"Wish you were some help, old son," Pop said out loud.

He sighed and closed his eyes again. Where were those boys? Where the hell were they? To think they'd landed men on the moon, yet two little boys could not be found. They'd stared at the map, tried to get inside their heads, but they really seemed to have vanished without a trace. Henry had been adamant they'd gone fishing, told him how much Tom liked it. Pop thought it was doubtful, but the river still had to be searched, and thoroughly this time, not just by a few blokes in a boat with some hooks. Even though nearly every child in the district could swim, water had still claimed too many, particularly the little ones. Little Flynn could have fallen in somewhere, and Tom might have had to jump in after him. After that, with clothes on, even a grown man could get tired quickly and start to go under. It was either look in the river again, or sit quietly up the back of the church and pray.

He opened his eyes. The girl was over in the old siding now, the heat haze from the tracks making her limbs tremble and flicker. Just half a year ago she had been skinny and shapeless—a little girl. He thought of the boys lost out in the bush and was seized by the sudden realisation of how much he loved her, the precise size and shape of it revealed to him without alteration as if he had always been loath to believe it. He couldn't remember the last time he'd told her as much, or the last time he'd really held her the way he had when she'd been younger. He watched her a little longer until he realised his mouth was dry again. He heaved himself up and went to the front of the car and unhooked the waterbag from the bumper and took another good long drink from it.

Grace followed the rusting rails through the long grass. In front of the old sawmill there were sidings and steel-edged humps for the loading and unloading of trains that had not stopped there for years. The old stationmaster's office stood empty at one end of the main platform. She tried the door of the little wooden hut and it creaked open on rusted hinges. Inside she found a bank of seized levers, coated in dust and cobwebs, and a clock on the wall stopped at seven minutes past three—an eternal afternoon. She closed the door and sat outside by the rails and waited with her hand on the hot steel and then, almost as though she'd wished it, the rails began to quiver under her fingertips. She thought of Darcy racing the train and she put her ear down to the rail and fancied she could hear its faint song. Presently she heard the train's horn sound off in the distance. She stood and climbed the siding to wait, looking over to her father.

Pop heard the blast of the horn as well but the race they had an interest in had also just begun. It was raining down there and the track was heavy. He pictured the horses, well fed and fairly sparkling with condition, not like the working hacks up here, some with their ribs showing, scratching their flanks against ironbark posts and flicking flies away with a judder of muscle. The racecourse would be like a path to horse heaven for those nellies.

The caller began his call. He sounded like he was selling cattle, auctioning first place off to the highest bidder, and then, fluttering across the country, came news of the winner, the placegetters, the dividends on the last race, odds on the next—always a next race like waves against a shore. He wondered what the odds were now of finding the boys alive. If he could find God's bookie he would certainly ask him. What were the odds?

He stood and slapped his overalls and squinted out from under the brim of his hat in the direction of the arriving train. Grace stood on the siding with her hand up to shade her eyes. She waved to the train as it appeared round the bend, her arm smudged near the shoulder with pale dust, her long dark hair halfway down her back just like her mother had worn hers years ago.

"Gracie!" he called, not able to help himself. "Be careful now!"

She turned and flashed her eyes at him. He strode up to the siding and raised his hand as well as the train slowed. The driver showed them his pale palm. Pop put his hand down on Grace's shoulder.

"Our horse came second."

"Damn."

"Hey now. Enough of that."

The train rumbled on, the wheels squealing on the steel curve, and then it straightened up and came alongside the platform.

"Step right back now, girl," said Pop, as the engine passed in a billow of hot, smoky air. Grace glanced up at her father. She thought his eyes were far too dainty a blue for his stern look, but she stepped back anyway.

When most of the train had passed and they could see where it ended a face popped out of the guard's van. It was a youthful face with a shock of straw-yellow hair blowing up in the train's wake and a huge smile formed from wildly angled teeth. As he came closer Pop saw that the young man had his foot on a wooden box and was getting ready to shove it out the door of the van.

"They're late," said Pop. "They're not stopping."

He pulled Grace back and watched as the young guard disappeared back into the van. Then the box came flying out and fell with a thud against the sandy gravel of the platform. The guard looked back at them from his door, dust swirling up between him and them. His shoulders were shaking and he was hooting with obvious glee. Pop stared after him, unmoving, the box at his feet, until the guard and his wild smile had faded from view.

"Silly bugger," he said, finally.

He turned to his daughter. She was standing stock-still, staring at the box, the way he'd seen her do during certain games when she'd been younger, or the way she did when she saw a snake.

"Come on. It's all right. Give me a hand."

Grace looked up at him. The sun had buried his face in black shade so she couldn't read his expression, but she trusted his voice and, breaking her stillness, bent and lifted the box with him and carried it to the car, surprised to find it not as heavy as she thought it might be.

Henry Gunn was waiting for them down by the boat ramp, a terrible uncertainty in his eyes, as if he doubted the veracity of the air he breathed and the earth he walked upon.

"The outboard's broken down," he croaked. "I'll row."

Pop nodded. He had Grace help him unload the box of gelignite and then he sent her home with a quiet word. After she'd gone they headed upstream from the ramp until they reached Henry's house and then another mile or so along from it they stopped to set the first charge, in close to the bank where the river curled around on itself. It was just one of a dozen places along the river where two children might have fallen in, drowned, then been caught on an underwater snag.

Pop tossed the charge towards a spot where the great bole of a redgum leant out over the water. Henry watched him, slouched over the oars like a hunchback, like a beaten man, his neck and shoulders corded with hard muscle. Pop detonated the charge and there was a thud and muddied water lifted up in a thick geyser and then crashed back to the surface like a fountain being turned off, the shock wave setting the boat rocking. A mass of leaves and black, waterlogged branches broke the surface and rolled back under like living things and all about them was the stirred-up detritus of the riverbed—hag's fingers of twigs gloved with lace of green weed.

They continued up the river in the same manner until dusk, Henry dipping and feathering the oars and manoeuvring the boat, Pop throwing out the charges like bait. Both of them waited in the aftermath of each blast, hoping for a result, yet not hoping for the body of a drowned boy, swollen and pale, with dead, staring eyes, to be loosed from the depths. Yet sometimes the pale underbelly of a stunned and rolling catfish, twelve inches below the surface, could have been a boy's arm or leg, and when they saw one their hearts jumped up into their throats until they could see for certain what it was, and each time it was not a boy Pop looked over at Henry and wondered how he could endure such cheap torture. Then, when the light was scarcely enough to see by, Pop called it a day.

"Tomorrow we can do down below the ramp," he said. "Steele's Reach."

Henry nodded and began to row.

Two days later Pop Mather went into the kitchen of the station house and made himself a pot of tea with much more care than he usually took—warming the pot, warming the cup, putting the milk in first— and then he sat out on the station house's back verandah in a steamer chair and watched the sun set. One of the tracker dogs had followed a trail that afternoon, way out to the west, but then had lost it. Pop couldn't believe—if it actually was the boys—how far they had travelled. He went through his plan of action for the next morning and then he closed his eyes for a moment. He dozed for a few minutes but when he woke it seemed hours had passed. It was dark, and his back was as stiff as the southerly that had loped in, all bluster and show, when he hadn't been looking. He reckoned the clouds that had come with it, swirling over the town, would barely shed enough rain to damp down the dust.

After a while—he thought it might have been five minutes or so but was unsure until he looked at his watch and saw that fifteen had ticked away—he stood up and stretched his back. He heard a plaintive sound from inside the house and looked round the doorjamb to see what it was. Grace was standing under the hall light in her new dress and Lil, pins in mouth, was on the floor adjusting the hem. Pop could tell by the look on his daughter's face that she wasn't enjoying herself at all.

He'd forgotten all about the dance. It had been postponed from Saturday, and while some had voiced their opposition, he thought it was probably about time it went ahead. God knew they could all do with something to cheer them up. Christmas was just over a week away now and he doubted whether anyone was quite ready for that. He took a last look at the evening sky before going inside. He gave his grimacing daughter a wink and then he went on into his room to change his clothes.

Grace didn't really expect Darcy to be there when she walked into the hall with her mother and father, so when she saw her sitting on a chair up the back she almost stopped dead in her tracks. Fortunately her parents had already peeled off from her side to talk to people so they didn't notice. Darcy looked up, caught her eye, then looked away again. Grace hesitated and then went to the side of the hall and sat down. Slowly, more people arrived, but the mood and the volume of the evening remained subdued and very seldom did anyone raise their voice or even laugh out loud. She avoided dancing when the music began and every so often she would glance over at Darcy to see what she was doing. Sometimes her brother Sonny was sitting beside her and sometimes she saw Charlie Perry, who worked on the Steeles' farm, whispering in her ear. She liked Charlie and was a little jealous of Darcy sitting next to him, a little hurt by the fact that he was the only boy who hadn't come and asked her for a dance. She was thinking about slipping out the side door and home when her father sat down beside her.

"You and Darcy have a falling out?" he asked.

She shook her head. Pop didn't repeat the question, just leant back and crossed his arms and sat like that beside her for a good five minutes.

"Why don't you just go and say hello," he said, finally. "Wouldn't do any harm, would it?"

Grace shook her head again. Pop sighed and wandered away. She watched him go, feeling as though she'd let him down somehow, but also a little annoyed at him.

She waited until neither Sonny nor Charlie were around and then she stood and began to walk. When she was a few yards away from Darcy she stopped. Darcy was barefoot—her shoes discarded under the chair beside her—and she wore the pale cream dress borrowed weeks ago from Grace's own wardrobe. It was too small for her across the bust and she looked uncomfortable and self-conscious in it. Pinned to the bodice was a wilting carnation and around her neck hung the cowrie shell Grace had found on the beach last summer and brought back for her. They both looked up at the same time and their eyes met. Grace saw the unhappiness in her friend's eye and was instantly ashamed of herself. She had just taken her first step forward when all the lights in the hall suddenly winked out. She stood there for a moment in stunned surprise, her eyes adjusting to the dark, people jostling past her, some making gibes about the county council and their beautiful timing. She heard people pulling out drawers in the kitchen at the back of the hall and then matches were struck and candles lit and her surroundings reappeared, but altered subtly, as if the darkness had changed something, moved things around, worked some curious magic. She looked back to Darcy, who was now fiddling nervously with her hands. Without another thought she went and sat down beside her and took one of her cool, dry hands and pressed it between hers. They sat like that for a few minutes, saying nothing amidst all the commotion, and then Grace squeezed her hand tightly and Darcy lowered her head and rested it against the top of her friend's arm. Grace looked down at the top of her head and, despite a much deeper current of confusion running through her, was sure she'd done the right thing. After a while she lowered her head until her mouth was right over Darcy's ear.

"How can I help you if you won't tell me what the matter is?" she whispered. She felt her friend take a deeper breath, as if she were about to speak, but then she let it out again, and Grace began to wonder, despairingly, whether Darcy would ever answer.

7

Tom took a few more shaky steps and then stopped. There was a road beneath his feet but its flat hardness felt more like the deck of a rolling ship. The road glistened with dew and there were lights shining upon it. He blinked and looked down at his feet for a moment and then he looked up at the source of the lights and began to walk towards it.

It was much further than he thought possible and more than once his legs nearly gave way beneath him, but he kept walking, a determination untainted by reason or any other consideration keeping him moving. A sound grew and swirled around him. It was like a swarm of wasps, maybe a whole plague of them. He thought he heard words in the sound but he was also quite certain it was not speech and had nothing to say to him. He stopped and sucked in air until the sound receded back into nothing and all he could hear were the trees on either side of the road and the leaves rustling in the slight evening breeze. He walked on, his head down, until he reached the gate of the house. He put his hand on the gate and rested for a few moments and then he opened it and walked up to the front door and knocked. Golden light streamed from the windows. He thought he could smell food. A flustered-looking woman opened the door and stared at him for a moment, her eyes growing slowly wider and wider.

"Tom Ferry!" she breathed. She crossed herself as if he were a ghost and then she brought up her big arms and embraced him. He looked into her eyes and saw the worry, the big buttery dollops of concern, and was overwhelmed, lost for even the simplest of words. Then the woman's children came and thrust their heads between the doorway and their mother to blink and stare at the ragtag boy on their front step. Then she looked through him, past him, behind him, already looking for his little slip of a brother, his little shadow.

"Where's your brother, Tom? Where's Flynn?" asked the woman—over and over—but he could not answer her, and could not even begin to. Things began to whirl around him then. One of the children raced by, up the road, into town, shouting at the top of his lungs. Tom stepped back and sat down, pulling his legs up and hugging his knees. The woman came and helped him up and together they walked down the path and out onto the road. When he next looked up there was a whole crowd of people running towards him. There were girls in nice dresses, boys in suits, men and women following behind. He could see the hall in the near distance, the people standing on its front steps holding candles, their flickering shadows falling in every direction.

Grace Mather was one of the first to reach him. She stopped a few yards away, sucking in breaths like a Gift runner, and just stared at him. He saw Sonny, his sister Darcy, and then everyone was around him, all talking at once, all making no sense. Sergeant Mather elbowed his way through the crush and bent down and put his hand on Tom's shoulder and peered hard into his face. There was a hush as he began to speak.

"It's Sergeant Mather, son—Pop Mather," he said quietly. "Can you tell me your name?"

Tom nodded. "Thomas Ferry," he said.

"Good boy," Pop said. He let the air out of his chest through rounded lips and then helped Tom to his feet. "All right," he said, turning round. "Give him some room, folks. Let's get him to the doc."

An opening appeared through the people and Tom took a few steps along it before Pop picked him up and carried him the rest of the way to the station house. When they arrived Pop set him down on a chair in the kitchen, a wide-eyed audience of children peering round the doorjamb at them both. Pop swung the door shut and jerked his head and then there were only the two of them. Lil had set a candle on the table and Tom stared into the flame.

"You look like you've been through the wars, Tom," Pop said.

Tom nodded and was about to cry but then he gritted himself and stopped it.

"I don't know what's happened to Flynn," he said. "I don't know where he is."

"That's all right, Tom. We'll work that one out soon enough."

Pop looked at the boy. His face was pinched and pale and his large green eyes seemed about to fall out of their orbits. His clothes were about to give up the ghost and his bare legs were covered in scratches and scabs and there was a nasty-looking gash across his forehead. He appeared in serious need of a decent feed, a hot bath, and a good bed, but other than that he seemed in fair physical shape.

"Wait there a minute, son, then we'll get you home."

After he rang the doctor he had Lil fry up a couple of eggs for Tom to eat. Between tiny mouthfuls of egg and bread Tom told scraps of his story. A kangaroo, Flynn running, something about smoke. Pop listened and let him take his time. His nerves seemed to have taken a beating. He'd lost track of the days and was confused about the sequence of events leading up to the Saturday afternoon they'd gone missing. Soon the words dried up. Pop went into his room and came back with some clothes.

"Here's a clean shirt of mine you can change into. Some shorts. They'll be too big but, well, better than what you've got on now. Can you manage?"

"Yes."

Pop handed him the clothes and left him to it. Grace watched from the half-open door of her bedroom down the hall. She saw him stand naked by the table for a moment—not a boy any more, but not a man either—then climb into her father's huge clothes.

The doctor arrived soon after, a little out of breath, to look Tom over. He peered at his forehead and shone a light into his eyes.

"How did you get this bump, little man?" he asked, as he cleaned it up, but Tom didn't answer.

"He's taken a decent knock there," he said to Pop, "but not too serious. He needs food; nothing too heavy, a bit of bread and such to start with."

"Can he go home?"

"I should say so. Though I'd like to see him tomorrow, look at him with some decent light."

"All right. Thanks, Doc," said Pop, motioning with his head.

"It's good to have *you* back home, Tom," said the doctor, "ah . . . anyway."

Pop drove him home after the doctor had gone. He made some comments about the search they'd made but Tom said nothing. When they reached Henry's house they walked up the path together and in through the open door. Pop rapped on the doorframe as he passed it.

"Henry?"

Pop stood in the doorway, squinting into the darkened house, his big palm in the middle of Tom's back. The room was still except for the flicker of the television. Pop cleared his throat, waited until it seemed part of the couch broke away, stood, came towards them. Henry was not as tall as Pop but he was shored up by long hard days in the forest and seemed almost twice as big.

"Henry," Pop repeated. "No one's been down?"

Henry stared hard at Tom, then shook his head as if he didn't trust his eyes.

"He knocked on the Reillys' door about half an hour ago," said Pop, then paused. "I thought someone might have come down to tell you."

Henry shook his head again.

"No. No one came."

"Henry," Pop continued, in a soft voice. "Flynn wasn't with him. I'm sorry. He doesn't seem to know . . . tomorrow we'll . . ."

He didn't know what else to say so he pushed Tom forward, gently, like a consolation, though he did not mean it that way at all. Henry stood there with his hands hanging by his sides, staring down at Tom, who could not bear his gaze and hung his head. He looked instead at Henry's shirt where it covered his flat belly, where it was grey, threadbare, odd-buttoned. He heard Pop continue on with other details but they seemed unrelated to him, seemed to be about some other boy named Tom. Suddenly his sight went grey, with red stars floating, and then black, without any stars, and he fainted.

"Thank you . . . for bringing him," said Henry, standing over his stepson, after they'd revived him somewhat with a wet cloth.

"Where's Ellie? She should—"

"She's in bed. The doctor gave her something to sleep."

"Ah. Well. I see. He wants to see Tom again tomorrow. I expect he'll come down in the morning. I'll be down as well."

"All right. I'll see you then."

"There's still hope, Henry," said Pop, softly.

Henry nodded, but Pop could see he barely believed it.

Tom woke up on the floor, on the threadbare red carpet of the living room, spluttering. Water had been thrown across his face. The front door was closed behind his head and Pop was no longer there and Henry was coming towards him from the kitchen, unhitching his belt. His stepfather hoisted him up by the front of his oversized shirt, forcing his breath from his chest.

"Where's Flynn?" Henry sobbed. "Where's my little boy?"

"I—"

Without another word Henry stood him against the door and pressed his face hard against the wood. With a high little moan each time his arm lifted and with tears streaming down his cheeks, Henry swung the belt in a figure eight, the meat of it striking Tom across the back, the buttocks, the legs, twice each revolution. The pain was worse than kicking your toe into a table leg, worse than falling off a bike and skinning your knee, worse than biting down very hard on your tongue, but still nothing like the pain flooding his heart.

When Pop returned to the station house Lil had fallen asleep in her chair in the living room. He watched her sleep for a moment before heading into the kitchen. He stared at the hearth for a while and then began to set a fire there, not because it was cold but because he needed to think, to calm himself, and looking into flames always helped. Grace came and leant against the kitchen wall.

"Why aren't you in bed?"

"I can't sleep."

Pop nodded. "Course not." He held his arm out to her and she slipped it over her shoulders and they both watched the fledgling fire crackle and hiss into life.

"Where do you think he's been?"

"I don't know. They found a trail yesterday, nearly eight miles west of here." He shook his head in bewilderment. "Unless someone found him, brought him back, or he walked . . ."

"Didn't he tell you anything?"

"No. Not anything that made sense."

"What about Flynn?"

"Sweetheart, I don't know. A boy's back where he belongs, and I thank Christ for that, but I can't help thinking I should be able to see what's happened, should know the right thing to do."

"You always do the right thing," said Grace. She slung her arms round his neck and put her head against the side of his. Pop lifted his hand and put it on hers.

"I just hope he can tell us something more tomorrow."

They both watched the fire for a little longer and then Pop pushed his daughter gently towards the door.

"All right, my girl," he said. "Off to bed now. Try to sleep."

Grace went reluctantly, but she wasn't about to argue. Pop stayed on to watch the fire and then, just after midnight, he heard the wind change and the first drops of rain hit the iron roof of the station house. He looked up at the flickering shadows on the ceiling and listened. The rain went from strength to strength until all other sounds were drowned out by the roar and in the morning it was still raining and for the next ten days it barely paused.

II

8

G ibson was dreaming when the telephone rang. He was drunk and couldn't speak properly and kept wearing himself out trying to make the milling figures around him understand that he wasn't sick, wasn't foreign, was just an ordinary bloke who'd had one too many to drink. The sound drilled through all the palaver and woke him but it still took a few more moments for him to realise where he was and what was required of him. He stood up and a plate of cold food clattered and broke against the floor. He looked down at the lamb chop, potatoes and peas. There was a half-empty glass of beer on the coffee table, a television screen of snow. He walked to the phone, turning the television off as he passed.

"Hello?" he croaked. His mouth still felt like a whole sink of ashes even though he'd slept most of yesterday. He couldn't remember making the meal now decorating the floor. The detective on the other end of the line gave him an address and hung up in a hurry, as if calling him had been an unwelcome, distracting task. He went into the bathroom and splashed water over his face, then put on a shirt he found hanging behind the door. Nothing more of the interrupted dream came to him, but a feeling of disconnection was left in its wake as if he had missed his cue and woken in the body of some other Gibson instead of his own.

He went to the lounge room and picked up the broken plate and the glass, carried them into the kitchen and set them on the bench. It took him a moment or two to realise that the strange flickering light in the kitchen was coming from one of the stove's lit gas rings.

"Fuck it," he said, turning it off.

He saw a cockroach struggling in the sink. He turned on the hot tap and let it run and then he filled a mug with steaming water and threw it over the insect. It wriggled for a moment, shat out some black liquid, died. He turned away and headed down the hall, plucking his jacket from the hook as he passed.

Once outside he stood on the step and took a few deep breaths before locking the door behind him. The morning was cool. The harbour, only a stone's throw or two away, was cloaked in a silvery mist and the running lights of the ferries further out were little more than red and green smudges in the murk. He walked down to his car and set off. By the light of the rising sun he could see, when he crested hills, the red-roofed patchwork of the sleeping suburbs to the south and west, the gold stitch of streetlights joining them together. In the rear-view mirror he saw his own neighbourhood appear and disappear, the little houses holding tight to each other like rows of people with linked arms. Fading paint, rusting roofs, streets ending at the harbour's edge, mixed feelings.

He lit a cigarette then rolled down the window to let the smoke out and wake himself up. Not much traffic, he thought to himself, and then he remembered it was Sunday. He flicked on the radio and listened to the squawk and crackle of interference, the flat tones of his colleagues. It didn't take long for him to reach the address. Smith Street. Right in the heart of Surry Hills. When he pulled up, the constable standing outside the front door directed him around the block and down a little lane.

"She's in here," said the sergeant he found at the end of it. There was no sign of Swain, but he lived further away and wouldn't be there for a while yet. Parked cars were dewed silver in the early cool of the morning. Weeds grew on the short stretch of back yard and a puddle glistened with flat oily rainbows. A warehouse loomed over the lane opposite the back of the house and cut out the light from the rising sun. The reek from a huge pile of rubbish in the next yard drifted into his nostrils. He sighed and rubbed his eyes and followed the man's blue-uniformed back. Instead of the usual tingle of anticipation in his belly he found himself fighting the urge to turn and run. On the back wall of the house someone had used charcoal to scratch the words *insanity* and *sadist* across the bricks next to a stick man being hung from a stick gibbet. An old game of hangman. Others of tick-tack-toe. On the ground a blackened circle where a fire had been. Empty flagons of port and sherry resting in the grass. Swallows nesting somewhere in the building chirruped and flashed over Gibson's head as he stepped through the broken doorframe. The interior was dim and musty, but he couldn't yet smell the body. That could wait. The sergeant took off his hat and yawned.

"Who found her?"

"The demolition bloke. He was giving the owners a quote. All the doors and windows were boarded up years ago. You want to talk to him?"

"Who?"

"Either," shrugged the sergeant.

"Yeah, but not yet." He liked to take a walk around first if he could, record some impressions of his own before those of others clouded his thinking. Today, though, there was something else, something which had smuggled itself in amid the untidy scrum of himself and his habits. He felt like he'd come to work and found someone else sitting in his chair and the feeling continued to unsettle him.

The sergeant wheezed, coughed, then lit a cigarette. Gibson looked at him. Barely in your thirties and you've seen it all already, haven't you, he thought to himself. Seen too many tired bastards like me as well, I bet, old before their time.

"Stay here, will you?"

The sergeant nodded and handed him his torch. Gibson walked through the kitchen and started up a short flight of stairs.

"She's in the bottom bedroom," the sergeant called after him. Gibson raised his hand in acknowledgement. He continued up the stairs and then into the front bedroom. It was very dark but Gibson resisted using the torch and let his eyes adjust to the gloom. Thin lines of daylight spiked in between the boards over the windows. He could smell rotting plaster and the floorboards moved and creaked as he shifted his weight. He flipped on the torch. Most of the wallpaper had sloughed off like old diseased skin. Where it still clung to the wall it was stained a dirty yellow; maybe cigarette smoke, maybe water from a leaking roof. There was a line of dust and rubbish along one skirting board where a last sweeper, years ago, had left it like a high-tide mark. The room's dimensions were very similar to his own back in Balmain and he wondered about the people who had lived here and what had become of them and why their home had been abandoned to the elements this way. His mind tossed up a few of the more intriguing possibilities, but then he concluded that the reasons were probably much more ordinary. He sighed and went back downstairs and looked around the kitchen more carefully. He turned on the tap in the sink and water coughed out. He shone the torch across the floor. There were body-sized shapes in the dust as well as footprints. Whoever had lit the fire out the back had slept there. Maybe a few days ago now.

The bottom bedroom was down under the level of the street, like a sump in the earth, with no sun and no warmth. He went and stood before the closed door, saw the fresh wounds in the wood where the workman's crowbar had forced the lock. His mouth suddenly went dry and his hand began to shake as he lifted it. The image of a dream he'd had years before flashed, unbidden, into his mind. Walking through a desert, dying of thirst, he'd come upon a stone structure with just a single door; wooden and painted blue. He'd stood before the door and had clearly heard the sound of running water coming from behind it. A fountain. A well. Salvation was to be had if he opened the door, stepped inside the cool interior, drank, but just as he'd been about to do so he'd seen the fresh blood running out from inside, across the doorstep, and he'd turned and run away.

He shook his head and squeezed his hands into fists and put one of them up against the wood. The hinges squealed as he pushed the door open a little way. He reached round and found the key still in the lock and then he pushed the door all the way open. In the silence that followed he heard a car go by in the street overhead, the whirr of fan and fan belt, hiss of monoxide. His eyes adjusted. Up high, the light from the grimy window barely illuminated the room and its solitary occupant.

She lay in her underwear on the only piece of furniture: a single bed hard against the wall. A rusted chrome frame. A flat base of diamond-shaped mesh to support a mattress. She looked as if she had died during a peaceful sleep—fingers interlocked over breastbone— but he could see the dark track where the blood from the wounds in her wrists had run down across her torso and dripped onto the floor. Down by her side he saw the knife where she'd dropped it.

"Shit, sweetheart, what'd you do this for?" he whispered.

She hadn't been dead very long; a few days or so at most was his estimate. She held something in her hands. Photographs. Holding his breath, he pulled them from her dead fingers as carefully as he could. He glanced at them briefly before putting them in his shirt pocket and then he slid the button on the torch forward and shone it around. Her clothes and belongings were in a pile near the foot of the bed. He took a deep breath and shone the torch on her body, starting at her feet, then up to her thighs. Very young, he thought. Very young. Fifteen, sixteen. Gently, he ran the back of his finger along the outside curve of her hip, then moved the torch along. Armpits unshaven. Hair quite dirty. Clean, it might have been a dark golden blonde, maybe the strawberry variety. He reached out and rubbed a lock between his thumb and forefinger as if he could assay it.

He shone the torch directly onto her face and stared, stricken. It had been disfigured, gnawed by rats or some other vermin. Her lips were missing—just a ragged smear now—and her nose, part of her cheek, some of her chin. She seemed denatured, godless, devised by a cabal of wasted jokers and cast out by the same from the world of the living; this room the terminus of all her dreams, all her desires. His heart began to thud painfully inside his chest and then his knees let go.

"Fuck me," he croaked.

He knelt on the floor for what seemed like minutes. When he was able he shone the torch across the floor and around the skirting board, the beam shaking along with his hand, a cool draught coming up through gaps in the floorboards. In one corner he saw a hole, its edges knurled by the sharp teeth of generation upon generation of rats. The floor was scattered with their droppings. He wondered how long they would have taken to strip her to the bone. He switched off the torch and stood—his knees popping—and turned to leave, the rat shit crackling under his shoes like so much black rice. He picked up the bundle from the end of the bed and then paused at the door to look back at her, shrouded—mercifully—by the gloom once more.

He could almost hear the sound of it. The dissonant chords of a particular and bloody evil. There was a cold, sharp smell—like ammonia, like vinegar—and his mouth felt instantly dry, as if it were suddenly full of salt. *Salt.* He could almost see the long turquoise swells lining up to break. He closed his eyes. Anywhere but here, anywhere but here, anyone but *him.* Then the long white curve of beach in his mind became not unlike a single rib, a breast. He felt faint then, and very queasy. As he walked from the room sweat broke out across his forehead and back and chest and he fought the urge to turn and make sure she had not risen from her bed to follow him.

"Sergeant!"

"Yessir!" The man tried to fold his newspaper but the middle fell out onto the muddy ground. Gibson looked at it lying there.

"Do you know what's happened in there?" Gibson asked, a little breathlessly.

The sergeant nodded, shrugged. "I think so. I've been in and had a look."

Gibson was about to shout, but he could see in the sergeant's eye the evidence of a desperate wish that he'd been able to resist his curiosity.

"She's not a pretty sight, is she," said Gibson, shaking his head, exhaling, his eyes flicking around the yard.

"No, but I've seen worse. Accidents and such. But when it's like that . . . intentional . . . so young . . ." He shrugged again.

"Yeah." Gibson nodded. "Yeah."

He stood with one hand on his hip, the girl's pathetic belongings in the crook of his other arm.

"There's someone asleep in there," he said, eventually, pointing to one of the cars in the lane. "Don't forget to ask him if he knows who's been dossing down in the kitchen here, all right? And if he saw her, obviously."

"All right," said the sergeant, a little surprised, but glad to be getting on with something.

Gibson walked up the yard and slid back out through the gap in the fence.

"You off already?"

"Swain'll be here in a while. He'll take care of it."

Gibson jumped into his car before the sergeant could say anything else and roared off down the lane. The sergeant watched him go, heard the squeal of his tyres as he braked heavily at the end of the lane, just missing the little old lady who'd stepped out in front of the car.

He resisted the temptations of the various hotels he passed as he drove, directionless, around the city. He wanted nothing more than to erase the memory of what he'd seen but he knew another day and night on the tiles might just kill him. He headed out to The Gap and sat for a long time staring out at the Pacific. He only remembered the photographs in his pocket when his hand went in there looking for his matches. He pulled them out. There were three. He fanned them and then looked at them closely in the bright light. The first, blurred and indistinct, was of a girl standing next to an odd-looking man with a glum expression on his face. *Me and Billy* was written on the back in childish printing. The second was an even more blurred photograph and no matter how hard he tried he could not make it out. The edge of trees, something there in the shadows maybe. An animal perhaps? He couldn't tell. Nothing was written on the reverse. The third photograph seemed to have been taken early, or maybe late, in the day, the sunlight angling in, hard shadows. Gibson stared. It was the same girl as in the first, but just a little older, her long hair slightly unkempt and fairer at the ends. She stood next to an elderly man in a black suit. She wore a dress that looked like it might be faded blue and there were darker marks at the seams where it had been let out. Her eyes, though hidden in the shade from her raised hand, could just be seen, staring into the camera, staring out at *him*. Gibson blinked, looked away, then back. She seemed like some bright-eyed sentinel on the border between two worlds, a knowing witness to the tricks of time; the here and now, the day—the world outside—and the past, the truth, whatever you wanted to call it, caught by the camera.

He closed his eyes and rubbed them and then he looked at the photograph again. Just a girl once more. Now she reminded him a little of his own mother when she'd been young, before she'd had the misfortune to meet his father, but then it hit him.

It was her eyes. She had the same eyes as Frances—the same sad, faraway look in them. He wiped his mouth and breathed out slowly. He could barely remember his sister's face now, but he remembered her eyes. He flipped the photograph over, his hand shaking once more. *Me and Father Carney.* Some sort of priest maybe.

He looked over his shoulder at the bundle he'd tossed on the back seat and then reached for it. He ran his hand through the clothes and came across a little cowrie shell on a cord of leather. Something of her personality. He turned it over in his hand before hanging it from the indicator stalk and continuing to look through her belongings. He thought for a while that there was nothing else of interest but then he felt something hard wrapped inside a blue cardigan. It was a bible, about six by four, in a cardboard slipcase. He slid it out of the case and flicked through the pages and then he turned to the inside cover. *Darcy Steele*, it said. *Angel Rock.*

"Darcy Steele," he whispered.

He flicked through the pages again. Words were written in thick pencil across the printed pages. He closed the book up, flicked through it again. The writing couldn't be seen unless the book was opened completely. He wondered about that for a little while and then he opened it up and began to read.

From the title page of Genesis to about halfway through the book she had kept a diary of sorts, the original text written over with large, childish printing in a soft grade of lead pencil. Sometimes he read the solemn words of the Pentateuch underneath and between her own clumsy lettering and the contrast had an odd and unsettling effect on him, as if her own words had become part of Genesis, Exodus, Leviticus, and Numbers, burrowing into the ancient texts and changing their essence.

The writing looked years younger than the age she looked in the most recent photograph. Words were often misspelt and the sentences crude, but she still managed to express herself well enough. He sensed an intelligence frustrated by a lack of skill. There were no dates but Gibson reckoned that there were at least two or three years' worth of events contained within the covers. She listed small events: her jobs around the farm she lived on, what she had for dinner, what the weather was like, wind, storms, rainbows, aeroplanes in the sky, sightings of birds, wild animals at the edge of the bush, the births of calves and kittens. He could almost see her in his head, walking around the farm, but the farm was swathed in darkness, and silent. Family members only appeared if they infringed on her domain in some way. *Sonny* helped her with a baby bird. Her father drowned kittens. Then there were a lot of entries about Father Carney, then some about *Grace*. The bulk of the diary, however, was concerned with *Billy*. If Gibson hadn't seen the photograph of him he would have said he'd been an imaginary friend, for he seemed to be a secret from everyone else in her circle. She saw him nearly every week and had what could only be described as adventures: expeditions to waterfalls, quests for gold in forgotten creeks, climbs to the tops of giant trees. Then Billy gradually faded from the pages. Darcy didn't say why. He suspected a gap then, maybe of a year or so, judging from the change in her handwriting. There was a little bit more about Grace, but then something caught his eye and made him go cold all over.

Something's watching me from the trees, read the entry. He closed the bible, sat and stared at it for a few minutes, and then repeated her words.

Something's watching me from the trees.

He drove back to the station and parked his car, then walked down to the café. It was still early. The streets stank of vomit from the night before as if signalling a new and unpleasant season. Grandad was standing outside the Quality hosing the concrete and sending a river of foul water along the gutter. The smell caught in Gibson's nose and made his stomach flip. Grandad nodded his head to him as he walked by as though he barely knew him. Once inside the café he ordered coffee and food although he had little appetite. He lit a cigarette. The ceiling fan reproduced itself in miniature in the sugar spoon. The clock on the wall tocked away and Grandad came in from the street and shuffled along behind the counter, making faces at empty cups and dirty plates, reading them like a medium might, passing them through the gap in the wall where steam billowed and Peter the dishwasher worked before a steel sink, already washing dishes from the early trade, a cigarette in his mouth and one behind his ear ready to go, the walls around him papered with a glossy harem of naked women as if it were a garage and not a kitchen. It was Gibson's favourite place to eat and it seemed to settle him now. Sometimes in the evening, after the café had closed, he would sit with Grandad and Peter at a table, eating and talking, playing euchre, a triangle of smoke, lamentation, caprice.

The food came. Grandad slid the knife and fork down and across the tabletop like an old cardplayer. Bacon, eggs, toast. Coffee. He tucked in, suddenly hungry, but his gums hurt when he chewed. Each tine of the fork seemed to have been sheared off roughly and carelessly. The metal, *Stainless 18/10* stamped on the reverse, felt underweight and crude and grabbed at the inside of his mouth. Grandad stopped by his table.

"You right, Gibson?"

"Why?" He wondered whether what he had just seen was written all over his face, whether he was pale, whether his hands were trembling.

"No reason. Just askin'." Grandad sat down opposite and helped himself to one of Gibson's cigarettes, lit it and sat there smoking and watching him eat.

"Listen," said Gibson, wiping his mouth. "What would you do with, say . . . a hundred grand?"

Grandad thought about it, resting his chin in the palm of his hand as if it tired him.

"Thinking of robbing a bank?"

"No. Go on, what would you do with it?"

"I'd pay off my house. Buy another one. You can't beat owning property."

"Mmmm. What about Peter? Go and ask him."

Grandad arched an eyebrow but then he went away. He came back after five minutes or so.

"Well, what did he say?"

"He said he'd be off to India on the next plane to sit at the feet of his guru and reach nirvana. Said he'd give the rest of the money to beggars."

"He's not serious, is he?"

"He had a straight face when he said it."

"The same one you're wearing?"

"The same."

Grandad gave the faintest of smiles and went back behind the counter.

"Wouldn't you leave your job? Wouldn't you leave town?"

Grandad shook his head. "Leave this?" he asked, his waved hand indicating the café.

Gibson smiled grimly and nodded.

"Thinking of selling the house?" Grandad asked, raising his eyebrows. "You won't get that much for it."

Gibson shrugged. "I'm thinking about it. Maybe when my mother dies."

Grandad gave him a strange look. "Things are the same wherever you go," he said, picking up a stack of plates and passing them in to Peter.

"Maybe," said Gibson, but Grandad didn't hear him. After a while he steeled himself and pulled Darcy's bible from his pocket. He started again from the beginning and then, with mixed feelings of relief and dismay, found that there wasn't a great deal more following the entry which had chilled him. It was disappointing, and he wished she'd kept writing, but the diary seemed to belong to her past—a record of happier times—and he guessed that that was why she had kept it with her.

He sat and smoked and drank coffee. He read the diary a third time and spent hours trying to conjure a solid reason for what she had done from the flimsy pages. In the end there was only the one line which offered any clue and he sat and pondered the words with glazed eyes and ash from his cigarette dropping unnoticed onto the table. In the afternoon he yawned and stretched and went and sat at a back table with Peter and Grandad. They'd locked up for the day and soon the table was covered in ashtrays and empty plates, tins of Signet and Three Nuns. Grandad poured shots of Johnnie Walker into ice-filled glasses and they toasted each other. While their wits were still about them they played chess and backgammon and then they started on chequers and cards. Gibson welcomed the way the drink took the edge off things and he was soon wisecracking as loudly as the others. It was past ten o'clock when Grandad called it a night. Gibson downed the last of his drink and then he and Peter staggered outside to Elizabeth Street and hailed a cab heading up to the Cross.

"Where'd *you* get to yesterday, you silly cunt?" spat Swain as soon as Gibson walked through the door of the station the next morning.

"Around," replied Gibson, mildly.

"I had to twiddle me thumbs there all morning before the fucking coroner turned up!"

"Ah, well . . ."

Erskine came into the room. "Shut up, Swain, will you?" he said. "It's Monday for Christ's sake."

"Her name's Darcy Steele," said Gibson. "She's from a place called Angel Rock."

"Angel Rock?" snapped Swain, leaning forward in his chair.

"Yeah. You heard of it?"

"Where's your head been, you sleepy bastard, Gibson? Up your arse? Those two little kids who went missing, the brothers, that's where they're from. Only been in every paper in the fucking country."

"Oh."

"Gibson," said Erskine.

"Yeah?"

"Come in here. I want to talk to you."

Gibson sighed, but followed Erskine into his office. Erskine shut the door behind them.

"I want to go up there," said Gibson, hoping to throw him by getting in first. His head was pounding from the night before and his stomach had only just settled down.

"Where?"

"Angel Rock."

"What for?"

"I . . . I just . . . I just need to go and have a look."

"Have a look? Sounds like you need a holiday, Matthew, that's what it sounds like."

"Yeah, maybe I do."

"What if I said you couldn't do either?"

Gibson shrugged. "I'm ready to quit. Right now. I'll walk out."

"All right, don't get hasty with me."

"I've just . . . had enough . . . for a while at least."

"Yeah? This girl got something to do with it?"

Gibson shifted in his seat. "Maybe."

"Cut and dried, isn't it? Opened her veins, Swain said. Door was locked."

Gibson flinched. Erskine's expression suddenly changed and he leant forward in his chair a touch and his look softened.

"Sorry, son. Sometimes I forget. You can tell me . . . this something to do with Frances?"

Gibson looked away and gave no answer.

"I can see it is," said Erskine, nodding. "But you've had suicides before, why's this one . . . ?"

Gibson shrugged.

"You wouldn't tell me anyway, would you?"

"I wouldn't know where to start."

Erskine sighed and leant back in his chair.

"You'd really quit if I said no?"

"Yep."

Erskine nodded. "Well, I suppose we should let the parents know, put 'em out of their misery. Ring the copper up there before you go, all right?"

Gibson nodded and unclenched his jaw. It felt like a huge weight had been removed from atop him.

"Yep," he said. "Will do."

Erskine leant further back in his chair and linked his fingers together behind his head.

"Kids that age, Matty, who knows why they do anything. My girls gave me a few heart attacks, I tell you."

"Maybe that's what I'd like to find out—if it was something . . . within her, or something else. I mean, she was only a kid, Bill, you know? Even younger than Frances."

Erskine nodded. "But kids sometimes . . . go to extremes," he said. "They can't see past what's directly in front of 'em. Can't see a better way out."

"No."

"And you can't go back and change that, or change what she did, any more than you can go back and change—"

"No," said Gibson, cutting him off. "I know."

Swain gave him a filthy look as he came out of Erskine's office but Gibson ignored it and asked him a question.

"Did you find anyone who saw her?"

"Nup, nobody except the old bird in the milk bar up the street. She bought some things there a couple of days ago. Old bird said she was barefoot, looked a little lost, but seemed happy enough. Only saw her the once, though."

Gibson nodded, and then he left. Outside, he looked up at the sky for what seemed like the first time in months. It was clear, a pretty blue, and the air felt fresh and mercifully free of the floating grime which seemed to settle on everything. He felt like he'd taken one foot out of the land of the dead and put it in the land of the living. He set off down the street whistling, making the tune up as he went along, thinking of all the things he needed to do.

He took a good look at his face in the mirror when he got home.

"Thirty-seven years old," he muttered.

He'd probably, he had to admit, always been unremarkable to look at. Dark eyes, sometimes green, sometimes slate-grey, a clump of greying, unkempt hair. Not strikingly handsome but not strikingly ugly, tall, but not outstandingly so, and pale, very pale, as if he'd been ill for a long time. He wasn't a pretty sight; even his whiskers were coming out white now, and his teeth were an unpleasant shade of yellow. He shook his head. It was, he reckoned to himself, with a bit of work, a face just about good enough for a new start, a second chance.

He cleaned himself up and made himself something to eat and then drove to the nursing home. His mother was asleep when he put his head through the gap in the curtains circling her bed. Her mouth was open and her head was propped up on two or three pillows. Her hair looked as though it had been washed and brushed and her lips were coloured with bright red lipstick and her cheeks were rouged. He went and found a nurse and brought her over to the bed, his hand on her elbow as if he had her in custody.

"What's this about?" he asked, pointing.

The woman looked tiredly at his mother and gave a faint smile.

"A woman from the boutique down the road comes in sometimes, does their hair, puts on a bit of make-up. She quite enjoyed herself."

The nurse shook his mother's arm. He nearly stopped her but his mother only opened her eyes for a moment and then closed them again.

"You must be her son."

"Yes."

"We don't see much of you."

"No, well, what's the point? She doesn't even recognise me any more."

"But *you* know who *she* is."

Gibson blinked. "Yeah. I suppose I do."

The nurse pulled up the sheets and straightened the blanket.

"She enjoyed it, you say?"

"Yes. She looked at herself in the mirror and oohed and aahed."

The nurse smiled at him and left when he nodded. Maybe she wasn't seeing what he was, but then she did not know his mother as anything other than the bag of bones she was now.

He sat down by the bed and stared at her, wondering—not for the first time—what she really knew of his sister's fate and what she'd never told him—and now never would. It was all so long ago and it was far too late but the thought began to gnaw at him and he wondered how he could ever stop it. Whatever she knew was lost forever in a dark and ruined mansion of remembrance and recollection. He pictured his sister wandering through it, a stub of candle lighting her way. He would never find out more about her and she would never be able to tell him herself. He bent over and kissed his mother's creased old forehead.

"Goodbye, Mum," he whispered. "Thank you."

In the evening, after he'd made his preparations, he climbed up onto the roof of his house and sat looking out across the city. Although he loved it, it sometimes seemed to him a city with too many lost souls, too many bad pennies, too many unhappy ghosts.

Over by the wharves arc lamps lit up the masts and upper works of merchant ships. He caught a glimpse of the *South Steyne* slapping through the chop and then a great nimbus of cloud swung around the moon and snuffed out its light. Pleasure boats, jaunty with strings of bunting and lights, passed by beetle-like in the new blackness. He could almost hear the chinking of the revellers' glasses as they toasted their cleverness and good fortune. He wondered if they would be quite so merry if they could see themselves from where he sat: almost inconsequential there between the empty shimmering jet above and the parlous substance sliding by just beneath their well-shod feet.

He decided to wait till morning to leave but he couldn't sleep no matter what he did or didn't do. Just after midnight he gave up. He locked the house, checked again where Angel Rock was on the map, and then set off through the quiet, empty streets. He thought about Darcy Steele as he drove and he became determined to press on through the night, to stay dreamless, to decide in the small hours, when his spirit, his resolve, was weakest, whether he really wanted to continue with the assignment he'd embarked upon, or make the promise to himself—to Darcy, and Frances—that he was considering.

As he left Sydney behind and drove north through the night he sometimes sensed a fluttering just behind his shoulder, always quicker than his eye as he turned his head. He thought at first it was the girl again, somehow conjured from her bed by his tired mind and given wings, but then, in the middle of the long night and a wide stretch, he stopped by the side of the road, the stars in full bloom overhead, and he knew that it was no more than his own death shadowing him, the black negative to his blood's red.

9

Tom climbed up behind the two big Canadian saws at the front of the sawmill and began to fill the butcher's two hessian bags with sawdust. Just like the Magic Pudding, no matter how much he took away from the heap it never seemed to diminish. He remembered how he used to read the story to Flynn and the pain bit into him anew and he cursed it as if it were a dog that wouldn't do what it was told and then he sat down in the sawdust and sucked in some deep breaths.

He and Henry had barely said a word to each other since the night he'd been found. Henry had to go back to work shortly after and soon he was spending more and more of each day out in the bush. When he'd been able Tom went with Pop up into the hills, searching for any trace of Flynn, trying to remember what had happened. Pop said it was the bang on his head that had knocked it out of him. Tom sensed it was hopeless, but he also sensed that Pop was helping him despite the fact that it was, and for reasons he didn't quite understand. Then, one day, Pop had taken off his hat and wiped his brow, looked at Tom, and Tom had known what the look meant. They stopped searching and went home.

Then he'd begun to dream—sporadically at first and then nearly every night—about the time he'd been gone. All he could remember of the dreams at first was the darkness in them, occasionally a flickering yellow light, but then he was able to recall the presence of something crouching in the darkness, something with teeth—man or beast, he couldn't tell—waiting, watching. He told Pop about the dreams—only Pop—and even though it helped it didn't make them stop. Then some people began to whisper that he knew more about his brother's disappearance than he was telling; that he was hiding some terrible secret, some terrible act of foolishness on his part that had caused Flynn's death. They said there was something very peculiar about it all, and even though Pop rounded on a few people in the street and pinned their ears back the talk did not stop altogether.

Until both tyres punctured he spent his days riding his bike along the long, straight roads of the valley floor and sometimes, sweating and straining, up into the hills west of the crossroads. He'd stop and look back down at the town, slapping the dust off his clothes, but he never saw anything to fill him with hope. He began to spend more and more time sitting in the long grass of the riverbank across from his house, peering into the water, a slight and unmoving figure beneath the hovering summer insects.

Christmas had come and gone. A church service had been held for Flynn a couple of Sundays before, but for Tom all the words had run together and made little sense. It hadn't done his mother much good either. Although she'd recovered a little after his return she'd worsened a good deal afterwards, as if getting him back wasn't quite enough. After a few failed attempts at returning to work she'd taken to her darkened bedroom, sleeping well into the mornings and then past lunch time as well. A nun from the church in Laurence had to come and feed her with a spoon for a whole week.

He picked himself up out of the sawdust and bent back to his task. As he shovelled he remembered, suddenly and vividly, the way his mother blew him and Flynn kisses at bedtime, the one time he'd watched her stand there in the dark as though waiting, or listening, the air warm and still, the sound of a storm rumbling far away, the wind picking up as it closed in, the flicker of lightning. She was the sweetness in his life, the balance to the severity of Henry, and there was something very wrong with her that he was powerless to alter. He realised then that it had been Flynn who had kept them all together. The thought stopped him in his tracks, made his mouth dry up, made him feel sick, and then a brown grasshopper, like the first drop from a grim storm, crashed to the ground near him and clambered off across the sawmill floor. The sun disappeared behind a cloud and suddenly the mill seemed an altogether more eerie place. He tied string around the last bag's neck and left.

He dragged the bags behind him as he'd always done. It was a long haul along the mill road and he kept his head down, the sweat soon beginning to run off him. He noticed some sort of commotion in the showground but he did not stop to watch. He crossed over the river on the ferry, then walked up the main street and stared in through the glass of the butchery window at the remains of the cattle and sheep and pigs, all laid low, all sectioned with band saws and razor-edged knives, all sitting now in little fields of their own, fenced off from each other with strips of green plastic grass. The butcher jumped when he came out from the back and saw Tom peering in.

"Tom!" he said, when he went inside.

"I've got your sawdust, Mr. Riley," Tom said.

"So you have, Tom. So I see. Didn't . . . ah . . . really expect you to . . . ah—"

"You don't want it?"

"No, no. I want it. If you want to continue on as before . . . ," the butcher said, feeling awkward, ". . . that's fine with me."

"I do."

Mr. Riley nodded and then he took the bags out the back and Tom waited by the register for his money.

"I'll tell you what," said Mr. Riley, when he returned. "Chappie from the circus was over this morning. He wants meat for his animals, but he also asked me about sawdust. Seems to me you could fill as many bags as you wanted and he'd take 'em."

He fished coins out of the till and handed them to Tom.

"You could go ask him. Mr. Newman his name was."

"All right. I might. Thanks."

"All right, Tom. Take . . . take care now."

"I will."

Tom wandered over to the park and looked across at the show-ground. There were rundown trucks and banged-up caravans, and a dozen or so men had begun erecting a patched and dirty-looking big top. He watched them for a little while and then he went over on the ferry and slipped in unnoticed between the serried ranks of vehicles.

He watched the men as they drove in long steel pegs with sledge-hammers, then used an elephant to hoist long wooden poles to the vertical. Threadbare red, blue and green pennants were strung in zig-zags over a lane of coconut shies and laughing clowns. For the first time in weeks his attention was held long enough for Flynn and his dreams to retreat from his thoughts and as the tent took shape he headed round to where there were trucks parked, eager to see more. Some of the trucks had cages behind the cabs instead of trays, and canvas covers—decorated with fading pictures of clowns and lions and trapeze artists—hung down over the cages to shade the animals inside. He wandered along through the trucks until he came to a cage containing a scurfy chimpanzee sucking hard on a cigarette. The chimp looked at him without any curiosity and then flicked the butt of the cigarette out onto the grass. Tom walked on until a rank, musty smell assaulted his nose. He stopped and looked about for what it might be. He walked to the end of the structure he was standing alongside and peered round its corner. At first all he could see was a stretch of steel mesh. Then, in behind it, vertical bars—like trees—appeared from the gloom. He moved forward, gradually, but still saw nothing in the blackness. He'd come to the conclusion that the cage was empty when one of its occupants suddenly came forward, paced to and fro, then retreated. Tom gasped.

"Wow," he whispered.

He stood stock-still and waited for the lioness to reappear. Soon she emerged from the back of the cage and paced along the bars as before. As his eyes adjusted he spotted another two lions asleep on straw bedding: another lioness, and a male with a threadbare mane twitching his tail at flies.

He was staring hard into the gloom to see if there were any more when the lioness came to the bars again, then stopped and looked out at him. Tom held his breath and returned her gaze, almost unable to look away. She held him there, taking in everything that he was, and in the depths of her sad, tawny eyes he saw much about her as well, and then something of himself. He let out his breath as she looked away from him and lifted her head to catch what little breeze there was, her nostrils flaring. She closed her eyes, held whatever it was she had found for a moment or two, then turned and returned to her pacing, her measuring of sadness, her melancholy.

Tom, his heart thudding, wondered what she had found drifting in the airy currents. The cage faced the east. Had she smelt the salt of the ocean, or something much nearer?

"Look out, kid!"

Tom, startled, jumped back to dodge two thick-armed men carrying a long pole between them.

"Um, where can I find Mr. Newman, please?" he asked the trailing one, when he'd remembered his purpose for being there. The worker jabbed with his thumb. Tom saw a short, very round old man wearing dungarees and a fancy Stetson. He walked over to him, sawdust his business, but his head brimming still with the lion's electric gaze.

After he'd spoken to Newman he went back across the river to borrow more bags off Mr. Riley. Grace Mather was at the far end of the main street when he turned into it and he couldn't help feeling a little nervous as she approached, remembering how pretty and grown-up she'd looked in her dress the night he'd come home. He put his head down, half-expecting her to not be there when he looked up again. When he did she was much closer and she was looking straight at him.

"Hi," she said, when they were abreast of each other.

"Hi," said Tom. "Ah, how're you going?"

"All right. What about you?"

He shrugged. "I'm supposed to feel better soon. That's what everyone keeps saying."

"Adults always say that," said Grace, flicking the hair out of her eyes.

Tom nodded.

"What are you doing?" she asked.

"Getting some bags off Mr. Riley."

She looked up the street and down before nodding. Tom didn't take his eyes off her face.

"Listen," she said, quietly. "Sonny Steele's been saying things. He says he's going to get you, and he doesn't care about . . ."

Her voice trailed away and she looked at the ground. Tom glanced down at his own bare feet.

"Tom?"

"What?"

"Where *were* you? Where did you go?"

Tom didn't raise his head.

"You still don't remember?"

"No."

He glanced up at her. It was hard to tell whether she really believed him, but he found himself wanting her to.

"Sorry," she said. "Anyway, just try and steer clear of Sonny."

"I'll try," he said. "Thanks."

"I just wanted to tell you that. Sonny's so awful."

"Yeah. He is."

They stood awkwardly for a few seconds more.

"See you later then," said Tom. "Thanks."

"That's all right. See you."

He continued up the street with his hands in his pockets, but he had to use all of his powers to resist looking back at her over his shoulder.

10

When the sun came up Gibson stopped to stretch his legs and eat some breakfast. He was sitting in his car with a full belly, thinking he was ready to continue, when his head fell back against the seat and his eyes closed. He slept right through until mid-afternoon and then he woke up with a start, a stiff neck and a dry mouth. It took him a little while to work out where he was and what the hell he was doing there but then he started the car and pressed on, eager to make up for lost time. He drove on into the evening, passing through a number of small towns until he saw, far ahead, a faint flash of lightning under a band of darker cloud. He stopped the car and stood behind the opened door with his hand cupped around his ear to listen for thunder but he heard none.

"Long way off," he muttered to himself. He jumped back into the car and pressed his foot down on the accelerator as far as it would go, speeding away down the road to chase the storm. He knew it was crazy, he'd seen the signs and knew what a kangaroo could do to the car if he hit one, but he didn't slow down. The needle hovered around seventy, eighty, the engine roaring, the evening air blasting in through the window and against the side of his head. Sometimes the road veered away from the storm, sometimes he seemed about to slide right under it.

"Come on, you big bastard!" he shouted. "I've got you!"

After half an hour the road began to rise again into low hills and he charged up them, only lifting his foot when he'd reached the top and begun to sail down the long bends on the far side, the tyres squealing on the bitumen. He saw the faint lights of a town flickering ahead and below like a constellation before clouds descended and hid them. Lightning flashed and lit up the scrub—pale-trunked paperbarks—on either side of the road and then thunder cracked directly overhead. In the wake of the crash he turned off the ignition and let the car coast to a standstill. Lightning flashed almost continually now and the thunder was right on its heels, cracking and booming and making the car tremble on its springs. He got out and lay on his back in the road, its store of heat working its way up through his clothes. Fat drops of rain began to crash down around him. A cooler wind washed down through the storm clouds and he shivered despite the warmth beneath him. The drops built in number and became a deluge. He lay on the bitumen and laughed as the rain hit his face and then he lifted up his arms as the rain soaked him, closed his eyes and just lay there, thinking no thoughts.

The rain eased, then stopped, the storm over almost as soon as it had begun, the clouds rolling away, worlds without end above him once more. He felt that the rain had washed away the last faint traces of uncertainty and reluctance from him, and although he was unsure of the new persuasion to which he had subscribed—and what he might be required to forfeit to it—he knew he'd done the right thing in coming and he knew he'd found the purpose he'd been craving.

It was about half past nine when, after another inspection of the map, he headed west and inland. He couldn't see much of the country in the darkness, but he was concentrating hard on keeping the car stable as he gunned down the quiet country roads, the tyres slithering around on the loose edges. He slowed over a crest and peered across to his left. The country spread out below was almost uniformly dark and broken only by the odd lonely light. According to the map he was close but he'd seen no sign. The road dropped down into a valley and he was wondering where Angel Rock might be hiding when he saw the sign for the turn-off to it. He was going so fast he had to slam on the brakes, the car eventually coming to a screeching halt a couple of dozen yards past the sign. Sitting in the middle of the road, the car slightly skewed, headlights spearing across an empty paddock, he listened to the engine tick over for a moment before backing up and turning. He drove for another half an hour along the valley floor and then he rounded a corner and Angel Rock appeared, spread out comfortably across the higher ground just to the west of a wide, dark river. There were maybe a couple of hundred houses and they all had the same pyramid-shaped corrugated-iron roofs, latticed verandahs, and neat little front yards. To the northwest a steep range of hills loomed, black against the starlit sky, and a rocky peak reared out of them, dominating the valley and town. *The* Rock, Gibson figured.

Gibson drove slowly into the town and then around it. A grid of streets, most ending against barbed-wire fences to the west and the river to the east. His headlights illuminated the eyes of cats and the odd dog as they went about their nocturnal duties. Moths spun like satellites around streetlights. He saw one or two old people sitting out on their verandahs, fanning themselves, but other than that the town seemed deserted. The main street was split in two lengthwise by a stretch of grass with two big fig trees at either end. There was a table, benches for people to sit, flowerbeds with no flowers. There was a bank, a butcher, a baker, a grocer, a newsagent with a barber's pole by the door, a pub. Somewhere, he supposed, was an unhappy dentist and a kindly old doctor who made house calls. He could see why someone might want to leave the place and never come back. When he thought of Darcy here his stomach knotted up in anticipation and his hand slid out and settled on her bible on the seat beside him and he stroked it like a familiar until he was calm enough to continue.

He found the station easily enough. He pulled his suitcase out of the boot and walked up the path to the door and knocked. A tall, white-haired man in his fifties, wearing a singlet and grey work trousers, answered it.

"Gibson?"

"Yes."

"Pop Mather. I spoke to you on the phone."

Gibson held out his hand for the man to shake and very nearly regretted it, his grip was so strong. He followed him inside, weary and bleary-eyed, but not so tired that he failed to notice a framed photograph sitting on a buffet in the living room.

"Come up through the range, or in from the coast?" Pop asked.

"Ah, the range."

"Good. Thought you might've missed the ferry if you'd come in by the coast. Meant to tell you."

Gibson nodded, but he was staring at the photo, struck by the same visceral jolt of recognition he'd had before. Darcy Steele and another girl were sitting on the verandah rail of a house somewhere, their arms across each other's shoulders, their bare feet and legs dangling. Darcy's head leant against the roof post. Her lips were red, her cheeks peachblown, her hair sweeping down across her face. The other girl's darker features and more reserved smile made her seem more serious, less . . . radiant, but that might have been an illusion. He knew well enough that photographs only ever contained a splinter of the truth or the whole box and dice.

"Couldn't have looked any prettier," said Pop. "Not even all gussied up."

"Yours?"

"Yes. That's Grace."

"Have you told her yet?"

Pop nodded. "Yesterday, after you rang."

"What about the parents?"

"Yes. They know."

Gibson nodded. He put down the picture and Pop took his case from him and showed him to a spare room. He'd barely returned from the bathroom, undressed, put his head down on the pillow, before he was dead to the world and all it contained.

In the morning he watched Pop's daughter as she came into the kitchen and sat down in a chair. Her eyes were very red and it was obvious she'd had little sleep.

"You all right?" Pop asked her.

"Yes." Her voicebox had tightened up so much she could barely speak, her voice just a faint squeak.

"Mr. Gibson's a policeman," Pop continued, his voice low. "He'd like to ask you about Darcy."

Grace nodded, then blew her nose.

"Grace, your father tells me Darcy was a friend of yours."

She nodded. "We were *best* friends."

"Pop says you haven't seen her for a while, not since before Christmas."

"No, I haven't. I . . . I don't know why. Mrs. Steele told me she was sick when I went to see her."

Gibson nodded.

"Do you know why she . . . ran away?"

"No. I don't know. Her parents are strict."

"How are they strict?"

"She . . . isn't . . . wasn't allowed out except on Saturdays. And only to see me."

"I see. When did you see her last then?"

"At the dance. The night Tom Ferry came home."

"She seem . . . unhappy . . . at all?"

"Yes," said Grace, wiping away a tear from her eye, "but she wouldn't tell me why."

"Did she ever talk about a man named Billy, or Father Carney?"

"She used to talk about Billy," answered Grace, her eyes flicking between Gibson and her father. "He used to take her to look for bird's eggs, things like that, when she was littler, when she was allowed out."

"That's all?"

"Yes. What's he got to do with . . . ?"

"What about Carney?"

"He taught her Bible stuff when she was little."

Gibson looked at her, at the fierce protectiveness in her eyes. Had Darcy's life been taken by another he doubted she would have shown any mercy to the killer were she ever to judge him. She reminded him of one of those sad-looking stone angels in graveyards with their heads at a tilt, listening to heavenly song so highly pitched only they and dogs could hear it. Up there with the beating of bees' wings, the fluttering hearts of the lovelorn—but altogether deaf to the appeals of the guilty. It didn't matter. She seemed a brave kid and he fell immediately for her spirit.

"I don't know that they've got anything to do with anything," he answered, softly. "I just wanted to know if she was . . . afraid of them, or anyone else for that matter, that's all."

She chewed over his sentence. "No," she said. "She never said anything to me like that. I didn't think she was afraid of anything."

He paused. He could tell she had a question of her own and he waited for it.

"Are you the one who found her?"

"No," he said, shaking his head slowly, "but I was there."

She looked at him a little awestruck, as if he knew mysteries. He could tell she wanted to ask something else—maybe a lot of things—but he could also see she didn't quite have the courage yet. Finally she just nodded, barely, tears welling up again.

"Thanks, sweetheart," said Pop. She looked up at him, wiping her eyes. He nodded to her and she pushed back the chair and walked from the room and as she did she looked back at Gibson over her shoulder. He wasn't quite sure of the combination of emotions in the glance—sadness, guilt, anger, at least—but it seemed obvious she wanted something more from him than he'd given.

"Sorry about that," he said to Pop, after she'd gone. "I thought she might . . ."

Pop held up his hand. "You want to go see Darcy's folks now?"

"Ah, yes."

Pop nodded.

"Is it far?"

"No."

They headed out of town along an unsealed road, passing a knot of rusted iron sheds and then a wrecker's yard. Cattle watched them as they passed, strings of saliva hanging from their mouths.

"What can you tell me about them?"

"Ezra's hardheaded, a hard worker. Keeps to himself. Fay was the local beauty in her day—believe it or not. Ezra was a catch himself when he was younger. His father had high hopes for him, but then he died young, and Ezra had to stay on the farm instead of getting an education. Sonny—John is his real name—is the other child. Not the brightest boy in the world. Bit of a grub really, and a bully like Ezra. He'll take over the farm, I expect."

They drove for a couple more minutes and then Pop slowed the car and turned off the road. He gestured up the slope and Gibson peered out through the windscreen. Like the other farmhouses he'd seen, this one was set well back from the road and connected to it by a short, rough track. It was encircled by a hedge and a number of sheds in varying degrees of dilapidation. He got out of the car on Pop's instruction and opened the gate in the fence, closing it again after Pop had moved the car forward. The closer they came to the house the more deserted it seemed. Curtains billowed out of open windows. A cat, sunning itself on a ledge, cracked open one eye, noted their approach, then shut it again.

"Ezra'll be out back. I'll go and find him. Why don't you go and introduce yourself to Fay?"

Gibson nodded. Pop strolled away in the casual, laid-back manner he had that Gibson had already begun to note and register. He turned to the house and stepped carefully up the heavily weathered stairs. He rapped on the door and after a minute or so it was answered by Fay Steele. Gibson peered at her intently from behind the facade of his manufactured half-smile. Any similarity to Darcy—except for her eyes maybe—had all but faded. Her hair, tied back in a ponytail, was grey and stringy and as she stepped through the doorway and into the light he saw that her skin was greasy-looking and rough, her finger-nails keeping half-moons of dirt beneath them. She wore a faded cotton dress and her breasts were pendulous under it, the nipples pointing to the floor like the tips of fingers.

"Yes?"

Her eyes were wide and glassy. So wide that Gibson could see his own dark silhouette in them, the bright yard behind him.

"My name's Gibson. I've come about your daughter. About Darcy. I'm very sorry . . ."

"Ah. You better come in then. My husband's—"

"Sergeant Mather's gone to fetch him. I'd like to speak to you both."

"Oh. All right then. Come in."

It was dim inside the house and its smell—thick and rancid—closed in upon him immediately. The sitting room he passed through was furnished with a suite of high-backed armchairs, all except one piled high with stacked magazines and newspapers, *Australasian Posts* and *Women's Weeklys* mainly, some garnished with shrivelled apple cores or spirals of orange peel. The ceiling was bedecked with dusty cobwebs and the carpet had worn through to its base of heavy twine. A huge television with a failing tube flickered in the corner. Drifts of cat hair softened the right angles where floor met walls. A pair of cats, then a half-dozen, trotted in silently to look at him, their tails upright, and began to rub themselves up against his legs. He pushed them away gently and kept up his inspection. The walls were empty but for one sallow print of a bush scene in a gilded frame and an old, faded portrait of a young soldier, rising-sun badge pinned to his slouch hat and shoulder. A colour photograph in a chrome frame sat on the same table that held the telephone. A younger Darcy. A school photo. She had the brown skin, freckles, and sun-bleached hair common to country children. A pretty oval face, the barest smile—as if she were just working one up when the photographer had caught her—and a clear, blue-eyed gaze which seemed it might grow more intense the longer he looked. He suspected the picture had only recently been framed and placed there.

Fay showed him to a seat at the kitchen table then filled a kettle with water and set it on the stove. The wall behind the stove and the stove itself were both so speckled with congealed oil that they were almost uniformly yellow, and on the floor beside the refrigerator was a pool of gleaming black liquor, rendered down from God-knew-what. The fridge wheezed to a halt and then there was only the sound of the water in the kettle increasing in temperature. Fay Steele stood by it, gazing at him absently.

"Do you mind if I take a look at her room?"

Fay Steele's eyes widened and then her hand fluttered up to her chin.

"Oh, well, I'd really rather—"

"I won't be a minute. Please? Just a quick look?" He gave her his reassuring smile and used his reassuring tone.

"All right then," she answered, breathily. "First on the right there."

"Thank you, very much."

Inside the room he found a chrome-framed bed with a crocheted bedspread over it and a wardrobe with most of its veneer springing off. Against the wall was a little white dressing table with a comb and a brush upon it and a chair underneath. A jewellery box with frilly tulle edging sat just under the oval mirror. He opened it and the ballerina inside stood to attention on her spring but no music played and she did not turn. Inside the box were a few plastic bangles, half a dozen marbles, some feathers, a bird's egg. He took out a cat's-eye marble and put it in his pocket and then he pulled open the two small drawers in the dressing table. They were both empty. He heard the kettle begin to sing and Fay to move. He opened the wardrobe door. There were her dresses, still hanging. He ran his hand across them, smelt the faint smell of *girl*. There were drawers built into the wardrobe and he pulled open the first one and sifted through the underwear it contained. There was nothing of significance, and nothing in the second or the third. Then he heard a heavy tread at the front of the house. He exited the room promptly and walked back down the hall.

Ezra Steele was a big man, even after he'd taken off his heavy gumboots and even after he'd sat down. He wore grey bib overalls, a check shirt, a shapeless hat, and he smelt faintly of cowshit. Gibson introduced himself and sat down in the chair opposite when Steele declined his hand. He waited, saying nothing, until Pop returned from the kitchen with Fay and a tray of tea and biscuits. Steele glared at him from under his black brows, his fingers tapping against the arm of the chair. Suddenly Gibson felt all at sea and so unsure of himself that he would have got up off his seat and walked out if Steele's look hadn't already pinned him. There was nothing for it but to continue.

When Pop and Fay had poured the tea and settled themselves he began. He caught Steele's eye as he lifted the cup to his lips.

"Let me just say how sorry I am for your loss."

"Thank you," whispered Fay. Ezra said nothing. Gibson watched his eyes flick over to his wife, watched hers drop to the teacup she cradled in her hands.

"I just want to get a few details, clear up a few things in my mind."

"Yes," said Fay.

"Sergeant Mather tells me Darcy had run away before?"

"Yes, half a dozen times."

"Do you know why she did?"

Fay shook her head, suddenly tight-lipped.

"Did she ever try and . . . did she ever try to . . . take her life before?"

"No."

Gibson nodded. Ezra Steele stared at him, his bottom lip jutting out. He paused, then began again.

"You didn't tell Sergeant Mather she'd gone missing straight away. Why was that?"

Ezra spoke up, his voice deep, gruff, each word sheared off with a blunt razor. "She didn't go *missing*. She *ran away*."

"We . . . we . . . ah, thought it might have been best if she'd run off, you know, for good," said Fay.

Gibson raised his eyebrows. Pop leant back in his chair and sighed and ran his hands through his hair. Gibson asked them why but neither answered.

"When, *exactly*, was the last time you saw your daughter?"

Steele breathed out through his nose and looked up at the ceiling for a few long moments before answering.

"Just after Christmas."

Gibson saw the glance Fay shot him, but he'd already decided from the look of him that the information was untrue, that he had better subtract at least a week from the time. He looked from one to the other but didn't press the point, just pretended to write down the date in his notebook. Fay Steele watched him, chewing her lip.

"When she left, she didn't leave a note?"

"No," said Fay.

"Are you sure?"

"Yes," said Ezra.

"Was there an argument? A fight?"

"No."

Steele took his eyes off Gibson after answering and looked down at his hands. They were huge, and seemed roughly hewn from stuff that barely resembled flesh. His chest rose and fell. Gibson began to think it was time to go.

"All right then. Thank you very much."

Fay looked about to say *our pleasure* but stopped herself in time. Ezra Steele shook his head, but not in answer to any question. Fay Steele's eyes became bright and shiny, and then she started to sob, pearly tears rolling down her cheeks.

"I'm sorry," Gibson said again.

He looked across at Pop and Pop motioned that it was time to leave. Gibson stood and went to the door, then glanced back after he'd stepped through it. Fay hadn't moved and she didn't look up as her husband went to close the door behind them. They walked down to the car and as they were getting in Gibson saw a boy standing up by one of the sheds, watching them. Pop saw him too. "Sonny," he whispered.

He was just on six feet tall and already heavy in the belly for such a young man. He wore a pair of dirty overalls open at the front and his pale, soft chest glistened with sweat. He flicked his head to one side to get a greasy bang of hair out of his eyes and then ran his forearm over his mouth. Pop raised his hand in greeting but the boy did not acknowledge him, just turned and went back to whatever task it was that occupied him.

They sat at the bar of the Angel Rock Hotel and watched Hughie Bean fill two schooner glasses with Pilsener. They watched him in silence and when he'd finished they lifted up their glasses in unison and Gibson said cheers and each took a long sip.

"That's better," Gibson sighed. "I think we earned that."

They sat and neither spoke for half a minute or so. It was Gibson who broke the silence.

"Sorry about the little bloke you lost."

"Yeah, thanks," Pop said, staring at the surface of his beer. "These things happen . . . but the place won't be the same for a long time."

"How's the one who came back?"

"All right, considering. He doesn't remember much—which may be a blessing—but he has nightmares. Who wouldn't?"

"Nightmares? What about?"

"He can't really say."

"What do you think . . . someone up to no good?"

"What do you mean?"

"Someone, you know, kidnapped them or something?"

"No, I don't think so," Pop said, giving him a strange look.

"No one's got a grudge against the family, the parents?"

"No."

"You sure?" asked Gibson, unconvinced.

"Well . . . Henry and Ezra *have* been at each other for a long time—their kids are even at it now—but that's got nothing to do with it."

"What're they fighting about?"

"Started with them both liking the same girl years ago. That's about it."

"Who was the girl?"

"She's dead now—look, Ezra had nothing to do with it. He came out to look for little Flynn with me for Christ's sake. Searched for days."

"You saying you trust him then?"

"I *know* him. I have faith in people, Gibson. Up here, if we don't have that . . ."

Gibson nodded and sipped his beer. "I have faith in evidence and that's about it."

Pop turned to him.

"Why're you here, Gibson?" he asked, his tone suddenly and unexpectedly inquisitorial. Gibson picked up his glass again, slowly, and took a good sip.

"What do you mean?" he asked, innocently, wiping froth from his top lip.

"I mean I rang Erskine after your call. I know him from way back. He said that, strictly speaking, you're on holiday. Said that, officially, there's nothing for you to do here."

"That's about right."

"Well?"

"Well . . . you could call it something I need to do."

"That doesn't seem a good enough reason to go poking your nose in where it doesn't belong. You'll have to give me a better answer than that, Gibson. If you don't, *nobody* will talk to you, believe me. I'll see to it. I don't want to have to do that but I *don't* want people upset. What happened just now was bad enough."

Gibson looked at him and saw he was serious. Behind the bar Hughie was suddenly staring at him with suspicion in his eyes. He let out a sigh.

"What else did Erskine say?"

"Nothing else."

Gibson nodded and then he looked at Pop and made a decision.

"Look," he began, "when I was twelve, my sister, Frances, committed suicide. I don't remember anything about it. Blocked it all out I guess. Anyway, we were very close. She was something of a hero to me—my best friend, really. She took the family car and drove it out into the bush and then she swallowed a bottleful of my mother's sleeping pills. She was only seventeen. She left a note to tell us why she'd done it but it took months before the car was found and by that time the insects and the weather had got to her note and turned it into pulp."

"Jesus, Gibson. I'm sorry."

"Yeah, well, you know, we just had to accept it. It knocked all the faith out of me, I can tell you. I hadn't really thought about her for years, but then, when I saw Darcy like that . . . it brought it all back." He stopped and took a swig of beer. "Kick me out of your town if you must, Sergeant, but I'm determined to find out a few things. There's no mystery as to the *how*—Darcy locked herself in a dingy little room and cut her wrists—it's the *why* that troubles me. I mean, if I could find that out . . . Maybe it's too late for Frances, but maybe it isn't for Darcy."

Pop didn't answer for a while.

"It's shocking what happened," he began, "but I don't see what you can achieve by being here. You didn't know this girl at all."

"That's right, I didn't. But I'm hoping to change that. I just want to get to know her a little. That's all. Maybe then it might make a little more sense."

"Look, Gibson, it's just that I don't want the town stirred up again," Pop said, a little less insistently than before. "You can see why I wouldn't. The Steeles need their peace, Henry Gunn and his family. Things need to settle down. There's been too much grief here. If you go looking for things that aren't there I'm just afraid, good intentions or not, you'll cause more people to suffer."

"Well, that's not what I'm here for. I've got no intention of causing anyone harm."

They sipped at their beers and were quiet for a time until Gibson asked Pop another question.

"So . . . why do *you* think she did it?"

Pop looked at him and sighed.

"I don't know. It's just one of those mysteries of life. One of the grim ones."

"What if there's something concrete? A reason."

"Then it'll come out."

"Only if someone looks for it."

"It'll come out, eventually," Pop repeated.

Gibson shook his head. "You're a religious man, aren't you, Pop? I can tell. I'm not, myself. Not really. I don't believe justice just happens by itself."

"Neither do I. It comes from God."

"Well, we sort of agree then. Maybe your God's using me. Maybe I'm His emissary. How do you know I'm not?"

Pop narrowed his eyes and peered at him. Gibson had the feeling then that Pop had underestimated him, just slightly, and had only just realised his mistake.

"Maybe there were . . . *reasons*. I have looked into some possibilities."

"Like what?"

"All the running away. Who knows what she got up to, or who she met."

"I think I know what you're getting at. You know what the coroner said?"

"What?"

"Said she was a virgin."

Pop stared at him. "You sure?"

"I'm sure *he* was. You seem surprised."

Pop paused, rubbed his whiskery chin, then nodded.

"I am. There've been stories, rumours, since," he said.

"Stories, rumours," Gibson repeated. "Listen, if you'd had any . . . doubts about Darcy before, would you have let your daughter run around with her?"

"Probably not."

"All right then." Gibson drained his glass and clapped it on the bar to gain Hughie's attention.

"Now," he said, "what can you tell me about a man named Billy and this man here? These were found with her." He gave Pop the photos he'd found in Darcy's hands. Pop slipped on his glasses, looked at the pictures, then blinked and shook his head.

"This man's name is Adam Carney," he said, pointing. "The other is Billy Flood. Ezra told me he'd caught Billy hanging around the farm a few times lately. He seemed to think he'd come to spy on Darcy, but, well, Grace says Darce was on good terms with him." He put the photographs down on the bar and tapped them, shaking his head once more. "Billy . . . well . . . I don't . . . I don't know . . . gee, I haven't seen him for years. I know he used to turn up on people's doorsteps scrounging for food, that sort of thing."

"What is he, itinerant?"

Pop didn't answer for a long time. "I better tell you about Billy," he said, finally.

"Well, yeah, sounds like you'd better. You've got a face like thunder."

Pop grimaced, then began.

"In nineteen fifty-one, when he was a boy of sixteen, seventeen, there was an . . . accident, near here. Annie, Billy's sister, drowned."

"How'd it happen?"

"No one quite knows."

"This the girl the feud's over?"

"Yes. Ezra and she were engaged to be married for a while, but then Henry came into the picture and busted them up, or some such nonsense. Anyway, there were rumours she was pregnant with one or the other's child, but that was all rubbish. No one really knows what happened. Billy was always an odd sort of boy, delicate, you might say, but then, at the funeral, he went right off the rails. His father had to put him in an institution. I went and saw him once or twice. It seemed to me the pain he'd felt was so great it made his mind shut down, made him forget everything, even his own name, for a very long while. I saw him not long after he'd gotten out of the hospital, probably be nearly five years ago now. He was deathly pale, and weak, like he'd come back from a war, but he was determined to start his life again. I had to admire his determination. He stayed away from people as far as I knew, stayed out in the bush. The next time I saw him he was a different man again—his own man—but then he started drinking. Maybe things just caught up with him like they caught up with you."

Gibson returned Pop's gaze with no interest and then he reached into his pocket and pulled out his notebook and began to jot things down.

"His parents still around?"

"His mother's dead. Horace is a preacher. An evangelist. Horace's . . . teacher, I suppose you'd call him, was an old feller named Adam Carney. Father Adam everyone called him. Horace and his two youngsters lived with him up until the drowning. Horace left then but Adam stayed on in the house. He was there up until a couple of years ago, but now he's down in the old people's home in Laurence, in a pretty bad way, I believe."

"Can you tell me where this house is?"

Pop nodded and told him, but then he didn't say anything more for a minute or two. He seemed to be thinking about things he hadn't thought about for years. Gibson tried his best to be patient. The country sergeant had a quiet, measured way of speaking, as though he was used to being listened to, used to giving orders, used to having them carried out. Gibson thought it might be more fruitful not to interrupt him too much, but let his sentences play out, reveal the man and his thinking.

"When I was a young bloke Adam used to preach around here sometimes, just as a layman. This was before the war, when nearly every man and woman was a churchgoer and competition for souls was pretty fierce. He was a fire-and-brimstone man, hell and damnation, and he was only young, not even forty. Eventually he got so intense, so . . . picturesque, that the minister had to ask him not to come. So he'd stand up on the war memorial, or in the park by the river, and preach, until people were coming from miles around to hear him. They'd bring their picnics and sit out on the grass to hear this firebrand preacher."

They sat for a time and then Pop gave Gibson a dry grin. "You're right about me being religious, Gibson. In my own way I am, but I always felt pretty shabby next to old Adam. That old bloke was touched by God all right. But then things changed. War broke out. People didn't want to hear about hellfire and punishment. They wanted . . . hope. Rainbows. Adam stopped preaching altogether. It took a long time but he settled right down until he was the gentlest, kindest old man you could ever hope to meet. And listen, Horace Flood was a hard man when he walked into this town: a brawler, gambler, crook, drinker . . . you name it. That all changed after one day listening to Adam. And I know for a fact that Billy kept visiting Adam right up to when he went into the home. Adam told me so."

"And your point is?"

"Just that Adam had faith in the boy. If you're thinking, because of this picture, that he had anything to do with . . . what Darcy did . . . then I think you'd be barking up the wrong tree, that's all."

Gibson lit a cigarette. He sat smoking silently for a while and then he asked Pop another question that took a while to be answered.

"What do you think went on in that house, Sarge?"

"I don't know, Gibson. I really don't. Ezra's a bit of a tyrant, but look, you saw him, he's like a mean dog when it comes to protecting his own."

Pop stood then and flattened his hands out across the bar and looked down at them.

"Listen, Gibson," he said, "I have to be going. Darcy's body is coming up on this morning's train. I thought I'd go over there, make sure there're no hitches."

"When's the funeral?"

"Tomorrow."

Gibson closed his notebook and slipped it into his pocket.

"What was she like?"

"Darcy? Darcy was . . . she was a good kid really. Bit too excitable though, and an overactive imagination, but I always thought she was good for my Grace. She's always been a little on the quiet side, you see."

Gibson nodded.

"So, where do you think I should start looking for this Billy Flood character?"

Pop sighed and half shook his head. "I don't know. Maybe you could try the old house. Apart from that . . . I know Billy used to do a bit of work down on the cane farms a couple of years back. He was drinking then. I heard they had to throw him in the lockup a few times. You could go ask the copper down there. Last I heard of his old man he was out west at a place called Mount Wright. It's his home town and he buried his wife and daughter out there. He might know where Billy is but I very much doubt it. Afraid that's the best I can do."

Pop downed the last of his drink and then leant in a little closer to Gibson.

"If you *do* find him, go easy. Believe me, he's not as tough as he looks. Ask him to come see me. He knows who I am."

He picked up his hat and walked to the door.

"So, you going to let me stay?"

Pop gave him a wry smile. "I'll let you know."

"Hey," Gibson called to his departing back. "I looked pretty hard last night but I couldn't see any angel in the rock."

"No? Well, there's a trick to it. Light's got to be hitting it just right. Even then, well, it's a bit of a stretch. People say whoever named it had had one too many."

Gibson smiled. Pop left. Gibson raised his arm and little finger to Hughie Bean and ordered another beer. He took his time drinking it and then he slouched outside and squinted up at the bright, empty day he found there.

After a while he wandered down the street to the grocer's shop and bought a pack of cigarettes from the big, talkative lady behind the counter. He ran a cursory eye over the other shops he'd seen the night before and then he walked down towards the river and the park that hugged its gently curving course. He strolled past the war memorial, running his eyes over the unfamiliar names chiselled into the marble, and then he carried on along the riverbank and up to the ferry ramp and the rotting posts of the old bridge alongside it. He walked in a long ragged circle around the town until he came to a little rise. From there he could see the whole town spread out before him, the valley stretching away to the northwest, the river—a fine river—glittering in the hard midday light. A dog barked. He thought the scene was very pretty, very peaceful, and the water made him feel like the Harbour once had, when he'd been a child, before he'd pulled one too many bodies out of it. He took the picture of Darcy from his pocket and stared at it. Again he felt a little hollow, a little alone, a little out of his element. He couldn't really blame Pop for his devotion to the living of Angel Rock, his ambivalence towards the dead, and he knew that he couldn't rely on him for much more in the way of help. As Pop had pointed out in his gruff but fair way, his claim to it was little more than threadbare. He sighed, flicked away his cigarette, and tried to imagine Darcy walking the streets below, killer and victim both, but he could not.

He walked back up to the café for a bite to eat before heading up to the old Flood house. He was the only customer. He sat by the window and looked at the dead insects in the ravine running along between the glass and its frame. He ordered coffee but what he got was undrinkable. He caught the eye of the smiling proprietress and ordered a pot of tea. He wasn't hopeful about the food he'd ordered. He reckoned that with the time they seemed to have on their hands out here the least they could do was get their food right, but when the plate came he could only sit and look at it for a few moments, his eyes wide, his surprise of the pleasant variety. There was a steak an inch thick, two of the yellowest-yolked eggs he'd ever seen, a mountain of vegetables, and two thick slices of fresh white bread.

"Get it down ya," said the woman, smiling.

"Thank you," he said, and tucked in.

When he was finished he paid the woman and complimented her on her cooking and left. He went to the car and looked at the map he'd drawn of Pop's directions and then he set off.

It took him half the afternoon to find the place. The hills above the town were crisscrossed by a network of unnamed and unsignposted shale tracks that seemed bent on leading him away from where he wanted to go. When he finally found the head of the track he was after he realised he'd already driven past the spot at least twice. He stopped the car in a cloud of pale dust and slammed the door behind him. He caught a glimpse of a structure away through the trees and he set off down the track towards it.

He soon regretted slamming the door so hard when the quiet closed back around him and he realised what he'd disturbed. There was very little breeze and the trees about were still and silent. There was no sign of movement from the house and no sign that it was occupied. Some of the weatherboards at its front were rotting and loose and its triangular roof was red with rust. Back behind it he could see more sheds and outbuildings in similar condition. He went up to the front door. There was some kind of dark stain on the lintel over it and he reached up and touched it with his fingers. Small brownish flakes came fluttering down. He wiped his hand on his trousers and gave a little involuntary shudder.

"Hello?" he called. "Anyone home?"

Silence.

He turned the knob and pushed open the door and looked down into the hall, his eyes adjusting to the gloom.

"Hello?"

Even though it was quite airless and smelt like it had been closed up for some time it seemed much cooler inside. He waited, listening, but heard nothing except his own respiration. He moved down the hall, looking into the rooms on either side as he went. They were empty of everything but dust and decades-old blinds and curtains but on the back of one of the doors he found markings that caught his attention. They were made with pencil and recorded the increasing heights of two children over nearly a dozen years. *Billy* and *Annie*. Gibson passed his finger over the old marks and then turned away. He walked down the hall and into the living room. One of the windows was open and a stained and ragged curtain hung down from a warped wooden rod. The floor in front of the window was rotting where rain had blown in over the past few years. The room reminded him of something, but no matter how hard he tried he couldn't quite pin down what it was. He took hold of the curtain and the fabric crumbled between his fingers. He stood there a little longer, frowning, and then he moved on to the kitchen. It was empty too but there was a slightly less abandoned look to it. He opened the stove's firebox door and sniffed. The ashes were cold, inconclusive. Pop was right. No one had lived there for a long time.

After a quick look around the house he headed back down to Angel Rock. His thoughts kept distracting him from his driving and before very long he was lost again. By the time he'd found his way again and pulled up in front of the station house it was getting late. He looked back up at the hills to where he reckoned the house was. The setting sun had turned the clouds over them as pink as fairyfloss. Later, after dinner, he went back outside and looked that way again. The stars were out, the breeze was out of the east, and the evening was clear and achingly beautiful.

He set off towards the river and then took the road that ran out past the ferry. Lil Mather had been only too helpful when he'd asked her where Henry Gunn lived—he doubted Pop would have been so forthcoming. He was curious about what Pop had said about a feud between Henry and Ezra Steele. He'd seen feuds escalate until they enveloped the innocent before and the possibility had to be ruled out.

It took about fifteen minutes to reach the house. He walked up the steps and looked in through the open door before knocking. He could see Henry Gunn asleep on the couch inside. He was still wearing his work clothes: blue singlet and shorts, gaiters around his boots. "Cold Cold Heart" was crackling out from a pair of battered speakers and as he stood there the record hit a pothole of a scratch and skittered back a few bars. When he looked back to Henry his eyes had opened.

"Who are you?"

"My name's Gibson. I'm a detective."

"Yeah? You don't look like one."

"So people tell me."

"What do you want? You come about my boy?"

"No, I didn't. I . . . ah . . . just wanted to ask you about something."

"What?"

"Pop Mather was telling me about Billy Flood, about how his sister drowned."

Henry rested his head back against the arm of the couch.

"Yeah?"

"He told me you and Ezra haven't got along since then."

Henry muttered something under his breath.

"Listen, does this have anything to do with my boy, because—"

"Maybe it does."

"Maybe? What's that supposed to mean?"

"It means I'm just trying to find some things out, just trying to get the lie of the land."

Henry eyed him suspiciously, but then he lifted himself off the couch, went into the kitchen and brought back two bottles of beer.

"You want one?"

"No, not right now."

Henry shrugged and then gestured to a seat. Gibson sat.

"You staying at Pop's?"

"Yes."

"He send you down here?"

"No."

Henry nodded. The record stopped playing and in its aftermath Gibson could hear crickets chirruping outside. Henry glanced over his shoulder and then leant forward.

"I think I know what you're getting at," he said, quietly. "Don't think I haven't thought it myself. But Ezra Steele didn't have anything to do with the boys going missing . . . or only Tom coming back. The thing about him, Gibson, is that he's a piss-weak, yellow coward. So's his boy. Ezra knows if he ever touched *anything* of mine I'd go over there and kill him with my bare hands . . ."

Gibson nodded. It was hard to doubt him.

"And Sonny?"

"Same thing."

"Why don't you tell me about Annie Flood? Pop said no one actually saw her drown."

Henry lit a cigarette with his calloused, nicotine-stained fingers and then he passed over the packet. Gibson took one and lit it. Henry leant back and inhaled. Maybe it was because he was speaking about something other than the disappearance of his boy that made him relax, as if he was glad of the opportunity.

"No, no one saw her go under, but that's . . . I mean, she was an odd girl. She liked to go off and do things on her own. Sometimes she was just giving Smith the slip."

"Smith? Who's he?"

"Smith was a mate of Horace Flood's. His right-hand man. They knew each other before they got religion. Met in a boys' home, I believe."

"Why did Annie have to give him the slip?"

"Oh, it was like he owned her, and Billy. He bossed 'em around and made them do this and that. Horace was too busy with his damn church to notice. Smith basically raised them both after Mrs. Flood passed on.

"He used to put all kinds of funny ideas into their heads," Henry continued, with a slight laugh. "Some of them silly, some just plain . . . mean."

"What sort of things?"

"Oh, he used to tell Billy all the time that he was slow in the head and that slowies were useless and couldn't be allowed near women because their seed was bad. And he was forever telling Annie that he'd marry her one day. That there was nothing she could do to stop it, that her father had already agreed to it."

"I thought she'd been engaged to Ezra?"

"Yeah, that's right. He asked her. I suppose she must have said yes.

Fuck knows what happened but nothing ever come of it. Then I started taking her out. Ezra still hasn't gotten over it. Hates my guts to this day. Anyway, Smith blamed me and Billy for what happened to Annie. That's the kind of bloke he was."

"He blamed you? Why?"

"I don't know—that we weren't looking out for her or something? God knows what the fuck he expected us to do—God knows me and Billy would have saved her if we could have."

"Where's this Smith now?"

"Don't know. Haven't seen hide nor hair of the sorry cunt for twenty years."

Gibson ashed his cigarette and rubbed his chin.

"What about Billy?"

"Nope. Haven't seen him for years either."

Just then came a sound that Gibson, at first, thought was some kind of animal in distress. The wail rose and rose and then trailed off into silence. A boy—dark-haired and good-looking—but with worry and concern in his eyes, appeared in the hallway. He stopped when he saw Gibson sitting there and he looked over at Henry, his forehead creasing.

"It's all right, Tom. I'll go. Gibson . . ."

"I'll go. I'm . . . ah, sorry," he muttered. He walked down the path feeling like an intruder, and as he made his way back into town he looked back over his shoulder at the darkened windows of the house and shuddered.

12

At three o'clock, just after they'd arrived back from the funeral, the telephone in the station house rang. Grace looked up from where she stood in front of the kettle, her eyes still red and weepy. Pop heard Lil's soft footfalls as she came out of her room and walked up the hall to where the phone hung on the wall, then the murmur of her voice, then her step once again.

"It's Reg Pope," she said, her head appearing around the door.

"What's *he* want?"

"He didn't say, just said it was very important."

Pop sighed and heaved himself up off his chair, then patted Grace's shoulder as he passed by.

"Yes, Reg, what can I do for you?"

The old man's voice was faint and crackly down the line and Pop didn't catch his first sentence.

"Speak up, will you, Reg? I can barely hear you."

"I need to see you, Mather!"

"What about?"

"About that girl."

"What, Darcy Steele?"

"Yes. Can you come up?"

"Can't you talk to me now?"

"No, not on this blasted thing!"

Pop replaced the receiver, his ear ringing from the crack it had made as Reg had hung up. He rubbed his chin and wondered what the old coot could possibly be wanting to tell him. He picked his hat off the peg near the back door and then stepped into the kitchen.

"Tea'll have to wait, love. I have to go see someone. You'll be all right till I get back?"

Grace nodded.

"Good girl."

He drove out of Angel Rock toward the Popes' place, peering out through the windscreen and rubbing away condensation with the back of his hand. There was a steady drizzle falling from the low sky and the hills around were swathed in ragged grey sheets of cloud. Usually he loved days like these—the fresh smell of the rain, the earth drinking it in, the creeks swollen and full—but today felt as oppressive as any summer heat wave because of the funeral.

He came to the crossroads where the boys had been dropped off by Artie McKinnon and he slowed and turned the car onto the road up to the Popes'. Soon the sealed road ended and the shale track which replaced it became slick and slippery the further it wound up through the hills. The ceiling of cloud sat just above the trees, softening the edges of everything. Drops of water falling from the overhanging trees drummed on the roof of the car like so many fingers. The tail of the Falcon slithered around on the rutted track and Pop wondered how on earth the Popes' big Roller managed it, even in the dry. He passed the old Flood house, then the turn-off to the dam and after another fifteen minutes of slithering came round a corner and spotted the Popes'. When he reached the gate he turned off the engine and looked down at the house. With no heirs to consider, the brothers had let it fall into general disrepair. It hadn't seen a coat of paint in more than twenty years and was way out of true now, thanks to the wet and, more than likely, the termites. He got out of the car and hoisted himself over the gate and walked down the blue-metal drive to the house. Reg was waiting for him just inside the open front door.

"Come on," he said, turning down the hall. Pop took off his hat, shook it, and followed him. He could see, despite the gloom, the shiny tracks on the walls where the rain was leaking down through the roof and ceiling. He could hear water dripping into buckets and saucepans and there was an odd smell in the air. It wasn't a bad smell—more like being inside a damp cave or standing next to new-turned earth—and soon he didn't notice it at all.

Reg limped along the hall to the kitchen, leaning heavily on his walking stick and huffing and puffing. Pop had never seen him looking so old. He'd worked too hard all his life, but the last few years of his retirement, his supposed slowing down, hadn't seemed to have done him much good at all.

"All right, Reg, it's a filthy day and I've come out against my better judgement—"

"Spare me, son, I don't want to hear it," said Reg, but not in the same cranky tone he'd used on the phone. "Not at my age."

He shuffled across to the bench and leant against it, then looked at Pop over his shoulder.

"I've always said my piece straight. I want to tell you something. Sit yourself down. You'll be wanting a cuppa, I suppose?"

"Only if you're having one, Reg."

"I bloody am now," Reg muttered. Pop smiled to himself. He watched the old cocky go about the business of tea-making and didn't interrupt him. His brother Robert didn't seem to be about. When Reg had finished he passed the mug with one quaking hand, threw the tea-spoon down on the table with the other.

"Now, I want to get something off my chest," he said, pulling out his chair.

"This sounds like a confession," said Pop, stirring sugar into his tea.

"It is a confession. Of a sort. Something I need to tell."

"What about the pastor?" said Pop, unable to help himself. "Why not tell him?"

"I don't believe any of that mumbo-jumbo!" Reg said, emphatically, and Pop caught a glimpse of the grumpy old sod he'd always been and relaxed a little.

"But you've been going to church for years."

"Yep. That's right—very observant, young feller!—but I've changed me mind about a lot of things recently. Decided you're the only bloke around here I could tell this to."

"Me?"

"Yes! Don't make me change me mind!"

"All right. Sorry. Go on."

"Anyway, I've been thinking about a lot of things. A lot of things. Like that young girl of Steele's."

"Darcy."

"Yeah," said Reg.

"You know something about . . . what she did?"

"Listen, wait a while and let me finish. I'm tellin' ya, aren't I?"

"Yes. Go on. I won't interrupt."

"Me and Robert, we never were married. You know it. Whole valley knows it. Don't ask me how we both missed out because I don't know. But us being not married didn't mean we didn't have . . . you know . . . *needs*. You follow me, man?" he finished, gruffly.

"Yes," said Pop, his heart sinking a little.

"Now Robert, he was the quiet one, but he's the one who took matters into his own hands and looked for women who'd be . . . friendly with him, you follow?"

"Yes."

"I never could bring myself to do it," he said, shaking his head. "Just bloody . . . couldn't. Anyway, a few years back we were out on the road, in the car, when we sees this young girl walking alongside the road, holding out her hand like she wanted a lift. Crikey, we said to each other. Young thing like that. What's she doing out here on her own? So we stopped and picked her up. I'm not sure Robert's intentions were altogether honourable, but when he saw how young she was, he pulled his head in. She spun us a big old story about this and that but I knew who she was. Robert didn't, but I did. I'd seen her before, with her mother. I knew she was Ezra Steele's girl. Anyway, she sort of invited herself home, on account of Robert's chivalrous nature and me keeping quiet and her being a bright spark, making us laugh with her stories."

"And what happened?"

"She stayed for a good few days. She cooked for us. She did. She'd recite from the Bible to us in the evenings. She could do that, you know. Whole parts of it. Nothing else, just the Bible. Bright as a brass button."

"And what happened?" Pop said, softly.

Reg stopped, mopped at his mouth with his handkerchief, his big old hand trembling, the two outside fingers stiff and near useless.

"I used to look at her while she'd have her bath," he said, his voice shaking. "There it is. That's what happened. Three nights in a row. What's more, son, I think she knew I was watching. I'm nearly damn sure of it. But she never said a word."

He thumped the rubber tip of his walking stick against the floor, a tear working its way out of his rheumy eye and his bottom lip quivering.

"That's it? You never did . . . anything else?"

"Nope. Nothing else. Just the looking."

"What about Robert?"

"No. Like I said, he had other means. I know my brother. He wouldn't have ever . . . not like I did."

"How many times was she here? And for how long?"

"After that first time . . . half a dozen times more. Sometimes for a few days, sometimes a week or two."

"Didn't you think her parents were looking for her? Were worried about her?"

"Yes, of course, man! But I couldn't help meself, you see! Now take me down to your bloody station, Mather, and throw the bloody book at me!"

Pop sighed, looked at the old man, tallied a few things up in his mind before continuing.

"What about just before Christmas? Did you see her then?"

Reg didn't answer.

"Reg?"

"Yes, God love ya! I'm gettin' to it.

"A few nights after that young Tom turned up in town. I don't sleep much these days, you see. I take the car out some nights. Thought I'd take another look for the other little bloke. Anyway, *she* was on the side of the road like the first time. I was going to take her home, Mather, I swear, but she just had a way about her. You'd just do what she wanted, and . . ."

"Where'd you take her?"

"All the way, all the way to Sydney."

Pop swore softly under his breath and shook his head.

"Well, it's done now, I suppose. How was she? Did she seem . . . unhappy?"

"No. I didn't think so. Once or twice I got the feeling things weren't all right with her, but she never said."

"She say *anything* that made you worry?"

"No. We talked about a lot of things. Good things mainly. She did ask me what I thought came after dyin'."

"What did you say?"

"I said I didn't know, but that some said heaven, that I was hoping for something like that myself. And we talked about how it might be and I think she had her own ideas. I never thought . . ."

"And where exactly did you leave her?"

"We got lost. I don't know where we were, but she hopped out, thanked me, and off she went."

"Just like that?"

"Just like that."

Pop sighed. "I wish you'd told me this sooner, Reg."

"I know."

"Is that everything?"

Reg nodded.

"Well, I don't think you've got anything to worry about from the law."

"You're not going to arrest me?"

"What law have you broken?"

"You're the flamin' walloper, man! You tell me!"

"I *am* telling you. She's gone now. I don't see that what you told me had much to do with how she ended up."

"You reckon?"

"Yes, I do."

Reg's miserable expression eased just a fraction, but then his bottom lip began to quiver. Pop didn't know whether he felt pity for him or contempt.

"But I'd keep it under your hat, Reg. Don't tell anybody else. Don't want Ezra finding out. That wouldn't do anyone any good."

"No."

Pop drained the last of his tea and stood. "I have to be off. I've a girl of my own to be worrying about."

Reg nodded. "She thought the world of your Gracie, you know. Be sure and tell her some day, if she don't already know."

"I will."

Pop made a show of looking around. "The house is in a bit of a state, Reg," he declared.

"Yes, it is," agreed Reg, almost cheerfully, the relief surfacing from deep within him. "It's falling down around our ears. Don't want anyone livin' in it afterwards so it'll die with us too. Way it should be."

Pop stopped at the front door to put on his hat and then looked out at the rain.

"Where's Robert got to anyway?"

"Town. He'll be back before the light goes. Can't see in the dark too well now at all."

Pop gave a slight smile and shook his head.

"All right then. I'll see you."

"Yep."

He was about to turn away when a thought occurred to him. "Reg," he said.

"Yep?"

"You remember that time you saw a big cat?"

"Oh, now don't go bringin' that up, son. I've heard more jokes about that than I've had hot dinners."

"Tell me again. I won't joke."

Reg looked at him warily, then shrugged.

"It don't bother me any more what anyone thinks. I know what I saw. I saw a big cat all right. A grey one. A lion, I'd say—big as that anyway. The meanest-looking beast I've ever seen. I saw it. I know I did. If you can't trust your eyes what can you? Where does it end? Does it mean I can't be sure of the sky? The trees? Damn thing gave me a look that sent me cold all over." He looked up sharply at Pop's face for any trace of amusement but found none.

"What you want to know for?"

"I don't know . . . I thought maybe . . ."

"One took the boy? No," said Reg, shaking his head. "They won't touch our kind. They stick to taking cattle and roos and that's that."

Pop nodded, then clapped the old man on the shoulder and turned to go. When he was halfway to the car he looked back. Reg was still standing there in the doorway with one hand on his hip, the other stretched up against the side of the doorframe, his chest heaving like he'd just run a hundred. Pop didn't think he was long for the world. He lifted his hand and the old man returned his wave before shuffling back inside the house and closing the door.

As he drove back down to Angel Rock the cloud cover began to break up. Shafts of sunlight struck down through the gaps and lit up sections of the valley floor as neatly as spotlights. He didn't quite know what to make of Reg's story, or even how he'd responded to it. Both troubled him, but the story had also filled him with a strange elation, as though he'd been given some glimpse of the essence of the girl, something to at least offset the memory of her grim, spiritless funeral; the priest droning, Fay and Ezra torpid, Sonny glum and scowling. Standing there with one arm round Grace, the other holding an umbrella over the two of them, he'd thought both girls had deserved much better. He remembered the funeral of Annie Flood, years ago, just after the war, when he'd been both veteran and wet-behind-the-ears copper. That had been more of a celebration than anything else, and one of the most moving things he'd ever seen.

He was driving along a straight stretch, Reg's story intertwined in his head with thoughts of funerals and spectral cats, when he rounded a bend and saw a young girl standing by the side of the road. Running around at her feet were three tan puppies, their bellies darker where they were wet from the grass. He braked to a halt and turned off the ignition and climbed from the car, the fresh smell of the rain still in the air all around. The girl stood before a closed gate and a letterbox on a post. He could see a house further up the slope. Hanging from the letterbox was a sign. *Puppies. Free,* it read.

He walked towards the girl and saw that she had gathered the puppies together by grabbing the string that trailed from each one's neck. He guessed her age at only six or seven. Her feet were bare and her arms were thin and very brown. She held the strings with both hands and the puppies writhed against each other and choked themselves as they strained towards him.

"Hello," he said.

"Hello."

"Are you in charge of these puppies?"

"Yes," she said shyly, nodding.

"What sort of dogs are they?"

"They are called mongrels."

Pop laughed. "Is that what your father calls them?"

She nodded. "And Mum."

She looked up at him through her fringe and he smiled at her and she put her head to the side and looked back down at the ground.

"This one's a boy, these two are girls." She pointed, and then her finger went into her mouth as if she had lost something in there. The puppies licked his fingers but then the little one she'd indicated as male wandered off and started pressing through the wet grass at the side of the road.

"He's a little quieter than his sisters, isn't he."

"Yes."

"I like him."

He picked up the little puppy and inspected him. His tan coat had smudges of a darker colour at the ears, shoulder and tail. He licked Pop's face with a warm, pink tongue. He put the dog down with his sisters and dug out his wallet and took from it a crisp new five-dollar note and handed it to the little girl.

She shook her head. "They're free."

"I know. This is for you, anyway."

She smiled at him, wide-eyed. He saw the gap where her two front teeth had once sat and he remembered Grace at the same age. She took the money and held it at its corner as though it were a flag or pennant.

"Thank-you-very-much," she said, remembering her etiquette.

"You're welcome."

They watched the dogs play for a few moments, saying nothing, the money still in the girl's hand but, for the moment, forgotten. It was quite still now, getting on to evening, and stalled up behind the girl's home were phantom heights of lavender and gold-edged rain clouds. A figure moved behind the screened front door of the house and paused there to watch.

"You'd like to keep all of them, wouldn't you?"

The little girl nodded.

"I know someone who'll look after him real well. I promise."

She nodded again.

"He'll be loved."

She didn't want to give any away but she knew she must, knew that a farm could not have so many dogs. She looked at him and even though he felt they'd come to an understanding he could see that when he left his words would have little effect on her heartache. She pushed gravel forward with her toe, her arms behind her. A wallflower and her dull suitor.

"Goodbye, then."

"Bye," she answered, softly.

Before he could change his mind he picked up the puppy and put him on the floor of the car. Almost at once he began to cry. When he waved goodbye to the little girl she had pulled in the remaining two pups and they were rearing up against her legs like tiny horses. She lifted her hand to wave but then didn't and Pop watched her in the rear-view mirror until the road turned and she slid off the glass.

13

Grace sat behind the western wall of the old boatshed, the last of the afternoon sunshine finding its way through holes in the rusting metal and falling across her in beams as if she were the centre of a magician's box-and-sword trick. Through her tears she watched the river roll by, knees drawn up before her and her chin resting in the vee they made. She was staring, not really seeing anything, when she became aware of a young man walking directly towards her. For a moment, until her eyes focused on him, he seemed closer than he actually was and she started, annoyed at his intrusion, but then she realised that he was still on the other side of the river. She recognised him then. Charlie Perry. He wore a jackaroo's hat, jeans, a blue Jacky Howe, and his tanned arms were dark with tattooist's inscriptions. As she watched he took off his hat, then his jeans and boots, then his shirt, but it was not until he was on the jetty, about to jump into the river, that he saw her sitting there in the shade of the boatshed. He stopped and looked across at her and grinned. She didn't make any sign that she had seen him, just turned her head a little to the side, as though she'd been watching something in another direction and not him, and then, just as she realised it was probably her knickers he could see and was grinning about, he leapt out into the river. While he was still underwater she jumped up and ran back across the park and up the street without looking back. When she arrived at the station house Pop was on all fours in front of the open pantry door in the kitchen, a piece of meat between his fingers.

"What on earth are you doing?"

Pop looked up, trying not to laugh.

"I've got a wilful pup on my hands . . . and I don't need another."

"A puppy? Whose is it?" She dropped to her knees and peered over Pop's shoulder.

"Mine. I bought him this afternoon. Then I remembered your mother doesn't care for dogs, then there's you and—"

"I don't mind them when they're little," said Grace, cutting him off. "Let me have a go."

"Be my guest, but he's already turned his nose up at my bit of fillet."

They swapped places and Grace shuffled forward on her knees. The pantry was dark and cool and smelt of potatoes and onions.

"He's in the cupboard there," said Pop. "I think he's behind that big saucepan."

Grace had to put her head right down and nearly against the floor before she could see the pup. His dark little eyes gleamed out at her from the back of the cupboard.

"You must have frightened him."

"Might have been the car."

"Yeah."

She began coaxing him out. Pop listened to the gentle little sounds she made and marvelled. He eased himself up, sat down at the kitchen table and left her to it. After ten minutes or so she emerged with the still trembling puppy in her arms.

"He's all right now. He's probably hungry, or missing his mother."

She continued stroking his little body for a few more minutes. Pop watched, his jaw resting in his palm. Grace went to the refrigerator and poured milk into a saucer and set it before the little dog—who promptly set to.

"The circus is on tonight," Pop said, softly. "I thought you and me could go."

Grace didn't look up. "I don't really feel like it," she said.

"Oh well," said Pop. He waited a little longer. "Darce liked the circus, didn't she?" he said, as nonchalantly as he could.

"Yeah. She loved it. She wanted to join them. Be an acrobat or something."

"She'd probably be going then, if she were here."

"Yeah, she would."

"Why don't you think about it? Do us good, I think."

Grace nodded but he could tell she wasn't quite convinced.

"Pop?"

"Yes."

"I heard a story the other day."

"What kind of story?"

She took a deep breath and repeated almost word for word a story Hughie had told him just last week over a beer. It was one of a batch circulating the town. A girl answering Darcy's description had arrived in a town far out to the west one Saturday night, not that long ago, and had taken on each and every patron of the town's pub on a mattress laid out in the weeds behind it. Black, white, young, old, fat, thin, ugly and uglier; for what they could spare, just the change in their pockets, she had taken them all on, and only then, when there were no more takers, had she wandered off into the night, a slippery glass jar full of guilt money in her hand as if she had sat begging in the street all night.

"What do you think?" asked Grace. "Why would people tell stories like that about her?"

Pop looked at his daughter. He didn't know what to say. She looked at him steadily. It struck him then—hard—that she had indeed grown up and he had the uneasy feeling that he'd let her down, not told her all he knew of the world, all she needed to know.

"You knew her best, kid. She was *your* friend."

"She was my only friend."

"I don't think that's true."

"May as well have been."

"Anyway, you knew her good points, knew her bad, isn't that right?"

Grace nodded. "She could be a bit of a dill sometimes."

"There you go. Only someone who knows a person's failings and still likes them—loves 'em—can call themselves a good friend. *You* were a good friend to her. Nothing can change that. Nobody can take that away from you. People want to tell stories? Let 'em. Doesn't change a thing."

Grace considered his words, then nodded.

"Gracie . . ."

"What?"

"Did you ever go with Darcy up to the Popes' place?"

"No."

"Darcy ever say anything about going up there?"

"No," said Grace, a look of puzzlement on her face. "Why?"

"Oh, nothing. Old Reg thought he'd . . . he thought he'd seen her, that's all."

"Oh."

They watched the pup chase the empty saucer around the floor and lick the last traces of milk from it.

"You don't want to keep him?"

"No. He'll grow up."

Pop nodded. "I was thinking Tom might like him. Might help take his mind off things. The butcher could keep him in offcuts. What do you think?"

Grace shrugged. "He might."

"Would you mind taking him down there?"

She looked up. "Why me?"

"Because I asked you to. Because I've got other things to be going on with."

She frowned and sighed but after a while she grudgingly agreed.

"Good girl. I'll see you later. If Tom doesn't want the pup just bring him back. I'm sure I can find someone who'll have him. Tell him if he wants him, he should spit in his mouth, be his dog forever then."

"Yuck," said Grace.

"Oh, and ask him if he wants to go to the circus tonight. Tell him it'd be my shout."

"All right."

She picked the dog up off the floor and tucked him into the crook of her arm, then opened the back door and walked down the path. She dawdled down through town, out along the road to Tom's, quite enjoying the warmth of the pup against her skin, the beat of his little heart. When she came to the house she went up to the open front door and knocked but, even after half a minute had passed, there was still no answer. She knocked again, harder, then called down the hall.

"Anyone home?"

A door to her right creaked open and Tom's mother peered round it at her. Her hair was flat against her head, her face was very pale, and her eyes were underscored with dark rings.

"Yes? Who is it?" she breathed.

"I'm sorry, Mrs. Gunn. I didn't mean to wake you."

Ellie Gunn pulled her dressing gown around her and stepped out into the hall. She squinted at Grace and looked her up and down.

"I'm, ah, looking for Tom."

"What's your name, honey?"

"Grace. Grace Mather."

"Pop's girl?"

"Yes."

"Of course. I thought I knew you." She reached out and began to stroke the side of Grace's head with the back of her hand.

"Are you a friend of Tom's?"

"Ah, yes."

"He's a good boy. He'll be handsome too. His father was a beautiful man. A bastard, but handsome."

"Oh . . . really."

"Yes. Listen. Men will want to put their things in a pretty girl like you. Don't let them. Babies will . . . break your heart." Tears began to roll down her cheeks and she stepped back inside her room.

"I don't know where Tom is," she said, her voice a bare whisper, just before she closed the door on the world again. "Maybe he's . . . maybe he's out back."

Grace blinked, collected herself, then walked through the house and down the back steps. She couldn't see Tom anywhere and was about to go home when she heard her name being called. She finally spotted him in the frangipani tree. He was climbing down.

"Hello," he said, when he was back on the ground.

"Hi."

"What've you got there?"

"A puppy. Pop wants to know if you'd like him."

Tom didn't answer. Grace handed him the pup. Tom's eyes fixed on him as if he were some kind of puzzle to be solved.

"Pop says you don't have to take him if you don't want to." Tom looked at her, then looked back at the dog.

"He says if you do, you should spit in his mouth."

Tom's forehead creased. "Why?"

"I don't know. He said he'll be yours forever if you do."

"Oh. Right."

"So . . . you want him?"

Tom nodded. "Yeah."

"Good. He drinks milk, but you could try him with meat and stuff. Pop says you could get scraps off the butcher."

She turned and started off, but when she was at the corner of the house she stopped.

"Oh, yeah. Pop wants to know if you want to go to the circus. He said he'll pay if you don't have any money."

"I'm going. Mr. Newman gave me a ticket for bringing the saw-dust."

"Oh. All right, then."

"Are you going?"

"I don't know yet. I . . . don't think so."

"There're lions over there, you know. You should see them."

Grace nodded, waited for another moment, but Tom didn't say anything else. He was engrossed in the pup once more and she felt a tug of jealousy that she'd had to hand him over. She turned and began the walk home.

Tom watched her go. He watched her bare feet on the road and then he noticed the scars on her left calf, a series of long jagged lines, cream-coloured against the slightly darker skin around them. Every-one in town knew that a dog had bitten her when she was little and now she was scared to death of them, but Tom suddenly didn't want to know what everyone else did. He wanted to know more. He wanted to say something to Grace about Darcy Steele but he didn't know what and he didn't know how. As she disappeared up the road he thought to himself that the scars just made her other calf seem all the more perfect.

"Say thanks to Mr. . . . . say thanks to your dad," he called after her. "Say thanks very much."

She half-turned, giving him the barest glance.

"I will."

He walked into town not long after she had left. Across the river the circus was gearing up for its performance. He quickened his pace, the new puppy in his arms. He went down Gibbs Street until he reached Coop's Universal and then he stopped. The grass coming up through the cracks in the path was very high and he remembered, a little hor-rified, the deal he'd made with Mrs. Coop to come and pull it up. He saw too that one of the shop's front windows was broken and had been boarded up. He went inside. Mrs. Coop was bustling around with a mop and bucket.

"Hello, Mrs. Coop," he said.

"Hello!" she replied, looking up. "Who's that then?"

"Thomas Ferry."

"Thomas Ferry. Thomas Ferry." She held her hand up to her fore-head as if trying to remember a message for him she'd been entrusted with.

"Tom!"

"Here's that money I owe you," he said, as recognition dawned on her face. "With a bit of interest." He handed her a twenty-cent piece. "Sorry I forgot."

"I'm sure you don't owe me any money, Thomas, but your father, that's another story!"

"Oh well, put this towards what he owes." He set the coin on the counter beside the till and it was then that he noticed the smell. In the cold case were two rancid hams covered in grey mould. The refriger-ator that held all the milk and soft drinks was silent. He put his hand to the glass—it was warm.

"What's the matter with the fridges?"

"Buggers cut me power off! I don't know what happened to the bill. Should be back on soon, I'm hoping."

"Oh," said Tom.

She slumped down on her stool and looked set to cry.

"Here, I'll help you, Mrs. Coop. Can you hold him for me?"

Mrs. Coop took the pup and, still sniffing, held him up to get a bet-ter look.

"What's his name, then?"

"He hasn't got one yet. I only just got him."

He managed to remove the hams without too much fuss by cover-ing them with newspaper and lifting them out. He took them outside and threw them in the bin.

"What happened to the window?"

"Someone threw a stone through it a couple of weeks ago. Vandals, Sergeant Mather says. I'll give him bloody vandals . . ."

Tom helped her finish mopping the floor and then he went outside and pulled up all the grass he could and put it in the bin with the meat. When he finished he went back inside and looked around at the shop's dusty stock.

"Do you have any tins of dog food, Mrs. Coop?"

"There, up by your head, Tom. Feller came and bought up a lot last week, but there's a few left. Take as many as you need."

"I only need one or two. I've got money."

"No. You take as many as you want. Not much call for the stuff anyhow. And you're such a good boy . . . and your little . . ."

She began to look like she would cry again. The pup coped with the sea swell of her heaving bosom as best he could. Tom went over and patted the flowery expanse of her shoulder.

"I'm sorry, Tom," she said. "Silly old lady, I am."

"No, you're not."

He sat and talked with her for another quarter-hour or so. They talked about Angel Rock, Mr. Coop, the world—not what was wrong with it but just how it was—and then Mrs. Coop was quiet for a time. Finally she looked up at Tom and smiled.

"You know, Tom," she said, "I think I've had enough of this grocery business."

"You have?"

"Yes. Too right. Starting now I think I'll start selling something else."

"Yeah? What?"

"Well, you know I've sat here for thirty-five years doing my sewing between customers. Doilies mainly. I've got mountains of them out back. I'll sell them, and other things as well."

"That's a good idea."

"It is, isn't it?" she said, blinking. "People'll always need a good doily. What's a cake without a doily, what's a plate of sandwiches?"

"Nothing," said Tom, shaking his head slowly, his voice grave. "They'll come from all over Australia to buy 'em."

"They might! They just bloody might!"

"You could call it *Angel Rock Doilies*."

"Yes," she breathed. "Or *Heavenly Doilies*. Yes, that's the shot."

Tom thought she was going to hug him, but then, maybe, she forgot she was going to, her mind racing, and just patted him on the back instead. The puppy began to whine and he asked her if he could borrow a can-opener and a bowl. She heaved herself up off her seat without a word and went out back to her residence, returning after a while with both the items he'd asked for.

"Thank you," said Tom. He opened the tin, emptied a little of the food into the bowl, put it on the floor, then set the dog down before it.

"He's eating it!" Tom said, suddenly and unaccountably happy for the first time in what seemed like years.

"My word, he is! And *he* sounds like *he* needs a name as well."

Tom nodded. "Any ideas?"

"Oh no. I'm not a one for making things up. You'll think of something, I've no doubt."

Tom nodded, but when the time had rolled around for him to be on his way he'd come up with nothing that seemed to fit. He said goodbye to Mrs. Coop and made his way down to the ferry. It was tea time but the thought of going home with the dog when Henry was there made him feel a little sick. He sat and waited for the ferry to arrive and decided he'd eat later, after the circus, then go home and try to hide the pup out in the yard somewhere.

When the ferry came he clambered aboard, along with a good number of other townsfolk going over to try their hand at the circus's sideshow stalls. A few of the adults greeted him but some of the younger children just stared at him with wide eyes. He was the first off the ferry when it touched the far ramp, jumping down before the gates were opened, the ferrymaster's growling rebuke sliding off his back. He didn't go straight into the collection of tents and marquees in the middle of the showground but skirted round the darkening edges to where the lion cage was. He'd nearly reached it when he came across three boys sitting along a fence smoking cigarettes. He stopped in his tracks. One boy he'd never seen before. The second he knew but was much older than him. The third was Leonard. When Leonard saw him he whispered something to the boys and then slipped down from the fence rail and hurried off through the caravans and trailers.

"You Tom Ferry?" asked the one he knew.

"Yes."

"You're the one that lost your little brother, right?"

"I didn't lose him."

The boy shrugged, as if Tom was just splitting hairs.

"What's your dog's name?"

Tom looked down at the pup and a name came to him out of the blue, easy as an amen.

"Ham," he said.

"Ham?"

"Yep. Ham."

"What's that mean, then? You can eat him if necessary?" The boy's friend laughed and he turned to him and nodded his head.

"No. He's named after a flying chimpanzee."

"A flyin' monkey?" Both boys looked at him as if he had lost his marbles.

"Yep. All the way into space."

"Ah yeah? Jesus aitch. Wasn't that a dog?"

"A dog went another time."

"So why didn't you call a dog after a dog's name? That bugger there"—he pointed, his face serious—"ain't a friggin' monkey."

Tom shrugged. "I didn't like the dog's name. It was Russian." He put the pup down on the grass but he didn't seem to want to stray too far.

"Ahhh." The boy nodded. "Russian. A commie dog. I wouldn't name nothin' after a commie dog neither."

"Got a bit of kelpie in it," said the other boy.

"Yep. Kelpie," said the first. Tom remembered his name then. Charlie Perry. He'd seen him once or twice working with one of the timber gangs.

"And somethin' bigger than a kelpie. Kangaroo dog," Charlie continued.

"A lab. Look at how solid he is."

"Maybe it's all three, with a bit of dingo for brains."

"Yes," said the other boy, nodding gravely.

"I'm joking, numbskull."

"I knew you were."

"You better watch out, matey," said Charlie. "Cockies'll shoot that mongrel soon as they clap eyes on him."

"I don't think they will."

Charlie took a cigarette from behind his ear and lit it.

"Suit yourself," he said.

"I will."

The three of them watched as the puppy chewed at the frayed hem of Charlie's jeans, trying them out for taste and texture. Before too long Leonard reappeared. Sonny was with him. They stopped by a circus truck about two dozen yards away and stared at him. Sonny sucked at the cigarette he was smoking and then threw it to the ground before him. Tom picked up Ham.

"See you later, then," he said to Charlie and the other boy.

"Yeah, see ya."

Tom set off towards the brighter centre of the showground, where the big top stood, where strings of lights were strung between poles. He didn't spare Sonny and Leonard another glance. He made his way through the growing crowd of people to the cage of lions. A tarpaulin had been strung just in front of the cage to shield them but Tom had no trouble slipping in behind it. He sat down on the grass in the half-light and crossed his legs. He held Ham in his lap, the smell of the lions like a solid thing in the air before him. A mechanic's lamp fastened to the side bars illuminated the floor and walls of the cage. Tom was surprised to see how shallow it really was. All three lions were pacing back and forth but if they saw Tom they made no sign that they had, apart from a barely discernible pause, a sweep of their eyes in his direction. He saw the flare of their nostrils as they sensed the pup, saw them take in deep draughts of the air beyond the bars, measure him, then turn away, finally, all questions having been answered.

He watched them intently for nearly ten minutes. They rubbed the tops of their heads against each other's shoulders and scratched themselves against a length of wood bolted to the bars at one end of the cage. They yawned and showed their great teeth and sometimes one would loll out a thick pink tongue and lick another's face. To Tom it looked as though they were comforting each other, raising each other's spirits, and he watched, mesmerised.

"I wish you were here to see this, Flynn, boy," he whispered.

One of the lions suddenly made a deep coughing sound and Tom felt Ham quiver in response to it. Tom looked down at him. His ears had pricked and he was staring intently up at the cage with his dark eyes. Tom didn't think it was fear that gripped him, but something else, something between animals that he could never be privy to. He watched him for a little longer and then he turned the pup over onto his back, opened his mouth, dropped a ball of spit into it from his own. The pup grimaced and licked his chops.

"You're stuck with me now, boy," Tom said softly.

"There used to be creatures like these about in this country, you know, long time ago." Tom, a little startled, turned and looked around for the source of the words. They seemed to have come from a man squatting in the gloom just off to his right. Tom was sure he hadn't been there when he'd come in. He wore a white shirt with the long sleeves rolled up to his elbows and a black tie. A jacket was slung over his forearm. A hat with a low, wide brim cast a deep shadow across his face. Tom could really only see the bottom of his jaw and the light from the lion's cage glinting on his eyes.

"Ah, you think?" asked Tom, remembering himself.

"Oh, yes." The man nodded. "Their spirits are still about, if you have the eyes to see them. They'll come if you call, if you've got the right voice."

Tom looked at the man, not sure whether he was being serious or pulling his leg.

"I don't know whether I'd want one to come," he said. "Not really."

"You know, in their own country," the man continued, ignoring Tom, "these big cats know where they are by feeling the currents of underground rivers. They feel them through their paws, feel them in their bones, smell them."

Tom stared. "Yeah?"

The man nodded slowly. Tom saw the white of his teeth as he smiled.

"In Africa, boys your age kill these, cut out their hearts and eat them. For courage. For courage!"

The man laughed, but there were too many humourless notes in the sound and Tom felt uneasy.

"Boys your age!" said the man again, laughing all the more.

Tom looked down at the grass.

"You want to see their tricks? What the tamer's taught them?"

Tom was about to answer when another voice, much louder, cut in.

"You're not stirring them up, are you, son?"

Tom looked up and saw one of the burly circus workers standing just inside the canvas.

"N-no, just watching."

"Well, you can pay like everyone else. Go on, piss off."

Tom jumped up and ran, his ears and cheeks burning with humiliation. He didn't pause to see what had become of the man in the shadows. As he ran the public address system crackled and squealed into life and the booming voice of Mr. Newman began to call for the crowd to start making its way inside. Tom squeezed back his tears and delved into his pocket and hurried away towards the big top, hard-won ticket in one hand, Ham in the other.

The sawdust he'd gathered was strewn across the single, spotlit ring. The smell of the rosewood, turpentine and pine shavings mingled with the musty scent of the damp canvas overhead and the perfumes of the women around him and made his head spin. He found his seat in the middle of one of the little stands and sat down. He settled Ham in his lap and then glanced around. Across the ring he spotted Sergeant Mather sitting in a front row, his arms folded, Grace next to him. He couldn't see Charlie, or Leonard, or Sonny, and it wasn't until Mr. Newman strode out into the middle of the ring with a microphone that he saw them, slouching in the darkness between two of the stands, so far back they were almost against the tent wall. Then the lights around the edges of the tent winked off and he couldn't see anything but the ring. Mr. Newman, his voice huge, his tongue stretching out words to ridiculous lengths, introduced the first act, and everything else faded away.

There were jugglers first, then a little girl who did tricks on the back of a short-legged pony, then clowns who pretended to get drunk and belt each other, and a young woman in a sequined costume who hung upside down from a swing and struck poses. There was a man dressed as a genie who conjured a rope from a jar which his monkey assistant promptly climbed, so high he was almost lost in the darkness at the top of the tent. Then the clowns returned dressed as matadors and proceeded to fight with two dogs dressed as bulls. After the clowns Mr. Newman re-entered the ring on the back of the elephant Tom had seen the day before. He clambered down the elephant's shoulder and then tapped its leg with a long staff. The elephant stood on two legs on a red and blue stand, counted to ten, sucked up water from a bucket with its trunk and blasted it at an unsuspecting clown. People laughed hard and then the elephant departed and then there was a man—Tom recognised him as one of the clowns from before— who took pieces of burning tissue paper in his mouth and then seemed to exhale flames. When he'd finished with the fire he picked up a long-handled whip and snuffed out lit candles with its cracking end. Then he called for volunteers from the audience and when no one came forward he strode around the edge of the ring until he came to where Pop and Grace were sitting. He stepped across the footlights and held out his hand to Grace as though he was after a dance. At first she refused to go, refused to budge from her seat. The spotlight fell upon her and Tom could see, all too plainly, her unwillingness. He held his breath. Pop bent and whispered something in her ear after what seemed like a very long time had passed, and it was only then that she stood and took the performer's hand. He could see Sonny and Leonard snickering to each other and a wave of blind fury made him grind his teeth together. The whipcracker called for applause and the crowd gave it in spades, relieved that someone else had been chosen. A clown, smoking a cigarette, wandered into the ring. He pretended not to notice the presence of the whipcracker, or the fact that he'd interrupted his act. The whipcracker had Grace stand to one side and then he called the clown over.

Who? Me? asked the clown, silently, pointing to his chest.

The whipcracker responded with a curl of his finger. He stood the clown in the centre of the ring and had him bend forward. The clown began to fret. He ran around in circles and the whipcracker admonished him to keep still. Then the clown began puffing away on the cigarette as if he might smoke it away and escape his fate that way, but the whipcracker, quick as a wink, snapped out his whip and knocked the cigarette from the clown's painted lips.

Then it was Grace's turn. The whipcracker walked her over to the centre of the ring, put an unlit cigarette between her lips, then walked back, very slowly, to his mark. Tom's heart began to hammer away even harder. Even though he'd seen the demonstration of the whipcracker's skill he still wasn't convinced that there wasn't some trick to it, something Grace couldn't possibly know. He jumped—not of his own volition—to his feet, and was oblivious at first to the calls from behind for him to sit down, only slowly becoming aware of the whispered chorus of his name all around. *Tom Ferry. Tom Ferry.*

When the whipcracker noticed the commotion he glanced up at him. Red-faced, he sat down, his legs rubbery, grateful for the dim light. The whipcracker turned back to Grace. She stood with the cigarette between her lips, her chin up, her eyes blazing, defying the whipcracker to knock it out or face the consequences. Tom was struck then by how pretty she was—amazed that he'd never really noticed before—and how brave she was being, especially after the way she'd been chosen, as though she'd taken her fear, her trepidation, and rendered them into different things altogether.

The whipcracker took long, slow aim then eased back his arm. The crowd went silent. Tom held his breath and almost shut his eyes. With a quick flick from his wrist and an accompanying loud crack the whipcracker caused the end of the cigarette to fly off into the air. Grace didn't move back an inch, but she flinched and her eyes squeezed shut reflexively. When she opened them again she took the remaining stub of cigarette from her mouth and looked at it, then smiled with relief.

Tom, in the dark, smiled along with her—for her—and then watched as she walked back to her seat, flicking her long, dark hair back over her shoulder. Pop gave her arm a quick squeeze as she sat, then whispered something to her and kissed the top of her head.

The whistling, roaring noise in his ears subsided as the lights dimmed once more. After a minute or so, Mr. Newman, almost whispering into the microphone, announced the lions and the lion-tamer. The curtains at the far end of the tent slowly drew apart to reveal the three lions, each sitting on a pedestal, all enclosed within an oval cage. The lion-tamer, his face masked, had them jump from one pedestal to another, then through hoops, then over one another. He opened one of the lion's mouths and seemed to put his head in it. Everyone gasped. As a finale, he had the smaller lioness, snarling and showing her teeth, leap through a ring he'd set aflame. Tom thought it was the most amazing thing he'd ever seen, but it also left him feeling faintly dejected.

After the lights had come on and the crowd had begun to make their slow, chattering way homewards he slipped away through the dark, still a little dazed by all he had seen. He made it home without being accosted by Sonny or anyone else. He shut Ham in the laundry and then went inside. He found Henry asleep on the couch in front of the television set, empty bottles strewn all over the floor in front of him. He went and turned off the set and looked down at his stepfather. It wasn't quite hatred, but he couldn't name what he did feel as he stood over him. At least with Henry like this and his mother always asleep he'd been able to do as he pleased for the past few weeks. He bent and picked up Henry's cigarettes and removed a couple from the pack. He spied a box of matches and put them in his pocket with the cigarettes and then he went out and retrieved Ham from the laundry and took him into his room.

He lay awake for a long time, just thinking. Just before eleven o'clock, he heard Henry stir and mutter and curse, then one of his Hank Williams records began playing. About three songs in, the needle jumped and squawked across the vinyl. Henry let out a burst of obscenities and Tom heard him storm from the house. He slipped from his bed and curled his head round the door just in time to see Henry, standing on the front step, fling the black disc out across the road with all his might. It sailed out over the river, finally arcing down and slicing into the water with a faint, wet chink. Henry stood there for a moment, swaying slightly, and then he went out the gate and headed into town. Tom, not at all curious about where he was going, went back to bed.

When he finally fell asleep the dreams returned. He stood in an open field before a thickly timbered slope. He was all alone and it was very dark but then the moon rose above the trees and lit everything up with its silvery glow. Then, from the edge of the trees, a shirtless man came walking, straps of raw muscle jerking him forward like a bloody marionette. In the crook of his arm he carried a small, pale child and in his other hand a huge, black shotgun. Tied around his head and covering his nose and mouth was a ragged piece of dark gauze—a doctor of antimedicine on rounds. Through the cloth Tom could see that his mouth was full of long, sharp teeth and on his slow and rubbery dream legs he turned and ran—ran for his life.

14

Gibson had woken very early that morning and left the station house in the pale dawn light to the sound of warbling magpies and the sun just turning the tops of the hills to the west of town a fine shade of gold. He was on the front step of the police station in a town called Woodburn a little after half past eight. The local copper was hung over and grumbled constantly, but described Billy to him and the truck he reputedly drove.

"He cuts firewood up in the forests most of the year. You might find him, if you're lucky, but if he doesn't want to be found he won't be. That's how I see it."

With that he reached into his desk drawer and pulled out a scrap of paper and a pencil. He sketched a rough map and handed it across the desk. Gibson thanked him and then he went and bought a cup of coffee and sat on a covered picnic table by the river. He smoked a cigarette while a rain shower came and went.

When he continued westwards an unbroken blanket of low grey cloud descended and the day became gloomy enough for headlights.

"Miserable," he said to himself. "Fucking miserable."

He drove west and it was only when he climbed into the ranges that the clouds thinned and the day brightened. Further west and the country began to look like it had only ever heard rumours of rain. He stopped in Tenterfield for a bite to eat and when he mentioned the rain on the coast to the young waitress in the service station café she said they'd had no rain for many months. She said it with her eyes wide open as though she were talking about the Second Coming or a visitation of angels. She said there were bushfires burning to the west of town. He expressed what he thought was sufficient disbelief at the absurdities of the weather and then watched her blue-uniformed bottom as she walked back to the kitchen, his thoughts suddenly as libidinous as any eighteen-year-old's. He wondered whether all the good country air was to blame.

He inspected the policeman's scrap of paper, then his own map. The state forest he'd sketched was crisscrossed with roads and logging tracks and fire trails. Even if Flood were there he might look for weeks and still not find him.

He set out anyway. With very little breeze to disperse it the smoke from the bushfires veiled the horizon in every direction. He saw no green Bedfords on the way to the forest and when he arrived there he settled down to the task of driving up every track he thought he could follow on the map. Some of them were overgrown, shrubs and long grass slithering by underneath the car, and some petered out into nothing. Up and down the heavily timbered hills, the pale sky appearing and disappearing. He followed fire trails where the land was burnt and blackened on one side and full of life on the other. Crows watched his progress from their dead tree perches.

He stopped and asked everyone he came across whether they had seen Billy or his green Bedford. Some said they had seen it a few weeks back, a month. Some asked him if he was a cop and what he was wanting Billy for and he answered that he wasn't a cop but a relative with important news. Maybe it was because he didn't look much like a cop that they believed him. He followed directions and edged closer to the area some had said Billy frequented. He met an old-timer by the side of one track and asked him. The man said he hadn't seen Billy but spoke of a particular spot. Gibson asked him to show him on the map and he leant into the car and traced the track to it with a grimy finger. He asked him if he wanted to know why he was looking for Billy but the man just said no and walked on.

He found the track about an hour later and headed down it. He searched until mid-afternoon and then, when the fuel gauge had dipped down below the half-full marker, he stopped the car and traced the path back to town on the map and wondered how long it would take him to get back there. When he looked up again through the windscreen he saw green. He blinked. He blinked again and saw the curved outline of a vehicle through the trees. His heart started to drum in his chest. He pulled his Smith & Wesson from the glovebox and stuck it in between his belt and the small of his back and then he opened the car door as quietly as he could and hopped out.

His ears were still ringing from the noise of the car but, gradually, he began to make out the sounds of birds, the throbbing of an engine somewhere in the gully just beyond the truck. He walked on, his shoes crunching in the gritty earth. Tiny green finches flitted around him. When he reached the Bedford he put his hand on its bonnet, gingerly, as if it were not quite real and might dissolve at his touch. He licked his lips and immediately wiped them dry with the back of his arm, surprised at how nervous he was. He walked round to the side of the truck and looked in through the window. Nothing out of the ordinary. A cardboard box, scraps of paper. The seat, the steering wheel and the gear stick were all polished by long hours of hard use and all needed a man of flesh and blood to operate them. Then he saw the black outline of a rifle, its stock scored and battered, on the floor. He tried the door but it was locked. He walked round to the other door. Locked too. He moved along to the rear. The truck's tray was half full of neatly stacked wood.

He licked his lips again and walked towards the sound he could hear. It was some sort of small engine. The trees around him were ironbarks and bloodwoods, their trunks rough, dark, grim. Overhead, as he walked, smoke came curling through them. Everything else, except for the engine noise, seemed silent. The birds had all stopped singing, then the engine spluttered and went silent too. Gibson stopped, looked up, listened, continued on. Before he had taken another dozen steps smoke was all around him like a mist. It was as though a giant wave had broken over the country, changing the light to an eerie, otherworldly yellow. His shadow became weak and soft-edged where before it had been blacker and sharper. He shook his head and cleared his throat and called.

"Billy Flood!"

There was no answer. His voice sounded puny and unfamiliar. He walked down into the little gully and found a saw straddling a fallen log. The blade was halfway through. Stacked beside the saw was a small pile of freshly split wood and next to that a deeply worn chopping block. A fire nearby had burnt down to embers and beside the embers was a shapeless gunny sack and a small wallaby, partly skinned, its head missing, the red meat drying at the edges. Long-bodied black ants clambered over both.

"Billy Flood!" he shouted again.

The smoke became thicker and the breeze which had begun only a few minutes before freshened and Gibson thought again of what the waitress had said about bushfires. He waited for a couple more minutes, called a few more times, and then a man appeared, quite casually, from behind a tree.

"Yes?" he said.

He had a large forehead with thick veins straining at the temples, thick and high cheekbones, a scrub of dark beard. His skull seemed two sizes too large for his skin and his hair was long and lank and hung to his shoulders and might have been fair if it had been clean. His clothes were patched and dirty and on his head was a battered felt hat, stitched and mended with brown string. It would have been hard to guess how old he was had Gibson not known they were around the same vintage. He was an average height, but thick with muscle, and a wedge-shaped logsplitter rested on his shoulder. In his other hand was a rifle. Gibson's insides went a little cold. He thought he must have circled round to his truck to collect it—unless he had two.

"Yes?" the man repeated.

"Your name is Billy Flood?"

"Yes."

Flood leant the rifle very deliberately against a tree and then took the splitter off his shoulder and rested its head on the ground and crossed his hands over the end of the haft. His face was blank but Gibson saw the suspicion in his eyes.

"Son of Horace Flood?"

"Might be. Who are you?"

"Gibson," he said. "Police."

Gibson saw a shadow flit across the man's face.

"What do you want?"

"To talk to you."

Flood walked forward until he was only a foot away from Gibson's chest. Gibson braced himself, his hand creeping up towards his gun.

"What about?"

"Darcy Steele."

Flood stared at him, his brow furrowing, and then he stepped back. "Tea?"

Gibson was caught off guard by the question and blinked a few times before replying.

"Yes . . . if you're making some." His reply sounded odd and overly formal, belonging to another time and place, and he almost laughed at himself. Flood, however, seemed not to notice as he set the splitter next to the rifle and gathered up a handful of twigs. Gibson sat down slowly on the log and watched as he rekindled the fire and produced a half-full billy of water from alongside the log.

"What about Darcy?" said Flood, as he set the billy in the flames. Gibson noticed that one of the fingers on his hand was just a stump. He also saw long scars running up his arm from the wrist.

"You know her?"

"Yes."

"Seen her lately?"

"No."

"You sure? Haven't been around the farm lately?"

"No. Not the farm. The dogs." Billy hung out his tongue and panted to demonstrate.

"When was the last time you saw her then?"

"A while ago. Big old Ezra saw me and set a dog on my tail. Had to run hard."

"Did Darcy see you?"

"No, I only saw her, from the trees."

Gibson nodded, swallowed.

"Billy, how long ago was that?"

"Don't know," Billy answered, shaking his head. "Last year?"

Gibson nodded and looked down at the fire. Billy was staring intently at him when he looked up again.

"What's the matter with her, mister?" he said. "Something happen to her?"

"Yes," answered Gibson, softly. "She's dead, Billy. She . . . killed herself. She killed herself."

He held his breath and watched Billy's reaction, but there was nothing counterfeit about it—nothing at all.

"Killed?" Two tears began to roll down his cheeks.

"Yes. Suicide. By her own hand."

Billy froze, seemingly unable to continue. A look of utter disbelief took hold of his face.

"Why'd she do that?"

"I don't know. I had a sister. She did the same."

"You trying to find out why?"

"Yeah, something like that. Make the tea, Billy. It'll help."

Billy said nothing more for a while, but then nodded, almost imperceptibly. When the water finally boiled he dropped in the tea leaves and when they had brewed he poured the tea into a tin mug and shook in sugar from a paper bag he pulled from his pocket. He picked up a twig from the ground and stirred it round, then handed the mug to Gibson. He swirled the remaining tea round to cool it, sluiced in sugar, then began to sip straight from the billy's lip.

Gibson studied him as he drank. His forearms were covered in grazes and the grazes were crusted with fine sawdust. His hands were large—the skin waxy under the bush grime as if his diet was deficient—and his fingernails were thick, yellow, uncut. He felt sorry for him then—just plain sorry—without having to shore it up with anything like a reason.

"You've been out here a long time, Billy. Must get lonely."

He thought Billy hadn't heard him but then he saw his head nodding slightly, a faraway look in his eyes.

"No," he said softly. "I like it."

"You know, Darcy kept a diary. She wrote down a lot of the things you used to do together."

"She wrote 'em down?"

"Yes. They were important to her."

Billy nodded. "To me as well."

The breeze picked up and more smoke swirled in through the trees.

"Isn't that fire getting close?" asked Gibson, looking up, a little alarmed.

"No, it's a long ways away yet."

Billy looked down at the ground before him and didn't respond to Gibson's next few questions, didn't even seem to hear them. He asked him whether he'd seen the boys but Billy just shook his head slowly.

"She's not really dead, is she, Mr. Gibson?" he said, finally, beseechingly. "You've been pulling my leg?"

"No, I haven't."

"But did you see her? Did you see her dead?"

"Yes. I saw her."

He began to cry then. It seemed to be finally sinking in, causing great ructions in his poor, muddled head. Gibson reached over and patted his shoulder.

"Billy . . . if you've done anything . . . bad, you should tell me. I can help you."

Flood seemed to consider the offer as he wept but then his green eyes flashed and Gibson retracted his hand reflexively.

"Mister, I might have done bad things as a youngster. I don't remember now. I got kangaroos in the top paddock, trouble in the brainbones. I know it, but I'm not a slowie. I know what I know and I know I never did anything bad to that little girl. She's one of God's angels and He'd blast to hell anyone who done harm to her. You say she's dead, but I . . ."

Suddenly he looked up at the trees and took note of something they seemed to be telling him. Gibson watched him and wondered what words the kangaroos had whispered in his ear, what paths they'd led him down, what things he'd been shown.

"I've atoned for my sins," he said, continuing. "Like him on the cross. Like Jesus. You see?"

Gibson nodded. "In the hospital."

"Yes," he whispered. "In *there.* Everywhere. Couldn't do nothin' bad after that. Nothin' bad ever."

Even as he asked his final question Gibson heard the faint crackle of fire.

"Billy, do you remember a man named Smith?"

Billy's eyes opened up wide and his torso began to rock to and fro ever so gently. Without another word he stood and picked up his rifle and his splitter and walked from the clearing. Gibson jumped up to follow him, but when he reached the point he'd last seen him he stopped. He looked all about but couldn't see which way he had gone.

"Billy!" he shouted.

He peered out into the smoky bush but saw nothing man-shaped. The breeze that had brought the smoke strengthened again—strong enough to bring down the tiny pale flowers from the eucalypts overhead. White and pale pink, they swirled down around him as he imagined snow might do. Except for the faint sound of the fire it was eerily quiet. He felt then as though he were standing in a cathedral and watching the hallowed spaces over the altar, before the crucifix, waiting for something to appear; where wine might become blood, and bread, flesh, and that he might be shown the mystery at the heart of everything. He stood like that for a few more minutes, the smoke swirling through the trees, until he became aware of small creatures moving through the undergrowth in the opposite direction to the origin of the smoke. Then he realised that the flowers weren't flowers at all any more, but floating ash, and the fire was very close, maybe just over the crest of the next small hill.

His copper's instinct was too strong to turn his back and flee. He cursed himself for not heeding Pop's warning, for being so blunt, for not seeing the full extent of the damage in Billy. He walked back up to where the truck was still parked and looked inside the cab. He thought he heard a peal of laughter but became certain after a time that he'd only imagined it. What he didn't imagine was the crackling and hissing. Maybe a hundred yards away a fire front was bearing down on him, the yellow flames leaping up, the smoke shutting off the sun. He ran to his car and turned it round and drove for his life down the track.

He kept going until it was nearly dark, east and back down into the rain, wondering whether Billy had been caught by the flames. Somehow he didn't think so. His eyelids began to flutter with a sudden weariness and after another quarter-hour had passed and there was still no sign of a town he pulled off the road towards a structure he'd spotted away through the trees. It was an old bush sawmill made out of corrugated iron. Rusted circular saws were lined up along its half-wall like ammunition for some grim weapon. He got out of the car and stretched and in the last of the day's light he poked about in the mill's remains. He found some old tools but rust had seized and misshapen them and he could scarcely guess their purpose. He thought he might try to light a fire but then decided not to bother. Instead, he settled himself along the back seat of the car as best he could and wound down the window a little and watched as bright stars and then whole galaxies appeared in gaps between clouds. They lulled him to sleep and he began to dream.

He dreamt he sat way up high under a crystal-clear sky, a sky white with haze at the edges, barren of clouds and long unacquainted with them. Just behind his shoulder were the iron gates of a graveyard. Beyond the gates were new graves with mounds of earth beside them and men filling in others with shovels. There were cracked and broken gravestones and crosses of unseasoned wood, the sap like petrified raindrops underneath the blue or white wash. A horse and cart driven by a small boy went in through the gates and he stood and followed it. The cart carried a coffin underneath a white cloth and he walked behind it to where a large number of people stood crowded together.

"Who died?" he whispered to the man at his elbow.

"I don't know," the man answered. "But they must have been great. Or very important. Possibly both."

The man leant on a shovel and Gibson realised he was the gravedigger who'd dug the grave they stood before. His torso was bare and his skin was coated with a fine, pale dust.

The white sheet was whisked away and a lidless coffin revealed. Gibson joined the queue that formed, then waited until the shuffling line brought him by the cart. Inside the coffin a beautiful young woman lay on a bed of tinsel with her hands crossed over her breasts and her long dark hair arranged round her face to frame it. She was dressed like a bride in a white silk dress with a fine edging of lace and ribbon, her lips painted dark plum and her cheeks rouged. Her eyes were closed and a string of bloodstones lay round her neck. When the queue had passed, four men lifted the coffin from the cart and placed it on a wooden bier. They carried the bier to the grave and were about to drop it in when they heard Gibson's shout.

"Stop! Isn't anyone going to say something? Where's the damn priest?"

The gravedigger made his way to the side of the grave and readied himself to begin shovelling.

"Priest isn't coming," said the man, his damp face a bright shade of red. "It's a sinner's burial."

"What's her sin?"

"Killed herself."

He stared, struck dumb, at the young woman in her coffin.

"Say something," said the man, "if you're going to."

"I don't know . . ."

"Make somethin' up," said another. "She's gettin' heavy."

It was then, as he looked around for inspiration, for an ally, that he saw his father. He was standing at the edge of the circle, watching him. His face in the shade of his hat seemed completely expressionless at first, but then he saw a glint of something like amusement in his night-dark eyes and a familiar curl to his top lip. He beckoned to him, holding out his forefinger and curling it up like a worm, again and again, as though he were a disobedient pupil.

With a surge of anger and defiance he looked away from his father and stepped forward to the lip of the grave. Then, even as a few words came to him, even as he licked his lips before saying them, the four men holding the bier suddenly let it go. A cloud of dust came billowing up. The dream Gibson sank to his knees and looked up into the powdery sky—maybe he'd fainted, maybe he was praying—and he saw, fluttering on wings of gossamer and sunbeams, a whole host of angels. They seemed indifferent. He cursed them. Then the dream rewound like a film on rusty sprockets and the men were standing again at the sides of the grave hole and holding the bier and this time he jumped forward to stop it falling—but jerked awake before he could, a cool sweat on him, the sound of his second shout still ringing in his ears.

15

Tom woke to the sound of a puppy whimpering. It was very faint and it took his sleepy head a few moments to realise that Ham had crawled in under the bed and that that was where the sound was coming from. He reached down and coaxed him out and the little dog came and licked his hand and then began to skate around on the slippery floorboards. Tom played with him for a while before taking him outside and letting him run on the dew-covered grass. He had a thought as he watched the pup taste its freedom after being cooped up all night, and the thought grew into an intention.

There was no sign of Henry in the house. Tom wondered where he might be but didn't give it another thought after a while. He showered and put on some clothes and then he went and opened the door to his mother's room and looked in on her. She was just a lump under the covers, but he could hear her breathing and see the slight movement it made.

"Mum?"

"Mmmm?"

"Can I get you anything? Do you need anything?"

"No."

She rolled over and said no more and Tom turned away and closed the door gently behind him.

Outside, the sun was trying to shine, but it was still cool enough for mist to be rising off the river's dark surface. He walked up the road towards town, towards the ferry, almost as excited as the puppy at his side. Just before he reached the ramp he looked over and saw, to his dismay, that apart from a few caravans with washing strung between them, the entire circus had already moved on. He sat down on one of the posts near the ferry ramp and stared at the vacated showground, feeling like someone who'd missed their train. He picked Ham up and held him close to his face.

"I was going to let them out," he whispered. "Maybe that would have been stupid. Maybe they would have been chased and shot or something, but maybe they would have found their way to the sea, tried to swim home. What do you think?"

The pup squirmed but didn't answer him.

He sat for a long time and then he decided that he'd still go over and see if he could find some trace of them. It was not much of an alternative to his first plan and the last of the excitement he had felt before drained away.

The ferry was over on the opposite ramp. No cars arrived as he watched and it stayed put. He couldn't even see the ferrymaster inside his cabin or see his smoke. He thought of swimming the river, but then he remembered that he had Ham to think of now. He couldn't risk it. Couldn't risk . . . The *death* word flitted darkly through his head. Even unspoken, chased away, it made his heart jump up into his throat like a greasy little acrobat.

He waited another half-hour, kicking stones along the road, and then a fully laden timber jinker came belting down out of the hills. The ferry spluttered into life and came splashing across. When it arrived he walked down to the ramp and watched as the timber jinker, black exhaust pouring from its pipes, roared up onto the deck. The ferrymaster stared at him through the swirling smoke, his long beard lifting like a flag in the morning breeze, and then he came and closed the gate behind the jinker. Tom went and walked round the lumber truck, breathing in the sappy smell of the fresh logs and running his fingers over their rough bark. The driver slumped against the door of the truck's cab and closed his eyes. Tom went and sat on the railing by the front of the ferry. He held tightly onto Ham as the ferry began to move but the pup was more interested in taking in the new smells than running and jumping into the water and Tom relaxed a little. When they reached the mid-point of the river the ferry's throbbing little engine suddenly cut out. Tom felt it begin to drift in the current, then the steel ropes which guided it across caught and held it with a low, moaning creak. He turned round to see what the matter was. To his surprise he saw the old ferrymaster heading his way, pipe in mouth, eyebrows wild. He stopped directly before him and scowled down, the smell of his strong tobacco making Tom's head spin.

"You're Tom Ferry, ain't ya?" he said, his voice deep and croaking.

"Yes."

"Why don't you listen to me when I tell you to go easy, when I say to wait?"

Tom didn't answer.

"I don't want anyone falling off, or slippin', or hurting themselves. That's all. That too much to ask?"

"No."

"No. All right then. I don't want to see anyone hurt, that's all. Not just you. You're not so special. Not anyone."

Tom nodded.

"You'll be more careful from now on?"

"I'll be careful."

"You'll wait until I say you can get off? Until I open the gate?"

"Yes."

"All right then."

The ferrymaster stared at him a little longer, sucking on his pipe stem, before turning away. Soon the ferry shuddered back into life.

Once on the far side Tom waited for the old man to open the gates. On the bank he glanced back, but the ferrymaster was heading back to his cabin, his job done. Tom watched him a little longer, puzzled, and then the jinker came rolling off the ferry and past him. Sawdust and dirt swirled in its wake and he screwed up his eyes. When it had gone he continued walking up to the showground. Off to one side of it he found where the ring had been; a circle of trampled grass and sodden sawdust. He wandered around and found where the tent's pegs and poles had left scars in the ground. There was plenty of rubbish about as well, and elephant dung, but that was about it.

He went and climbed up into the showground's grandstand and looked down at the remnants of the circus. He wanted to talk to someone about the lions, and what the strange man in the hat had said about them, but, as the sun rose higher and the morning ebbed away, the remaining cars and caravans all packed up and left. A council man in a truck came along a little later to clear up the rubbish. Tom watched him for a while and then slipped away through the show-ground buildings and headed for the sawmill. It was about ten or eleven o'clock and he was getting hungry, but he wasn't ready to go home just yet. He dawdled along the riverbank and then headed into the mill yard. The yard was filled with stacked timber and rusting machinery and jinkers and skidders and trucks that work had worn out and he'd never before tired of exploring it. Today, though, it seemed more than a little dreary. He wandered around for a quarter-hour, kicking at things, Ham in tow, and then a strange sound came his way on the breeze and was tugged away as quickly as it had arrived. He stopped and turned his head to and fro until he heard it again, fainter this time. It seemed to be coming from down near the fence where wood was stacked in great oblong piles to season. He picked up Ham and began to step quietly towards the sound. It became louder as he approached one of the stacks and he stopped at its corner and peered carefully round its edge.

Sonny was on all fours in the weeds, his trousers around his knees. Charlie Perry was kneeling behind him, grunting rhythmically. He'd rested some sort of magazine on Sonny's back and was staring at the open pages as his hips moved back and forth. Sonny's forehead was creased, as though he were at school trying to work out a long sum on the blackboard. Tom could see his stiff dick slapping against his soft, pale belly.

Tom, scarcely able to believe his eyes, was about to back away when Charlie suddenly eased up, his torso bowing back. He shook his head, then shuddered and pulled himself clear of Sonny. Tom saw a string of fluid gleam in the sunlight for an instant before dropping away. Sonny snatched up the magazine from the ground where Charlie had let it fall and wrapped his hand around his own dick. Tom watched for a moment or two more and then Sonny lifted his head and, for one horrible instant, looked straight into his eyes. Tom bolted. He ran, but after five minutes of running he slowed up and tried to see if they were following. He couldn't see them, or hear them. He kept going anyway, jogging down to the ferry, looking over his shoulder every few minutes. The ferry didn't take too long to come once he'd arrived and the ferrymaster, thankfully, didn't say a word to him and barely glanced his way as he boarded. Relieved, he sat down and began to wonder about what he'd seen. There was something very disturbing about it but also something faintly comical and ridiculous. He realised how little he knew of the world and all its mysteries and the thought exasperated and wounded him in almost equal measure.

He walked into town with his head down and his jaw clenched. He thought about going in to see Mrs. Coop but decided against it. Instead, he walked down to the Catholic church and, as he had done many times before, continued down beside it until he came to the overgrown garden of the convent. While Ham explored he went and sat down on the jetty at the bottom of it. He watched the pup appear and disappear in the bushes like a tiny jungle beast and then he pulled one of Henry's cigarettes from his pocket and lit it with a match, inhaling as deeply as he could. He looked down at the water and watched the current spiral and eddy along the bank and round the jetty pilings. He took another draw of the cigarette and hung his head down between his knees when it began to spin. When he looked up a minute or so later Flynn was there in front of him, standing on the water, rubbing the smoke from his eyes.

"Sorry, mate," Tom managed to say, but the wispy outline was already gone, and there was nothing in its place but light sparkling off water and an old promise ringing in his ears, loud as a church bell, unkept.

I promise you, Flynn. I promise you we'll get home.

He sat for a long time and then wandered home, his heart like a stone inside him. He found Pop Mather sitting on the front step looking at his hands and his heart sank even further.

"What is it? Is it Flynn?"

"No. No, son. Sorry. I'm here about Henry. He got himself into a bit of bother last night. Me and Mrs. Mather have been thinking about it and we think it'd be best if you came and stayed with us for a bit. Just until Henry . . . settles himself."

"What'd he do?"

"Had a bit too much to drink. Caused a bit of bother. Had to lock him up . . . for his own good."

Tom nodded. Pop saw the relief flicker across his face, then something else—maybe pride—settled there. He seemed about to protest and Pop felt such a flood of affection for the boy he was taken by surprise.

"But what about—"

"What? I won't hear a word," he said, lifting his finger. "Not a word. I've already told Henry."

Tom nodded.

"Good boy. Now, can you give me a hand with your mother?"

He liked the station house when he got there—he liked it a lot. He liked its musty, churchy smell and he liked its wooden floors and high, high ceilings. He liked the fact it was made out of bricks. The walls felt much more solid—safer—than the weatherboards of his own home and he liked the thought of his mother sleeping behind them. He continued his exploration, peering round the doors of all the open rooms and running his fingers over those of the closed, Grace's among them. Twelve rooms in all, not counting the laundry out the back or the halls. Far too many, he thought, a little wistfully, for Pop's small family.

The police station was joined to the station house by a length of verandah and just before the door leading to it he found a tall bookshelf crammed with books. He ran his finger along the spines until he came to a hefty dictionary. He pulled it out, sat cross-legged on the wooden floor, and opened it up in his lap. He looked up *lion. A large greyish tan cat native to Africa and southern Asia.* He wondered how close southern Asia was to Australia. He flicked a few pages. *Lose, lost, losing: to come to be without, by some chance, and not know the whereabouts of.* He sat for a long time looking at the definition and then he looked up Sonny's word again. *Whore. A prostitute,* it said. He looked up *prostitute. A person, especially a woman, who engages in sexual intercourse for money as a livelihood,* it said. He looked up *intercourse* and *livelihood* and then he closed the book and thought about his mother and what he knew about her, then what he knew about Sonny Steele, and finally drew some kind of comfort from the comparison. He looked up one last word, one that had crept into his head earlier that day at the jetty and wouldn't go away. *The disembodied spirit of a dead person imagined as wandering among or haunting living persons,* said the book of *ghost. Imagined,* it said. He wondered if he'd imagined what he'd seen Sonny and Charlie doing as well. He looked down at the dictionary, closed it and put it back on the shelf. Mysteries. The world was full of them.

He was still thinking about it when he went to bed that night. Grace had said barely a word to him all evening and that troubled him as well. He didn't want to stay in the station house if she didn't want him there, no matter how much he liked it.

Around midnight, when he finally fell asleep, he dreamt the dream again. The figure without a face stepped out of the trees and came for him. He ran and ran and ran—until he wondered how he could possibly keep on going.

16

Gibson eased out of the car and rubbed at his neck. It was very early. More rain had fallen during the night and pools had formed where it had rilled off the mill's roof. He bent and drank and then he walked over to a tree to piss. On the slope below a small mob of grey kangaroos moved through the trees and nibbled at the grass there. He was so close he could hear the soft thud of their hind legs and tails against the ground, the sound of their cropping teeth, but then his piss slapped against a leaf and their grey heads all went up as one and they bounded away down the hill and disappeared into the mist at the bottom of it.

Later that morning when he saw the sign to Laurence he remembered Pop telling him about Adam Carney. He stopped and got directions and in a few minutes he pulled up outside the nursing home.

The nursing home was dim and quiet inside and he couldn't hear anything for a time except the subdued chatter of nurses coming from somewhere out of sight, but then the moans and calls of the old people began to seep through closed doors and move along bare corridors to where he stood. He looked around. The place was much the same as the home his mother was in and a wave of guilt suddenly rose up and threatened to wash him away. He steeled himself and stepped forward and by the time he reached the nurses' desk he'd regained enough of his composure to show them his police identification and ask the whereabouts of one Adam Carney. One of the younger nurses offered to show him where he was and he followed her down a long

hall and into a far wing and muttered clumsy answers to her loaded
questions.

The nurse left him by a door and after she had gone he opened it.
He heard cursing in a rasping, fluttering voice, hanging in the air like
broken birdsong, and then a gust of fetid air, loaded with the smell of
age, sickness and shit, came rushing out. He screwed up his nose and
peered in, the room slowly emerging from the gloom. An empty bed
and another with a wizened old man upon it. He stepped into the
room and shut the door behind him and walked forward to the bed.
The old man, his eyes closed, looked as if he had been lying there for
years. His skin was pale and paper-thin—his life barely contained
within it—and the veins at his temples were a deep ocean blue. His
emaciated arms had bandages attached to them and the ends of the
bandages were tied to the bars at the side of the bed.

"Mr. Carney? Adam Carney?" he said, softly. Nothing.

"*Adam Carney,*" he said, a little louder, but still the man made no
sign he'd heard.

Gibson waited. He was wondering what he should do when the old
man recommenced his cursing. When he stopped soon afterwards he
seemed to sense some other presence in the room.

"Father . . . Adam? Can you hear me?"

The old man's lids flickered open and he looked up at Gibson with
eyes childlike and unfocused. Gibson saw him for a moment as his
mother once had, as a baby in a tiny cot, put down at evening to sleep,
his whole life ahead of him, and a little constellation of hopes and
promises turning above his head that were wholly unrelated—and as
distant as Saturn—to this fate.

He'd been summoned to similar bedsides before, like an odd priest
for the unbelieving. As a representative of society's laws he'd heard
final confessions—some old sin or misdeed that was better off forgotten—or final appeals for recognition of an old offence. Sometimes
he'd just been an ear to bend, a source of sympathy and vindication.
Maybe some had hoped that in their last hours, even in their state of
least grace, a corporeal judge might stride in, berobed, ancient, find in
their favour, promise justice, anodyne, consolation, but all they'd got
was him, a tired man in a cheap suit.

Adam Carney seemed to require nothing of him. His flickering eyes closed again and his hollow chest rose and fell as if he were sleeping. Gibson pulled up a dusty chair from underneath the window and sat down by his side. There was nothing on the stainless-steel chest of drawers beside the bed but a plastic pitcher of water and a stopped clock. He put his hand on the handle of the top drawer and pulled. Inside, among the socks and underwear, he found an old pair of spectacles and a wristwatch with a yellow, battered face. The second drawer held nothing but spare pairs of pyjamas, but in the third was a squat wooden box adorned with the faded logo of some long-defunct oil company. He lifted it out and set it upon his lap and lifted the lid. Inside, amongst the various papers and odds and ends, was a dismantled Brownie Hawkeye, its delicate black innards filled with dust and old spiders' webs. By its side was a stack of prints nearly three inches high, and the rubber band which held them gave up the ghost as he removed it. He held the first print up to the light and then the second and then he let out a soft whistle. In amongst the old pictures of starched and straight-laced church folk there were many of Darcy Steele. They'd been taken by trees, in clearings, on creekbanks. There was a series taken in an old wooden church with what looked like a white sheet wrapped round her. One of them was blurred, the side of the girl's face as pale, as diaphanous, as her makeshift garments. At the bottom of the pile were a number of her swimming in a creek, her wet dress hitched up round her waist, smiling and laughing. Then there were others similar to one of those he'd found in her hands—an unfocused shape surrounded by foliage—but they shed no more light on what the shape might be.

He looked down at Adam Carney. He put his hand on his shoulder and shook it—gently at first—then much more vigorously. The old preacher made a gurgling sound and then his chest, covered in grey hair and the barnacles of the aged, rose up, shook, subsided. His eyelids flickered again and his mouth began to fashion a word. Gibson waited, a little breathless himself, for it to come.

"Water," he rasped, finally.

Gibson lifted down the pitcher and looked around for a glass. There were none so he lowered the pitcher to the old man's face and proceeded to pour a thin stream of water down between his dry lips. His head sank back down into his stained pillow after he'd swallowed, but then, after a few minutes had passed, his eyes reopened and he looked up.

"Father Adam?"

The man's lip trembled. "Yes?" he began, in a weak, quavering voice. "Are you a true man, possessing a soul . . . or another unclean spirit . . . come to torment me?"

"I'm a man," said Gibson. "Not a spirit."

"Not one of His angels come to collect me?"

"No. Not an angel. My name's Gibson. I'm a detective. I want to ask you something."

"Yes?"

"Darcy Steele. These pictures you took of her . . ."

The old preacher's forehead rippled and he nodded slightly. He closed his eyes and seemed to take an age to open them again.

"Yes, Darcy. I saw in her . . . something long gone from the world, from . . ." His voice trailed away.

"In the stillness . . . in her eyes . . . there I saw God . . . saw His face . . . His plan . . . the way it was in Eden . . . when the world was very young."

"You tried to . . . capture that? With a camera?"

Carney didn't answer, but his breath began to wheeze in and out of his lungs as if the question had disturbed him. Gibson knew he didn't have much time. He held up one of the pictures with the blurred subject.

"And these . . . what are they? What are they of?"

Carney strained to see the photograph, then slumped back.

"It would not permit itself to be photographed . . . always around her . . . an angel . . . a protector . . . a devourer of time . . . God Himself . . . I don't know."

"You gave one of these to Darcy?"

"She came to me . . . wanted proof that all I'd taught her was true. That there was more to the world beyond what can be seen. This is all I had."

"But what *is* it?"

The old man wheezed again and a wet cough rattled out of his chest, then another, and another. When the coughing subsided Gibson fancied he saw a faint smile ghost across Carney's face.

"You know," he began again, his voice little more than a whisper, "I found her one morning in a peach crate . . . by a creek . . . where I'd camped after a revival. Far to the west it was. That day as fine a day as there has ever been . . . her eyes the same colour as it. Such an angel. I carried her all the way back to the Rock . . . but she never cried . . . not once. I brought her to Fay. Fay took her. A good woman to raise her."

Another fit of coughing took hold of the old man. Gibson leant forward.

"I'll get a nurse."

"No. No. He'll be along directly."

"Who?"

"The Almighty."

"Oh. Right."

"And what about you, son? I see something on your heart. Something you must confess."

"No. There's nothing."

"Yes. I see it in your face. Clearly."

"No," said Gibson again, shaking his head emphatically. "Nothing."

The old man's eyes grew wet and his lips began to quiver. He raised his finger and his mouth trembled—an old prophet about to append words to the world it could not do without. Gibson waited but no words came and the old man drifted back to where he'd been before he'd disturbed him. The years, the seasons, the sun, wind and rain, all the words he'd ever spoken, seemed engraved in his face, plain to see. He didn't have long to live. Gibson's heart fluttered a little and he felt the sudden need to get out of there lest he be caught in the wake of whatever spirit came to claim him.

As he passed the nurses' station on the way out a sister came and stepped into his path.

"What's this all about then?" she asked him.

"What's what all about then?"

"Don't be cheeky. Why is Mr. Carney so interesting all of a sudden? You're the second visitor he's had lately."

"The second? When was the first?"

"About a month ago."

"A man?"

"Yes."

"What did he look like?"

"Oh, a real scruffy type. I almost didn't let him in, but he said Mr. Carney had saved his soul, so I thought it would be all right."

Gibson reached into his pocket and pulled out the photograph of Billy and Darcy.

"Is this him? Is this the man who was here?"

The nurse peered at the photo for a few long seconds, but then she shook her head.

"No," she said. "He was much older."

As he drove he wondered who it could have been. Maybe Smith, maybe Horace Flood—maybe neither of them. He went over and over what Carney had said to him, glancing every so often at the photographs now spread across the seat beside him as he did. It was easy enough to believe what he'd said about Darcy's origins but the sheer strangeness of the photos and the explanation given for them seemed to cast doubt on everything. The photographs were proof of something, that was for sure, but of what he couldn't quite tell. He tried to remember the name of the town where Pop had said Horace Flood had moved to after the drowning and when he had it he pulled out his notebook and rested it against the steering wheel and wrote it down, his hand shaking ever so slightly.

When he reached Angel Rock he parked in the main street and headed up to the station. Pop, on his way out somewhere, was just locking the door behind him.

"You smell like a bushfire and you look like a dog's breakfast," Pop said when he saw him.

"Thanks," said Gibson.

"Did you find him?"

"Yeah, I found him."

"You did? Well? Did you ask him about the boys?"

"Yeah, I did. He never saw them."

Pop sighed and nodded. "What about Darcy then? Did he say any-thing about her? Shed any light?"

"Ah, no, but he was . . . pretty shaken up when I told him. The poor bastard."

Pop nodded.

"Anyway, how . . . ah . . . how'd the funeral go?"

"Yeah, fine. Expected to see you there."

Gibson said nothing. Pop slipped his keys into his pocket and cleared his throat.

"Listen, Gibson, if you're going to be here a few more days . . ."

"Don't worry, I'll find somewhere else."

"Let me finish. It's just that Grace needs to settle, get back into a routine. If she sees you around . . ."

"Say no more."

"Good. Thanks, Gibson. I appreciate it. I've got an idea about where you could stay, if you're interested."

"Fire away."

"The convent down behind the church there is empty. There's a kitchen, everything else you'd need. Why don't you go down and have a look. I'll talk to Father Tuckey if you're interested. How's that sound?"

"Sweet. Sounds good."

"All right."

Pop had already passed him on the path when Gibson blurted out his question. "Listen," he said, "you know a man named Smith?"

Pop stopped in his tracks and turned round.

"I know quite a few."

"This one was—is—an associate of Horace Flood."

"Oh, yes. I know him. He left when Horace did. Why?"

"I was, ah, talking to Henry about him. Seems he blamed Henry and Billy for Annie Flood's drowning. When I mentioned his name to Billy you should have seen him."

"What are you saying, Gibson?"

Gibson took a deep breath.

"I think he's come back. I think he's got the little boy."

"You think he's *what*?"

"I think he found them and avoided the searchers and then he let the older one go because he wasn't Henry's."

Pop looked about, as if he thought he might be dreaming.

"The boy's dead, Gibson," he said, his voice low and forceful. "You haven't been spouting this nonsense to his father, have you?"

"Tell me this: if he is dead, then why haven't you found him?"

"Why? Because those valleys out there are riddled with old mineshafts. If he isn't at the bottom of one there are foxes, and dogs which could have carried him off. If he drowned in the river he could have been swept all the way down to the sea. *That's* why we haven't found him."

"But what—"

"You saying he came here, found the boys when hundreds of us couldn't, just to get back at Henry? That's the biggest load of old cobblers I've heard for a good long while. Why wouldn't he just front Henry, sort it out like a man?"

"Because he wants to inflict the worst kind of pain—the loss of a loved one."

"But what did Henry ever do to him?"

"I told you. He blames Henry for Annie's death. Did you know Smith used to tell her they were going to be married?"

Pop didn't answer but Gibson could tell he didn't.

"Gibson, listen," said Pop, leaning in close to him, "don't you think I'd know if someone like that was around? Don't you think someone would have seen him and told me they had?"

"Not necessarily."

"Not necessarily? Christ on a bike! Gibson, all I can say to you is you're wasting your damn time."

"I'm not. What if I'm right and that's what's happened? It means there's a reason for—there's a chance the kid's alive."

Pop nodded wearily. "How about some proof then, Gibson. That'd help."

"Darcy kept a diary. She says in there that someone watches her from the trees. It's Smith. I can feel it."

"A diary? Why haven't you told me this before? Where is it?"

Gibson pulled it from his pocket and handed it to Pop. He showed him the passages.

"She say anything else?" Pop snapped, after he'd read them.

"Not too much."

"Proves nothing, Gibson. You know it doesn't. The only monsters running around in this valley are the ones in your head."

"Fine."

Gibson turned on his heel to go when he remembered the other photographs he'd taken from Adam Carney's drawer. There was at least one of Adam Carney as a younger man, surrounded by his followers. He found a good, clear one and waved it around under Pop's nose.

"Here. Just point Smith out for me, Sarge. That's all I ask. If he's here. Just point him out."

Pop reached into his pocket for his glasses and put them on. He seemed to take an age to inspect the faces in the photograph, but he finally pointed to one.

"This is Smith," he said. "Here."

Gibson looked, and then he nodded.

"Thanks," he said. "Thanks very much."

Pop gave him the sternest of looks, warned him again to keep his theories to himself, and then walked down the path and got into his car. Gibson watched him drive off then he headed up to the café for something to eat. As he passed the shops he noticed that at least three of them had had their front windows smashed. Curious, he stopped at the butcher's and poked his head round the door, inhaling the shop's strange smell of blood and sawdust.

"Someone smash your window, mate?"

"Yeah. Henry Gunn. Drunk. Can't get too upset about it. The man needed to blow off steam. The sarge sorted him out."

"Yeah, right."

"Get you something?"

"Ah, yeah, all right. Those steaks look pretty good. One of them."

The butcher picked up one of the steaks, weighed it, then wrapped it up. Gibson paid and left.

He continued on up the street and got a sandwich from the café and then headed down to the convent Pop had told him about. It didn't take him long to reach the neat little complex of buildings between the church and the river. He tried the door of the main building and found that it wasn't locked. He walked inside and began looking around. He found a chapel and a library and various offices. The two wings of the building held the kitchen and the dining room and the little cells where the nuns must have slept. The laundry and bathrooms were in a separate building just behind the main building and joined to it by a footpath of worn paving stones set into the earth. In the courtyard formed by the two wings was a water trough fashioned from a block of granite with a ball cock and float mechanism to keep it full, but the neat green lawn that had once framed it was overgrown now with thistles and billygoat weed. Behind the laundry was a triangle of land that must have once been a garden. It was bordered by peach and citrus trees but the space within was waist-high with more weeds and the smothering vines of pumpkin and choko. He went down to the little jetty at the end of the garden and sat down and ate his sandwich and then lit up a smoke. The river was a broad reach before him and stretched away like a lake. A rusted iron ladder was bolted to one of the piles. He couldn't quite imagine the nuns climbing down it and swimming, no matter how hard he tried.

He went back into the kitchen and plugged in the refrigerator and put the steak in it. Finding a jar of tea bags in a drawer and a dusty kettle, he boiled water and made himself a cup of tea. He walked up the wide central staircase of the convent and sat at the mother superior's desk to drink it. The room was warm, bright, and still. The steam off the hot tea spiralled up and joined, for a few moments, the gentle waltz of dust mote and sunbeam. Out the window he could see the roofs of the town stretching away, the Rock rising out of the bush, Jack's Mountain away behind that, then the long escarpment that formed the valley's western border. There was a floor-to-ceiling bookcase on the opposite wall but all the books had been removed, all the knowledge gouged out, all the mysteries gone, all the past, all the explanations. He could still see the impressions of the books where they had nestled in the dust.

He pulled out the photograph he'd shown Pop and looked again at the man he'd pointed out. He was tall and dark and wore a black suit, but other than that he was quite unremarkable. Maybe it was the fact that his dream of the night before was still so fresh in his mind that made him think of his father. There was something about the man that recalled his father's disregard for anyone's feelings but his own. It was in the eyes, it was in the way he stared forward, almost oblivious to the camera. It was in the way the others left an almost unnoticeable gap between him and themselves. In that way at least he was unlike his father, who'd always been the toast of any he'd been with, the centre of attention, the life of the party.

He put down the photo and rubbed his eyes and then ran his hands over the desk before him. There was no graffiti inscribed in the wood or the inserts of leather. He pulled open the first of the desk's drawers but it was empty. Others had scraps of paper, broken pencils, inkstains. From the deeper bottom drawer he pulled out a heavy black telephone. He looked behind him and found a socket just above the skirting board and plugged the telephone's lead into it. He sat the phone on the desk before him and looked at it for a moment as if, given half a chance, it might ring. When it did not he picked up the receiver and held it to his ear, as though someone might be there all the same; some ranking nun, God Himself. All he heard, however, was the blood rushing through his ear, the same trapped ocean his mother had introduced him to with a shell on a beach somewhere, such a long time ago now. He hung up the receiver and pulled the lead from the socket.

In the afternoon he moved his things down from the station house and set himself up in one of the convent cells. Then, in the early evening, he went and sat out on the jetty again. A night-bloomer's perfume lingered in the air and down on the river all was quiet. An ever-so-gentle breeze moved through the trees, their leaves rustling and whispering like a costumed cast in the wings of a great theatre. He smoked another cigarette and then he went inside to the kitchen and heated up a skillet over the blue flames of the gas range. Then, from the refrigerator, he retrieved the good, thick steak he'd bought from the butcher and when the skillet was hot enough he dropped the meat onto the hot metal. As the smell filled the kitchen and his mouth began to water, he sat down at the table and looked up Mount Wright on his map of New South Wales.

17

The dream woke Tom again during the night but he wasn't as frightened by it as he had been at first. He looked around. It was very early and the room was still quite dark. The window glowed dimly with silvery morning light and he could just see the outlines of the room's furniture: the end of the bed, the wardrobe, the dresser. He tried to go back to sleep but couldn't. He opened his eyes, closed them again, and then, from the bedroom down the hall, he heard a short, strangled scream. He jumped out of bed and ran to Grace's bedroom and opened the door. She was sitting up in bed, her face awash with tears.

"What is it? What's the matter?"

"Someone . . . was . . . out there," she said, her words barely intelligible.

"Where?"

"Out there! Under the fig tree!"

Tom went to the window and looked out.

"There's nothing there," he said, turning to her, no derision in his voice. "You might have been dreaming."

"No, I wasn't! He was standing there! He was standing there, without any clothes on and he had *dead* eyes."

Tom didn't know what to say. The memory of her at the circus, waiting bravely, chin up, hands behind her back, for the whipcracker to strike, came to him. He didn't like seeing her frightened.

"Do you . . . do you want me to get your parents?"

"No," she whispered, leaning back against the bedhead, wiping her eyes. "No. Maybe you're right. Maybe it was a dream."

Their eyes met for a moment, then Tom wheeled round and headed for the door.

"Where are you going?"

"Outside."

"No! Don't be—" she began, but he was already out the door. He heard her follow him down the hall, into the kitchen, then out the back door. Soon they were both standing on the wet lawn at the side of the house in their bare feet. The grass was an unspoiled plain of dewed silver right up to the trunk of the fig tree.

"Nothing there," said Tom, shaking his head.

"There *was* someone there," Grace whispered. "Can't you feel . . . something?"

They both stood still and silent and, whether it was because he wanted to believe her or there really *was* something there, just for a moment he felt the sensation of eyes on him, of being watched, of being *seen*. Over in the hills behind the town, where the fig tree's wild cousins huddled together, the darkness seemed impenetrable. Anything could be in *there*. The hairs went up on the back of his neck and a cold shiver fluttered its way down his spine. Maybe there *had* been someone out there, but they had not stood under the fig tree.

"I'm going inside," Grace whispered at his side, her teeth chattering. Tom took one more look at the fig and then followed. Back inside the house he hovered outside the door to his room for a few seconds before heading back to Grace's room. The door was not closed and he poked his head round. Grace was back in her bed, the covers pulled up to her chin, chewing her lip, but looking up at the doorway as though waiting for him to appear. He stood there for a moment and then went quickly to the window and pulled down the blind. He stood by the foot of her bed and put his hand on the bedpost.

"Pop says dreams can seem very real," he said softly, after a few moments. "But they . . . they can't hurt you."

"It wasn't a dream," Grace hissed. "I've seen *him* before!"

"When?"

"When we were out looking for you and Flynn."

Tom frowned. When Grace said no more he started back to his room.

"Tom?"

"Yes?"

"Pop's going to ask you if you want to come out fishing with us. You don't have to say yes if you don't want to come. I tried to tell him you mightn't want to."

"Where? Out . . . in the bush?"

"Yeah. Out west."

"Oh."

"You don't have to come."

Tom nodded and then he left the room.

"Tom?" he heard her call.

"What?"

"Close the door."

"Oh. Sorry."

A few hours later when the sun was up he saw her in the hall, her hair wild from sleep. The bright morning light streaming in through the window fell across her as she turned his way and he saw the dark roundels of her nipples through the thin material of her nightdress. It was only when she crossed her arms over her chest and hurried away towards the bathroom that he realised he'd been staring and that she'd seen him doing so. Appalled, his cheeks burning hot, he went and sat down at the kitchen table and tried to smile at Mrs. Mather.

"I want to take you kids out for a bit of a walk," Pop said, a little later, standing by the toaster. "A bit of a fish. Blow a few cobwebs out. What do you think?"

Grace crunched down on her toast and didn't even look like replying. She hadn't acknowledged Tom's presence since coming into the room and Tom almost turned Pop down because of it. He was about to tell him so when Grace looked directly at him. He paused for a moment, torn, unable to decipher her expression, her slightly wrinkled brow.

"I—I'd like that," he stammered, finally.

"Good lad. Grace?"

"I'm not a kid. I've had a bloody debut."

"Oh, I'm sorry. Would the *young lady* care to join us?"

Grace glanced over at Tom again. Tom looked down at the fat yellow knob of butter sitting on a plate before him.

"All right, then. Suppose so."

"Good girl. We'll head off this afternoon, then." He took his plate over to the sink. "Oh," he said, giving Grace a stern look, "and that'll be enough of your language, young lady."

"Sorry," said Grace, softly.

Pop smiled, winked at Tom, then left.

Tom glanced across at Grace. She didn't *look* so angry any more. It was hard to tell what she was thinking, or feeling. Maybe her cheeks were a little red but her face was deadpan as she glanced at the newspaper Pop had left open on the table.

"Sorry about . . . *before*," he said.

Grace half shrugged her shoulders, took a semi-circle out of her toast and began to munch on it nonchalantly. Tom let out his breath. He thought he saw her cheeks turn a few shades redder than they had been before but he couldn't be sure. They sat in silence, awkward, until Mrs. Mather came in from feeding his mother. Grace finished her toast, wiped the crumbs from her fingers, and made a move to stand. Before she did, and just after Mrs. Mather left the room again, Tom spoke again.

"I saw a man down by the convent yesterday."

Grace looked up, surprised.

"I know," she said.

"Oh. Do you know who he is?"

"Yes. Mr. Gibson. He's a policeman."

"What's he doing there?"

"He . . . he came up about Darcy."

"Really."

She licked a fleck of jam off her knuckle then stood.

"Yep."

"Do you think he might help me look for Flynn?"

Grace froze, staring at him. "You don't think he's still . . . alive, do you?"

"I don't know. Maybe. I might go down and ask that man what he thinks."

"You'd better not."

"Why?"

Their eyes met across the table where the question still lingered. Grace didn't look away for a long time.

"I'll ask him," she said, finally, her voice low. "I'll go and ask him for you."

Tom spent the morning helping Mrs. Mather and sitting by his mother's bed, talking to her when she was awake, watching over her when she slept. Mrs. Mather came and went from the room and sometimes she would laugh at something and his mother would give a sad little smile. The sun fell in through the open window and Tom would close his eyes and let his eyelids turn the light red. Every so often his mother would comment on something she could see outside as if she were seeing things for the first time, and he realised that they were making something new, propping it up with simple words so it might grow stronger.

Grace went down to see Mr. Gibson as she said she would but came back saying she couldn't find him and his car wasn't there. In the afternoon he helped her and Pop load the station wagon with gear and food and then they set off. They drove up into the hills for an hour or so before leaving the car by the side of the road and continuing on foot. They walked for another hour until they emerged from a stand of gums out into a green valley with a river, narrow and dark, winding along at the bottom of it. Pop stopped and turned back to the edge of the trees and threw down his swag.

"And you thought I'd forgotten how to get here!" he called to Grace, who'd gone ahead. Grace smiled and retrieved a billy from her own bag and set off down to the river to fill it, Ham loping along behind. Tom looked about. The sky was clear and the land was silent except for the odd crow and stray gusts of wind rattling the leaves of the trees overhead.

"I've been here before," he said.

"You have?"

"Yes. Henry brought us one time. Flynn was only little."

Pop nodded and patted Tom on the shoulder.

By the time Grace had clambered back up the bank with the billy, Pop, with Tom's help, had gathered enough wood to start a fire and was just putting a match to the little pyramid of twigs and leaves. When the fire was blazing Grace placed the billy in the centre and they all sat back in the shade of a tree and waited for it to boil. When it had, Pop unwrapped the fruitcake his wife had made and portioned it out and then he made tea to wash it down with.

They set off with their rods not long after, following the river upstream to where it spread out into broad pools. They fished for the rest of the afternoon but caught nothing. Late in the day they trudged back up to their camp and sat and watched the day wind down. Pop relit the fire and Grace put a fresh billy in it, but dozed off while waiting for it to boil. When she woke Pop and Tom had already made one billy of tea, drunk most of it, and had been down for more water to brew another. The smell of tea and smoke was all around her and the fire was just a curled red cat of coals. Later, after they had eaten and the sun had set, they lay in their sleeping bags listening to the night. After a while Pop propped himself up on his elbow and leant over to Tom.

"I'm sorry, son," he said quietly. "I didn't think about how hard this must be for you out here."

"It's all right. Really."

"You sure?"

"Yes."

"Good."

Tom waited. Pop seemed to want to say more but was having trouble starting.

"You know," he said, finally, "I had a good talk with Henry the other day. He's sorry for what he's done, all his drinking. He's not a bad man, Tom, just a hurting one."

Tom nodded.

"You have to understand how much young Flynn meant to him. To your mum as well. The little feller . . . held them together. Myself and Mrs. Mather, well, we don't see eye to eye on a few things, but we both love Grace like blazes. If anything happened to her I think we'd be even worse off than your mum and Henry."

Tom looked over at Grace's sleeping form and nodded.

"But he was *my* brother too."

"Yeah. I know. I know. Look, one day, when your mother's . . . better, she'll be there for you. Until then . . . I told Henry what a fine boy he has in you. I told him he should take more care."

"You did?"

"Yep."

Tom looked at his fingers for a while before continuing. "I don't think Henry . . . I don't think he . . . I don't think he's ever *wanted* to be my father."

"I don't think that's the case, Tom," said Pop, his voice grave, "but if it is . . . then more fool him."

Pop lay back in his sleeping bag and closed his eyes.

"Good night, Tom," he said. "I'm good for sleep. I'll talk to you some more tomorrow . . . after we catch a few champion fish . . . all right?"

"All right. Good night then."

"Good night."

The night was cloudless and bright with a full moon. Tom looked up at it for a little longer and then fell into a deep, dreamless sleep.

18

Nestled by the river the little town of Angel Rock still looked to be fast asleep when Gibson left at first light, but also, maybe, about to produce the impossible, about to reveal true beauty, or something close to it. He looked up at the Rock. Just as Pop had said, with the light as it was, he could just about see why they'd named it. He could see how the sail-shaped piece of rock at the rear might be mistaken for a wing, the piece of rock below it for a head—of sorts—but then the sun's rays dropped further and it changed before his eyes. He *could* see a face now, but if it belonged to an angel it had to be the most misshapen, rough-headed angel of all time—or maybe it was hiding its face, resting its forehead on its arm. It reminded him of something else, something he'd seen once before, a long time ago, but he couldn't think what, or where, and as he rolled quietly out of town the light changed again and the impression faded away and the Rock became indeterminable stone once again.

The morning was uneventful but once he was in the ranges the Holden began to overheat and he had to stop a few times to let the engine cool. He went down into a gully the third time it happened and found a beautiful little creek, the banks crowded with ferns and moss-covered rocks. He replenished his bottle of water, drank, then sat there for a few minutes watching the clear water roll over the stones and green weed of the creekbed. He put his hand down into the water's cool caress, wondered whether Angel Rock, the whole world, wasn't somehow similar—just a surface to be broken through, the dark machinery of existence—mysterious, dusty, cold-hearted—there for the seeing beneath. His dream of the graveyard came to him and he wondered whether that place, that Gibson, existed too, somewhere. He looked around and up. Nothing but trees and the sky, so quiet, so empty—yet not at all so. Not at all. He shook the water from his hand and walked back up the slope.

When he cleared the range he let the car coast down the roads and the overheating stopped. The afternoon flashed by as he put his foot down, only stopping again close on five o'clock to relieve himself by the side of the road. He hadn't seen another car or truck for nearly an hour now and the only sounds he could hear were his piss hitting the ground and the slow ticking of the car's engine as it cooled. Ahead was a small range wooded with dark-leaved eucalypts. A layer of bluish haze hung like smoke over the strip of hills, as if the trees were burning but not being consumed. When he drove down through them he saw an understorey of dull khaki shrubs and earth the colour of cold ash and when he crested the next hill he saw a town down in the valley below. Beyond the town there was land stretching out in great spools of peach and ochre, olive and rust; a mantle of sky glowing ultramarine and electric overhead.

He drove into the flat, two-street town, pulled over into a park and fell asleep across the car's back seat, exhausted.

He dreamt of Darcy, walking ahead of him, just out of reach, beneath trees, then through the deserted streets of Angel Rock. He followed her, sure that if he could only catch up, her touch would be like nothing he'd ever known. It would lift him like a crisp blue swell, wash over him, take his breath away—maybe keep it—but be worth that, even that.

He woke with a smile on his face, wondering how his mind could resurrect her—someone he'd never met—so precisely. Up through the window he could see myriad stars, bright and clear in the black void of night. He thought he should have felt more alone, but he didn't. He closed his eyes again, hoping there might be more of the dream to come.

The next thing he knew a skinny little Aboriginal boy was tapping at the glass just above his head. Bleary-eyed, half-asleep, he reached into his pocket and passed the tapper a dollar bill through the gap he'd left at the top of the window. The boy took the note and scampered away, laughing and hooting to his mates. Ten minutes later Gibson heaved himself out of the car and washed as best he could in the small sink of the public convenience he found in the park. He walked over to the hotel when he'd finished and ordered a breakfast of eggs and chops and bacon and listened to the complaints of the publican as he ate it as though he were some kind of travelling confessor. When he went back to the car the boy was standing by it, his two little friends watching from a safe distance.

"Your tyre's flat, mate," the boy said, pointing to the offending item. "I was tryin' to tell ya." He held out his hand and grinned a toothy grin.

Gibson smiled. "*You* didn't let it down by any chance, did you?"

"Nah, mate."

"Swear to God?"

"Swear. Cross my heart, hope to die." The boy spat in his palm and held his hand out for Gibson to shake.

"That's all right," said Gibson. "I believe you." He fished another dollar bill from his wallet and handed it to him. "Go on, don't spend it all at once."

All three boys watched him as he changed the tyre and then waved as he drove off. He kept going for a few more hours until he came to another little town spread out along the banks of a brown river. As he drove down the main street a funeral procession came out of a church. Most of the town seemed to have turned out. Gibson stopped by the hotel and waited for the procession to pass.

An old drunk came and leant on the banister of the hotel's verandah and looked at him. A finer example of pickled manhood he could not have hoped to find. The man came down the steps and stopped by the car's window.

"A funeral," said the man. "Won't be long."

"Yeah," sighed Gibson. "I'm plagued by 'em."

"*Plagued,* are ya?"

"Yes."

"Crikey, that's no good!"

"No. How far is it to Mount Wright?"

"Mount Wright?"

"Yeah."

"Awww, you're nearly there, lad," said the man, winking. "Come and 'ava drink. Do you good. We're havin' a bit of a wake."

Gibson nodded to the procession. "Who died?"

"Old coot . . . name of Spratt . . . thought he'd been dead for years meself, truth be told!"

The old man screwed up his face, cackled madly at his own joke, then stumbled back up the stairs to the cool of the bar. Gibson shook his head, envying him just a little.

The procession cleared from the street and snaked along over a bridge to the river's opposite bank. He followed at a distance until the hearse and accompanying cars turned off down a lane. He could see a cemetery at its far end. He pictured the souls of old river folk, bobbing, floating in the ether, waiting for the resurrection, eyes opening after an age of sleep, as though no time at all had passed. He planted the accelerator, leaving it all behind in his dusty wake.

He drove out of town for a few miles and only then did he pass a sign and happen to look at it in his mirror as he passed. *Mount Wright*, it said, in reverse. He shook his head, turned the car round and drove back into town. When he pulled up by the hotel, the drunk saw him and began to laugh like a drain.

"Told-ya you were nearly there!" he spluttered.

"Clown," muttered Gibson, getting out of the car and going up to him.

"I'm looking for a bloke named Smi— named Horace Flood," he said.

"Horace Flood?" The man turned and shouted into the bar. "Hey! Any of you bastards know a Horace Flood?"

Out of the gloom came some murmured responses.

"Yeah. Long gone though."

"Lives up Sapphire way, I heard. Up near the border."

"That's the preacher."

The drunk relayed the words to him as if he was hard of hearing.

"Doesn't live here any more?"

"Doesn't live here any more?" the drunk shouted in.

"No. Been gone years."

"No, mate, gone years, the fellers reckon."

"Wife and daughter are in the cemetery," said someone inside.

"Wife and—"

"Yeah, I heard. Here." He gave the man a ten-dollar bill. "Drinks all round."

The drunk looked at the note, then held it up to the light.

"Aww, beauty!" he said, finally, sounding like he meant it. "Good-on-yer, mate!"

Gibson drove down to the cemetery and looked around through the stone angels and plastic flowers until he found the graves. He stared down at them for a while, then looked up at the boundary fence of the graveyard and across at the empty fields beyond. There was no one watching from a distance, no one kneeling at other gravesides with prop flowers and false tears. The mourners at the old man's funeral were still huddled together around his open grave. He'd left a big family behind. Children, grandchildren, great-grandchildren by the look. One or two glanced over at him, but they had other, more pressing concerns and soon paid him no more heed. He turned his own attention back to the graves.

The mother had died many years before her daughter. *Drowned,* said her daughter's headstone. *Annie Flood. Drowned.* The words set into the stone. What man or woman hadn't dreamt of going that way, hadn't imagined sinking down into the depths? Set in stone beside her name like that it seemed to him she could never escape it. It changed everything that had gone before. Everything she had been, thought and seen in her short span. All drowned.

When he looked up from his reverie he found the funeral party departing, their dust rising sluggishly into the air and falling back as they passed. He wiped the sweat off his brow and flicked his wet finger towards the dusty earth, then he turned and left Flood's family to their rest, hoping the next world was treating them with a touch more kindness.

The country beyond the town consisted of broad plains of drab mulga and vast stretches of nothing. He'd never been so far from all he knew. There were flickering mirages at the end of long straight sections of road as if the sky was merging with the earth in a sleight of smoke and mirrors. Crows danced around carrion in the middle of the road, punching their steely beaks into the meat right up until the last possible moment, as if they thought he might stop and have a go at the rotting flesh himself. At a quarter to two he saw a ragged sign for Sapphire. He turned off the road and stopped. He was up high and could see for dozens of miles in every direction, the blue of the sky consistent from horizon to horizon. To the southwest lay a long, low mesa, but there was nothing else on the plains except a single pillar of spiralling air, made visible by the dust it carried. He watched it weave across the earth, then vanish. If there was a town out there he couldn't see it. There was no Damascus, no Jerusalem. Desert, yes, but no temptations: no panoramas of naked flesh, no palaces stuffed with gold, no fountains of perfume, no cities to sack. He climbed back into the car and followed the road down into the nothingness for another hour before Sapphire slowly revealed itself to him. In a fold, a ripple, a knurl in the landscape the sun was glinting off something man-made, but it still took another quarter-hour before he reached the source of the reflection. The road came to an abrupt halt. On either side of the last fifty yards of it were a dozen corrugated-iron shanties. Gibson turned off the car and looked about, tired and parched. The land surrounding the settlement was gritty and bright in the sun and dotted with knee-high tussocks of spiny grass. Small yellow flowers, their stems trembling in the warm breeze, pushed out of the red, gibber-studded earth. He eased out of the car and stretched his arms up over his head and then he walked up to the nearest house and knocked on the door. No answer. None from the next or the next or the next. A town of ghosts and a deathly quiet. He didn't know whether to be relieved or disappointed.

He set about examining each shack more closely. Most were occupied by nothing more than dust and cobwebs. Some seemed more recently inhabited and these he examined for clues as to their owners, but he found no evidence of Flood or Smith in any of them. Finally he came to the last shack on the western side of the street, set a little further away from its neighbour than any of the others. Its door was locked, its windows heavily curtained. He walked round to the rear. A few old tools leant against the back wall but other than that there was nothing. He broke the lock on the back door with an old spade and then he dropped to his knees in the doorway and peered at the fine layer of dust on the floor. Nothing disturbed its uniformity. It had been some months at least, maybe years, since anyone else had entered. He stepped inside and pulled back the curtains to let in some light. There was only the one room; a fireplace, table and kitchen press at one end, a bed at the other. Set over the fireplace on two rusting iron spikes was a mantel shelf fashioned from an old railway sleeper. On the rough wooden surface sat a pipe, a Capstan tobacco tin and a box of matches. The tobacco tin was empty. He picked up the pipe. It was smooth and cool to the touch. He was vaguely disappointed, as if expecting a small coal to still be alight in the bell.

The pipe was the only evidence he found of any vice, or indeed, anything that tempered the dwelling's feeling of utter cheerlessness. He stepped forward to examine the kitchen press. The plates and bowls stacked in it were either of battered tin or turned wood and the utensils were worn-down relics, decades old. In the kerosene-tin pantry box he found near-empty tins of flour, tea, sugar, and salt. He moved to the bed. It was made up with grey army-surplus blankets. A small table beside it supported more dust and a candle-stub on a tin lid. He sat down on the bed and felt under the pillow with his hand but found nothing. He opened the drawer in the table and pulled out a thick, leather-bound bible and an old shortbread tin with its tartan paintwork all but worn away. He flicked the bible open. High on the inside of the front cover he found the owner's name printed in thickly inked capitals.

SMITH.

He let out a long breath and then began to leaf through the thin, grubby pages, his hands trembling just a little. Soon he found the first of the underlined passages. There were many more underlined and cross-referenced with other books, chapters, and verses, some with scrawled annotations, exclamations and question marks. Proverbs was thick with weaving lines. As was Job, Lamentations. Smith seemed to be a man who liked his sadness neat.

He put the bible down on the bed and prised open the tin's lid. Inside was a sheaf of papers, about two inches thick, tied up with brown string. He could see that they were covered in fine, closely spaced handwriting. He untied the string and read the first page, then the second. It was some kind of treatise, but it felt as though he had come into an argument halfway through and the gist of it eluded him. There was an even greater abundance of footnotes and marginalia. There were numerous crossings out and long-winded references to other works, but it was the lengthy, roundabout, barely legible sentences that stymied him. He flicked through the pages, saw a name begin to appear again and again, sometimes underlined in an angry red. Horace Flood. He sampled the prose around the name. Declamations, condemnations, vitriol. A great schism seemed to have developed between the two men. Although he tried he could not seem to get to the crux of the disagreement until he turned a page and found the beginning of the pages—the whole thing had been cut like a deck of cards.

Annie Flood was the subject of the first half of the screed—Annie and no one else. Page after page described Smith's absolute devotion to her until Gibson began to feel a little ill. Obsession seemed too mild a word for it. He flipped over another page and found a photograph of her pinned to the paper. It was yellow with age and mildew but he could still make out her features well enough. He thought he could see some resemblance to Billy in her features but it was her similarity to Darcy Steele that took his breath right away.

As he stared, a loose leaf of paper slid from the pile and onto his lap. He picked it up, still a little dazed, and looked at it. The page was filled with a passage copied out in thick black ink:

> While he yet spake, there came from the ruler of the synagogue's house certain which said, Thy daughter is dead: why troublest thou the Master any further? As soon as Jesus heard the word that was spoken, he saith unto the ruler of the synagogue, Be not afraid, only believe. And he suffered no man to follow him, save Peter, and James, and John the brother of James. And he cometh to the house of the ruler of the synagogue, and seeth the tumult, and them that wept and wailed greatly. And when he was come in, he saith unto them, Why make ye this ado, and weep? the damsel is not dead, but sleepeth. And they laughed him to scorn. But when he had put them all out, he taketh the father and the mother of the damsel, and them that were with him, and entereth in where the damsel was lying. And he took the damsel by the hand, and said unto her, *Talitha cumi;* which is, being interpreted, Damsel, I say unto thee, arise. And straightway the damsel arose, and walked; for she was of the age of twelve years. And they were astonished

with a great astonishment. And he charged them straitly that no
man should know it; and commanded that something should be
given her to eat.

He looked back and forth from the words to the picture of Annie
Flood and wondered. He wondered whether Smith had returned to
Angel Rock, seen Adam Carney's pictures of Darcy, then gone and
seen her in the flesh and been tipped over into some kind of mad-
ness—and vengeance against Henry for Annie's death. He didn't
quite understand how Darcy had become so entangled in Smith's poi-
sonous vendetta but it was impossible to know what effect his lurking
about might have had on her.

He knew he was right about Smith, knew in his gut that he had
something to do with the missing boys, and with that knowledge firing
him he began to look more urgently at the pages, trying to find some
clue as to what he might have done with Flynn; where he might have
taken him. A name that he'd seen in the first half of the papers began
to appear again. *New Eden.* New Eden. From what he could gather it
seemed to be the place where Horace Flood had gone after Mount
Wright and Sapphire. He kept looking and finally found a description
of the place, and then, after another half-hour, enough information to
find it. He tied the papers back up and headed outside.

He put the bundle into the car and began looking around the
houses for a small, boy-sized grave. When he couldn't find one he let
out a sigh of relief and tramped up into the barely perceptible hills to
the west to clear his head and to see what could be seen. To the north
he could just make out the darker smudge of the dingo fence along
the border, but in the other three directions he saw nothing to suggest
men had ever set foot there. The collection of corrugated-iron shacks
that was Sapphire seemed like toys from the heights as though, simply
by walking up there, he'd grown to be giant-sized. Maybe that was the
hook that had brought Smith and Flood out to this beautiful elemen-
tal emptiness; the temptation it offered those in it to believe they
were more than other men, greater, closer to God. He saw them then,
and other men like them, kneeling in the dust on the hill's crest,
wholly pious, holding up bibles to the empty sky as if more words
might be added to them in bursts of holy fire. Maybe there was temptation here after all.

He walked back down to the empty town and sat on the bonnet of the Holden, surveying the main street and its traffic of scampering lizards as the day drew slowly to a close. Small birds flitted to and from their perches in the eaves of the abandoned shacks. The hills where he'd stood an hour ago turned shades of lavender and magenta. The sun lowered, and even the smallest things on the plain before him cast long shadows. Then, like dyes thrown at things invisible, the light from the setting sun picked out the outlines of massive structures as they rolled away from him across the sky. He saw mountains and great ruins, galleons with acres of sail. He saw them shimmer into life, then slip away under the grey pearl sheet of the darkening sky, fading to nothing.

Despite the urgency it was too late and his eyes were too tired to make the journey to New Eden in the dark. He didn't want to sleep in the car again so he went looking for somewhere else to spend the night. He found a decent mattress in one shack and carried it across to another which still sported a little iron stove. He set a fire and warmed a tin of beans on the hotplate and when he'd eaten he fastened the door closed with a piece of wire and lay listening to the faint, comforting sounds of the stove. He thought of his mother and his sister and Darcy, and he whispered to them in the dark.

"I think we're getting somewhere, girls," he said.

He heard a dingo's mournful wail somewhere out in the country, far away, but there was no answering call and he fell asleep, finally, still waiting for one. Then, in the dead of night, the front door swung open and crashed against the wall of the shack. He started awake, staring at the open door for almost a minute, disoriented, his stomach twisting with a black, irrational fear. A gust of wind picked up something outside, a piece of tin maybe, and banged it against the side of the shack. The sound shook him from his frozen stupor and he pulled himself up and went to the door and wired it shut again and then he took his revolver out of his bag and the box of ammunition with it. He lay back down, loaded the weapon, then put his finger against the trigger's cool steel. He lay there for what seemed like hours, holding the revolver over his chest, loading and unloading it in the dark until his hands were bloodless and numb, and the click, click, click of the bullets became the sound of claws on the iron roof, something pacing to and fro, waiting for him to emerge.

19

In the morning the valley was flooded with a silver mist as though a strange inland sea had risen while they slept. They took it in turns to walk down to the river's hidden edge and splash and wash themselves awake before eating a breakfast of porridge with Sunshine milk and golden syrup. By the time they'd finished, the sun had crested the hills to the east and found rainbows in the steam coming off their mugs of tea. They packed up their gear and walked downstream, the mist thinning, the sun soon flooding the trail with warmth and light. They walked for twenty minutes and then they came to another spot that Pop reckoned looked promising. They stopped and fished, but still had no luck. Finally Pop, with a sigh, put down his rod, rolled a cigarette, found a pleasant spot to smoke it. Grace sat down beside him.

"Looks like it might rain this afternoon, or tonight," he said.

Grace nodded. It seemed a reasonable forecast even though there were no clouds and as she looked around and nodded again she saw that he was amused by her unquestioning acceptance.

"Over there." He pointed with his cigarette hand to a long escarpment jutting out of a line of grey hills in the middle distance. Just behind them was a haze and behind the haze, or inside it, she could just make out a small collection of fluffy white clouds. She nodded and then glanced over at Tom. He was sitting by a tree with Ham at his feet, his line slack in the water. He was staring out across the river, his eyes glazed. She wondered what was going on behind them.

After a while they continued downstream. As they went Grace kept one eye on the clouds and one on Tom. By mid-afternoon the clouds had risen like dough, dwarfing the escarpment and threatening the sun. Tom hadn't changed. A gust of cool wind lifted her hair and she breathed deeply from it.

"Storm's coming," said Pop. "Looks like we'll have to sit it out."

They headed up the side of the nearest hill to see what shelter could be found. Pop pointed to a cluster of rocky outcrops. They walked to them and Grace found an overhang that looked large enough to shelter the three of them from the worst of the rain and any falling branch or tree. They sat down and Pop draped his oilcloth coat over them and they waited while the storm brewed overhead and the air became charged with its electricity. Tom lifted Ham up to his chest and felt the race of his heart and tried to calm him. The day darkened very suddenly and then the massive thunderhead broke from its moorings with a flash of light and a crackling rattle of thunder and headed straight for them. Grace looked anxiously at Pop but he was staring out expectantly, steady as a rock, a faint smile on his lips. He looked at her and gave a wink and she managed a weak smile in return. A great surge of air swerved up the valley, sending leaves and dust flying into their eyes and birds rocketing for shelter. They heard the roar of the rain as it approached and then all at once it was over them, a bedlam of rain and thunder and lightning. Pop laughed at the noise—distant cousin of birdsong, water over pebbles—but put his arm round his daughter's shoulders. There was a deafening crack as a great electric key reached down and tried to unlock the earth. The flash dazzled Grace and she squeezed her eyes shut and saw the jagged blue line repeat and repeat. Then, after only ten minutes or so, it was all over. The rain died away until there were only the big drops from the trees above clattering down onto Pop's coat.

"We're right? We're all in one piece?"

"Yep."

"Yep."

They stood and breathed in the cool air and watched the storm cloud as it bore down on the valley, declaring itself with long, echoing rolls of thunder.

"If that doesn't wake up the blinkin' fish I don't know what will," said Pop.

They walked back down to the river and along it for a bit until they came to a point where the river elbowed its way between two spurs with a chatter of rapids before opening out into a calmer reach. The sun emerged from behind the clouds and lifted wisps of steam from pools in the rocky bank. They put down their loads to stop and look.

"If I was a fish that's where I'd live," said Tom.

Pop laughed and agreed with him. He dug into his swag and pulled out a bottle of beer.

"Put this in the water will you, Tom?" he said, handing it to him. "Don't frighten the fish, though!"

"I won't."

Grace went down and found a shady spot on the bank. Below her a large rock jutted out and caught the river current, the sun sparkling on the disturbed water. She pushed a wad of bread onto the hook of her fishing line and threw it in the water and then watched Pop as he assembled his fly rod and began casting out across the pool. She sat and waited and grew very sleepy listening to the breeze in the rushes and the water gurgling past the rock. She watched Tom as he walked along the bank. He was a little ungainly still. Although he was growing fast he was still just a boy, just a sweet, gentle boy, and not at all like Sonny, or Charlie, or any other boy she'd ever met for that matter. Just looking at him made her sad. She wanted to help him, but she didn't know how.

"Getting any bites?" she called.

"No."

For a while he looked as though he was going to say something else, but then he moved away downstream with his dog at his heels.

Pop fished until the shade left his daughter and her arms went a little pink. He had no luck—not even a nibble, and nor did Tom.

"Good fishermen out of luck," he called to him, giving up. He walked over to Grace and sat down with her. The sun began to sink behind the hills and the river became a stage, its black surface like a polished floor, for the birds to dip into and soar over. The breeze stopped and everything but the river and the birds stilled. Grace threw her line in again, then a turn of light underneath the water's surface suddenly became a splash and the arching leap of a golden perch. Grace laughed and began to pull the fish in. For a while it felt like the river itself on the end of her line but then the perch tired and she landed it, held it up before her for Pop to admire, swinging like a pendulum, its exact pattern of opalescent scales gleaming in the fading light, its mouth gasping for water like a desert traveller.

"Got a deal going with St. Peter?" asked Pop, lifting his eyebrows.

She shook her head, smirking. "No."

She laid the perch on the ground and twisted the hook from its mouth, then unrolled Pop's fishknife from its square of leather. She held the fish and pushed the knife down between its eyes and into its brain to kill it, then made a cut along its length from mouth to tail. The internals seemed delicate, miraculous, inside their shell of pale flesh and silvery skin. She pulled them out and threw them into the river and then walked down to the water and washed her hands of the bloody residue. Pop had already started to gather wood for a fire and Tom had wandered over to see what was happening. Grace walked over to where Pop had bent over the fire and handed him the fish.

"You can scale it," she said, "while I try and catch another one for you."

"Thanks," said Pop, shaking his head, grinning. "And one for Tom while you're at it."

Tom came and sat down by the fire and they both sat in silence watching Grace try for another fish. She stood in the golden afternoon light, insects describing circles around her, intent on her task, oblivious to them both.

"Look at that," said Pop, almost to himself, shaking his head. "That's some kind of miracle. Beyond praise that is."

Tom looked and knew what Pop meant. They watched her and, to their amazement, she caught another fish within five minutes, this one an even better size than the first. After that, no matter what she tried, she could not catch a third.

"Two're enough, girl," said Pop. "Come and sit."

By the time the last light had gone they'd cooked the fish and eaten them. They sat, contented, looking into the fire. Pop handed his daughter a tin.

"Roll me some durries, will you, Grace."

"Greyhounds or racehorses?"

Pop didn't answer, just gave her a pained look.

"Why don't you go and get that bottle out, Tom."

Tom went down to the water and retrieved the beer bottle from where he'd set it that afternoon. Pop took it from him and opened it and filled his mug.

"Just remember something," he said, pointing to the bottle. "This isn't Henry's problem. Henry is Henry's problem. Beer is an honest drink and nothing beats one after a hard day. Here, have a taste."

Pop handed the bottle to Tom and Tom took a swig.

"What do you think?"

Tom wiped his mouth. "It's not real nice."

Pop laughed. "That's what Gracie says too!"

Grace handed him the cigarettes she'd rolled.

"Thanks, sweetheart."

Pop could tell by the look on her face that he'd embarrassed her somehow in front of Tom. He sat smoking and sipping at the beer. Grace climbed into her sleeping bag and then rested her head against his thigh. Soon her eyes closed and her mouth fell open and her legs began to twitch. Her brow furrowed from whatever dream had taken her in hand.

"She's always been like this," Pop said quietly. "As a youngster she'd run around set on one thing until she'd mastered it. I used to find her flaked out in all sorts of places, all her steam gone."

Tom looked over at Grace, uneasy that Pop was talking about her while she slept.

"Her grandfather—my father—taught her to fish. I think the skill's skipped a generation, but at least he showed me his best spots."

"Is he still alive?" asked Tom.

"No, he passed on a few years ago."

"Oh."

Pop looked at the boy. He seemed suddenly troubled.

"What is it? You been having those dreams again?"

"Sometimes. I've been dreaming about lions too."

"Lions?"

"Yeah."

"Good dreams?"

"Yeah. Mostly. I'm walking through the bush and they're with me. It feels good, like they'll protect me if anything bad happens."

"Sounds good."

"I . . . I wanted to let them out."

"Who?"

"The lions from the circus."

"Oh, well, that wouldn't have been such a good idea. I'm glad you didn't. They don't belong here. They probably would've died."

Tom remembered the kangaroo he and Flynn had found by the side of the road and the wound in its shoulder. He remembered how spooked it had been, like cattle sometimes got when dogs chased them.

"What about kangaroos, wouldn't they be able to eat them?"

"Yes, but I think cattle would be a better bet for them, and I don't think the cockies would let 'em get too many before hunting them down."

Tom nodded. Pop waited. Finally Tom spoke again.

"Do you still . . . see him . . . sometimes?"

"Who? My father?"

"Yeah. I mean, do you *imagine* that you see him, walking down the street or something?"

"You asking me if I see ghosts, Tom?"

"Suppose so."

"You seeing some?"

"Just one."

"I see. Don't really believe we *see* 'em myself. I think it's more like our minds . . . project things that only *our* eyes can see. Some people might call them ghosts. I call them angels, because they look out for me and tell me things. Some people reckon children can see things that adults can't, but I don't know about that myself."

"What do they say?"

Pop smiled.

"*Don't be afraid,* they mostly say. *Don't be afraid.*"

Tom thought about it.

"So they're not people who died and aren't at rest?"

"No. I don't think so. I think it's the people left behind who often aren't at rest. That's why we need to see them."

Pop lit another cigarette and took a long drag on it while Tom thought about it.

"Listen," he said. "When I came back from the war I used to see a lot of the blokes who didn't come back . . ."

"Tell me about them."

"Well, I was only twenty when I joined up—just a boy still in my head. Just before I was due to start my training I went down to Sydney to see a few relatives there. Well, I saw 'em, but then I had a night to myself. I went and got a room near Central, stayed there that last night. That's when it really hit me, what I was going to do, and where I was going. I looked around at the walls of that room and I thought: if I'm killed I'll never be able to just do this again, lie in a room and think, go outside and have a feed, talk to people. It really hit me. So I got down on my knees and prayed. I was just a boy, all on my own, and I wanted some kind of . . . reassurance. Someone to tell me it would be all right, whatever happened. Someone to tell me not to be afraid."

"Did you get it?"

Pop pulled on his cigarette, the glow lighting up his face.

"I got it. I think I got more than I bargained for. Something came into that room to visit me. I couldn't see anything, but I felt it."

"What was it like?" breathed Tom.

"It was like . . . it was like . . . well, you know those lions from the other night, it was a bit like if you went and stood there in the cage with them—not knowing a plumb thing about lion-taming—and knowing that whatever they decided to do there wouldn't be a damn thing you could do to stop it. You follow?"

"Yeah, I think so."

"But it *did* nothing. It just *was*. I didn't sleep a wink afterwards, just lay on that lumpy bed all night with my heart beating so hard it hurt. And somehow it came to me that I'd be all right. I just knew it. I just *knew* the war wouldn't kill me."

"And it didn't."

"No," said Pop, with a smile, "it didn't. But it tried, and the harder it tried the cockier I got. By the end of it I was the oldest bloke in my outfit. That's when they started calling me Pop and I started to really worry about them. They were only young—just boys like I'd been— but they thought they were men. I wanted all those boys to live. I wanted them to live, but I knew, like I knew I was going to live, that some would die. Knew it. See, that was the bad part of knowing I'd be all right—I had to watch too many of those boys get shot up, killed. I didn't ask for that, just like you didn't ask to go missing, but it still happened."

"You don't see those boys any more?"

Pop squinted, then threw his cigarette away into the dark.

"No, not like before. But I *see* them, and I remember I'm not just living my life for myself."

"How d'you mean?"

"Well, those blokes never got to come home, or see their sweethearts again, or get married, or have kids of their own. I consider that, 'specially when I'm cranky about something."

"What about your father?" Tom asked.

"What about him?"

"You didn't say if you saw him."

Grace changed position and slid her head off Pop's thigh. Pop rolled up his jumper and put it under her head.

"No, I don't see him," he continued, his voice soft, "but I . . . *sense* him sometimes. 'Specially in a place like this, where I used to come with him."

Tom nodded, then stroked Ham's belly as he stretched out to soak up the fire's warmth.

"Sometimes I wish my father was still with us."

"Yeah, well, maybe you'll see him again some day."

"What about your mother, is she still alive?"

"No. She died when I was not much older than you. I remember her pretty well. My old man came up here into the hills, a bit further out and higher up, just before he died. He always said he would when it was his time but I never really figured he'd do it. I found him curled up by a cold fire, covered in snow. It'd snowed up there for the first time in years. I was . . . heartbroken by that at first, that he'd died alone, but then I remembered what he'd always said. He used to say he didn't want to be a burden and he used to say that while his wife— my mother—was in his head, fresh and young as the day he'd met her, he'd keep going, but the moment her memory started to fade he'd know it was time to go. He couldn't bear the thought of that happening. I knew then that he hadn't died alone up there, but that she'd been with him. It did me good, that. It made it easier. It made me realise that a memory like that, of someone who's gone, can help you for the rest of your whole life. That's what I tell Gracie about young Darce, and that's what I want you to consider as well."

When Pop looked up at Tom he saw the tracks of two tears down each of his cheeks shining in the firelight.

"Sorry, Tom," he said, pulling his handkerchief from his pocket and handing it to him. "Didn't mean to be upsetting you."

Tom mumbled something and wiped his eyes and then he stared into the fire for a long while. Pop watched him and waited. It was another five minutes before he spoke again and it dawned on Pop that he was summoning up courage.

"Is he really dead, Mr. Mather?"

"I think so, Tom," said Pop, gently. "I think he must be."

"They thought Jesus was dead, but he came back."

"Yeah."

"And the astronauts, when they were on the other side of the moon, no one knew if they were going to come back. They could have been dead."

"Yes."

"But they came back."

"Yep, they did."

"He's too little to be wherever he is without me . . ." Tom spluttered. He turned away from the fire and began to cry steadily. Pop thought it was for the best. It was best for him to accept it, with all his heart. It was the only way he would start to mend.

He lay there for a long time, thinking, watching his daughter sleep, and then Tom moved so that Pop could see his face. Pop reckoned that some of the strain, some of the care, had gone from it, but he knew it might have been wishful thinking. They were both quiet for a while, lying on their backs, looking up at the moon and stars. He began to point out to Tom the constellations along the great track of the Milky Way, from Canis Major through to Sagittarius. The constellations got him thinking about the sea and navigating by the stars and he began to tell Tom about Ulysses and his wanderings. After a while he looked over at the boy, thinking he'd fallen asleep, but his eyes were still open, his ears still listening, his head full of things that hadn't been there before.

"Keep going," he said. "Please?"

"All right."

He told him of Theseus and the Minotaur, how Ariadne had helped him find his way out of the labyrinth. He told him of Daedalus and Icarus and he told him of Oedipus and how his father had left him, feet pierced and bound, to die, and then he stopped, realising the story was probably not the best in the circumstances.

"That's pretty bad," said Tom, filling the pause.

"Those old storytellers didn't pull their punches."

"Keep going. What happened to Oedipus?"

"You sure?"

"Yep."

"Well, Oedipus went to this town that was having troubles with a sphinx."

"What's a sphinx?"

"Body of a lion. Head and, er, chest of a woman. With wings."

"Not a real thing."

"No. Not real.

"Anyway, this sphinx was hanging around outside this town and anyone it came across it would ask a riddle, and if they couldn't answer it it'd eat them."

"What was the riddle?"

"Let me see. Let me get it right. *What goes on four feet, on two feet, and three, but the more feet it goes on the weaker it be?*"

"That's it?"

"Yep."

Tom lay thinking about it for a while and then he said: "I can't get it."

"You don't want to sleep on it?"

"No. I'd never get it."

"You sure?"

"Yep."

"A human being. That's the answer. When we're little we crawl around on all fours, when we're adults we walk upright, and when we're old we use a cane—three legs."

Tom nodded slowly. "And Oedipus got it?"

"Yep."

"And what did the sphinx do?"

"She, ah . . . jumped off a cliff. Which was not much good for her, but good for Oedipus, because he got to carry on."

"Maybe that's what happened to Flynn. He wouldn't have known the answer either."

"Maybe."

Pop looked over at Tom after a while and saw that his eyes had finally closed for the night. Unable to sleep himself, he sat up and watched the river's black surface and the moon's reflection upon it. When the fire died down around midnight he threw on more wood, the bright yellow flames pushing back the darkness and the things it contained for a little longer. Grace gave a whimpering little moan as her dream resumed. He didn't have the heart to wake her from it, but just sat there, watching her sleep, watching the firelight flicker across her beautiful, troubled face.

20

Gibson left Sapphire just as the sun was showing itself in the east. He was glad to see the back of the place. Horace's land was on the western side of the Great Dividing Range and further south and he thought it would take until lunch time to drive there. It took much longer than that and by the time he reached the little town of Deepwater it was the middle of the afternoon. He bought a more detailed map from the service station and studied it closely. The land was a few miles from the nearest sealed road and there didn't seem to be any vehicle access to it from anywhere. He headed out of town along the road that swung closest to the property and when he reckoned he was as near as he could get he parked the Holden under a tree and set off on foot.

The land was dry and rock-strewn and covered in ironbarks and grey-leaved peppermints. He was soon wet with perspiration. After toiling for an hour he came upon a dirt track winding up into the hills. He followed it for another half-hour and then he turned a corner and found Flood's settlement spread out below him. New Eden. He eased down onto his haunches and took a drink from his bottle of water. Below him, tucked between two small hills, was a motley but orderly collection of tents and makeshift dwellings. One of the tents was an old circus big top complete with painted decorations and he couldn't help but smile. A creek ran down out of the hills and on either side of it the land had been cleared and planted with vegetables. He could also see a few scrawny cattle in fenced pens and some sheep that looked as though they needed shearing.

He sat up on the rise for a few minutes, just watching the settlement and sipping at his water until he'd drained the bottle. He made his way down to the creek, but by the time he reached it and had wet his face and drunk, the sun had set and the moon was already sitting plump and pretty in the southeast, the early evening air so calm and clear he could see the rocky details of its unlit regions. To the south the Milky Way was a diamond-strewn isle in a dark and beautiful sea, and far away on the eastern horizon lightning flashed faint and silent.

He followed the creek down towards the settlement and when he was only a few dozen yards away he began to smell meat cooking and hear children laughing. Lanterns hung from trees. Fires were burning and he could see children running around in the firelight chasing each other. He could see women in long dresses, some with babies on their hips. He'd rarely seen such a peaceful scene, and nothing that had ever brought, welling up inside him, such fierce yearnings to join in, to belong.

He waded across a shallow part of the creek, his shoes filling with water and his trousers quickly sodden. He moved forward, then paused by a tree and watched as the women began to carve meat off a spitted beast, sawing with long knives, closing their eyes against the smoke rising off the beds of glowing coals. They piled plates high with the steaming slices and then carried the plates across to trestle tables set up under sheets of canvas. The men appeared from the main marquee, all dressed in white shirts and black ties with dark trousers and polished shoes. He couldn't see Smith and there was no way of knowing which one was Horace Flood. It was only then that Gibson realised he'd lost track of the days. It was Sunday.

They all sat down at the tables and everyone went quiet as grace was sung, the song drifting over to Gibson and making him think of his childhood and Sunday lunches with his mother's parents after church. His stomach rumbled as he watched them eat and he wondered why he just didn't walk up and invite himself to dinner.

When they had finished their meal the men filed back inside the tent and the women set about cleaning plates and seeing to children. Gibson sat down to rest his aching legs and think about what he should do. He lit a cigarette in his cupped hands, then took his revolver out of his bag, unloaded it and dropped the bullets into his pocket. He'd nearly finished smoking the cigarette when two girls came round the tree he had his back against and saw him sitting there, the gun still resting against his thigh. Between the girls was a small child and for a brief, heart-stopping moment he was certain it was Flynn Gunn, but when he looked again he saw that the child was also female. She wore dungarees and her blonde hair was cropped short. The girls stopped in their tracks. The oldest of the three was about thirteen or fourteen, slender and dark-eyed, and the middle one was about eight or so, fairer, with a round, cherubic face and ruby lips. Both wore dresses like the older women but their feet were bare and dusty.

"Hello," he said, after a long pause, sliding the gun down to the ground and out of sight. "Ah . . . what are you doing?"

"We're hiding," said the cherub, her eyes sparkling. The older one, without taking her eyes off him, immediately let go of the little one's hand and covered the cherub's mouth with her hand.

"I see."

The girl pulled her sister's hand away. "What are you doing there?"

"I'm, ah, waiting to see Reverend Flood."

"Oh."

They blinked at him a little while longer and then watched, wide-eyed, as he rose to his feet and threw the butt of his cigarette to the ground. It hissed in the dew, winked out.

"We have to go now," said the older girl, pulling the other two with her and hurrying them back towards the camp.

"Bye, then."

"Bye," said the little one, over her shoulder.

Gibson swore under his breath. There was nothing for it now but to go over. The older girl would almost certainly tell someone about him. He stuck the gun into his bag and hurried across to the old circus tent, glad to be doing something at last. He slipped straight inside through two loose flaps of canvas. The interior was warm and lit dimly by one gas lantern out the front. There was an empty bench before him and he sat down on it as though he were just a latecomer at a wedding or funeral. He held his breath for a few moments but no one in the congregation seemed to have even noticed his arrival and after a while he relaxed a little. He lifted his head and peered up at what was happening at the front of the tent. A man was standing, speaking, his arms describing some great event or other. His sleeves were rolled up, revealing the blue smears of tattoos. Gibson wondered whether it was Horace Flood. He would have taken him for a hard drinker by the shot veins in his nose and cheeks. He wasn't very tall and he had a hangdog expression on his face that never changed once while Gibson watched. He moved around the lectern like someone who'd been doing it for far too long and Gibson had almost made up his mind about him when the man looked his way and found his eyes. The man's eyes were dark in the dim light, but also slightly disconcerting, as if he *knew* things—knew his sins—and wouldn't hesitate to expose them, there and then. Gibson, despite wanting not to, looked away first.

The women began to drift inside in ones and twos. It didn't take long for him to be noticed as the benches near him filled. He saw women whisper to their menfolk. Some turned round and observed him, nodded back when he nodded at them. Hymns were sung. "Bread of Heaven." "Abide with Me." Gibson almost wished he could sing. Then one of the men came and sat down beside him.

"Can I help you? Do you want food?" he whispered.

Something about the man's manner instantly set his teeth on edge.

"No," he said, his tone far too belligerent.

"Well, I think you should go, then."

"What if I don't want to go?"

"We think it would be best if you did."

"What if I'm after salvation? What if—"

"You frightened some young girls."

"Frightened them? They didn't look frightened to me."

"Please," said the man, after a pause.

"I'm here to speak to Reverend Flood. I'm a policeman."

The man changed then, and seemed to take him at his word, as if it were his habit to believe what people told him without question. Gibson felt a little silly. After another moment the man slid away along the bench. The atmosphere changed inside the tent almost straight away. The women began to leave and it wasn't much longer before the service petered out altogether. The man who'd spoken to him went and whispered something to the preacher and he looked Gibson's way before exiting the tent through a flap in the canvas behind the lectern. Gibson stood and left the same way he'd come in and then skirted round to where he thought Horace Flood would be. He saw him walking towards a smaller tent, his shoulders hunched, and set out after him. He moved quickly for his age and Gibson didn't gain on him at all for a time and his wet shoes, squelching comically, didn't help matters. When he did catch up he noticed the patched elbows of the old man's suit, the mending stitches around the sleeves.

"Flood? Horace Flood?"

The man turned and answered. "Yes?"

"My name's Gibson. Wondered whether I could have a word with you."

"Of course," Flood answered, calmly, entering the tent and motioning him to sit. Gibson sat down.

"What can I do for you, Mr. Gibson?"

"I'm looking for this man." He pulled out the photograph from his pocket and pointed. "I believe he's a friend of yours."

Flood took the photograph and peered at it in the flickering light of the lantern. After a while he put it down and reached over and picked up a pipe and a tin of tobacco from a small table. He filled the pipe and lit it with a match and started puffing. Gibson sneezed but Flood didn't seem to notice.

"What is your business with Mr. Smith?"

"I want to ask him about a town called Angel Rock," answered Gibson, his heart beginning to thump, "and a few things that have gone on there recently. Why don't you just tell me if he's here."

"You're wasting your time, Mr. Gibson."

"Maybe I should be the judge of that."

"You're wasting your time because Mr. Smith passed on, nearly a year ago."

It took Gibson a few moments to absorb Flood's statement and when he had he rejected it absolutely.

"Mr. Smith is dead," Flood said again, as if he had read his thoughts.

"He . . . he can't be."

"He is. I assure you. I give you my word."

Gibson looked at him. He looked into his calm, grey eyes and his certainty began to ebb away like so much water.

"But I thought . . . I was sure he'd gone back to Angel Rock. I was sure he'd taken Flynn."

"Flynn?"

"Henry Gunn's son. Henry told me Smith blamed him for your daughter's death. I thought he'd gone back . . . to get even with him."

Flood puffed on his pipe and looked around, as if inspecting the tent, and then he nodded.

"After Annie drowned," he began, "Henry did come to me. He told me of Smith's fascination with my daughter. I found it hard to believe, and as for his accusation that Smith was somehow responsible for her death . . . well, I can tell you, Mr. Gibson, he loved that girl like she was his own—he would never have harmed her. No one knows what happened that day, but so many things changed that I can only come to the conclusion that she was called home for a purpose. Many good things—this place, perhaps—might not have come into being."

"So you didn't believe Henry at all?"

"No. Not until some years later. It took that long for me to realise that Smith hadn't seen what I had the day we both gave our lives to Christ, the day Adam Carney baptised us. I had no idea that his heart hadn't been changed as mine had."

"What did you see?"

Flood ignored the question and continued. "Mr. Smith was still enslaved by his baser desires. It took time, but finally his habits were uncovered."

"What happened?"

"I banished him."

"No, I mean, what did he do?"

"He pursued a young woman who was . . . inappropriate for him."

"That's all?"

"He forced himself upon her."

Gibson nodded. "And for that, all you did was send him away?"

"No, you must understand. He was a part of this family. I trusted him implicitly. I heard his version of events and I almost believed him too, but I sent him away; I banished him from New Eden, for the good of my people, although I wasn't wholly certain, and I told him he could never return. This was the harshest penalty for him for, you see, Mr. Smith never had any kin of his own and for some of us, to belong is all that matters, to be bound by faith, by loyalty, or by blood. But the price we pay for the bond is that even the smallest crimes cause a far greater hurt."

"What are you saying?"

"You know it to be true, I think."

"I'm not sure I know what you're getting at."

"Then why are you here, Mr. Gibson? Why did you come all this way? Are you kin to this boy?"

Gibson shook his head. "Tell me how Smith died, and where," he said, tersely.

"In Melbourne. In a boarding house there. I was called down as his next of kin. There'd been a fire. Two others were also killed."

"You saw the body?"

"I buried the man."

Gibson shook his head again. He couldn't believe it.

"Now, Mr. Gibson, I have duties . . ."

Gibson felt everything slipping away. He wanted to ask him about Billy, but, in the end, Flood was right; it was his own kin—his sister—that had brought him all this way.

"Listen, you preached about heaven just now—that's where you'd all rather be, right?"

"Certainly."

"Yet suicide is a sin?"

"A grave sin."

"What about an unhappy kid, promised all this glory, mightn't they want to take a short cut to it?"

Flood shook his head. "Life must be endured, Mr. Gibson."

"But how're children supposed to know that?"

The eldest of the girls who had seen him by the tree came running in before Flood could answer. She stopped and stared when she saw him. Flood held out his arm to her.

"Mr. Gibson, this is my daughter, Evangeline."

"We've met."

Gibson looked into her wide, luminous, fearless eyes—eyes that had seen nothing else but this valley and its peace—and felt like weeping. He saw the trust she had in her father and he knew then what he'd said was true—Smith was dead.

"You remarried?" he managed to say, pulling himself together.

"Yes."

He stood abruptly after another moment. "I should be going."

"I'm sure we could find you a bed for the night."

"No. I really should be going."

He turned and left the tent but stopped a few yards from it and looked back. Flood stood at the entrance, his arm round his daughter's shoulders.

"Take care of them, Reverend," was all he could think of to say.

"I will, Mr. Gibson. I will."

He followed the moonlit track out of the valley and found his car where he'd left it by the side of the road at about eight o'clock. Out on the highway despair began to creep into his thoughts, blooming like a drop of ink in water, growing and growing until he could almost feel its presence round the car. He'd been wrong about Smith and being wrong was the worst kick in the guts he could remember. Little Flynn *was* lying dead at the bottom of a mineshaft somewhere just as Pop had said and Darcy . . . Darcy would share the same fate as his sister and he was powerless to prevent it.

He hunched down over the wheel and stared at the empty road and its broken white lines of division as they passed beneath him. New Eden to Angel Rock. The two places felt like a pair of lonely ports with nothing in between but a black and empty sea.

He descended into the valley just before dawn and found it blanketed in thick fog. He remembered crossing the harbour bridge as a kid one morning and seeing the whole of the city flooded by the same, nothing clear of it but the arch of the bridge, a few buildings, and everything else drowned under the eerie silver. He glimpsed the dark bulk of the ranges out to the west and then he slid down into the mist.

The car's headlights made little impression down the road and he slowed. In the mirror he could see the fog, stained red, swirling and writhing in the car's wake like a dancer's gown, like a live thing. He wound down the window and hung out his head. Nothing but soft, watery white all about. Even with the sound of the car's engine he could tell that the land around was empty and that he was the only disturbance in it.

He drove on. Sometimes the ghostly limbs of nearby trees loomed out at him and once, overhead, through a gap in the mist, he saw the waxing moon, skimming along, tailing him. After a half-hour he thought he must be nearing the town. The fog began to change. It cast itself into shapes that settled, obstacle-like, across the road before him and across the paddocks on either side of the road. Some looked almost solid, able to cause damage to the steel of the car, and he flinched as he reached them, pierced them, swept through. Others were wispy and spectral and if he saw objects or faces in them he permitted no names to form and attach. He felt he could have been flying the way the shapes came and went like clouds, one after the other, leaving him untouched yet slightly damper. Then, suddenly, there was no more mist, and the land, grey and still, stepped back into the spaces it had occupied. He breathed a sigh of relief and sped up, driving the next few miles thinking only of bed and sleep, imagining the pillow already under his head. He crested a rise and saw the outline of the Rock against the grey dawn sky. He put his foot down and roared down the hill. The road ploughed through a stand of tall gums and then took a sweeping left over another little rise. The car rocked on its springs as it cleared it. He sawed away at the wheel to line up the next little right. When he was halfway through the corner he saw, up ahead, a whole little fleet of tiny, tremulous moons, all a soft amber-rose and all floating a few feet above the ground by the side of the road. It took him a moment to realise what they were and by then he was almost upon them. The kangaroos, a dozen or more, were standing still as totems on the grass verge and some were on the road itself. All their heads were turned in his direction, as if they'd been waiting a long time for someone to appear down the road, maybe for a man named Gibson in particular, their glowing eyes ready to see to the quick of him. He braked, swerved. As the car flashed by he glanced out the left-side window, catching glimpses of curved backs as the creatures bounded away into the darkness. He pictured his own pale face looking out of the roaring metal box of *car* and realised they'd probably been just as startled as he. He looked back to the road, but in the next instant there was a grey shape in the beams that seemed to fill the whole windscreen. Almost simultaneously he blinked, ducked, and swung the car over to the right. He heard a bang as the car's bumper collected a marker post and then he squeezed his eyes shut again as shards of white-painted wood clattered up and over the windscreen and roof. When he opened his eyes a second later the car was still off the road and skittering along in the wet grass and loose gravel at the side of it. The next marker post along flashed by, inches from the corner of the car, its reflector taking the glare from the headlights and blazing it back a seething red. Gently, he steered the car back onto the road and slowed down, until the faded white lines on the road were just gliding by underneath the car, each with a distinct beginning and end. He looked in the mirror but there was nothing behind but an empty road. It had all happened too quickly to curse, or think, and his heart took a long time to wind down and stop pounding against his ribs to be let out.

21

Grace stared up at the curtained window. It was morning but it was still dark in her room and very warm and airless. They'd returned from fishing the evening before and even though the whole time they'd been out there she'd barely thought of the man she'd seen, once back in her room she kept seeing the vivid image of him every time she closed her eyes. His black, staring eyes and his pale, hairless skin. Frustrated, she tried thinking of something good to force the image of him away. She closed her eyes and imagined she was dancing in her best dress with Charlie Perry, that she was kissing him, that he was holding her in his arms. It seemed to work and after a while she rolled over onto her stomach, wriggled around on her mess of bedding until the nubby seam of the blanket was in the right place, then began to slide her hips back and forth against the seam until a tingling warmth began to build and spread. Her brow furrowed and she thought of his hand on her bottom, of him touching her, and then she concentrated instead on the sensations beginning to radiate out and up into her belly, making everything feel delicious, making her breaths puff out faster and faster. She felt the beads of sweat break out on her brow and she thought she might have to bite her tongue to stop herself making a sound, but then a sudden banging noise made her freeze. She lay very still, not breathing, her heart pounding away inside her. It had sounded like a knock, and so loud she thought it had been on her own door. There was nothing else— no call, no following knock—just a distant clang that made the bed tremble beneath her. She hopped up and opened the door and then stood there, breathing hard, listening. More muffled sounds were coming from the station. She walked down the hall and opened the door to the connecting passage.

When she put her head round the doorway the first thing she noticed was her father's back. He was standing just inside the room with the two cells in it, his shoulders heaving as if he'd been working hard, his arm out and resting on one of the bars. He was looking down. He didn't hear her come in and it wasn't until she was by his side and had let out a gasp of amazement that he even realised she was there.

"Who is it?"

"It's Billy. Billy Flood," Pop said, pointing back towards the house, but Grace had already turned on her heel and run.

"Tom!"

"Wha—?"

She shook his shoulder again. "Wake up!"

"What? What is it?"

"Come and look! It's the man I saw. It's the man I saw when we were looking for you. It's Billy Flood."

"Huh?" He sat up on the bed and rubbed his eyes. "Who?"

"Just come and look!"

When he stood up she got behind him and pushed him along the hall to the station. Pop was sitting at his desk inside.

"Just a look," he said, sternly, more to Grace than to him. She pushed him round the corner. At first he couldn't see anything. Even though the sun was up it was very dim inside the cell. All he could see was what looked like a scruffy pile of blankets or clothes, but then, as his eyes adjusted, he saw the man's face. His head was back and his mouth was open and he was snoring loudly.

"It's him," Grace whispered beside him. "He was out at the Steeles'. He climbed through the window into Darcy's room and put on some of her clothes. Look, he's still got her dress wrapped round him there." She pointed. "Pop says he's really really drunk. Said he fought like a Kilkenny cat all the way here."

They looked at him a little longer, at his lank mane of hair, at his yellow teeth, at his waxy skin, and then Pop cleared his throat to get their attention and made a shooing motion with his hand.

When Pop went to have his lunch they slipped back into the station to look at Billy once again.

"Come on," said Grace, urgently. "Pop'll be back in a minute."

They expected him to be asleep still, but when they peered round the door and in through the bars they saw that he was very much awake. They froze, staring, and Billy stared back at them until almost an inch of ash fell down onto his chest from the end of the cigarette he was smoking. They looked at one another and then Grace stepped forward.

"You frightened me!" she blurted out. "Why'd you do that?"

"Didn't mean to."

"What were you doing?"

"Heard those boys was missing. Thought I could help."

"Why didn't you search with everyone else?"

"Do things better on me own."

Tom stepped forward. "Billy," he breathed.

"Yeah?"

"Did you find . . . anything?"

Billy squinted at him through the smoke, but didn't answer.

"Tom's one of them," said Grace. Billy sat up to take a better look.

"My little brother. He's still missing."

"Yeah, I know. Thing is, maybe I know where to look for him."

Tom glanced over at Grace. "You do? Where?"

"Tell us," Grace hissed, "or I'll get Pop!"

Billy looked at each of them in turn and then he shook his head. "No, if he comes, I won't say nothin'."

Tom stared at him, aghast. "Why not?"

"Just won't. Won't tell him."

"You have to!"

"Don't have to do nothing I don't want . . . but . . ."

"But what?"

"I'll show *you* all right." He tapped his forehead, then pointed at Tom. "Right up here it is. Fresh as daisies."

"You'll show me?"

"Don't listen to him, Tom! Pop will make him tell!"

Billy sprang up from the bed and came to the bars and gripped them. Tom and Grace jumped back.

"If you let me out," he said quietly, to Tom, "I'll take you there. Right now. If you don't, I won't tell. I won't ever tell. Not Pop, not no one. I hate being in a cage."

"Don't listen, Tom! Don't listen! Pop will make him tell!" Grace grabbed his arm and began to pull him towards the door. "Let's go!"

Billy glared at her. "You're Darcy's little friend," he said.

"Yes," said Grace, stopping what she was doing and staring up at him.

"Why don't you just go away."

Tom looked at her. He didn't know whether she was about to cry or fly into a rage. He took her hand off his arm and held it, then turned her to him.

"Where are the keys?"

"Tom, no! You can't!"

Billy smiled, and from the gap between his front teeth came a snake of blue smoke, its head wriggling and dissolving a few inches out from his mouth.

"Up on the wall there, kid," he said.

Tom looked. Behind Pop's desk hung a loop of brass with a brace of heavy keys attached to it. He headed over to it.

"Tom!"

"I have to! You heard him. He won't tell Pop."

Grace watched him lift the keys down and return to the bars.

"You promise you'll show me?"

"Yep."

Tom handed in the keys and Billy took them and began to try each one in the lock.

"I'll meet you up under the Rock," he said. "Have to go get me truck first."

"When?"

"'Bout an hour."

A key turned in the lock and Billy pushed on the door and stepped out. Grace backed away and Tom went and stood by the station's front door. Billy paused there on his way out.

"Don't forget, you promised me," said Tom.

"Yep," said Billy.

They watched him walk down the path and then turn right into the street. He didn't look back. They stood for a few moments and then Tom turned to Grace.

"Are you coming?"

"I can't stay here. Pop'll kill me."

"It's all right. I'll tell Pop I did it. He'll understand."

"I'm not sure he will," said Grace, shaking her head, then looking towards the station house. "Quick, we have to go before he comes back."

"I have to get Ham."

Grace rolled her eyes as Tom headed back to the yard. She couldn't stand waiting for him inside the station so she went and stood in the street, glancing nervously around at the few people about. When Tom returned with Ham in the crook of his arm they set off.

They made for the cemetery and walked up through it and then followed the old sliprail fence that separated the bush from the paddocks. After a few hundred yards they jumped the fence and slipped in under the trees. When they reached the tumble of rocks at the base of the Rock they stopped to catch their breath.

"Do you think he meant here?"

"Must have," Grace panted.

They waited there for an hour and then for another but still Billy did not appear. Tom had a sick feeling in his stomach and when he looked at Grace he could tell that she did too.

"He's not coming," she said, finally, and he didn't argue with her. She stood and started walking back towards town. He stood too, but stopped to listen one last time. There was nothing but the wind in the trees overhead and the chattering of a small bird close by. Nothing else. He followed Grace at a distance for a while, then stopped again and looked around. Nothing behind him. Nothing up the slope either. He picked up Ham and put him in the crook of his arm, continuing along behind Grace, but every so often the sensation that something was following, ghosting along through the trees above and to his right, returned, and he would stop and listen and stare off into the puzzle of green, brown and grey.

When he heard something rustling through the undergrowth up

ahead he stopped. A red-bellied black snake slithered out across the path and then disappeared into the grass on the other side. He put Ham down to sniff the track of the snake and then he closed his eyes and listened. He could almost feel the spin of the world beneath him. He threw out his arms for balance, dizzy, and then his arms went cold and his hairs pricked as something brushed by him. He opened his eyes and spun around but there was nothing there. He shook his head. Grace was calling him. He could hear the annoyance in her voice and his heart sank as he caught up.

When they reached the cemetery they looked down at the town and then at each other.

"We have to go and tell Pop what we did," said Grace.

"I did it, not you."

"He's going to kill me anyway."

"I'll say you were somewhere else."

"He'll know you're lying. He's a policeman, remember? He'll just know."

Tom nodded. He felt empty inside and unable to think straight. He waited for Grace to make a move so he could follow.

"I can't face him just yet," she said, her face pale.

"What do you want to do?" he asked, a little surprised.

"I know somewhere. We can get a drink. Aren't you thirsty?"

"Yeah, I am."

Tom followed her along the cemetery fence. They skirted the town before cutting through a back lane to Springline Road. They stayed on the road for half a mile and then crawled under the barbed-wire fence at its side. He followed her in through the trees until they came to the creek. Grace went to the edge and drank. She sat down and wiped her mouth with her arm and began to pick up small stones from the ground to throw into the water. Tom stood in the shade for a moment and listened to the water tumbling over the rocks and the soft rustle of the trees overhead. Ferns dipped gently in the breeze and dappled sunlight fell across the little clearing they were in. By a tree was a little collection of boards and a circle of river rocks and as he went and drank at the creek himself he wondered who had put them there and for what purpose.

They sat for what seemed like another hour, Grace throwing stones ever more forcefully into the creek. A cloud came over and plunged everything into gloomy shadow and it began to look like it might rain. Tom edged over to where Grace was, very slowly, until he was only a few feet away, but even then she didn't acknowledge him or look up.

"Did you . . . did you and Darcy used to come here?" he stuttered, waving his hand at the boards. "Was that your cubby?"

She looked up and glared at him.

"*Yes.*"

She stood and took a few steps away and then, before he could say anything else, she stopped and turned on him.

"I bloody *wish* you hadn't let him out!" she shouted, her voice fierce. "I bloody well wish you hadn't!"

She turned round and ran. A little stunned, Tom hesitated for a moment before following. He didn't want this. He didn't want *her* to be angry with him as well. He needed her, needed someone beside him, and the sight of her disappearing away through the trees made him feel even sicker, even emptier than he had before. His vision became blurred by tears and he stopped and dropped to his knees. His gut wrenched and the water he'd drunk earlier and what was left of his breakfast came up and out of him, bitter and hot. He retched and retched until there was nothing left and when it was finally over he sensed her near him. He was too ashamed to look up.

"What's the matter?" she asked him. She still sounded angry.

"I don't know."

She pulled him up by the arm and helped him over to the water.

"Drink," she said, and he did.

She waited for him to feel a little better and then she put her hand on his shoulder.

"Come on," she said, firmly, but in a gentler tone. "We have to go back now. We really have to."

He nodded.

He followed her for ten minutes or so through the trees and then he saw something move up ahead of them and off to the right. At first he thought it was Billy crouching there but when he was a few steps closer he saw it wasn't him at all.

"Grace," he whispered.

"What?"

"*Stop.*"

"What is it now?" she snapped, turning round.

Leper, one of Sonny Steele's dogs, was standing in the long grass on the other side of the creek. He was a big dog; a mostly black mongrel with heavily muscled shoulders and a square head. He looked as if he had been put together using only the meanest parts of half a dozen other dogs. As Tom watched, Leper's ears pricked up and then flattened against the top of his head and his tongue came out and did a circuit of his snout.

"Just keep walking, slowly," he whispered to Grace.

Tom thought she seemed quite calm really, for someone who was supposed to be afraid of dogs, but then she began to back away, tripping over bushes and tussocks of grass as she went. Tom tried to follow her but then Leper saw Ham, who hadn't seen or smelt the bigger dog yet, and crossed the creek. Tom, his heart thumping madly in his chest, opened his mouth and screamed out a warning.

"*Ham!*"

He imagined, in a flash, Leper swallowing the little dog whole, like a giant bean. He saw himself cutting open Leper's belly just in time, giving Ham a second bloody birth. Then he realised that he had no knife, and that Leper wouldn't swallow Ham whole, but would crush him instead between those awful jaws.

Ham saw or sensed Leper coming and yelped like he'd been kicked. There was a clump of lantana bush nearby and he headed straight into it. As the big dog came past after him Tom threw himself across his back, digging his fingers into his coat to try and halt him. He flailed his arms, felt the dog's domed skull under the loose skin of his head, but then Leper shook himself free of Tom's grip and turned, momentarily, to see what had had the nerve to get in his way. Growling, the dog looked down at Tom sprawled on the ground. Tom smelt his wet fur, his hot, meaty breath, heard his breath hissing through the narrow races of his nostrils, and then the dog lifted his head and leapt off after Ham. Tom pulled himself up. He could just see Ham wriggling away through the maze of lantana, but he could also see that the big dog was intent on forcing his way in behind him.

"Grace! Help!" he yelled, but Grace had put her head down and her arms round her ears. She didn't even look up.

He looked around. The only weapons he could see were the stones in the creekbed. He went and picked one up—his legs shaking—and carried it over to where Leper was thrusting his head and shoulders into the undergrowth. He was very close to Ham but had been slowed by the lantana and seemed unable to move forward any further. Ham crouched only a foot or so away from Leper's jaws and was so still that Tom, for a moment, thought he was already dead.

"No, you don't, bastard!" he yelled. He lifted up the rock and brought it down as hard as he could upon Leper's back. The dog yelped, although after that there seemed to be no other effect, as if he were dealing with a dog with workings of cog and pulley rather than flesh and bone, but then he began to growl and pull himself free of the lantana. Tom knew he was angry and he knew there was only a little time—and maybe one chance. He went and picked up another rock from the creek and threw it at the dog just as he was about to wriggle free. Leper's back legs buckled, then straightened out again. He turned himself round, struggled to his feet, walked away with his back legs stiff and swinging from side to side. Tom followed him. He picked up the heavier rock he'd thrown first and hoisted it once more at the growling, snarling dog. The rock landed a glancing blow on the dog's head and stunned him into silence. He stood for a moment, licking his chops, his back legs trembling. Tom picked up the rock again and threw it as the dog tried to escape through the grass, dragging his back legs behind him. When he stopped for a moment Tom took the opportunity to get closer and take more careful aim. He lifted the rock and brought it down across the top of the dog's head with all his strength. He heard a wet crack. He picked up the rock and threw it again. This time the rock's sharper edge opened a vein in the dog's head and blood scythed out across the bank. Tom lifted the rock, brought it down, again and again, until the dog's fur was soaked with his own blood and there was blood on Tom's own arms and legs. Finally, breathing hard, he stopped and let the rock fall from his hands. Leper twisted over onto his back, his jaws working soundlessly, and showed him his belly as if begging for a scratch. Then he went still. A bow of yellow piss shot up and his legs kicked out. A shit came churning out of his arse and fell into the grass.

Tom stared down at the dog's body and prodded it with his foot. The rock had flayed off a flap of skin near the muzzle and Leper looked as though he was grinning. Tom turned away and went over to Grace.

"Grace," he said. "It's all right now. It's dead. I killed it."

Grace lifted her head, slowly, until she could see the body of the dog.

"See?"

"Yeah," she whispered. "I see."

He left her and went back to where he'd last seen Ham. On hands and knees he fished around in the lantana until he had hold of his back legs and could pull him free. The little dog was trembling violently and he could feel no pause at all between the beats of his heart. He stood, cradling him like a baby, and walked back to Grace.

"He's all right. Ham's all right."

"Good. That's good."

He put Ham down and went to the creek and washed the blood off his hands and arms. Ham sniffed Leper's still body from the tip of his tail to his wet nose. Tom finished washing and then helped Grace to her feet.

"Come on," he said. "We should go. Sonny might come."

"Yeah. Okay."

22

There was soft rain falling in the courtyard when Gibson shuffled past on his way down to the showers. He looked at his watch. It was just after three o'clock. He'd slept most of the day away, but his head still screamed to be horizontal, and cushioned. He yawned and looked at himself in the mirror. He thought he looked about five years older than the last time he'd inspected himself. He shook his head, picked up his brush and shaving soap, and began to build up some lather. When he had a good amount on the end of the brush he lifted his hand up, but then he stopped, staring at the whiskery Gibson before him. It was a minute or so before he blinked and realised he'd come to a standstill, stalled. He shook his head again. He shaved and rinsed his face then slapped after-shave onto his raw skin, the evaporating alcohol making him sneeze.

He walked into town and when he reached the main street he saw Pop sitting on the police station's front step smoking a cigarette, a grim look about him. He crossed the street and walked up the path. When he reached Pop he saw, inside the station, Grace and Tom sitting with their backs to the wall on two wooden chairs. They glanced up when they noticed him and he saw their shoulders move as each let go of the other's hand. Grace looked back down at the floor. Tom looked out at him with a clear, steady gaze, and only after quite a time did he look away, as if he had seen quite enough and all he needed.

"Gibson," said Pop. "Thought I'd seen the last of you."

"Nope. Still here."

He gestured to Pop's office. "Your prisoners don't look too happy in there."

Pop didn't look round. "They're not in my good books."

"Why, what happened?"

"Billy Flood turned up out at Ezra's early this morning. Drunk. I had him in a cell out back to sleep it off. These two," he said, jabbing his thumb over his shoulder, *"let him out."*

Gibson looked up at them. Grace looked away, shamefaced. Tom inspected his hands. Gibson let out a long, incredulous whistle as Pop continued.

"He told young Tom he'd show him where to find Flynn. Said he wouldn't tell anyone if he wasn't let out. I don't doubt Billy's learnt some cunning in his time, but if these two learn nothing from this they'll sure remember how hard those chairs were."

Gibson almost smiled. "How long they been there?"

"Couple of hours."

"You're a hard man, Sarge," Gibson joked weakly.

Pop gave him a look. "No, I'm not. I've just never been quite so angry in my life. I think they're getting off pretty light."

Gibson nodded. "You've had a look for him?"

"No point. He'll have headed for the bush."

Gibson went and sat down beside him. "Borrow a smoke?" he said.

"Here," said Pop, handing him the tin. "Help yourself."

They watched cars pass in the street as the day began to wind down. Every so often someone would see Pop sitting there and wave or raise their hand and Pop would give a slight nod in return. Gibson smoked and watched and thought.

"You look tuckered out, Gibson," said Pop, after a while. "You hungry?"

"No, not really."

"I am. Getting close to feeding time. You won't join us? These two won't be eating tonight."

"No. Thanks anyway."

The lowering sun caught the webs of spiders in the trees across the street and gilded them. It lit up tiny insects in the evening air as they described arcs and things unknown. The belly of a passing cloud turned shades of red, orange, and purple and then the streetlight elements flickered on inside their glass cases. A magpie atop the metal-capped power pole began to sing evensong to its fellows across the valley and a band of grubby kids came tearing out of a lane. Girls with a hopscotch panel at their feet threw stones onto the footpath and watched each other's turn, oblivious to all else.

"This is a good place, isn't it," said Gibson.

"It's as good a place as any."

"Think you'll ever leave?"

"Nope. What? Thinking of moving here?"

Gibson shook his head. "No. I don't think I'd fit in somehow."

Pop nodded and looked intently at Gibson for a time.

"What's the matter, son? What's happened? All the fight seems to have gone out of you."

"I went out to see if I could find Smith," said Gibson, after a long pause.

"And?"

"He's dead. Horace Flood told me that."

"Oh. I see."

"You know, I came up here because I thought if I could find out why Darcy did what she did it would help me understand why my own sister did the same. Then I thought I'd found some kind of reason why somebody would want to take young Flynn. I thought it was Ezra Steele at first, but not even Henry agreed. I thought if he was capable of that, maybe he was capable of . . . anything."

"You're talking about Darcy."

"Course I am, but I've ended up with nothing."

"That's hardly a sin, Gibson," said Pop, putting his hand on his shoulder briefly. "You saw some hope and chased after it."

"Yeah."

"Look at Billy. Look at what he went and did this morning. Maybe he saw the same thing in Darcy that you did. We're only human. We see the things we want to see."

"Yeah, maybe. But when I found her down there I thought I'd walked into the one place in the world I was needed most. You know? Now why did I think that? Why?"

"Why? You mean why *you*? Why here? You're talking about designs beyond our understanding."

"And you're talking about God again."

"Maybe I am, but you're asking for a reason and that's all I can come up with."

"But it's not so much to ask, is it? To know why? To have a little peace?"

"No, of course it's not. But you've tried, Gibson, what else can you do? I'm sorry about your sister, but maybe for some questions there are no answers. Maybe . . ."

"What?"

"Maybe you've been looking in the wrong place altogether."

"Where do you think I should be looking then?"

"I don't think you've even set foot there."

"Where?"

"The country of the mind, Gibson," said Pop, catching his eye. "The country of the self."

Gibson shook his head and tried to give Pop a dirty look but his heart wasn't in it.

"I'd just get lost," he said.

Pop smiled. "Oh, I don't know. I really don't. But look, one day, young Tom will remember what happened when he was lost. I know it. Maybe the same will happen for you."

Gibson nodded and watched the girls play hopscotch until Pop spoke again.

"What will you do now?" he asked, softly.

"Go home."

"Good. It's the best place to be."

They sat for a while longer and then Pop nudged him, indicating a man coming up the street. He was very tall, his limbs ponderous, his shoulders round and his back beginning to bend forward in a hump. He walked with a long but very slow, almost stiff-legged stride. Ezra Steele.

When Steele saw them he stopped in his tracks and stared. Gibson stared back until the big man turned away, blank-faced, and walked to his car. They watched him as he pulled out and drove away, his head not deviating to the left or right.

"Now there goes a man with something on his chest, Gibson," said Pop. "One day I'll find out what it is, and believe me when I tell you, although I lack a saint's temperament, I have the patience of the best of them."

23

An hour or so after he'd finished breakfast Tom wandered down to the convent with Ham and sat on the jetty with his legs dangling down over the river. The day was hot and muggy and barely a soul was to be seen out in it. After he'd been sitting there for a while he heard a rapping knock behind him and he turned and looked back over his shoulder. Up through the trees he could see Pop Mather standing before the convent's side door. The man who'd come to the station house the day before eventually appeared to answer it. Pop spoke to him for a while and then left. Tom turned back to the river.

A little later he heard a car roar into life behind him and whine its way in reverse back up the long convent drive. Curious, he stood and dusted off his hands and walked towards the convent building. The man had left the door open. Tom went and peered inside. He looked around behind him at the empty garden before stepping into the cool interior, Ham at his heels. It was quiet and peaceful inside the convent but Tom found nothing of interest until he wandered into the kitchen and found Gibson's photographs spread out on the table like an unfinished hand of patience.

He recognised Darcy Steele amid the photographs and a vein began to throb in his temple. He put out his hand, wavered for a few moments before picking one up. He looked at it for a second and then slipped it into his top pocket and headed for the door. He went back and sat down on the jetty and looked at the photograph in the bright sunlight. There was something sad and beautiful about the picture and its effect was a little mesmerising. He had just begun to entertain the thought of going back inside and getting another when he heard his name being called. He peered back through the foliage and saw Grace, with Ham in her arms, wandering down to where he was. He swore softly and stuffed the picture back into his pocket and with cheeks suddenly afire he went up to meet her.

"Tom," she said, when she saw him, "Pop wants you."

"How'd you know I was here?"

"I thought you might have come to see Mr. Gibson."

Tom nodded. "What's he want me for?"

"How should I know?"

"Does he want to send me back to Henry?"

"Don't you want to go?"

"Not without my mum."

"He said you could stay as long as you wanted," said Grace, her tone softening.

Tom turned and headed back to the jetty.

"Aren't you coming?"

"In a while. Not yet."

Instead of leaving as he half wanted her to do she came and sat down beside him.

"I'm sorry about yesterday," he said.

"Wasn't your fault."

"Do you think . . . do you think they've found Leper yet?"

"I don't know," said Grace, her voice miserable. "Maybe."

"Maybe we should go and bury him."

Grace didn't answer.

"He wasn't a bad dog really. I saw him once with Darcy. He'd do anything she said. Anything."

Grace still said nothing.

"I know Darcy was your friend," he said, tentatively. "I'm sorry about what happened. I'm sorry she died."

Grace shrugged.

"You think about her a lot?"

"Yeah, of course," she answered, testily, "but I don't really want to talk about her, all right? *You* should understand that."

"Yeah," said Tom, nodding, "I do."

◇☯◇☯◇

They sat for a while and then Tom heard a bar of harmonica music come floating down on the breeze. He shook his head and it faded away to nothing, but then, minutes later, he heard it again, coming from somewhere not too far away in brief, airy snatches. He ignored it for as long as he could and then he gritted his teeth and looked at Grace.

"Can you hear that?"

"Yes," she answered, nodding her head.

"It's a harmonica."

When they heard it again they thought it might be coming from the convent behind them, but the next time it came to them they decided that its source was further away still. They walked downstream a little until a fence stopped them. Here the music was stronger. They crawled under the wire of the fence and crossed a paddock, then another with a little pony in it. The pony came over and sniffed at Ham's track.

"I used to come down here with Darcy sometimes," Grace whispered. "There's a house further along. It's where the ferrymaster lives."

Tom nodded and they continued on. They followed an old path that wound down through lantana and cockspur and huge thickets of blackberry and then they came to a sun-filled clearing. In amongst the long grass they saw the bleached and scattered bones of half a dozen or more long-dead cattle.

"It's spooky," whispered Grace.

It was also very quiet and they realised that they couldn't hear the music any more. Neither of them could say whether it had faded away or just stopped.

"Which way's the house?" asked Tom.

"This way, I think."

They started off, but just before they left the clearing they spotted a tawny little kitten, its eyes only just open, taking a few trembling steps out from a jumble of bones. Ham went and licked it and the kitten opened its mouth wide and gave a high-pitched meow.

"Come on, its mother must be around," said Grace, nervously. "You shouldn't get between a cat and its kittens."

Tom picked up Ham and they walked on until they could just see the house through the bushes. It was half covered in creeping vines and shielded by a clump of tall tobacco bushes and some of its windows were boarded over. They crossed the open ground just before it and then went up the steps to the front door. Tom knocked.

"Anybody home?" he called, but there was no answer. They went back down the steps and walked down the side of the house and round the back. Billy Flood was sitting there cross-legged and barefoot before the ashes of a small fire. He had a handful of twigs and leaves in his hand. As they watched he put them to the ashes and blew on them, as if he were the very discoverer of fire and they were at the beginning of history. The fire flared into life and they watched him place more fuel quickly and expertly around the flames, and then, although they'd made no sound, had barely breathed, Billy suddenly looked up to where they were, his eyes dark in the shadow of the old hat he wore. He stood. Grace jumped.

He was wearing a black dinner jacket in fair condition and trousers to match. In the buttonhole of the jacket was a flower, dried and brown, as if he'd recently been a guest at a very long wedding. It was a rose, as frail as old paper and closed, but the petals' leading edges were still pouting, shaping to kiss. A loop of frayed twine was slung diagonally across his chest and from it, at his waist, hung a battered little sack. Slowly and deliberately he pulled from the sack a pipe and a round tin. He filled the pipe bowl with tobacco from the tin, tamping it down with the long nail of his forefinger, then he bent over the fire, pulled out a burning twig, and carefully lit the pipe. He puffed away until it was well alight, looking unconcernedly at Tom and Grace through blue wreaths of smoke.

Tom put Ham down on the ground and went and stood across the fire from Billy.

"Why didn't you meet us where you said?" he demanded.

Billy shrugged, but he looked almost repentant.

"We got into a heap of trouble."

The information made no impression. Billy lifted a billy of water out of the grass and set it in the fire.

"Does the ferrymaster know you're here?"

"Course. He always helps me out. Gave me these strides," said Billy, pointing to his pants, "and this here doodie."

He tapped the pipe with his finger and grinned a gappy grin. He looked more comical than anything else and Tom had to bite his lip to stop from laughing out loud.

"This what?" he asked, stepping forward.

"This pipe here. This here doodie."

They stared at each other and Billy blinked smoke out of his eyes as he puffed on the pipe. Tom thought he could see a whole raft of sadness in him. Despite his silly grin it was plain to see, and he wondered whether people saw the same in him.

"Was that you making the music?"

"Maybe."

Tom chewed his lip and gave Billy a hard stare. Billy couldn't match it and he hung his head.

"Billy, if you won't *show* me where to look, can't you just *tell* me?"

Billy considered his request for a few moments and then answered.

"I can tell you that."

Tom waited impatiently but Billy said nothing. "Well, where?" he said finally, exasperated.

Billy's forehead creased and he looked down at the fire and threw on a few more sticks.

"Near a big stand of yellow box. Hard to get to."

"Show me. Draw a map in the dirt."

"Nuh, too hard. Too many turns and so forth."

"Show me, then," said Tom, his desperation growing.

"Can't. Haven't got enough fuel. Got no money for it."

"I'll get you money."

Billy peered at him through the smoke, his eyes narrowing. "Got some money, I'll take you," he said.

"Is it far?"

"It's a good way. I got a truck."

"Let's go, then," said Tom.

"Now? What about me tea?"

"Can't you drink it later?"

Billy grumbled for a while and then decided that yes, he could. He picked up his boots and started pulling them on. Grace came and stood next to Tom.

"You don't have to come," he whispered to her.

"You're not going by yourself!" she hissed back.

"He won't hurt me, if that's what you think."

"How do you know?"

Tom shrugged. "I think he's probably safer than a dog." Grace shot him a look.

Billy set off. "Follow," he said.

They headed down to the edge of the wrecker's yard where cars whose panels no one needed any more stood like deserted islets amid the weeds. Billy's truck was parked between two rust-ravaged saloons. Billy climbed up into the cab and Grace and Tom followed him. Inside there was a newly tanned kangaroo skin covering a gaping hole in the seat's upholstery and Grace screwed her nose up at the smell. Billy bent down to the gutted dash and poked about amidst the hanging wires until he found the two he was looking for. He muttered spells and incantations and prayers to the patron saint of internal combustion and then brought the two wires together. After a few anxious moments when the engine sounded like it would rather die than start, the truck belched and blatted into life. Billy cackled with laughter and Tom and Grace looked at each other and then Grace shook her head in disbelief.

They roared down through the ranks of dead cars and up to the gate that opened onto Springline Road. The yard owner was nowhere to be seen but Tom didn't care about the reason why. They drove into town and pulled up near Mrs. Coop's shop. Tom jumped down and ran to the station house and into his room. Relatives, people he'd never met, had sent him money through the post when he'd been found. Pop said he should put it in the bank but he hadn't yet. There was a lot. Bright-orange twenties and sea-blue tens. He thought two of each would be enough. It seemed like enough for a man to drive clear to Sydney. He ran back outside without seeing Pop. Grace was looking worriedly out through the window. He swung up and shuffled past her.

"Here," he said, brandishing the notes. "Let's go."

Billy took the money, then stared at it in his hand as if it might disappear at any moment.

"Sweet," he said, when it didn't.

They headed out to the crossing and then up the road to Jack's Mountain. Tom watched everything intently while Grace fiddled nervously with the quarter-glass window. Soon they were in the township and there they stopped outside the little general store. Two petrol bowsers were set into the footpath before it.

"Better duck down," Billy whispered. "Folks always think I'm up to no good."

They bent down and stared at the filthy floor of the truck while the shopkeeper came and filled up the tank. Billy went inside and paid for the fuel and when he came back he handed Tom a handful of notes and coins and looked at him almost bashfully.

"Got some more baccy," he said, as they drove off. "That all right?"

"Yeah. Fine. You keep it."

"You sure?"

"Yep."

While Billy drove he pulled his pipe from his pocket and managed to pack and light it with one hand and sometimes with both, steering with his elbows resting on the big wooden steering wheel. They came to a series of creek fords and Billy went roaring through them, the white arches of water finding their way up through ragged holes in the cab floor and wetting Tom's feet. With all his senses alert and heightened, Tom felt like he was back in the truck with Flynn and Henry.

"This is the way? Really?" he asked, a little breathless.

"Yeah," answered Billy, suddenly serious. "This is the way."

"But it's the wrong way. It's the *opposite* direction to where we wanted to go."

Billy could only shrug his shoulders. They drove for what seemed like an hour and then Billy pulled the truck off the road and killed the engine.

"Round here . . . somewheres."

"We have to walk now?"

"Yeah."

They hopped down from the truck and slammed the doors shut behind them. Tom put Ham down on the grass and he promptly went and cocked his leg against the front wheel of the truck and pissed on it.

They walked in under some trees, Billy looking up and around as they went, and then they came to a gate locked with an old and rusty padlock. They clambered over and when Tom took Grace's hand to help her down and she didn't let it go afterwards his heart just about grew wings and flew away. Beyond the gate was an empty paddock, and at the edge of it Tom saw water twinkling in the sun.

"There," said Billy, quietly. "The bees were over there, and I found you"—he pointed with his finger and chin—"there."

He was pointing to a little bank under some trees. Grace let go of Tom's hand as they walked over to it but he didn't even notice. He was looking down at the ground to see if there was some trace of him or Flynn, some evidence, but he could see nothing.

"Are you sure it was here?"

"Yes. Sure as sure."

Tom walked from the bank to the edge of the creek—about a dozen yards. He could feel Grace's eyes on him, and Billy's. The creek was narrow, deep and fast-flowing. He put his hand in the water, looked at the light dancing on the surface. He put his other hand up to the scar on his forehead and rubbed at it.

"What is it, Tom? Are you remembering?"

Tom looked at her and shook his head. The memory was as mysterious as an underground stream, as black and snakelike, headless and tailless; a black echo of lightning deep deep down inside the earth—inside him—but unreachable.

"Maybe," said Billy, demonstrating, "you came running down here, and then you *whacked* your head against one of those branches yonder."

Tom looked, and began walking up and down the bank, staring at the ground, staring at the branches. Grace followed him and Billy went and leant against a tree to pack his pipe.

"Why was I running?" he asked, but neither Grace nor Billy could answer him.

They looked around for another half-hour but all they found were the remains of an old campfire a few hundred yards away. Tom looked down at the blackened circle and turned over pieces of charcoal with his toe.

"What is it?" asked Grace.

"I don't know. I don't know. I feel a bit . . . sick." Tom looked back to the creek. "Maybe he drowned. Maybe he drowned here."

Grace took his hand in hers. "We'll come back with Pop," she whispered to him. Tom nodded and together they walked back to Billy.

"It's not a bad place this," said Billy, when they reached him. "There's good honey from them trees. The best."

Tom looked up.

"Should see the sun on 'em in the morning. Beautiful. But down there, along by this creek, lots of old shafts with rotten lids. Big fat seam of gold running under the hill. All gone now, though."

He looked back at them and noticed their long faces. He knocked out his pipe against the trunk of the tree he stood by and cleared his throat.

"Back to town then?"

Grace nodded, but Billy made no move to leave. Instead, he looked intently at Tom's face. Grace grew nervous, but then he reached deep into his jacket pocket, pulled something out and handed it across to Tom.

"I . . . found this," he said, a little sheepishly, "on the ground here. You know it?"

Tom took the harmonica from Billy's outstretched hand and held it up to the light. He turned it round and read the words inscribed in the metal.

The Miniature Boomerang, they said. *Albert's System. Tangent Tempered Reeds.*

24

Gibson was sitting at the convent kitchen's long dining table, shuffling through photographs, off in his own little world, when there came a sudden knock at the side door. Startled, he jumped up to answer it. Pop Mather was there, with a dark look on his face.

"What is it?"

"I've just had a phone call."

"Oh?"

"Not good news. It was Erskine. They've been trying to get hold of you. Your mother . . . your mother passed away yesterday morning."

The words didn't surprise Gibson—he'd imagined them enough times during the last few years—but he still felt the blow land somewhere deep within him, and almost heard the cold, hollow clang of it.

"Oh. Thanks for coming down. Thanks for . . . letting me know."

"Can I do anything? If you need to ring anyone . . . relatives?"

"No, no, there's no one else. Thanks. It's all right. It's something I've been expecting. Thanks for coming to tell me."

"I'm sorry," Pop said. "Come up to the house if you want. Use the phone."

"Yeah, maybe I will. Thanks."

After Pop had gone Gibson went and stood under the shower for a long time. He tried to remember a prayer, any prayer, from his childhood, but the only words that came to him were from his father's funeral: *Earth to earth, ashes to ashes, dust to dust; in sure and certain hope of the Resurrection unto eternal life,* so he said them over and over while the steam billowed up around him.

When he finished he went into his room and pulled the .38 from his bag and just stared at it for a long time, finally tucking it under the mattress like a dirty magazine. He went and dressed himself in his cleanest clothes and drove up to the hotel. At the bar he ordered a whisky and a beer and when he'd drunk them he ordered another pair. He sat there and lost track of the time and when his head was buzzing and his nose was numb he left the hotel and headed out to the Steeles'.

He liked the sound the gravel made under his shoes; the *crunch, crunch, crunch.* It felt like you were really getting somewhere when your shoes made a sound like that. He lit a cigarette and after another five minutes of crunching he rounded a bend and eased up. A ute was parked on the grass verge, its headlights wide-eyed and glassy. On the grass he saw a roll of barbed wire and some sort of tool for tightening the strands once on the fence. A tethered dog in the bed of the ute began to bark at him as he neared and as it did so a figure appeared from the far side of the utility. Head, then shoulders, then torso, like a man climbing out of a trapdoor. John Steele. Sonny to everyone but his mother.

The boy took a last look at him when he was a dozen yards away and then he picked up a piece of rag and began to wipe his hands on it. Gibson raised his hand in greeting. He didn't feel drunk at all any more.

"Afternoon."

"Afternoon."

Gibson pointed to the few head of cattle grazing just beyond the fence. They were black and dark brown and their coats were glossy and slick in the rain and they looked in prime condition.

"They yours, then?"

"Yep."

"It's good country around here, isn't it."

"It's fair."

Gibson nodded.

"Thought I might try and climb the Rock later. Must be a good view from the top. Must be able to see a good long way."

Sonny shrugged. The dog whined and pulled at its chain and panted, the pink mat of its tongue racing in and out between the white spires of its canines, a ridge of serrated teeth sprouting from the red-and-black skin of its gums behind them. Gibson looked at Sonny's hand and saw that he'd cut it and was stanching the blood with the rag, not wiping his hands as he'd first thought.

"You all right there?"

"Yeah. It's not deep."

"The wire get you?"

"Yeah."

Gibson nodded. "What's your dog's name?"

"Blackie."

"Vicious-looking sod. Doesn't seem to like me too much."

"He doesn't like your perfume. He doesn't like sissy smells."

Gibson almost laughed. As he continued up the road he felt Sonny's eyes boring into his back.

"Watch out," the boy called to him, a hint of waggery in his voice. "Other dog slipped its lead. He's round here some place. You wouldn't want to run into *him* smellin' like that."

Gibson nodded, raised his hand, and kept going for another ten minutes until the farmhouse appeared on his right. He walked up to it and was about to knock on the jamb of the open door when he saw Ezra sitting just inside it. Steele nodded, but when he went to take a seat the farmer growled at him.

"Don't sit, you're not staying."

"Ma!" yelled Sonny, who'd appeared at the door behind him. "Cut me hand!"

Ezra looked up at his son. "You finished that job yet?"

"No," said Sonny, his face glum.

Fay Steele, wringing her hands in the dirty pinafore she wore, appeared from the kitchen.

"Mother, would you get a bandage? Some antiseptic?"

"Methylated spirit?"

Ezra looked at Gibson and smirked.

"That would smart a little, wouldn't it, Gibson? But it'd get out the poisons right enough."

He turned to his wife. "No, not the metho. Something else. Go with her, son."

Sonny glowered at Gibson and then he followed his mother into the darkened rear of the house.

"Your cattle . . . are they for milk or meat?" Ezra looked up at him as if he was simple. "Only I had a steak the other night. Bought it from the butcher in town. Wondered if it was one of yours."

"My father had milkers. I run beef. Any fool can tell the difference."

"Ah, well, not the first time someone's called me that."

"What do you want, Gibson? You don't want to be wasting my time with boneheaded questions."

"No. Suppose I don't. Can I ask you something?"

"What about?"

Fay Steele returned with a little brown bottle of Mercurochrome in one hand and Sonny in the other. Ezra, his eyes flashing, dismissed them both with a jab of his chin and then began to push himself up out of his chair. Gibson could tell it wasn't to embrace him.

"Did she ever tell you about someone watching her?" he asked, backing away towards the door. Ezra looked up at him, blinking like an owl.

"When? When did she first tell you?"

Ezra shook his head dismissively, but then he slid back down into his chair, somewhat paler than before, and rubbed his grey-whiskered chin.

"She always had an imagination," he said, without much conviction. "She was always making things up."

"Did she know where she came from, Mr. Steele? Did she know she wasn't yours?"

Fay Steele came barrelling back into the room. Ezra's mouth clamped shut. She went and stood by her husband's shoulder and put her hand on the top of the armchair. There was something in her eyes that he hadn't seen before—a determination—that was both unexpected and touching. He knew she'd overheard his question.

"Go now, Mr. Gibson," she said. "I think we've had enough upset."

Gibson nodded. "Yes, you're right," he said, as he stepped back through the doorway. Sonny appeared in the hallway.

"What about you, son? Don't you owe your sister something?"

Sonny didn't answer him but lifted the rifle he was holding and aimed it at Gibson's chest.

"All right," Gibson muttered. "I'm leaving."

He walked down to the road with the three of them watching behind him. His head began to throb and he knew tears were close to the surface and once they came he wouldn't be able to stop them. He almost ran back to the hotel and there he drank some more and when he was feeling better he called Hughie over and asked him some questions.

"White?" asked Hughie, in response to his slurred query. "Or black?"

Gibson half shook his head, puzzled for a moment before understanding.

"Ah, white, I s'pose. Shit."

Hughie nodded and gave him directions to a house in Laurence. It didn't take long to drive there, despite the car weaving all over the road, and despite his unreliable vision. The house was in a wide street and there was no one about. Cheap weatherboard houses. He found the number he was after and knocked on the door. A young woman answered and peered out at him through the flyscreen. He wondered how things were done.

"I'm looking for someone," he muttered. "A friend."

"A friend?"

"Yes. A *lady* friend. The publican, at the hotel, said I could . . ."

"Oh."

Gibson thought for a moment that he'd been made the subject of a practical joke and cursed himself for a fool for stumbling into it so blindly. He could see them all laughing in the bar, or maybe they were behind him now, sniggering. He turned. They were not. He turned back. The young woman was holding open the door and motioning him inside. He walked in. An older woman was sitting at the kitchen table smoking a cigarette, one leg crossed over the other, her hair a masterpiece of peaks and valleys the like of which he hadn't seen in years. He nodded to her and she nodded back and then she held out her hand for his money as if it had been owing for years.

"How much?"

She told him. "And nothin' silly," she added, with a dry smile, showing her big yellow teeth. "That's my go."

He handed over the notes and the woman folded them and made a show of tucking them into the front of her bra as if she'd seen it in a movie once. She gestured to the room the girl had gone into and he went ahead. When he opened the door she was in front of the dressing-table mirror brushing her hair. He stood for a moment and watched her. She looked at him out of the corner of her eye and then picked up an old-fashioned atomiser from the table and puffed perfume out onto her neck. She did it stiffly, as though the other woman had coached her, before turning very slowly to face him. He took a good look at her and wondered at this strange commerce and why it was that the coloured paper in his pocket should give him access to her bed, her body. She was younger than he'd first thought—plump, blameless—and growing more and more uncomfortable before his gaze. He felt sadder than he could ever remember, a little desperate, very drunk. He knew it wouldn't help but he couldn't stop himself.

"Please," he said. "Stand there. Take off your clothes."

Her slippered feet whispered over the linoleum and then stopped on a fluffy pink mat at the foot of the bed. She took the chewing gum from her mouth, set it on the metal end of the bed frame, undressed, then stood by the bed with her hands over her crotch, suddenly bashful. A vein pulsed in her neck. He knelt before her and put his arms round her naked body and pressed his cheek against her soft belly for a long time, just running his hands up and down her back and trying not to care about anything else.

25

The drive back to town passed in silence, but when the truck shuddered to a halt in Gibbs Street and Grace hopped down Tom stayed put and shut the door behind her.

"I'll see you," he said, leaning out the window as the truck moved off again. Grace, alarmed, followed along the footpath.

"Where are you going now? When will you be back?"

"Later."

"I don't think you should . . ."

"It'll be all right. Don't worry!"

Grace stopped and cupped her hands round her mouth. "Just be careful!" she called after him.

He watched her in the side mirror as they drove off and he saw her kick a rock and then give them one last look before turning away. Billy drove back to where they'd started from and they sat there not saying anything for a few minutes.

"I really thought I'd find him today. I really thought so."

Billy looked over at Tom and then shook his head. "It's too bad," he said.

"Yeah."

"Say, you want to see something?"

"What?"

"A good place. Where I go when things are no good. You'll like it."

Tom shrugged feebly, but as Billy climbed down from the truck and strode away towards the road he followed. They cleared the Steeles' fence and headed up along an overgrown track. Before long they slipped in under the cool shade of trees and then rocks began to loom up out of the understorey like remnants of an ancient and ruined structure. They climbed up and up and the rocks grew larger and larger. They stopped before one massive boulder and Billy climbed up on top of it and then pulled Tom up behind him.

"Where are we?" Tom asked, panting.

"Look," said Billy, pointing away through the trees, "there's the town, and the Rock's right behind us. There used to be a castle up here, long time ago. All fallen down now."

"Bullshit," said Tom and laughed.

He turned round and craned his neck. Up behind them he could see the Rock's massive foundations of lichen-covered boulders. Ferns and staghorns traced the path of a tiny stream.

"It *is* a good place," he said, turning back. "I like it."

They sat quietly, looking down at the town and catching their breath. He could see dust rising from the hooves of a ridden horse, blue smoke winding up from chimneys, the tops of eucalypts trimmed with new red leaves. He could see the station house, the church, the tall trees down near the convent, even his house out along the river road. He pictured himself in it, then tried to imagine Grace down there in her room.

Magpies came and fought running skirmishes through the trees. Occasionally a crow or a currawong would get in the way and the magpies would band together to see it off. Tom watched Billy watch the magpies and wondered about him. There was something about him that suggested he knew things about the world no one else did. He'd never been game to ask Henry a lot of things but Billy seemed a better prospect.

"Why do you think birds aren't just all black or all white?"

"Don't know. Why don't their colours all run together in the wet?"

Billy tried hard not to laugh at his own joke. Tom didn't. Billy grinned and took out the makings of a cigarette. With his nicotine-stained fingers he pinched tobacco out onto a paper and licked the gummed edge. He noticed Tom watching him.

"You want one?"

"Yeah."

Billy finished rolling his and then made another. He lit both cigarettes and took a deep pull on his and held the smoke in his lungs for a long time. Ash flew in the breeze as Tom followed suit.

"What happened to your finger?" he asked, as his head began to spin.

"Cut it off."

"Why'd you do that?"

"It was botherin' me."

Tom nodded. Somehow it seemed reasonable. He waved his hand at the town below.

"You used to live here, didn't you?"

"Yep, but not down there, in a house just up behind us a ways."

"Near the dam?"

"Yeah, up behind there. Lived there a few years. Remember the place but don't remember myself in it."

"How's that?"

"Don't really know. Got put in the hospital down there near Newcastle. Can't remember much before that, when I were here. Can't even remember my mother's face, or my sister's."

"You can't?"

"Nope."

Tom contemplated Billy's words and hoped he would never forget Flynn's face. It seemed impossible, but a lot of things had seemed that way before.

"Why'd they put you in there?"

Billy looked at him as though he should know.

"After my sister . . . you know . . . drowned up there."

"In the dam?"

"Yeah."

"I thought that was just a story."

"No. Not a story."

"You don't remember that either?"

"Nope. None of it."

Tom said nothing for a few moments, just looked down at Ham and stroked his head. He couldn't think what to say next.

"You know what they do in hospitals such as that?" said Billy, breaking the silence.

"No, not really . . . what?"

"They feed you gunpowder and kerosene and then plug your finger into the 'lectric. Blows your head clean off."

Tom grinned and Billy laughed.

"How long were you there for?"

"Ah, fifteen years or so. Something like that. Don't remember much about them days neither. All I've got to show for 'em are all these scars . . . and my hospital teeth."

Billy pulled up the sleeves of his shirt and showed Tom the long scars on his arms and then he slipped his false teeth out, the gums pink as coral, and let them dangle on his bottom lip. He gobbled them back up again after a while and smiled the merest ghost of a smile.

"How'd you get all those scars? Fighting?"

"No."

"How then?"

"Battles with meself."

"You did them?"

"Yeah."

Tom nodded, though he didn't quite understand. Billy's eyes had glazed over.

"Some of those old fellers in there," he said, quietly, ". . . mad as larks they were, mad as cut snakes. Never were sane, I reckon. Never were."

"What about you?"

"What about me?"

"You were sane?"

"Yeah, I think I was, long time ago. What kept me going in there was the Good Book, Jesus Christ himself. The church service on a Sunday."

"I haven't been to church much. Henry doesn't like it."

Billy turned to him, disbelief writ large on his face.

"But the Lord Jesus . . . he's God. He shed his blood for you. For me too. A man who sheds his blood for you is a brother always and a man who gives his life for you, well, that's another thing altogether. That's what the Lord done."

Billy's words came out at a hundred miles an hour and it took Tom a few moments to respond.

"Jesus came back to life after he died?"

"Yeah, he did. And he raised other people from the dead as well."

"How could he do that?"

Billy shook his head. "I don't know, but Father Carney told me he seen it done, with his own very eyes."

"You can't believe everything you see with your eyes. I've seen my brother. I saw him standing on the river, and he couldn't have been there because he's . . . because he's dead."

"Maybe you're a bit mad as well, then."

"Yeah, maybe."

"Don't worry. I see all sorts with these eyes. Good things . . . bad. I seen the Lord Jesus once, by a river too. A real funny feller he was. Let me eat his grub and everything. I thought he were as real as you and me sittin' here but in the morning he was gone and not a trace of him."

"What else have you seen?"

"Like you, I seen a few of the dead. After I been drinkin' a bit I see 'em."

"You ever seen your sister?"

He nodded. "I told Father Adam. He said it weren't her but a shade of her. He said I should not be drinking."

"What's a shade? A ghost?"

"Yeah, something as real as a dream but not quite. I'm not talking about dreams. Dreams are a different thing altogether. I'm talking about seeing things with the eyes in your head." He jabbed the stump of his finger up at his own.

"I know you are."

They smoked for a while and Tom's head began to spin again.

"Who's Father Adam?" he asked, stubbing out the cigarette on the rock.

"Old Father Adam. Adam Carney. Good mate of my old man. Helped raise us. He used to help me, after I got out of the hospital. He used to settle me down, help me with the drink, but then he couldn't help me no more either. Not even him."

"You drink a lot."

"Pretty much."

"Does Father Adam still live around here?"

"Used to."

"Why don't you go and see him?"

"Don't know where he is," he said. He stood abruptly and clambered down off the rock and went over to where the stream trickled down over the rocks to drink. When he came back Tom was ready with another question.

"Why'd you go into Darcy's room the other day?"

"Why'd I *what*?"

"Go into her room. Darcy's."

Billy scratched his head. "I don't remember."

"You don't remember why?"

"I don't remember doing it."

"You were drunk."

"Yeah, I suppose. That drink, it'll do it."

"You didn't see Darcy, did you? Before she ran away?"

"No, didn't see her."

Tom chewed on his lip.

"Billy, you should go and find where Father Adam is. Maybe you wouldn't need to drink any more. Maybe you could live a normal life."

"Normal? Strewth! Normal. I don't know if a normal life is a thing for me."

"Don't you want to live in a house, and have a wife, some kids?"

Billy looked at him in amazement and Tom knew from the look that he'd never really thought about it before.

"No, I don't want them things," he answered, quietly. "God don't want them things for me. Normal people don't see the things I do. My wife would have to be mad along with me, and we'd have mad children. Too damn right we would."

Ham began to whimper a little, and then he stopped and pricked up his ears. He lifted his nose into the air and sniffed. Billy and Tom both watched him.

"What do you think it is?"

Billy looked around. Something about the way he did—slowly, deliberately—put Tom on edge, but then, after a few moments had passed, Billy relaxed and shook his head.

"Food, that's what it is. He can smell food cookin'."

"Yeah, must be. I think he's hungry."

Tom stroked Ham's flank and put his finger in his mouth. His little teeth pressed down on his skin and Tom could feel his hot breath.

"He's a good little dog," said Billy. "Looks like he'd be a good gunnie."

"Yeah? One of the Steeles' dogs tried to eat him yesterday. I . . . killed it."

"You killed it? You killed one of big old Ezra's dogs? With what? A rifle?"

"No, a rock."

"A rock?"

"Yeah. A rock. I didn't want to. It just happened. I had to help Ham. I had to help Grace."

Billy nodded, impressed. "Maybe it had to be done," he said. "A mean dog like that, he would have used yours for a bit of fun. He would have played with him maybe, then killed him, or maybe he would have just killed him. Either way he'd be dead."

"Yeah, I suppose. I feel sick when I think about it, though."

"I've killed a lot of things. I always felt a bit sick. Sometimes it's just got to be done."

Tom nodded. He knew it was true.

"That Grace, she's real sweet."

"Yeah, she is."

Tom fished in his pocket, pulled out the photo of Darcy he'd taken from the kitchen table, and handed it to Billy.

"Here," he said. "I found it."

Billy took it from him and stared at it for a long time without saying anything. Finally he nodded, slowly, and thanked Tom. Tom said he was welcome.

They sat up there until the sun was low in the sky behind them. Billy began to tell Tom in a soft voice of all he had seen in the past few years in terms of trees and animals and rain and sun and clouds, his hands describing the tussles he'd had with cranky old kangaroos and dingoes and wild pigs. As darkness fell the sky emptied of clouds and birds and the brightest stars came out and claimed the vacancies. Underneath them, around the town, the darkening country spread out in every direction, barely broken by light of any description. To the south, just over the horizon, they could see the faint lights of another township but to the east and north there was nothing except the odd yellow light of a facing window and sometimes a car's head-lights. Away down the valley they could see fires flickering orange like the eyes of animals.

"Burning off scrub," said Billy.

"Yeah."

Every so often a plume of bright orange sparks would reach into the sky as the fires began to collapse into themselves and when the wind blew in a certain direction they could smell their smoke; the faint, sweet scent of burning rosewood. Tom breathed it in and wondered whether he could ever leave the valley, or whether he ever would. He lay back on the rock and watched the great black arc of the summer sky wheel around its load of stars, clearer and in greater number than he'd ever seen in his life before and each alive with its own colour. Meteorites began to spin and burn across the sky near the rising moon. He imagined the chimpanzee Ham riding up there, and all the astronauts, Flynn at the controls of a rocket—a long sleek thing—in a helmet, exploring out past the planets.

"Wouldn't it be good to go there one day," he whispered.

"Where?"

"The moon."

"The moon?"

"Yes."

Billy had a strange look on his face.

"Don't you know? They've been to the moon, Billy. They've landed on it."

"You're pullin' my leg."

Tom shook his head slowly. "No." He explained the mechanics, the rocket, the men, the *Eagle,* their walk, and how they'd planted a flag. Billy looked up at the moon while he explained and at the end he just shook his head.

"How'd they get back, then?"

"Flew."

"Flew? Down out of the stars, ay?"

"Yeah, sort of."

"I don't think they should've done that," said Billy after a while, shaking his head. "They shouldn't've done *that.*"

He seemed much sadder all of a sudden. Tom didn't know how to console him, or even if that's what he needed. He pulled the harmonica from his pocket and breathed into it for a while and tried to form a tune. Billy reached for it after a time and began to play. He played the same sad, beautiful song Tom had heard with Grace that morning on the jetty. Tom picked up Ham and held him before his face and looked into his dark eyes and then he lifted him up and turned him in all directions, wondering whether his animal eyes might see something neither he nor Billy could.

"See anything, boy?" he asked, but Ham gave no sign he had.

"Billy?"

Billy stopped playing and looked up. "Yeah?"

"You ever see a lion out here?"

"A lion? Nope. You?"

"No. I just dream about them sometimes."

"Well, that ain't the same thing as seein' 'em for real, is it."

"No."

Billy stretched. He looked to be getting ready to move on.

"What'll you do now?"

"Get me a feed, now I got some money."

He grinned his contagious grin, but Tom thought that the sadness of before was on him again and he hoped it wasn't what he'd said about the moon, or anything else.

"Better watch out for Pop."

"Don't worry, old Pop won't catch me again. Might buy some shells as well, plug meself one of Ezra's little poddies and have a good roast-up."

"Be careful."

"Yep."

Billy wiped his lips with the back of his hand and stood up. Even in the dark Tom could tell he was shaking a little. They set off, Tom following Billy all the way back down to the road. When they reached it they stopped and looked at each other.

"You be right now?" asked Billy.

"Yeah. I'll be right."

"Say sorry to your little friend. Didn't mean to be rude to her the other day. Just didn't like bein' locked up."

"I'll tell her."

Billy nodded. "You like her?"

"Yeah, I do."

"Good. That's good," said Billy, his voice suddenly sombre. "I'll see you, Tom Ferry."

He crossed the road and slipped away into the wrecker's yard. Tom watched him go for as long as he could and the thought came to him that he would never see the strange man again. For the first time he noticed how Billy walked, with his head down and wearily, as though he'd done far too much of it, or didn't much like where he was headed. After he'd gone Tom headed home. He felt a little empty inside. Ham fell asleep in his arms and his own head began to nod and his feet to trip. He walked right through town and then out past the ferry to his own home—not the station house. When he reached it he stopped, surprised at himself. He was about to turn round and head back to Pop's when he noticed that all the windows were in darkness. It didn't look like Henry was home. The thought of sleeping in his own bed, in the room he'd shared with Flynn, began to feel like something worth doing. He walked in through the gate and stepped softly up the steps. The door was open. He peered in round Henry's bedroom door. The bed was unmade and empty. He turned and tried the light but the bulb didn't come on. He tried another switch but that had the same result. He walked down into the house. It seemed very empty, and not quite the mess he'd expected. He went back to the front door and leant against the doorway. He looked out across the moonlit yard, at the river whispering by beyond the road. He made a decision and then he went back inside to the kitchen and found the blackout candles and a box of matches. He set one of the candles on a plate and lit it and carried it into the bathroom. He glanced at himself in the mirror as he washed his hands and face. So many things had happened that day. He'd held Grace's hand again, and he'd felt closer, somehow, to Flynn. He thought about Billy then and he thought about Flynn and then he looked in the mirror for the sadness. It was there all right, just like Billy's. Even holding hands with Grace wasn't enough to take it away.

He went and found a tin of corned beef in the kitchen cupboard, opened it, put some on the floor for Ham and ate the rest with his fingers. After he'd eaten Ham tore around the rooms, his toenails snare-drumming against the bare boards, his nose down, sneezing at the dust, maybe smelling faint traces of scent that were almost like his master's yet not quite. Tom took the candle into his room and lay down on Flynn's little bed. He fancied he could smell his brother's faint scent as well. Ham chased Matchbox cars around the floor until he wore himself out and then Tom lifted him up onto the bed and put his nose to the pillow.

"If you ever smell this smell I want you to tell me," he whispered, drowsily.

He lay and watched the yellow flame of the candle flicker and tremble. Ham put his head down on his paws, looking at Tom, looking at the flame. Tom watched the candle's reflection in his shining little orbs until the dog's eyelids grew heavy and closed. He yawned and huffed and soon his legs were twitching along with his dreams. Tom reached out and put his hand on one warm flank.

One day he'd find Flynn. He knew it. It would be a good day. He'd seen it happen in his head so many times now. It was always Pop who answered his knock—wearing a white shirt, the hair at the top of his chest spilling out like beach foam—but now Billy was there too.

This is my brother, he'd say to them, and they'd ask no questions but take Flynn from him very gently, very carefully, as if he were still alive. Then they'd all head up into the hills and build a bonfire of logs as tall as a house and they'd set Flynn's bones deep into the side of it and set the wood alight. They'd watch the flames build, half expecting a resurrection, for Flynn to come walking out of the darkness behind them, soft-skinned, to warm his hands at the fire, to tell them of their mistake. The wind would whip the fire and give it a voice, a roar. Billy would sit with a rifle across his knees as the roar summoned strange beasts out of the darkness. All the sad, exiled lions, all the ghosts of their ancestors, all the hiding things, all the things that didn't belong. They'd stay out there all night, calling just beyond the light, until the fire died down, until it was just a midden of embers glowing under grey ash, until the dawn came. Then he'd see his brother's glowing bones, the small yellow matrix at the balefire's heart, and he'd watch them diminish, become like nothing, sink down into the ash and disappear—and that would be that.

26

Billy Flood, his hat askew, repeated the steps of an age-old dance in the middle of the road as he swigged from the bottle of rum he'd bought at the back door of the hotel. He sang "Rock of Ages" and other old hymns at the top of his voice as he staggered out of town. The lie of Angel Rock—the river snaking by, the railway line—had long ago been branded into his mind, yet he didn't hate it, not even when he was sober, and not even when he remembered from long ago, as if it had been a dream, his father and Adam Carney harangue the town as though it were Sodom and call down fire and brimstone upon it.

As he swayed along the road and tried to remember the words to other hymns a carload of youths drove up and stopped to taunt him. He stepped off the road and into the bush to avoid them. He heard the screech of the car's tyres and the roar of its engine as it left but then a few minutes later it came back and stopped again. He saw the boys gather stones by the side of the road and then he saw them begin to pelt the dark spaces beneath the trees. Before he turned away he thought he saw Sonny Steele's round, red face. He headed up the slope and before long he was back where he'd sat with Tom that afternoon, the car and the boys forgotten. He climbed higher and higher up into the rocks, much further than he'd taken Tom, risking his bottle and his neck. When he'd gone as far as he could go—the moon-lit angel rock towering above—he slumped down on a great plane of broken stone, lichen-covered, stung and spalted by lightning, and drained the last of the rum. He threw the empty bottle high up into the air. As it shattered on the rocks below he fished the second bottle of rum from his jacket pocket and cracked the lid.

"God bless you, Tom Ferry!" he shouted to the sky, and then he drained a third of the bottle and not long after that he passed out cold.

When he opened his eyes again it was raining. He was lying on his back in a puddle by the side of a road. It was still dark. He couldn't remember anything of how he'd got there, or how the puddle had claimed him, but his head was still spinning hard from the rum and he didn't particularly care. He struggled to his knees and looked down the road, water rilling down his forehead and into his whiskers. He remembered Tom and his money. More money, more drink. He stood and started towards the lights he could just see through the rain haze, but before he covered even a few yards he saw *her.*

"*Darcy?*" he whispered.

She was up ahead, standing in the rain, her hair plastered to her scalp, her dress clinging to her body. He stopped and stared at her for a moment—a feeling in his gut like he'd just swallowed a big wet river stone. He let out a low moan, then turned and staggered away in the opposite direction. That was no good either. Standing on one side of the road's dividing line was his mother, and on the other, his sister— his sister whose face he couldn't recall any more, whose face, even now, was just a pale blur.

He turned back to Darcy but she had turned and was walking away down the road. He blinked the water out of his eyes and followed her. He followed her, not a thought in his head, not a question, just a thirst that needed quenching. He followed her all the way into town and then past the shops and up to the cemetery gate. He leapt over— barely aware of the rusted ironwork atop it gouging into his palm as he did—his blood up and carrying him like a river in flood.

He saw her one last time standing at the head of a grave and then she was gone. He went and stood where she'd last been. He stared down at the bare, rain-dimpled earth, at the runners of grass creeping across it like stitches over a wound. It was her own fresh grave—he saw her name carved into the wooden cross stuck in the ground. He began to weep, clutching at the broken ground, his shoulders shuddering. He cried for a long time, but when his tears finally ebbed it felt as if a small, warm fire of hope had spluttered into life deep inside him. He tilted back his head and closed his eyes and shivered as the warmth spread from his centre and out into his fingers and toes. When he opened his eyes again he looked down at the earth for a moment, his heart pounding, and then he stood and made his way over to the gravedigger's shed. He found a broken-handled spade propped up against it and he took it back to the grave and knelt before it. After a time he began to dig.

The earth was still loose from the burial and damp with the recent rain but it still took half the night to reach her. In the early morning it began to pour with rain again and the steep sides of the hole he'd dug began to collapse. Clods of earth fell upon his back and head and his boots sank further and further into the slurry of water and earth at his feet. He stopped and looked above him at the rough circle of slate-grey sky, only a shade lighter than the darkness. The rain ran down his forehead and dripped from his ears and he licked his lips and sucked in what he could to ease his drink thirst. He saw the hole filling and him drowning before he could finish and he moaned and doubled his efforts, the mud clearing the grassy fringes of the grave in long syrupy skeins.

When he finally heard the spade thud hollowly against wood he dropped to his knees in the pitch-black and sank his hands into the cold soup, tracing the outline of the coffin beneath him. He pulled at the lid but could not clear his own weight sufficiently from it for it to open. He flailed into the side wall of the hole he'd dug and made a space for himself, then put his feet down beside the coffin and forced the tip of the shovel into the join between coffin and lid and began to lever it up. He worked his way along the join as far as his reach extended and prised away until he had a gap between the lid wide enough to get his boot into. He put his hands in under the lid edge and lifted. The extra weight of the mud made it seem as though a grown man were standing upon the lid, but he grunted and strained and, slowly, the board cleared the slop, the catches giving way in a series of muffled cracks. He pulled at the lid until it came off completely and then he heaved it up and out of the hole. He paused, caught his breath, then bent and felt inside the coffin with his finger-tips. He found a ridge of material where he thought her head must be and then he felt his way down. He put his hands under her arms and lifted her out, holding her against his chest with his arm across her torso, then edged his way to the foot of the grave. He'd left a steep ramp rather than a sheer wall but it was still a struggle to pull himself up it with one hand and keep hold of her with the other, but he managed—finally—and lay on his back on the grass, panting, thunder rumbling overhead.

If there were any to shine a light on him when he slithered out of the ground they might have mistaken him for something recently human, recently interred himself, and the beneficiary of some form of resurrection—but there was no one, no witness, no one to even guess at his purpose and no one to testify to what they had seen. He hauled himself up and knelt beside the wet and muddy bundle he'd removed. He leant forward and set his forehead against it.

"Damsel, I say unto thee, arise," he whispered.

He prayed that his breath might be enough for both of them, his heart, but when she didn't move—not an inch, not a whisker—he began to weep again, his shoulders jerking uncontrollably. Amidst his weeping he realised what the problem was—he had too little faith. The only person he knew with enough was Father Adam. He picked Darcy up and began to walk. She seemed no weight at all in his arms and he carried her to the edge of the timber and stopped there for a moment and looked down across the town. The dozen or so street-lights cast soft yellow blooms in the swirling rain. Empty. A stage with no actors upon it. He stepped in under the cover of the trees and disappeared into the darkness.

III

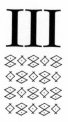

27

Tom almost dreamt the new day into being; knocking it up out of happier memories that had been waiting patiently to roll to the surface of the dark pool inside his head. The dream day had a clear blue sky and Flynn and Grace were there with him, not lions or fires or darkness or anything else, just Grace in a dress, and Flynn just as he remembered him. They were all holding hands and running on a beach somewhere and he was talking to them both at a mile a minute, making promises, telling them everything he knew and loved and hoped for and Grace was laughing and smiling back at him and little Flynn was just laughing.

He woke up. He rubbed his eyes and looked out the window for a few minutes, admiring the sky and remembering more of his dream—and then he remembered where he was. A sense of urgency gripped him. In just a few more weeks he'd be back at school. Today seemed like the last chance he'd have to take hold of something—he couldn't quite say what—before it slipped away, never to return again. Despite what Pop had said about Flynn, Tom didn't believe he was gone, not today, and not in his heart. He sat up, swung his legs onto the floor, found Ham and picked him up, then went as quietly as he could to the door. He tiptoed up the hall to Henry's room but he couldn't see him inside and neither was he sprawled on the couch. He half wondered where he was, but then the thought went from his mind almost as soon as it had come. He went to the bathroom and when he came back he saw the marks on the door where his mother had measured his and Flynn's heights. He pressed his back against the door and put his finger back against the door and turned round to look where it was.

"Nearly three inches," he told Ham.

Outside, the day that he'd dreamt up was cloudless and already warm. Everything was still wet and dripping from the rain during the night and the air was fresh and clear. Ham stopped at a puddle in the road and lapped at the water.

As he walked into town the small amount of hope he had for the future made a touch more room for itself and became something more than a feeble voice in the back of his mind. As he passed the ferry the ferrymaster lifted his finger off his pipe and acknowledged him with it, the first time he had ever done so. Tom wondered if he had seen Billy the night before but he didn't stop to ask. When he reached town Mrs. Coop was standing outside her shop, the breeze lifting her pink-flowered dress. She looked up from under her big straw hat and saw him and waved. He waved back. She held a tin of paint in one hand and a brush in the other. Behind her was the shop's brand-new title. *Heavenly Doilies,* it read. He smiled to himself and continued on down to the wrecker's yard. Billy's truck was still there but there was no sign of him. He went back up to the ferrymaster's house and knocked and looked around but there was no sign of him there either. He headed back to town, slightly deflated, but as he walked along the path he sensed something following him. He stopped and looked around. All he could see was the long yellow grass waving gently in eddies of warm air and the sun catching insects as they lit and circled, lit and circled. He opened his mouth to say something but then he closed it again and walked on, fighting down the urge to run.

When he arrived at the station house he walked up the back-yard path and into the kitchen. Pop and Grace were at the table eating breakfast. Both looked up at him in surprise, Grace with a spoonful of cornflakes halfway to her mouth.

"Morning, Tom," said Pop.

"Morning."

"Grace tells me you slept at your place last night."

"Ah . . . yeah. That's right."

"Might have been polite to come and tell me."

"Yeah," Tom mumbled. "Sorry."

"No harm done," said Pop. "Though you look like you could do with a good scrub."

Tom glanced at Grace and then he set Ham on the floor.

"Come on," said Pop, standing. "Come and say good morning to your mum before you wash up."

"Is she awake?"

"She is. Feeling better, she says."

He went along the hall to the bedroom his mother was in and peered round the door. Sun was shining in through the window and onto her bed. She looked very pale but she opened her arms when she saw him and gave him a hug when he went to the bedside.

"My boy," she said, stroking his hair.

"You look better, Mum."

"I feel better. You've been a good boy for Sergeant Mather?"

"I've tried."

He held his mother's hand until her eyelids began to flutter and she fell asleep. He watched her sleeping face intently for a while and then he bent and kissed her on the cheek.

"Listen," said Pop, as Tom sat down to breakfast. "I had a call from Ezra Steele last night. He says he found one of his dogs dead. Have either of you heard anything about it?"

Grace dropped the cup she was washing and looked round. She thought Tom looked about to spill his guts.

"Grace?"

"We didn't see anything," she said, looking Pop in the eye. "Isn't that right, Tom?"

Tom hesitated, then saw her eyes flash as Pop turned to him.

"Yeah," he said. "That's right."

"Well . . . good, then," said Pop, a touch doubtfully. After looking at them both for a little while he sighed and put on his hat and walked outside.

"Why couldn't we just tell him?" Tom whispered across the room.

"I don't know. It's just better. We can't do anything now. We just have to be quiet about it."

Grace continued washing up and Tom went and stood by her and picked up a tea towel. He breathed in her clean, girl smell while trying to look at the bare skin of her arms and shoulders without her noticing.

"Thanks . . . thanks for telling Pop where I was."

"Where were you really?"

"I was really at my house."

"What about Billy? Where'd you go with him?"

He told her where they'd gone and what they'd talked about and he answered her questions until she was satisfied and all the crockery and cutlery was clean and dried.

"I didn't tell Pop about him. I thought you should."

"Yeah. I suppose. I've already been down to the house this morning. He's not there."

"But you remember the way to the spot?"

"Yeah, but . . ."

"But what? What's the matter? Don't you want to go back?"

"Yeah, I do, it's just . . . I mean . . . I don't know . . . just not today . . . I'm not ready to find him today."

Grace bit her lip and was silent for a few moments.

"What about tomorrow?" she said, softly.

"Yeah. Maybe tomorrow."

Grace threw the sponge into the sink. "You can come with me, then," she whispered.

"Where are you going?"

"Up to see Mr. Pope. Pop asked me whether I'd ever been up at his house with Darcy."

"Had you?"

"No."

Tom nodded, frowning. "Why'd he ask you that?"

"I don't know. He said it was nothing important, but he was lying—I know he was."

Tom stood up. "I'll come with you," he said.

Grace smiled and pulled an old leather satchel out of a cupboard near the back door. She filled a bottle with water, slipped it into the satchel and slung it over her shoulder.

"I'm ready," she said.

They left the station house quickly and quietly and walked down the street towards the crossroads. They didn't see Sonny Steele in the shade of the milk bar's awning eating an ice cream—but he saw them. He licked his lips and trotted away in the direction of his house, his entire body suddenly slick with sweat.

The day remained clear and grew ever hotter, the sky all sapphire and lapis, the light sharp, a fresh snap of eucalyptus in the air and high kites of cloud. The sun hammered down and reclaimed the rain from the earth, and up on the road ahead the heat shimmer quivered like a genie set to appear. It took most of the morning just to clear the valley floor and start the ascent into the hills. Neither of them knew quite how far it was to the Popes' but neither wanted to ask the other.

They passed the old Flood house and Grace pointed it out to Tom. He stopped and stared at it.

"Should we go in and see if Billy's in there?"

"You can if you want. I'm not going anywhere near it."

"Why not?"

"It's creepy."

Tom looked at the blackened boards of the house, the rusting roof, the overgrown house yard and tumbledown outbuildings. He could see what she meant. It had a deserted, lonely look to it and the thought of wandering around it wasn't very appealing. Grace had already started walking and he had to jog to catch up to her.

When they reached the track that led down to the dam Grace stopped and pulled the water from the satchel and drank, then handed the bottle to Tom. They could see cars parked just down the track and the faint sounds of splashing and calling.

"Do you want to go have a look?"

"Yeah, okay."

They walked down and sat at the top of the broad stretch of grass that went right to the water's edge. There were a lot of people in swimming, and more sprawled on the shore and the grass.

"Feel like a swim?" Tom asked.

"No. Not while everybody's there."

Tom nodded and looked out along the curving dam wall to the thickly timbered slopes on the far side of the reservoir.

"This is where Billy's sister drowned," he said.

Grace shivered. "I wouldn't swim in there. I don't like the deep water."

Tom agreed that the water did look dark and forbidding, despite the full sun.

"Come on," he said, getting to his feet, "we can go further up. We can fill up the bottle."

There was a track leading away from the clearing and they took it. It was cooler in under the trees but the steepness of the track slowed them down and by the time the track meandered its way back down to the creekside they were even hotter and sweatier than they had been before. Tom suddenly put his hand on Grace's arm and his finger to his lips. A girl and boy were standing in the creek kissing. The boy had what Henry always referred to as an axe-handle. When he saw it Tom looked away, embarrassed, but Grace, with a glitter of mischief in her eye, picked up a rock and threw it down in their direction. The rock plocked into the water behind them and made them both jump. The boy looked about wildly until he spotted them.

"Hey!" he yelled.

"Come on!" Grace spluttered, snorting, dragging Tom back.

"What'd you do that for?"

"I don't know! Don't be such a spoilsport!"

"I . . . I'm not . . ."

"Come *on!*" she said, grabbing his hand.

He followed her away through the trees until they were sure the couple weren't behind them. The track continued alongside the creekbed and finally came to a halt at a quiet tree-lined pool. Grace went to the edge and stood looking at the water.

"This is more like it," she said.

Tom looked at the top of her back, the crest of backbone there like some ancient totem embedded. He saw the swell of her hips beneath the pale-green fabric of her dress. Abruptly, he put Ham down on the ground and took off his shirt. He went round to the deeper part of the pool and slid into the water, savouring the cool shock to his system. He swam around, watching Grace out of the corner of his eye. She sat down on the rocky bank and took off her sandals, then let her dusty feet down into the water. He caught a glimpse of her white underwear and the pale skin at the top of her thighs. He took a breath and ducked under the water, trying to stay down as long as he could, the strange echoing sound of the waterfall drowning out his thoughts. When his breath gave out he went to the side and clambered out. He sat on the rock edge, dripping and trying not to look at her.

"Maybe I should jump off the top there," he said, finally, indicating a rocky overhang on the other side of the creek.

"What for?"

Tom shrugged his shoulders.

"You don't have to prove how brave you are."

"I'm not very brave."

"Yes, you are."

"If *I* am then you are too."

"No, I'm not." Grace laughed.

"I saw you at the circus. That was brave. Coming outside that night, that was brave too."

Grace thought about it. "I wish you hadn't reminded me about that."

"Sorry. Anyway, Pop thought you were brave too."

"Yeah, he did. My mother went mad at him the next day when she found out."

"Why?"

"I don't know. They . . . don't agree about me. My mother . . . I think she'd like it if I stayed inside with her all the time, sewing or something. Pop says I should have my freedom. They fight about it." She looked distractedly down at the water. "Maybe it'll be better when I leave."

Tom gulped. "You're leaving?"

"Well, after school. I'm going to go to university in Sydney."

"Oh."

"Don't you want to leave one day?"

"I don't know. Maybe."

"Don't you know what you want to be?"

"I don't know. Work in the sawmill?"

"You don't really want to do *that*, do you?"

Tom thought about it. He supposed he mustn't.

"Maybe I could be a policeman. Maybe I could take over from Pop."

Grace rolled her eyes. "You don't want to do *that* either."

He looked at her. She was going. Just the thought of her leaving—even years in the future—made his heart sink and his mouth go dry. He couldn't think of what to say.

Grace stood and waded out into the pool, holding her dress up out of the water. After a while she looked up, shading her eyes with her hand, at the sky.

"It might rain later," she said, pointing to some hazy-looking clouds to the northwest. Even as she said it her foot slipped on the rocks and she splashed down into the water, backside first. Giggling, she regained her footing, half her dress now a darker shade of green. She stood and wrung out the worst of the water and then waded over to the bank and climbed back out. She walked over to a little clearing under a tree and sat down. She pulled her legs up and wrapped her arms round them. Tom looked up at the trees and then he glanced over at her and when their eyes met she inclined her head and inspected the ground before her, plucked a tiny purple flower from a ground bush and began to twirl it between her fingers.

"Come and sit beside me," she called out to him after a while, her voice thin and strange. He got up slowly and went and sat a few feet away from her. She held out three of the flowers she'd picked.

"Nice," he said.

"Just nice?"

"Beautiful."

Grace nodded. "But they don't have much of a smell."

She pulled one out of the bunch and put it in his top pocket. He looked down at it solemnly.

"Thanks," he said.

A gust of wind blew a strand of hair across her face. As her hand pushed it back he realised it was because he loved her that he felt so sick about her going away. It was the same feeling he'd had at the circus, but far stronger. It gripped his chest—like a fist round his heart—and made him feel giddy, but then, along with the pain, came a feeling of wonder and happiness. It washed over him, a rare and awful feeling, bought with blood, but all the more fierce for that. To look at her just made it worse and he turned away.

"What do you want to be?" he managed to say, his voice a little shaky. "After university . . . and all that?"

"A lawyer, or maybe a doctor. Something useful."

Tom nodded. "Good," he said. "That's good." He found himself looking at the scars on her calf and even though he knew she had seen him looking he was unable to stop.

"There was a pack of stray dogs that had been killing calves," she began, her voice low. "I was only five. Much braver than I am now. I'd gone to visit Darcy. You have to walk past that bit of bush?"

Tom nodded.

"Anyway, I felt them watching me, from in there, and then they came out and started chasing me. One of them got me by the leg and I fell over."

"What happened?"

"I must have been screaming pretty loud because Mr. Steele heard me and came running with his gun. The dog was trying to drag me away into the bush. Mr. Steele had to hit it with his gun before it would let me go."

Tom stared at the pale scars.

"What's the matter? You look sick."

"I don't know. Do you think . . ."

"What?"

"Do you think when you grow up . . . do you think you know why things are, why things happen?"

"Maybe. Maybe not. Pop says people see things better—understand things—when they're young."

"Yep, he told me that too."

Grace nodded and put her hand on his arm. "Tom," she said, "don't worry, we won't be young forever."

"No, I suppose not."

Ham snuffled past, his nose in the grass.

"Tom?"

"Yes?"

"Would you kiss me?"

He glanced at her. She looked very serious. He lifted his head and looked at the tanned skin at the top of her chest.

"Yes," he said, swallowing hard. "I mean . . . if you want."

She moved closer to him and put her hand up to the side of his head. She stroked his hair a little, then his cheek, and then she closed her eyes and leant forward. He closed his eyes too, then moved his head forward until his lips, very gently, touched hers. They were smooth and warm and very soft. They kissed for what seemed like a long time and then they parted. He opened his eyes to find her smiling at him and he blushed. She kissed him again, harder this time, and he felt the hardness of her teeth behind her lips, the warm jets of her breath against his cheek. They kissed until he couldn't feel parts of his body any more, but he didn't want to stop. When Grace finally pulled away and lay back Tom rested his chin in his hand and looked at her. Her lips were very red and her cheeks pink and her eyes very big. They looked at each other, their fingers intertwined, and they smiled but didn't say anything. After a while she took his hand and placed it on her thigh, just below her damp dress, and sat up to kiss him again. He didn't move his hand for a long time—he was too terrified—but then some deeper intuition took over that knew no fear at all and he slid his hand up her thigh—very slowly—and then down again. Her skin was cool and soft and still damp. She didn't stop him, didn't scream, and then her kisses changed, almost seemed to be encouraging him, and soon his hand was sliding up and down her legs—from the leg seams of her underpants to the scars on her calf—as if he'd been doing it for years.

"Further," she whispered, breaking away from his lips only for the time it took to say the word.

He brought his hand up past the side panel of her pants and onto her belly. Her dress gathered in the crook of his elbow and rode up. He glanced down at the pale bareness of her thighs. He felt her belly and the shallow well of her navel and then he ran his hand up over her chest, his heart in his mouth, and cupped her bare breast, feeling the rubbery nipple at its peak. Again, she didn't stop him, and he ran his hand up and down her body, sometimes kissing her, sometimes not, but never tiring of either, just amazed at the feel of her, the satin of her skin, and amazed it was happening at all.

"Put your hand down there," she whispered to him, finally. "Inside my pants."

"Are . . . are you sure?"

She didn't answer but looked from his eyes to his lips, kissed them again, hard. Her mouth was sweet and salt, hot and cold, all together. Her tongue stole in between his teeth and began to flick by his and that tied a great big knot in his belly.

"I want you to," she breathed into his ear, resting her forehead against his shoulder. He looked down at her neck, saw the vein pulsing in it, and then he moved his hand slowly down over her belly and slipped his hand in under the elastic of her pants. He moved his fingers around, feeling the hair, the hot, slippery structures further down. Her head fell back onto the grass and she closed her eyes and then Ham blundered in, trying to lick Grace's face—and broke the spell.

Tom picked up the pup and shook him and Grace laughed.

"That was really . . . nice," she said, after Ham had busied himself elsewhere.

"Yeah," he nodded.

They lay back down, resting their heads on their arms and looking at one another. They kissed some more and then Grace pushed back on his shoulder until he was lying on his back and then slid herself up and onto his body.

"I'm not squashing you, am I?"

"No."

It wasn't anything he'd ever glimpsed Henry doing with his mother—it was always Henry's back he'd seen—but Grace seemed to know what she was doing and that was good enough for him. For a while afterwards she seemed to forget he was even there. She closed her eyes, raised herself up a little, her palms on his shoulders, and began to move her hips. Very slowly at first, up a little, and down again. He counted the first half-dozen and then he didn't bother. He looked up at her instead, trailed his fingers down her side, felt her breathing, the ridges of her ribcage, her damp dress, her perspiring skin warm beneath it. He could see the stubble under her arms where she'd shaved, and a trailing drop of sweat, the fine sheen of perspiration on her forehead, her long lashes, her sweet nose, her white teeth, the line of her jaw and her princess chin, the faintest of dimples in her right cheek, her dark hair, her long arms. He saw it all but still she changed before his eyes, became something he couldn't have imagined and couldn't even have dreamt. She was off in her own little world and queen of it and he loved her even more. Her eyes opened. They were green, like his own, and so clear, their colour so fine, so beautiful, that he knew he'd never forget them.

"Don't look at me," she whispered, putting her forearm across her face in case he did anyway. All he could see was her embarrassed smile, but then it slowly faded as the movement of her hips against him became more insistent. Her head dipped to one side. The friction built and built and then he heard her take a breath, like a swimmer about to dive, and then she lifted her hips clear of him, drove down again, then wilted against his chest. When she'd got her breath back she lifted up her head and looked at him.

"That was . . . good."

"I didn't do much."

Grace smiled. "You're a good kisser. Have you been practising?"

"No."

She laughed at him and then leant her head forward until her forehead touched his. He looked down at her nose and lips and felt her warm breath against his skin and he closed his eyes and let the feeling he'd had before envelop him.

She'd slid off him and started running her hand down across the front of his trousers when they heard the sound. It was a snap, and in its aftermath, in the silence, they both hoped it had only been their imaginations, but when they looked at one another they knew it had been real.

"What was that?" Grace whispered.

"A branch falling, I think," answered Tom, looking around. "Maybe it was Ham. I can't see him anywhere."

"He'll be here somewhere."

"I'll have a look."

He stood, his head a little woozy, and began to look around the clearing they were in.

Grace straightened out her dress and propped herself up on one elbow to watch Tom. He disappeared behind some trees but she could still hear him calling Ham's name. She waited for him, looking up at the branches of the gum overhead, its smooth grey-green bark speckled with red sap. The breeze cooled her. She listened to the sound of the water, the calls of birds, and thought about what she'd just done with Tom. Even though she hadn't even been thinking about doing anything of the kind she was glad it had happened.

Minutes passed and still Tom did not return. There was no sound but the water, the breeze through the trees, the electric codes of insects.

"Tom?"

He didn't answer.

She stood and brushed off her dress, then put on her sandals and took a few steps in the direction he'd taken.

"Tom?"

She walked up the track a little way and as she crested a rise she saw, down in the gully below, a figure standing just near Tom. It was Sonny Steele, with a sickly grin on his face. He was holding Ham roughly by the scruff of his neck and the little dog was squirming around, trying to bite his hand, sick of the game. Sonny's dog, Blackie, was loose by his side and her legs went to jelly the instant she saw him.

"Tom!" she cried, but then someone appeared at her elbow, threw his arm round her shoulders and pulled her close. She whirled her head round and up, too startled to make a sound. It was Charlie Perry.

"Ooh, Grace, honey," he murmured in her ear. "Didn't take you for a cradle snatcher. Should try a real man next time."

At first she thought it was shame that made her face flush red, but she knew she wasn't ashamed. It took a few moments for her to find her breath, and then her voice.

"Wait till I tell Pop!" she spat.

"You won't tell anyone, sweetheart. Come down here with me."

"I can't! The dog—"

Charlie half carried, half dragged her down into the gully. He was carrying a rifle in his free hand. They stopped a few yards away from where Sonny and Tom were standing glaring at each other.

"Put him down!" said Tom.

"Did you kill my dog, you little cunt?"

"Put him down!" Tom seethed.

Charlie put down the rifle and then reached up and pinched Grace on the buttock.

"Did he kill Sonny's dog, Gracie?"

"No!"

He pinched again, harder, and Grace gasped and cried out. Tom turned and saw her as if noticing her presence for the first time.

"He had to—" Grace began.

"I'll tell, Sonny," yelled Tom, cutting her off.

"What? You going to admit it?"

"I'll tell. You put my dog down, and you let Grace go, and then you two piss off, or I'll tell. I'll tell everyone what I saw."

"*What?*" Sonny snarled.

"You know, near the mill," said Tom, looking him square in the eye.

Sonny's face drained of expression and his eyes went blank. His hand gripped Ham even harder and the little dog's lips drew back into a grimace.

"You killed my dog," he spat, his voice dripping with menace. "You let your faggot little brother die! No one'll believe *you!*"

Sonny reached up with his other hand and wrung Ham out like a wet towel and all four heard the wet pop as the small bones in his neck gave way. Sonny flung him away and his limp little body skidded to a halt in the grass and didn't move. Grace didn't breathe for a moment—no one seemed to—and then Tom launched himself at Sonny, a strange, hoarse moan escaping his lips.

For a time it seemed an equal fight. Even though Tom was smaller, Grace could see that he was strong for his age, and would maybe be as strong as Charlie in a few years, but as they wrestled and rolled across the base of the gully Sonny's greater weight began to wear Tom down and soon all he could do was try and defend himself from Sonny's blows. Blackie danced around them, barking furiously.

"Stop them, Charlie!" Grace screamed.

"You can't just kill someone's dog and get away with it," he muttered.

"Aren't they even now?"

Charlie didn't answer. She twisted round and looked up at him, saw the thick whiskers straggling out of his chin, his sweat, and felt nothing but disgust. She couldn't believe she'd fancied him for so long— the boy she'd known for years had gone and in his place was someone she barely recognised. He looked back at her, a strange expression in his eyes, and then he pressed his crotch hard into her hip. A cold panic gripped her.

"Charlie?" she said, shakily.

"Yeah?"

"Do you know why Darcy killed herself?"

Charlie shook his head. The question seemed to take the wind out of his sails.

"No," he said, and then his eyes grew wide. Grace looked round to see what had caught his attention.

Sonny, standing now, had pulled out a knife. They saw the blade flash in the light. He went for Tom with it, but Tom, still on his knees, caught his arm and held it. Gradually, Sonny's weight began to tell, and he forced the knife down towards Tom, his face red and streaming.

"Stop!" Grace screamed, but Sonny didn't. Instead, he eased his downward pressure—then suddenly reversed it. Tom came up with him a little way before Sonny bore down again, putting all his weight behind his knife hand. Grace screamed again. Tom wrenched back his head, but the blade sliced into his cheek and might have gone even deeper had he not pushed Sonny's arm aside at the last moment.

"Charlie, stop them!" sobbed Grace.

Grace wrenched herself away from Charlie as his grip weakened and picked up a stone and pegged it at Sonny as hard as she could. It hit him in the chest and he looked up, stunned. Blackie took a few steps towards her, growling and showing his teeth, but even as her courage and legs failed her the dog gave a whimper, then turned and skulked away with its tail between its legs. As Charlie grabbed her again she felt the hairs lift on the back of her neck. She heard a deep, menacing rumble and then a shiver ran up her spine and her breath seized in her chest. Something was coming towards them from the thick undergrowth further up the gully. She couldn't see what it was but could see the long grass and bushes move as it came closer.

"Shit," said Charlie, behind her. She glanced back at him, saw his big Adam's apple bobble up and down. Sonny, oblivious, had stepped back to survey his handiwork and she thought for a moment that he would stop, but then he approached Tom's crouching form again and brought back the knife for another blow.

"Charlie!"

Charlie relaxed his grip again and bent to pick up his rifle. Grace struggled free of his arms and grabbed the barrel before Charlie could and ran forward with it, swinging wildly. Sonny turned to her just as the butt came smashing into his face. He staggered back and then sat down hard, blood streaming from his mouth and nose.

In the silence immediately afterwards Grace realised that whatever it was that had been in the gully had gone. She went and knelt down by Tom. He was on all fours and fat red drops of blood were falling steadily from his cut face onto the bare earth. She ripped a strip of material from the bottom of her dress, folded it into a wad with shaking hands, then pressed it against his cheek.

"What happened?"

"I don't know. Something was there. Maybe . . . maybe it was Billy."

She looked back at Sonny. He was prodding at his face and looking at the blood on his hands.

"You stupid boy!"

"He deserved it," Sonny spluttered, blood spraying from his mouth. "He killed my dog. Got a beating 'cause of him!"

"You selfish pig! We came up here to find out about Darcy! Don't you care what happened to her?"

Charlie had retrieved the rifle and was standing looking at the undergrowth, the weapon trained there.

"Tell her, Sonny," Grace heard him say, in a low voice.

"What?"

Sonny scowled at Charlie and shook his head.

"Darce came and asked us for help . . . just before," said Charlie. "She said . . . she said a man was after her, that he had one of the boys."

"What did you do?"

"We . . . we told her father."

"And what did he do?"

"He didn't believe her. That was it. He . . . ah, chained her up in the shed, like a dog, for lyin'. He was always doin' it. He was always real tough with her."

"*Shut up!*" Sonny shouted.

"*You* shut up. Come on, let's go. Your nose's broke."

Charlie reached out his hand to Sonny but Sonny ignored it. He got to his feet by himself and, breathing hard, glared at them all before staggering off up the path. Charlie put the rifle up on his shoulder and nodded to them and then he followed.

"I swear, that's all we know about Darce," he said, walking away. "That's all Sonny knows."

Grace nodded to him and then she turned to Tom.

"Did you hear what he said?"

"Yeah."

"We have to tell Pop."

"Yeah." He tried to stand but the wound in his cheek opened again.

"Hold still and hold it there!" Grace scolded, and he did, until the bleeding was stanched and the stars stopped whirling around whenever he closed his eyes.

"I'm sorry," he said, dejectedly, after he'd recovered a little. "I should have looked after you better."

"Don't be silly."

Something shiny, lying in the grass, caught his eye. It was his harmonica. He picked it up, stared at it for a moment, then saw Ham's body lying a few yards away. Grace tried to stop Tom crawling over to him but he wouldn't hear of it. He knelt down and stroked the top of Ham's head with the back of his forefinger. He blinked away tears but Grace couldn't stop hers from flowing freely as she watched him.

"Come on, we have to go," she said, after a while, putting her hand on his shoulder. "They might come back."

Tom took a long, hitching breath and shook his head.

"I don't think they will."

"We'll go and get a lift off someone back at the dam."

"What about Mr. Pope?"

"Your cheek! We have to get home!"

Tom swayed a little, then looked over at Ham again.

"I'm taking him," he said.

Grace nodded. She went over and picked up her satchel and opened it up. Tom lifted Ham into it and buckled up the straps. His cut bled some more. Grace tore another strip from her dress and wadded it and handed it to him.

They walked back down to the dam but the people who had been there before had deserted the place. The day had clouded over and cooled and the water in the dam looked even blacker, a reservoir of something not meant to be stopped up. A fresh breeze began to pull the trees to and fro and Grace thought of Charlie and Sonny and Blackie out there somewhere . . . and the other thing, and she shivered.

When they reached the road again they stopped. A cloud slipped in front of the sun and all of a sudden the day became even more gloomy. A few drops of rain fell from a scudding cloud. Away through the trees to the west they could see black rain clouds wheeling around above the hills. The wind picked up and made a howling, rattling sound as it swept down through the trees. Grace grabbed Tom's shoulder and stopped him.

"There's a storm coming!"

"Yeah."

"What'll we do?"

Tom shrugged.

"We can't walk all the way home through it! Not in the dark!"

Tom didn't answer. He turned away as more rain began to fall and bent his head, his arm slung across the leather of the satchel. Grace stared at him, breathing hard. Something was wrong with him and it wasn't just his cut face. She looked around, frantic, for someone to help her, but there was no one, and she was close to a strange kind of panic when it occurred to her what they should do.

"We could keep going to Mr. Pope's," she shouted in Tom's ear. "He's got a phone. We could ring Pop. We could ring Pop and he'd come and get us!"

Tom looked at her uncomprehendingly. Grace grabbed his hand.

"Come on, Tom! Come on!" she cried, and they set off up the road, the day closing in by the minute.

28

Gibson thought he must be dead or blind or both. He tried to lift his head but a tremendous pain shot up into it and fireworks appeared and he had to lie perfectly still for ten minutes or more before the pain subsided. The details of a dream came vividly to him as he lay there. He'd been in a country hall, the woman from the grocery shop in Angel Rock up on the stage on a throne. The throne had been formed from the interwoven bodies of a dozen or more lion-like creatures with steel-grey coats, their claws and teeth digging into each other to hold the shape of the seat and the animals quivering and shaking with the effort. Jaw to haunch, flesh to tooth, no beginning or end, their glittering eyes watching him standing there before her, itching to leap up and tear him limb from limb. She'd just watched him for a long while, oblivious to her tightstrung seat, then dropped her index finger down and levelled it at his chest, her look neither kind nor unkind. His heart had gone as hot as a coal in his chest and he'd found himself on the floor, one of the animals standing over him. He'd seen the seams in its hide as if it had been, far back in time, stitched together from the offcuts of other, greater beasts. It had bent to him, opening its mouth, two long fangs filling his vision. A delicate cream colour, flawless, pristine, age-old, razor-sharp. He'd looked up into the beast's eyes as it had looked into his—iron-grey, traces of cornflower-blue, depths of black—then he'd lifted his arm, put his hand against its rough, cool side, seen its frame aglow in its flesh—bones sculpted from light—and he'd known the thing was beyond ancient and beyond comprehension. It had brought up its massive paw, unsheathed a set of razor-sharp claws, put one of the black scythes down upon his bare chest and swiftly undid it, lifting out his heart for all to see.

The hall, the beasts and the shopkeeper slowly faded away as he lay there until there was nothing left but stone-cold reality. He opened his eyes to slits and peered about. His top half was lying in leaves and grass and his lower felt in even worse condition. He looked down. His trousers were round his ankles and his pecker was in the dirt and there were smears of mud across his bare arse.

"*Fuck*," he croaked.

He couldn't remember anything of the night before. He got to his feet very slowly and pulled up his strides. It was merciless broad daylight. He tried to remember what had happened and where he was, but until he spied another man asleep in the grass alongside a number of long-neck beer bottles he remembered nothing. The man looked somehow familiar but he couldn't remember his name. He'd met him, and some others, after he'd been with the girl. Another pub. Much more drinking. That was it.

He looked around. He was in the back yard of a house. It looked like a fine day, half gone. He took a few tentative steps towards a nearby water tank, then stopped, wincing, as a dog began to bark somewhere close by. He continued, very gingerly, over to the tank, and caught sight of himself in the drum of water sitting under its tap. His face was stuck with pieces of dry grass and there were tracks across his cheeks where his drink sweat had run down through a fine layer of dust.

"You look like your fucking father," he muttered.

He bent to the tap and drank from it for a long time and then he walked round to the other side of the house wiping his mouth with his forearm. On the stairs leading up to the back door of the house sprawled a large woman with matted red hair, snoring away as though she were tucked up in bed. Her dress was torn at the shoulder and flies buzzed over the broad slab of her exposed breast. It and the front of her dress were both sticky with spilled liquor of some sort. Her legs were open and no underwear was in evidence. Gibson looked at her, scratched his head, and wondered what the hell they'd got up to. A chicken came scratching round the corner and then a lean, scarred dog emerged slowly from underneath the house. The dog looked at him for a while, looked at the chicken, then turned round, tripping over the chain attached to its collar. Sheepishly it picked itself up out of the dust and padded back in under the floorboards. When Gibson looked up from watching it there was a boy standing in the middle of the yard watching him. He was barefoot and thin and dressed in a dirty T-shirt. His grim, wizened little face gazed up at him from under a long fringe of dull brown hair. He continued looking at Gibson for a while longer and then he picked up a stone and shied it in his direction.

"Hey!"

The boy picked up another stone. Gibson set off round the house, passing by where Col or Ray lay snoring in the grass, and looked around for his car. His heart sank when he couldn't spot it—couldn't even feel the keys in his pocket. The boy came round the corner and fired off the stone he'd picked up. It caught Gibson a stinging blow behind the ear. He swore, then ducked off into the jungle of hedge and fruit trees at the side of the house as another stone slapped through the leaves above his head. He made his way down to the front of the house and there he stopped, panting, to look about. A driveway joined the house to a dirt road. Parked along the road was his car. It was about fifty yards away. He made a dash for it, the boy opening up with a hail of rocks and wild, unintelligible shouts; a burlesque of ancient war song that made Gibson's skin crawl. When he reached the car he glanced back. The house stood all by itself on a little rise in the middle of a swampy valley. The boy had stopped before it, his goal achieved. He stared at Gibson as he went to the window and looked in at the ignition. There were no keys there.

"Where are the keys, kid?"

"Fuck off!"

"Give me the keys and I bloody well will!"

The boy didn't answer him. Gibson sat behind the wheel and wondered if he could start it without a key. He reached down and struggled with the ignition for ten minutes before he managed to remove the casing and work out which wire was which. After he'd stripped the wires and touched them together the starter motor gave a whine. Gibson half smirked at the boy as he held the wires together again and put his foot on the accelerator. The starter tried its best but the engine refused to kick into life. Gibson, swearing, popped the

hood and looked underneath. He couldn't see anything wrong with
the engine but when he tried the starter again it still wouldn't start
and then the battery began to run out of juice.

"What've you done to my car, you little bastard?"

The boy gave no answer, just turned away as if Gibson was of no
more interest to him. Gibson, nonplussed, watched him walk back up
to the house and go inside.

There was nothing for it but to get back to Angel Rock somehow
and come back with Pop's car. He slammed shut the door and started
walking and then realised he had no idea which way to head. He
stopped and contemplated going back to the house, but had to decide
against it. There weren't even any other cars in the house's yard. He
turned back to the road and after half an hour he came to an intersec-
tion and a bitumen road. He sat down on the grass verge to wait for a
car to come along and then he remembered that his mother was dead.
He dropped his head into his hands and wept.

He sat by the road for a long time but no cars came. In the end he
flipped a coin and headed to the right, hobbling slightly, his legs stiff
and sore. His thirst bit into him and he realised—maybe for the first
time—how sweet water really was. He touched the side of his aching
head. There was blood but his skull seemed intact. He walked for
about an hour and then he heard an engine. He turned and saw a battered old ute coming down the road. He waved it down as it
approached, then peered in through the window at the driver when
he'd pulled up.

"Angel Rock?"

"Sure," said the man, slowly, studying him, a faint look of bemuse-
ment on his face. "Hop in."

"Bit of weather coming," said the farmer, as they drove.

Gibson looked. To the west, up behind the hills, sat dark and sour-
looking clouds and beyond them there were only more.

"Yeah," he croaked. "Listen, you got anything to drink?"

"You mean liquor-wise?"

"No, just water, anything."

"Course. Bag there. Help yourself."

Gibson picked up the waterbag and unscrewed the lid. It was almost empty and he drained it, his stomach cramping almost at once.

"Steady on there, mate. Don't bust your boiler."

Gibson wiped his mouth and grimaced. About twenty minutes later he began to recognise the outskirts of Angel Rock. They were heading into town along the road that ran along by the river. They rounded a bend and Gibson saw two houses nestled together. Across the road a trio of young boys were sitting fishing.

"That's Henry Gunn's place, right?"

"Yeah, it is. You know him?"

"Ah, yeah, sort of. Let me out here, will you?"

"Sure."

The farmer stopped the car and then hung his elbow out the window as Gibson came round to thank him.

"Take care now. Steer clear of those kiddies. Might give 'em a fright."

Gibson looked at the driver uncomprehendingly and then he bent and looked at himself in the ute's wing mirror. Trails of blood from the wound above his ear ran down across his cheek and neck. He looked a sight.

"Ah yeah, thanks, I'll keep it in mind."

When the farmer had gone he headed over to the boys. They watched him come and looked at one another a little wide-eyed. He went down to the water's edge and laved water over his head and washed away the blood from his neck. The boys watched him in silence. When he'd finished he looked back at Henry's house, then changed his mind and headed into town.

From the house Henry watched him stop by the river and wash and then continue on. Sometime later he finished the bottle of beer he was drinking, rubbed his eyes, then pulled on his boots and headed into town himself.

When Gibson reached his room in the convent he took his revolver out from under the bed and put it and his other belongings into his bag. He went and washed the last traces of blood from his neck and put on a clean shirt before heading up to the station house to ask Pop about getting a tow for his car. As he approached he saw Henry's truck parked outside and then Pop and Henry came out of the front door together. Pop locked it behind him and looked around. Something about the way he did it seemed slightly furtive—and completely out of character. Henry just looked baffled.

They headed up the street and he followed them at a distance. He couldn't quite see what they stopped to look at in the cemetery and he had to wait until they'd disappeared into the bush before he could move closer. When he looked down into the empty grave and saw whose it was he thought he was dreaming again. As a dozen questions rushed into his head he almost ran after the two men, but then he stopped and turned round and headed back down to the convent instead. He pulled his gun from his bag and stuck it in his belt, then he went back up to the street and began looking for a car to borrow. It was nearly five o'clock and there weren't many about and he felt the urgency inside him begin to spill over into panic. He felt like he was in the wrong place at the right time and was missing something—something he *had* to witness. Then he spotted the ute of the farmer who'd given him a lift into town and ran over to it. The keys were in the ignition and the old man was in the butchery. The butcher saw him as he started up the car and put it into gear, but then he gunned the engine and roared away. Country and western songs crackled out of the radio as he drove, but it wasn't until he reached the crossroads and a few stray drops of rain came and speckled the windscreen that he heard them and flicked the music off.

29

As they walked the breeze picked up and cooler washes of air began to sweep down across the valley. Pop, lowering his voice, described what had happened. Henry listened, open-mouthed and shaking his head.

"Rita Coop went up there to talk to her husband. When she came to me she was in hysterics. I had Lil put her to bed with some tea and Bex. Hopefully we'll be all right for a while yet. Hopefully long enough to find . . . the body, put it back where it belongs."

They followed the trail without any difficulty for a while and then the ground became rocky. Pop continued apace, undeterred.

"Should have brought . . . some water," said Henry, panting, wiping his mouth.

"Here," said Pop, handing him a bottle from his knapsack.

"Thanks."

They continued on, the Rock looming up out of the trees before them, and before long the broad expanse of the dam began to appear through the trees. They scrambled down to the shore and peered about. The water looked black. Pop thought that those who said drowning was an easy way to go hadn't seen this place. He turned to Henry.

"See anything?"

"No."

He bent and looked around at the bank. Even though the day was getting very gloomy there was still just enough light to see by. There were all sorts of tracks, but mostly of bare feet.

"Can't see his bootmark," said Pop, standing. "Too many people have been up here today. But if he came this way he must be headed for the house. There might be tracks across the top of the dam."

Henry nodded. He looked back the way they had come. The hills behind were now swathed in grey clouds and he could barely see the township below. Rain seemed imminent. When he turned back Pop was kneeling again, looking intently at the ground near the dam wall.

"What is it?"

Pop motioned him forward and pointed.

"What do you see there?"

Henry looked.

"I—"

"*That's* the print we're following. *That* . . . is Grace's. And that, I'd guess, is young Tom's."

Henry shook his head. "You sure?"

Pop put his hands on his knees and pushed himself up. He didn't respond to Henry's question but stormed away across the dam wall. Henry went after him.

"You sayin' that's my fault or something?"

"It's no one's fault."

"Look, I don't know—"

"By Christ, Henry! You've been drowning your damn sorrows for too long to know a damn thing!"

"Me? Do you know what *your* daughter's been up to today?"

Pop stopped and turned and gave Henry a cold stare.

"I just hope . . . I just hope, for both our sakes . . ."

He turned and walked on, but he kept talking.

"You know, Henry, back in the old days, when a child was stillborn, miscarried, you know what they did? I'll bloody well tell you. They gave the body to the father to bury, just like that. I buried three. Two boys and a girl. After that, me and Lil gave up on children, for years and years, and then Grace came along, a bloody little miracle. You know how much she means to us? If anything's happened to her . . ."

"I'm sorry . . . I—"

"I know losing your little bloke's been hard, Henry, but you've still got Tom to think about."

"I'm tryin', Pop, but I can't watch him twenty-four hours."

"No. No, you can't. You can't keep 'em locked up either. Look what happens when you do."

"Darcy."

"Yeah."

"Grace'll be all right, Pop," said Henry, his voice a little shaky. "I know it . . . and if Tom's with her . . . he's a good boy."

"Yeah, he is. But let's pray they're both safe at home and not out here. Let's just find Darcy now . . . and Billy. Let's get it sorted, before the day's out."

Henry pulled down his hat and nodded. They walked on and after a while it began to rain. Pop pulled a lamp from his knapsack and a box of matches from his pocket and handed them to Henry.

"Better fire it up. Light's going."

Thunder echoed around the hills and away to the east lightning crawled across the clouds like spiders across a ceiling. Rain began to fall more heavily, full-bellied and cold, working up to torrential. The tin plate on the top of the lamp began to sizzle and spit.

"Looks like it's settling in," said Pop, adjusting his hat.

"How far do you think the house is?"

"Not far now. Not far at all."

"Pop?"

"Yeah."

"You know this feller Gibson?"

"Yep. What about him?"

"He reckoned Smith might have come back."

"Yeah."

"Do you think he could be right?"

"No. Smith's dead."

"Oh."

"Listen, Gibson's mother just died. I had a talk to his boss when he rang about it. He's chasing ghosts, Henry. His sister killed herself. He's about as mixed up as Billy is about it. He told me as much, but what he didn't tell me was his mother shot dead his father not long after they found the sister's body. She spent six years in prison for it and Gibson grew up in a home. Erskine says he doesn't remember anything about it, but he's always reckoned it wasn't—"

"What?"

"Wait—you hear that?"

"No."

"Wait here a tick."

Pop slipped into the bush at the side of the track and vanished. Henry heard him moving up the slope, but then there was just the sound of the wind stirring the branches, the rain falling. The shadows the lamp threw began to spook him. He walked on for another twenty or so yards and stopped. Up through the trees he could just see Pop.

"Turn off the light."

Henry turned down the wick of the lamp and stood staring into the near-darkness. The sight of Pop, unmoving, the whites of his eyes glowing, chilled Henry's blood. After a few minutes of silence Pop came back down.

"Come on," he said, his voice grim.

They came to the fence that ran alongside the road and as they crawled under the wire Pop noticed something by the base of one of the posts. Some sort of bag. A piece of twine attached to it was caught in a barb of wire. He picked up the bag and pulled at the twine until it came free.

"What is it?" asked Henry, coming up behind him.

Pop upended the bag into his hand. There was a pipe, a new tin of tobacco, old coins: shillings, pennies, a sixpence, a piece of bone with a sailing ship carved into it, a curved yellow tooth about an inch long and a bent photograph of Darcy Steele.

"Billy's," said Pop. They looked at one another and then Pop put the objects back into the bag and they walked on.

30

As Gibson drove the clouds descended and by the time he reached the last steep and twisty section before the house the light had all but gone. He slowed down, the old ute creaking with relief, and then, through the silvery veils, the house appeared. It sat up behind the fence like a black limpet, full of bad graces, daring him to approach, to seek out its rotten heart, to steal its secrets. He stopped the car and stared at it for a moment and then he got out and continued on foot.

He knew it was Billy who'd taken Darcy. He thought he understood why too, but then he'd been wrong about Smith. Maybe he was wrong about Billy's motives too. Who knew what was going on in his mind, especially now that he was in the house he'd grown up in, the house where Smith had loomed large.

When he was only a few dozen yards away he stopped again, remembering the rifle in Billy's truck. He watched the house for a minute or two but he saw no movement and no light. He pulled out his revolver and searched around in his pocket for the bullets. He found a few and slipped them into the chambers and then stuck the revolver back into his pants and set off up the track towards the house. He held up his hand to shield his eyes from the rain and as he blinked water from his eyes he saw a faint light flare briefly behind a window, then snap out, as if a hand had snuffed it. The sight of it made Gibson's heart hammer even harder inside him and he licked his lips and wiped them with the back of his hand and then he put one foot forward and then the other, feeling for the grip of the revolver as he went.

He knew Billy was just a man, and he remembered what Pop had said about the only monsters in the valley being the ones in his head—the ones he hadn't fronted yet—yet he still couldn't shake the feeling of cold dread that crept up and took tight hold of him. He was dry-mouthed and shaky, but he went on. He told himself that it had always been on the cards, this walk into the unknown. He remembered the night at the roadside, the storm overhead, the rain coursing down just like this, and how he'd accepted a commission, not knowing what it required of him. Maybe now it was time to find out.

He trod carefully up the rickety steps to the front door and paused there. He shook the water from his hair and wiped his face and then stood before the door and composed himself. He was suddenly more afraid than he could ever remember. He saw himself as a boy and the boy was asking him how he'd come to be standing before this door, dripping with water, scared out of his wits. He muttered one of the first prayers of his life and then he put his hand on the doorknob and turned it. He pushed open the door and peered inside. It was very dark and all he could hear was a steady thrumming from the rain on the roof. He went inside. He could see nothing in the utter blackness before him and he thought for a moment that he might be defeated by the darkness itself. He remembered that the hall opened out into the old living area and he crept forward until his hand touched the closed hall door. He listened for a moment and then he pushed open the door very slowly.

There was someone in the room. He knew there was, even before he breathed in the odorous animal reek it contained. He took a single step into the pitch-black.

"Billy?" he half whispered. No answer. He saw a darker shape in the darkness, then heard the boards creak under its weight, then a scrape, and then a flaring match lit up the room. A man knelt in the middle of the floor like a supplicant, his torso bare, his feet shoeless. There was nothing else in the room—no furniture—just the long boards running from one side of the room to the other. The man leant forward very slowly and lit the candle sitting before him. In the light, Gibson saw that his back was streaked with dried blood. The blood extended out all around him, over the floor and up the walls.

"Billy, where is she, mate? What have you done with her?"

The man looked round and then up at him and as Gibson saw his face for the first time a cold, electric shiver ran up and down his whole body. He began to tremble, and the revolver, when he lifted it, shook along with him. He stepped forward, expecting the figure to dissolve at any moment, expecting to wake from the nightmare, but when neither happened he found his voice and whispered a name like an invocation.

"Smith."

The man Pop had pointed out in the picture had been tall and straight and young, but Gibson knew it was him. It was his eyes— black and burning with an unholy intensity. The will behind them seemed the only thing keeping alive his ravaged body. When he spoke his voice was guttural and almost inaudible.

"Get out," he rasped.

"No, Smith. Not on your life. No way."

Gibson licked his lips and circled round Smith's kneeling form, a giddy feeling of elation beginning to displace the dread in his belly.

"You're supposed to be dead. You're supposed to have died in a fire. Even Horace Flood thinks you did."

He knelt down beside Smith and put the revolver against his skull, just behind his ear. His hair was sparse there and his skull clammy with perspiration. Blue veins stood out in his frail, eggshell skin.

"So if I pulled the trigger it wouldn't mean anything, you already being dead."

"I . . . escaped the flames . . ."

"Yes. So I see. Just so we could meet. Just so you could confess your sins."

"I have nothing to confess. I remember nothing."

"You don't remember? I'll tell you. Twenty years ago a girl named Annie Flood drowned. I think you were there. I think she was running from you. Isn't that what happened?"

"I don't . . . I don't remember."

He hung his head and Gibson began to imagine the wretched, loveless life he must have led. He almost began to feel a little pity for him, but then it evaporated.

"Then . . . then you came back and you wanted Darcy, like you wanted Annie, but you couldn't get close to her, could you? You couldn't get close enough because of her father, because of his damn dogs."

"I was reborn. So was she."

Gibson frowned, hesitated, grasped for understanding. He remembered Smith's writings and the lines he had copied from the Bible and then he finally understood.

"No, Smith, Darcy wasn't Annie come back. She wasn't."

Smith looked up at him again, the barrel of the revolver sliding against the dirty skin of his neck as he turned.

"Untrue. She *is* here. Outside. Can't you hear?"

Gibson paused and listened, but then shook his head.

"Is that why you're here? Is that who you're waiting for? Annie's *dead*, Smith, and so is Darcy. *Neither* of them is coming!"

Smith blinked up at him and Gibson saw the same look of horror and alarm in his eyes that he'd seen in Billy's when he'd broken the same news to him. Smith, however, after a long moment, began to smile. It took shape very slowly on his thin-lipped mouth and then began to edge into his eyes. Another, altogether darker, side of the man surfaced from the depths like a body. Gibson could tell this side didn't believe him. His fear returned—hollow and wet-handed—but then it began to alchemise into anger. *Something's watching me from the trees,* Darcy had written in her Bible. *Something's watching me from the trees.* He gritted his teeth.

"It's *true*, Smith. They're both dead. You can't hurt either of them any more."

Smith didn't respond. His grin turned into a smirk and then just a look of sly resolve, as if he would yet prove Gibson wrong. Gibson kept the gun against his neck but moved his body back out of reach of his long arms.

"You can prove I've done these . . . wrongs?"

"I don't need to."

"Judge *and* jury? On whose authority?"

"My own damn authority."

"*Only the judgements of the Lord are true and righteous altogether,* Mr. . . ."

"Gibson."

"*Only the judgements of the Lord are true and righteous altogether,* Mr. Gibson," Smith repeated, his voice almost a whisper. "*More to be* desired are they than gold, yea, than much fine gold: sweeter also than honey and the honeycomb."

Gibson blinked, licked his lips. Smith glared up at him.

"Pull the trigger then, Mr. Gibson. Please."

Even though he knew the exhortation was some kind of ruse a polar cold washed over him as his eyes locked with Smith's. Maybe it was his own fury, his own need for retribution—a whole unfathomed sea of it—but he knew it would be all too easy to give in. Slowly, he lifted the revolver.

"Not yet, Smith," he said, his voice shaking. "Not yet. You tell me where she is."

Smith shook his head. "I don't know . . . what you are talking about."

Gibson swore and then he stood up and looked around. He backed up slowly and glanced into the two front bedrooms. He could barely see inside them but he thought a body might make itself obvious. They were empty and he went back to Smith and then circled round him and went to the steps that led down into the kitchen.

"Get down in there," he ordered, pointing. "Take that candle with you."

Smith rose slowly to his feet and picked up the candle with his thin, bloodstreaked fingers. There was something deeply disturbing about the man and his almost still slowness. When he reached his full height Gibson took a step back. Down on the floor he could see the old razor Smith had used to inflict his wounds. He kicked it away against the wall and then ushered him down into the kitchen.

"Sit down on the floor again."

Smith sat, but he didn't take his eyes off Gibson for a moment. Gibson looked around the kitchen. Where before it had been empty it now looked like a hovel. A pile of rags lay along the wall and he guessed it was where Smith had been sleeping. In the sink sat empty tins of dog food and down in one corner of the kitchen was a dark pile of shit. He screwed up his nose and then noticed the closed laundry door. He paused, knowing in his bones that something was behind it, knowing in his heart. He went to the door and put his hand on the doorknob and momentarily took his eyes off Smith as he turned it. He saw him move out of the corner of his eye and when he snapped his head round he saw that he had pulled a rifle from somewhere beneath the pile of rags and had already drawn a bead on him. He spun round, dropping his shoulder, but he had no time. Smith fired, his eyes full of nothing. The first bullet thudded into his centre and knocked him off balance. The next slug hit him in the shoulder as he tried to lift his own gun. He stepped back against the doorjamb and slid down it onto the floor. His vision went cloudy for a moment or two, and then waves of heat ran up and down his body. There was no pain, just a ringing in his ears. Veils of blue smoke hung in the air. He could hear high-pitched laughter, but he couldn't see Smith. The revolver was still in his hand and he lifted it, aimed for the laughter and pulled the trigger once, twice, three times. All he could see when the smoke cleared were pale marks in the wall where the bullets had splintered the wood. There was no sign of Smith. He set the warm gun down on the floor and flinched as he took a deeper breath. He touched his wet shirt and then looked around and wondered what he should do. The kitchen was very still. The candlelight flickered and, except for the peaceful sound of the rain on the roof, it was very quiet. He felt sad and helpless and about twelve years old again. He thought of his sister and mother and tried not to cry and then he squeezed his eyes shut and hoped the pain would not get too much worse.

He saw a number of things then, very clearly. He remembered a warm Sunday morning in Sydney. He saw himself coming home—only a boy—and walking up the stairs, then peering into his parents' room and seeing the sweating neck of his father as he plunged himself into a woman who was not his mother. He remembered how the breeze had lifted the curtains in and out, ever so gently, and he remembered how the woman had looked up and seen him there at the door, and he remembered that it was his sister's face, and he remembered the look in her eyes.

Even as the shock and the pain of the memory began to numb him his head swam and he saw himself again, but much later, as a nineteen-year-old vagabond, standing in the centre of Venice, dreaming of a grand romance, something to take away the pain of his childhood, and looking up at the winged lion of St. Mark, and his sister, his beloved sister, was standing there beside him, smiling. He knew then that she'd always been there, ever since she'd left him. She'd been with him at the side of the road on the night he'd driven to Angel Rock, and she was here even now. He knew too that it was a *lion* he'd seen in the rock above the town—not an angel at all—but a winged lion, a queen of her race, her brow heavy, her wings ready for flight, yet caught in the stone for eternity. She was a beast from some age long past and he knew then that some plan *did* exist, something far greater than him—than anyone—and unknowable into the bargain. He was glad he'd glimpsed it and was glad he'd been shown a world beyond fact, beyond evidence. Pop's world, but maybe also his own.

Even as the life ebbed out of him, he knew. He finally knew. Life was to see, to touch, to smell, to taste, to hear—and to *know*—and even though knowing was painful it was also like diving into a wave on a hot summer's day, then surfacing, floating, letting your body be lifted by the sparkling blue water. Lifted and lowered. Lifted and lowered. He could hear the rain on the roof and he listened to it as the warmth began to spread out from his centre like a tiny rising sun. He heard a faint sound then—a voice?—and just before his eyes fluttered and closed something else became utterly and entirely clear.

31

Billy surfaced from a dark, cold place and lifted up his head. There was a picture in his mind of the first day he had walked into Angel Rock and had seen Adam Carney, tall and lean and blue eyes blazing. He remembered him wading into the river to baptise his converts, the great sweep he'd made through the air with his arm, his finger pointing first to the heat-soaked sky, then the hills, blue-green and shimmering across the valley, then the river, slow and muddy, turning in eddies about his waist. Everything about the man had seemed to promise good things and the assembled followers had gaped, as if he'd been about to transmit Old Testament wonders across the great drift of centuries to where they stood, as if there might be more creation and new creatures to be named and the river itself might part and reveal marvels. He remembered his head reeling with Adam's words, spinning with haloes of fire and visions of the debauched world of the sinner and only the Lord God like a rock to cling to in the midst of it, until he'd been light-headed with newborn faith, and the land itself had been a chorus of agreement around him.

He lifted his head and looked around. He couldn't tell where he was, but Darcy Steele, wrapped up in her muddy cerecloth, was still by his side.

"I've brought her, dear Jesus, I've brought her to be raised up," he whispered, but there was no one to hear him.

Before him was a single lit candle, a miracle of light. He couldn't remember how it had come to be there. He looked around for other miracles, but there were none. There were bottles on a shelf instead, and a raging thirst inside him. He was in an old farm shed. He went and plucked a bottle off the shelf, sniffed at the lid, discarded it, then repeated the operation until he came to an old but nearly full bottle of wood spirit. He unscrewed the lid and the fumes, like the very genesis of flames, curled up unseen from its dark throat and into his nose. He threw back a belt and the liquid burnt down, cramped his gut, then came straight back up again. He tried again, and again, and when he finally succeeded and there was nothing left in the bottle he let it fall to the floor and soon after he followed.

He knew nothing else at all until he found himself outside and stumbling across wet grass. The shack was in flames behind him and then he saw that he too was ablaze. He wore a coat of flames—the finest thing he'd ever worn—but it was turning him to ash, to cinders. The pain of it wrung him out, doubled him over, and he fell, the flames hissing out against the damp ground. He crawled away to the foot of a tree at the edge of the sallow corona of light and there he rested his head and curled up into a ball.

A time later something came and stood over him and breathed in long draughts of his charred self. He thought at first it was a dog come to clean him up and he tried to bat it away with his hand, but a whole truckload of pain slammed into him when he moved and he hissed out a long hiss into the ground—his blood cold, his bones cold—until it eased. Then he felt the thing's teeth at him, tearing him apart, getting right to the quick of him, right down inside where his life was kept, and he moved into some kind of dream. His eyes, his ears, his arms, his legs—the whole box and dice of him—all changed, and there was no more pain. Slow flames, golden light, began to weave down towards him, illuminating everything and squeezing the trees into strips as thin as insects in amber. At the centre of the light he saw a figure with bright skin. Darcy. He wanted to laugh at the sweet impossibility of her. Darcy!

"Glory be, Darce," he managed to say, as she knelt down and put her hand against his forehead.

"You're all done here, Billy," she said.

"Yeah, Darce, I am," he breathed. "I am. I'm all done."

32

Pop reckoned they were close as something caught his eye away through the trees.

"Look, Henry. There!"

Henry peered in the direction Pop's outstretched arm indicated. Through the trees he could see flames.

"It's one of the sheds!" Pop shouted. "Come on!"

They could hear the rain hissing as it fell upon the heated iron roof of the shed. They held up their arms to shield themselves from the heat and peered in through the shed's open door. At first they could see only flames, but then they each caught a glimpse of a blazing bundle on the floor just inside the door. The heat beat them back and Henry stumbled and almost fell across an obstacle lying in the long grass. Henry held up the lamp and then Pop went and knelt beside the burnt and blackened form.

"He's dead," said Pop.

"Billy?"

"Yeah, must be."

Pop wiped the rain from his face and Henry looked back at the burning shed and then they both heard the first of the shots. At first they thought it was something in the fire but when they looked up to the house, a hundred or so yards away, they saw a dim light burning. Their eyes met and then they set off as one.

Tom and Grace sat on the cracked leather back seat of Reg Pope's Rolls-Royce and listened to him grumble about the road and the rain and the dark and foolish children. Tom put his hand down on the satchel containing Ham and looked across at Grace. She was staring out the window at the black, wet night, but seemed to sense him looking. She turned to him and gave a weak smile and he reached for her hand and she gave it to him before turning back to the window. They drove for another five minutes and then the car slowed for a bend.

"Look," Grace suddenly shouted, "it's Pop! Stop, Mr. Pope! Stop!"

Tom peered out into the blackness. Pop was standing in front of Billy's old house. In his hand was a black object and Tom realised it was a gun and that Pop was loading it. What surprised him even more was that Henry was standing by his side. The Rolls slid to a halt and Grace opened the door and ran across to her father. Tom followed. Away down the paddock he saw that one of the sheds was on fire.

"What is it?" Grace began, breathlessly. "What's the matter?"

Although he was surprised to see them Tom could tell there was something else far more pressing on Pop's mind.

"Henry, keep these kids here," he said, his voice sharp, and then he walked up to the house, lamp in one hand, gun in the other, and went in through the open front door.

The room was a far cry from what he'd been expecting when his eyes fluttered open again. Pop Mather was there and feeling for his wounds and saying his name over and over. The blood he'd spilled glittered in the lamplight.

"What happened, Gibson? What the Christ happened?"

"It's Smith, Pop. He's not dead. He's not dead. He must have run."

Pop shook his head.

"He was here!"

"Steady on, man, steady on. I believe you. Someone sure was, unless you shot yourself up."

"I—I saw the grave. I thought Billy had brought her here."

"We found her. Her and Billy."

Gibson nodded. "The bastard's killed me, hasn't he?"

"No," said Pop, taking hold of his hand. "You're not going to die. Not if I can help it. You've got a bullet in your gut and one in your shoulder. I've seen men beat worse."

Gibson smiled.

"Should I trust you?"

"You could do worse."

He felt himself slipping away, despite what Pop had said. Everything came back to him in a rush and he knew he had to tell it before it was too late. He reached up with his good arm and clutched at Pop's wet shirt, his grip weak as a baby's. Pop put his arm round his shoulders.

"Come on, son. Stay with me."

"I shot him, Pop."

"Smith?"

"No, not him. My father. It was me who killed him. Me."

"You remember?"

"Yes. I remember. He was sitting at the kitchen table, listening to the races. He was surprised to see me. *Me,* not my mother. Make sure they know it wasn't her. Make sure they know."

Pop nodded. "Erskine told me he always thought it was you. He said one day you'd remember."

Gibson nodded and squeezed back tears.

"And I remember why I did it. I remember . . ."

He was about to tell Pop everything when he heard the sound again. It was much fainter now, barely audible above the rain. A cough—then a deep, bronchial string of them. He reached up and tugged at Pop's hand, suddenly breathless.

"Sarge, the laundry," he gasped. "Look in the laundry."

Pop stood and lifted up the lamp and then unlatched the laundry door with his free hand and opened it. Gibson turned his head and tried to look as well. At first he couldn't see anything, but then he saw the glint of eyes underneath one of the concrete washtubs.

"He's alive," Pop whispered, awestruck. "Look at the state of him."

He was filthy and curled up in a ball with one grubby thumb in his mouth. Pop lifted his hand to the little boy but he shrank back under the tubs. They both saw the length of rope tied round one of his ankles.

"He's . . . he's petrified."

"But he's alive."

"Yeah, he is that," Pop whispered. "And I'd given up hope. We all had. You were right then, Gibson. I'm sorry. Maybe the man upstairs did send you after all."

"No, I was wrong. Smith didn't want revenge. It was Darcy he wanted. He thought she was Annie Flood back from the dead. He *did* find the boys, and he must have used little Flynn to get her to . . . co-operate. He was waiting for her to come. But she never did. That's how she thought she'd save him, Pop. That he'd have to give him back. She was a brave little soul, Pop. A brave little soul."

Pop shook his head. "Why the Christ didn't she just tell someone?"

Gibson couldn't hold it all in any longer and two hot tears began to roll down his cheeks.

"Maybe she did, Sarge. Maybe she did."

More people appeared in the doorway and Gibson slumped back against the wall, his vision wavering. They didn't notice the boy for a few moments but then he saw Grace's hand go up to her mouth. Henry Gunn stood there, his face ashen, and then stepped forward. The boy in the laundry shrunk back and Pop lifted up his hand to keep them still.

"Careful," he said. "Don't frighten him."

Gibson watched as Tom looked from the boy to Grace and then back again.

"Do you see him?" he whispered.

"Yes," answered Grace.

"Really?"

"Yes, Tom. He's really there."

"Why doesn't he . . ."

Tom stepped forward across the no-man's-land of six floorboards. The little boy didn't move, but his eyes widened.

"He's been scared out of his wits, Tom," Pop whispered. "Just give him a minute."

Tom gave a slight, dreamy nod and then he put his hand down into his pocket and pulled something from it. He held it up before him, enclosed in his fist, and then he unfurled his fingers one by one. The little boy looked from Tom's hand to his face and then back again. Tom lifted the harmonica and put it to his mouth, breathed through it, then set it in the middle of his palm and offered it.

"Go on, Flynn," he whispered. "Take it. It's yours. Remember?"

Flynn blinked at him.

"Flynn," Tom repeated. "Tom."

With painful slowness Flynn eased out from under his hiding place and stood. His torso was bare and pale and they could all see where his ribs pushed out against his skin. He stepped forward, his hand reaching out for the harmonica. Tom saw, along the inside of his arm, just down from the wrist, the burn scar from the day they'd gone missing, the day Henry's eggs had gone into the fire. Flynn pulled in a big hitching breath and his arm went up to his face as if to wipe away tears.

"Time to come home now, Flynn."

Flynn's arm wavered a little, and then he let out a long, slow breath and his chin went up and down ever so slightly.

"Yeah," he said.

Tom went to him then and dropped to his knees and wrapped his arms around his middle. He put his forehead down against his brother's little chest and left it there, his shoulders heaving and shaking, his tears flowing. When he looked up, after a long time, Gibson thought he saw equal measures of happiness and dismay and pain burning there in the boy's wet eyes. They were almost unbearable to behold, but he could not turn away, and he did not want to.

A Note About the Author

Darren Williams was born in Australia in 1967. His first novel, *Swimming in Silk*, won the prestigious Australian/Vogel Literary Award and was published in 1995.

A Note on the Type

This book was set in New Caledonia, the digitized
version of a Linotype face designed by W. A. Dwiggins
(1880–1956). It belongs to the family of printing types
called "modern face" by printers—a term used to mark
the change in style of the type letters that occurred
around 1800.

Composed by Stratford Publishing Services,
Brattleboro, Vermont
Printed and bound by R.R. Donnelley,
Harrisonburg, Virginia
Designed by Anthea Lingeman